# Hush

Tim Lebbon

&

Gavin Williams

This book was first published in 2000 by
RazorBlade Press, 108 Habershon St, Splott,
Cardiff,
CF24 2LD





Designed and typeset by
RazorBlade Press

Published with the financial support
of the Welsh Arts Council

Printed and bound by the Guernsey Press.

British Library in Publication Data.
A catalogue record for this book is available
from the British Library

ISBN 0-9531468 5 5

**Dedications/Acknowledgements**

For Gary, Max and Matt .... still, basically, insane
T.L

For my parents, of course- for patience above and beyond the call of sainthood (and sometimes even martyrdom!)
G.W

The authors would like to thank Tom Piccirilli, Brian Keene, Steve Lockley, Darren Floyd and Chris Nurse for all their help

All that we see or seem
Is but a dream within a dream.

*"A Dream Within a Dream"*, Edgar Allan Poe

# Part One:
# Blind Spots on the Sun

## 1. Storm Warning

*"Hush," says a voice from the darkness. "It's started."*

*He senses it, too, and shifts his balance, crushing neatly clipped grass flat against the wet earth. The light from the guttering braziers is thin and uncertain, revealing only glimpses of his surroundings: the shoulders of his companions; a cheek or nervously twitching eye; the tips of branches bowing nearer in the wind. Arrayed on the ground at their feet luminous designs have been painted, a constellation of glittering symbols woven in a tight, distorted spiral.*

*He grips the precious object which he carries even tighter, feels its cool smooth surface slip slightly in his grasp, and debates whether to wipe his hands on his trousers. Yes, but quickly: one, two, a nimble motion, skin momentarily rasping across cotton. But this doesn't work. A beat later the prickle of sweat is back again. The garden is cold, but he is damp with fear. Someone curses, terrified—perhaps the man who spoke? This is quickly followed by the unmistakable* ker-clack *of a shotgun cartridge being chambered. A woman coughs.*

*He can hear the noise now above the asthmatic wheeze of the wind. Not quite the rumble of an earthquake, nor really a tidal wave. Not an avalanche in the distance, nor a chanting crowd. It is all of these things and none of them, a ghostly white noise rising in ferocity.*

*The attendant change in atmosphere is hardly subtle. It actually feels as if the air has congealed, adhering in syrupy clots to his eyelids, forehead, throat. He suddenly finds it difficult to breathe. Pinpricks of light percolate on the film of his eyes.*

*Thirty feet to their left the undergrowth begins to churn. The trunks of trees creak hysterically, then splinter ... crack ...burst! Jagged shards of wood leap up into the air before shredding to inky shavings and spinning away to nothing. It feels as if a land-borne whirlpool is coming their way.*

*At that moment one of their crew lets out a desperate scream and steps back, across the hidden security of the gleaming spiral ...*

*... into blackness ...*

**

Jacob awoke to disorientation. The bedroom was dusky, the curtains still closed, which lent the gloom a strangely granular quality. Early morning, he concluded, then started violently as he realised that Maria was standing at the foot of the bed. She had a nylon rucksack over one shoulder and a collection of other day bags by her side. He couldn't see her face properly.

"What you doing?"

"I didn't want to wake you," she confided quietly, her tone subdued.

He grunted and tried to free himself from the tangle of sheets.

"You cried out," she said.

"I was dreaming," he croaked, rubbing at his eyes. "Something was coming, or I was going towards it. Dunno. A noise, like thunder." He shook his head like a drowsy dog. "Just another dream."

Maria said nothing. Jacob squinted at the alarm clock and winced: *5.30.* He swung his gaze back to her.

"Bags," he muttered, staring dumbly at the colony around her feet, the confusion of waking still making a moron of him.

"I'm going."

"Work? It's damn early …"

"Leaving."

There was a long pause. Jacob just stared at the bags, breathing heavily. "Fuck," he finally managed to heave out. "No."

"Yeah."

"No."

"Yes, Jake. It's too late. I didn't want to wake you-I mean-"

"No, goddamnit! What, you were just going to walk out?" He flung himself out of bed to confront her. She flinched at his sudden belligerence. Despite the fact that he was naked and cold—and now realised that he desperately needed a piss—he glared aggressively down at her, shaking with rage. She endured his hostility with resigned control.

"Jake, I don't want a fight," she said half-heartedly. She averted her eyes, as if the platitude had disarmed her, made her vulnerable. Angrily, Jacob pressed at the opening.

"What is this, M?" he demanded. The emotion had begun to vibrate inside him, and he spoke with a rigid jaw. "I thought we'd done this. Sorted it out. Time, you said. That's all it needs. We only talked about it yesterday. We talked about this. Please, M—"

Maria sucked hard on her lower lip, avoiding his gaze, eyes locked on the corner of the door jamb. She shook her head, and he could see that she was trying not to cry. The fury caught him fully then—fuck, the least she could do was cry! He tasted anew his hatred of her job, her therapist's discipline, its airless gulf of detachment.

"Today of all days!" he found himself shouting. "What kind of timing is this? Janey'll be here in two hours. It's half a day's drive for us to hit the demo on time, you know that. And we've got to pick up Morris and Bob on the way. Jesus! Why today, Maria?"

"If it wasn't this, it'd be something else, somewhere else. It's one thing after another. Animals, roads, disarmament—"

"It's i*mportant.* These things matter. If we're caring, *feeling* people, they must do!"

She looked directly at him for the first time. Her eyes were very bright.

"No. Not with you. Not really, not wholly. Just look at yourself." She stepped forward and tenderly traced the violet crescent of an old scar looped across his ribs. "Poll tax riots," she said, then she touched a ragged white mark on his temple. "Dockers' dispute." Then, a snag of scar tissue on his shoulder. One by one she ticked off his old wounds. "Legalisation of cannabis. Miners... euthanasia... argument over South African oranges...."

Her hand fell away. She looked sad and weary. "You're all revolt, Jake. You're a scream made out of skin."

Jacob seethed. "Look, Maria. Just listen! You couldn't be more wrong. See…" He limped on, but the words simply burnt away on his tongue. He cried out, spun around and lashed out at a nearby bookshelf, knocking a bracket from its mount. Roaring, he swept everything off his desk in one furious motion, as if trying to prove the sincerity of his initial violence. Maria punched him on the shoulder, and the red mist cleared. Jacob blinked the emotion down, appalled by his own lack of self-control.

"See, here it is!" Maria shouted. "This is exactly what I mean. These… *spasms* of unfocused rage. You spit in every direction at once, Jake, but the only person you ever hit is me!" She regarded him steadily, mouth tight, tears quashed.

"Fuck, fuck, fuck!" Jacob growled through his teeth, the words like grit in his throat. "Look, just … just stay there a minute." The urge to piss had become intolerable. He hurried into the bathroom, and as he urinated he pursed his lips, trying to force it quicker. He felt the familiar heat at his temples, the prickle of impatience… and maybe this was what Maria was on about. Maybe if he closed his eyes, breathed deeply…

He heard movement by the front door.

Still naked, he ran through to the living area. Maria was at the door, her palm resting on the handle. He stood about four feet from her, forlorn, his emotions tugged in every direction, from tears to rage and back again.

"Another day," he implored. "Give me that. When I get back we'll talk it through, M. We'll make it right. You know we will, we always do. I mean, what's one more day?"

"One more day is sticky tape, J. It's over. Face it. You're trying to put TCP on a gunshot wound." Her face softened. "Really... Please, J..."

"One day," he whispered. "I've just got this last demo. It's important."

Maria looked at the floor. After a heavy breath she opened the door and began backing out, the bags slipping from each shoulder, straps tangling round her slim frame like even they didn't want her to go.
Desperate, Jacob tried to call her back, "Who'll save me, M? Who'll save me from myself."

"Oh, Jake, I have a job, a life. I've tried to help you, I really have… I'm sorry. You're on your own now, baby."
Jacob followed her and stood shivering in the communal lobby. Maria had started to cry after all, but it seemed almost unexpected, as if she were willing herself not to notice. Tears streaked her cheeks but her expression remained perfectly calm. She reached out to brush his face.

Her fingertips felt like the sofest of feathers.

Without another word she turned and fled, sobbing loudly. The outside door slammed after her with a dull hand-clap. Jacob stayed there for a long time, naked, at the centre of the deserted lobby. Somewhere nearby a toilet flushed and the pipes whispered very softly, laden with regret.

## 2. Peaceful Protest

The crowd roared. Faces flashed before him. Hundreds of bodies jostled and bumped and shoved in their anger. Despite the chaos all around him Jacob felt more alone than ever—the eye of an approaching storm.

The voice of the crowd mingled with the residue of his dreams until he couldn't be sure which screams were real, and which were uncertain memory. His anxiety brought with it images of a lawn at night, the grass splashed with glittering designs. He tried to recall more details, but all that persisted was a sense of impending dread. He thought of Maria and his disquiet intensified still further. But Maria was gone. So all these fractured thoughts must be down to that. Must be.

The crowd shifted suddenly and Jacob was dragged along with them, his feet barely skimming the ground. There were renewed shouts from his right as protestors and police lines nudged each other, bumping like magnets of opposing poles. He raised his placard and began shouting himself. The venting of rage and frustration felt good, so cathartic that he ramped the volume higher and higher until he was bellowing himself hoarse.

"Stop vivisection NOW! End the cruelty! Vivisection is scientific fraud!"

He jerked the placard skyward, fighting for space with all those who wielded similar messages. The impersonal grey face of the complex beyond the fence stared back. The police held them from the gate, but everyone could sense the dangerous undercurrent, a wound spring of violence just waiting to uncoil.

The building stood about twenty metres back from the security fence, long and low and vulgar. Its one concession to aesthetics was a glazed central section which housed the main entrance. Otherwise, the walls were ash grey, two storeys high, punctuated at regular intervals by square, steel-mesh windows. There was no character to the building, it was aggressively utilitarian. Almost actively in-your-face with its functional crudity, and this made it seem intimidating, rather than simply neutral.

"We should tear the fucking fence down," Morris growled from behind him.

Jacob managed to turn his head and smile at the big Cornishman. He had to shout above the crowd to make himself heard, and even then he had the uncomfortable feeling that Morris had only really been speaking to himself. He was passionate, that was for sure.

"We'll have our chance, mate. Their time's coming sooner than they think!" He grimaced as the crowd rippled again. "Anyway, wouldn't do any good. We'd just get nicked. No publicity, just a fine. "

"Fine," Morris echoed, though the context was unclear. "Get in, cause a bit of rumpus. Shit in their beakers."

"All in good time," Jacob said.

"Tie one of those bastards up, stick perfume up his arse 'til he bleeds. Stick needles in their balls, see how they fucking like it! Bastards! *Nazis*."

Jacob laughed fiercely, joining in the chant for a round or two. He punched at the air so hard that his elbow began to burn.

With a roar the crowd surged again, this time against the police lines. Jacob stumbled and lost his grip on the placard, watched it tumble away across the sea of arms and heads. He hung onto the shoulders of those around him, struggling to stay upright while wondering what had brought on this unexpected charge. He felt Morris's big hands on his own shoulders, steadying them both. They kept slipping sideways, moving like a crab scurrying across a beach of melting tarmac, their roars turning to grunts of pain as the police line started to crumble.

The crowd haemorrhaged through a break in the police cordon, and Jacob was permitted a glimpse of what had suddenly enflamed the protestors: the main entrance gaped, and he could just about make out several people strolling briskly through the laboratory gardens. The rose bushes growing alongside the pathway were obviously flourishing. Rumour had it that the corpses of animals "used" by the facility were incinerated and then scattered over the grounds to encourage such hearty growth. That was so much ardent nonsense, he knew, but still, the lush red flowers *did* look like open wounds.

Jacob was one of the first to reach the gate. It was at least eleven feet high and virtually impregnable—certainly unscalable—but it could be shaken and pounded, and it was. The crowd screamed their fury between the metal slats, profanities and statistics mixed in with improvised speculation on the dubious lineage of the laboratory staff.

The small group of people who had come from the complex remained near the security outhouse, seemingly conscious that a fence—however strong—might not be able to restrain emotions as primeval as those vented by the crowd. There were seven of them, all bar one dressed in dark suits. The exception was a tall, slim woman, somewhere over fifty, whose imperial bearing made her seem to tower head and shoulders above the rest. Her face was drawn, yet dignified, her hair twisted into an elaborate bun on the top of her head, giving her the look of a firm disciplinarian. She wore a bright scarlet dress with what appeared to be a matching cloak clipped around her neck.

She was facing the gate, scanning the crowd intently, as if searching for something. She turned and Jacob saw that one side of her face was branded with a vivid pink slash—either the evidence of a terrible burn, or some breed of disfiguring birthmark. Her gaze tracked on and then seemed to linger… Shit, was she looking at *him*? Something cold trickled down his spine and grabbed his balls.

She continued her slow pan of the crowd but muttered something to her companions, one of whom took a camera from a small case at their feet and proceeded to video the assembled protestors.

This ignited a fresh burst of anger from those at the gate. Screamed threats which could never be realised stabbed at the group behind the fence. Jacob held onto the gate as the pressure built, passions flaring. His ribs grated against the unforgiving metal, but he did not shout. He stared at the woman.

The person with the camera—Jacob saw it was another woman, younger, and attractive after a stern, militaristic fashion—stepped forward a few paces and swept the camera along the fence. He frowned, wondering how clear those images would be with the speed she was moving. Surely not sharp enough so you could identify anyone? Or were they simply filming in order to provoke, and thus spur the demonstration into a full-scale riot that would require the employment of harsher tactics by the police?

Then the camera settled on him, and Jacob realised it was neither of these. He stared into the shiny black lens from ten steps away, imagined his face reflected there. The woman thumbed a switch and the lens swivelled, nosing closer to him as the zoom came into play.

There was motion behind her. The woman in red dropped a hand on the younger woman's shoulder, causing her to shift her camera sights along the fence once more, panning on. Only there was something wrong with the tall woman's hand—obscurely, it seemed too small, its colour too strange and its shape all wrong. Together with her scarred face this confirmed for Jacob the likelihood that she was a burn victim. But though it disturbed him he felt no pity for her. She was one of *them.*

He continued glaring at the group, hairs prickling up along the back of his neck, balls shrivelled up into his body. None of them looked at him, but he sensed in this a pointed distraction. Within seconds they had turned and strolled purposefully back indoors, much to the chagrin of the crowd. As they closed the door Jacob stared into the cold darkness of the interior, and a flash of something dreadful—too vague to be memory, too intense to be imagination—cooled him to the core.

**

The police had little trouble clearing the demonstration once the black-clad group had returned to the building. It was as if the scant minutes of heightened emotion afforded by the appearance of the group had sapped the crowd's energy. Their numbers dwindled quickly, until there was only Jacob, Morris and the core gang of activists. Soon they too were moved along, but Jacob noticed the look on Morris's face as Janey drove them back into Beckington. He stared at the building until it was completely out of sight, and even then he did not seem inclined to talk.

Jacob felt the same way. He watched Morris and nodded, almost imperceptibly, in time with the jounce of the van. He smiled to himself, tight and grim.

*Time for action.*

## 3. Direct Action

"It's all such *bullshit*!" Morris slapped his hand onto the tabletop. Their drinks sloshed in concert and a few nearby faces glanced round. Morris was on a roll riding high at the crest of it.

"The political 'system' in this country just simply isn't working, and people are despairing as opposed to being apathetic. It's atrocious! I mean, look, we live in a society where basic human kindness—fellow feeling for our brother animals—has become an act of *social responsibility*. I mean, what's the nation coming to? It's a complete failure of the democratic process," he curled his lip into a sneer. "The only option left open to us has got to be direct action, everything else is bullshit or prevarication. *Listen ...*"

Jacob let him run on without paying much attention. Morris was a true zealot, and sometimes his pop-eyed fanaticism left even Jacob cold. Especially on a night like this, without Maria. Without any hope of ever having Maria again. He bit his lip and made it hurt, bit in hard. Angrily, he glanced around the table at the others: Janey, captivated by Morris's spiel; Liam and Trev talking football as usual; Dogstar Bob rattling out old punk riffs on the edge of the table with his tatty drumsticks; Sondra gnawing apprehensively at her fingernails. What a bunch.

Apart from Bob—who never drank soft drinks after six o'clock—they were all on Coke or orange juice, though Jacob had barely touched his. Images of Maria spiked at him. Maria poised over the sink, rinsing her hair, twisting it into a slick dark rope to wring out the water. Maria asleep, her lips parted against the pillow, breathing deeply, her brows creased into dreamy furrows. Maria leaning on a ferry's railings, gazing out to the sunset, its fuzzy salmon highlights glowing on her cheeks and forehead, the wind loose in her hair... Maria, all Maria.

Earlier, Janey had tried to talk to him about the break-up, but he found that he couldn't get any of it out. If it was all his fault then the problem was all his, nobody else's. It was private, his sacred pain. He grimaced, swilled a mouthful of Coke around his mouth, as if to wash away the taste of his confusion.

The pub was getting busy. The air filled with smoke. Irritably, he glanced at his watch. *Hell*. He looked up.

"Time," he said tersely. Morris's face cracked in half with a vicious grin. Moments later they left.

**

Janey took them on an intentionally circuitous route to the Hellier labs. She wound right out to the city limits, then crawled laboriously back through the one-way system so that they could approach the Keerling industrial estate from an out-of-town, westerly direction. That had always been the plan, ever since Liam and Trev had reconnoitred their target a month ago.

Sondra took the passenger seat up front with Janey, nervously smoking straights, while the men lounged in the back. Jacob didn't join in with their forced camaraderie, but glared out back at the unfurling length of black asphalt. He clenched and unclenched his fists, his nails digging deeper into his palms and making red weals, question marks in his skin. He'd been biting back this anger all day—committing minute acts of emotional censorship—because the thought of Maria still niggled at him. It felt like she was constantly with him, watching his life from the sidelines with a disapproving frown. His cheeks burned. It didn't even make sense, his affronted pride growled. If his sentiments were right, then they were right—she couldn't quibble with how he'd arrived at the conclusions. It was senseless! Yet still, her ultimate rejection of him and all his beliefs churned fat and full in his stomach, indigestible and sickening.

After an hour in the van the lab came into view. Jacob experienced a flutter of disorientation as they approached from the opposite direction to last time, when the only thing on his mind had been the coming demo. Now, a myriad of new concerns were nagging at him, crawling beneath his skin. And the stakes were so much higher.

Janey drove very cautiously here, in case the police had left any cars dawdling in the demo's slipstream, but they saw no other traffic. She turned away from the service road which snaked around to the front of the lab and bumped over the curb. She flipped off the lights, heading directly for the rear of the complex. After a few sightless, heart-in-mouth moments they coasted to a standstill halfway through the horseshoe-shaped copse of trees which bordered the labs. The security fence was just visible through the undergrowth, but essentially they were hidden from view.

Jacob glanced at his watch: *11.50.* He grunted and folded his arms, attempting to try and find a more comfortable settle for his vigil. With a few muttered curses his companions followed suit. Dogstar Bob had even brought pillows.

**

A few hours later the cramped confines of the van had become stale with the accumulated funk of their bodies: sweat, deodorant and sour breath. The air was thick with anticipation, with fear.

Jacob was convinced he could detect subtle crackles of static whenever he rearranged his jacket, or shifted his head. While outside the night pushed at the window panes, the wind groaning, gasping and puffing like a man struggling to catch his breath. An occasional gust rocked the vehicle on its suspension and vibrated the back doors in their frame. The fingers of nearby branches bowed close to the van, their tips scratching noisily at the metal walls.

"I think—" Trev said suddenly, then caught himself. "Well, it's time, isn't it? I mean—" He looked imploringly at the others for guidance, particularly Morris and Jacob. Someone to ratify his permanently tentative opinions. No one moved.

"I can't believe we're doing this *again*," muttered Janey weakly.

"Spiky, spiky, spiky," Liam whispered under his breath. "You do not wanna get yourself caught tonight." He whistled through the gap in his teeth. "Tonight means time inside, no messin'." His voice was impressively level but his hands were trembling. After a moment he sat on them.

"Come on, let's get ourselves ballied-up," hissed Morris. Everyone donned Balaclavas or hood and scarf combinations, all except for Jacob, whose gaze remained pinned, unblinking, on the high fence. Morris nudged him. "Hey," he said tightly.

Jacob started and turned sharply, as if jerking out of a trance. "Ready?" Morris growled.

Jacob nodded. There followed a subdued commotion of shuffles and brisk activity as everyone checked their gear, rifling through their kit bags one last time. Trev took a very deep breath to accompany him outside, then slipped through the back doors. He carried a sealed plastic freezer bag—which Sondra had prepared that afternoon—and two lengths of rope with hooks sewn into their tips. Once he'd gone Janey performed a deft about-face, carefully manoeuvring the van so that it pointed out towards the road and a swift route of escape.

Then they waited, staring into space, chests tight with anxiety. Jacob debated whether to wipe his steadily dampening hands on his trousers, decided against it.

Sondra scratched frantically beneath the frayed black tent of her sweater, her thin shoulders poking sharply through the material. "Eczema," she confided, miserably. "Stress-related."

Jacob wondered if she was going to cry, and this brought on a fresh volley of Maria memories to unseat him. He cursed, *sotto voce*.

Ten minutes later there was a hurried rap on the back door and Jacob cracked it just enough to admit Trev. "Well?" he demanded once the younger man was inside.

"Done," he confessed breathlessly, looking worried.

"Rock your own roll!" announced Morris and launched himself out of the back of the van. One by one the others followed, all except Janey, who remained in the driver's seat to keep the motor turning over.

"Good luck," she hissed after them, but Jacob didn't even turn.

They darted through the trees towards the fence. Thorns snagged at their clothes, scrabbling for purchase in the folds. It wasn't too difficult to fix on their destination, though—the Hellier labs burned through the matted branches, bathed in the lemon-tinged radiance of five or six banks of sodium lamps.

As soon as they reached the security fence, Morris and Liam went to work on the sturdy links with heavy-duty bolt cutters. Within seconds they had created a sizeable gap in the chainlink, and they all tumbled eagerly through onto the grassy verge beyond.

There, they came across the evidence of Trev's expertise: a trio of slumbering Dobermans with the remains of the steaks Sondra had drugged still hanging in shreds from their froth-speckled jaws. The team stood nervously around the gently twitching bodies, while Trev detached hooks from the meat and coiled up the lengths of rope he'd used to lob the steaks over the fence.

"How long *exactly*?" Morris demanded.

Sondra looked as if she might be sick at any moment. She was staring down at the dogs, shivering, hands by her sides, fingers virtually hidden by the concertina sag of her raggedy sleeves.

"Sondra?" Morris pressed.

When she looked at him her skin—above the scarf lashed across her mouth—was lacquered a freakish yellow by the sodium lamps. "Er, thirty minutes, tops," she managed.

"You know what to do. Stay here and make sure," Jacob told her sternly. Then the men set off across the compound.

They made directly for the clutter of outbuildings tacked onto the main bulk of the lab. Their angle of approach had been carefully chosen. Coming through the fence at this point meant that the brow of the roof shielded them from the CCTV 'cam scanning the rear of the complex. However, once they got past that blind spot they'd be instantly spotted and recorded for posterity, to be reeled in by the law a few days later.

Which was where Dogstar Bob came in.

He dropped to his knee and—with a snake-like motion—drew out his custom-built crossbow. He carefully drew a bead, and let fly with a bolt. The missile thunked directly into the camera's eye, disabling it instantly. So far everything was going according to plan. However, now Jacob felt fear dash handfuls of crushed ice into his guts. The next few minutes—potentially, the most important of his life—were to be ruled by raw, uncut chance. There was no way they could properly plan for this next stage: they had to make it to the security station on the opposite side of the building before the night-duty guard decided to investigate the camera malfunction. It was a slippery variable they just couldn't calculate. The race was on.

Morris sprinted ahead and Jacob matched him as best he could, while the others fanned out behind. As his feet whispered across the grass, Jacob weighed up their chances: if the guard was too slow then he could lock himself inside the office and simply phone the police; if he reacted too quickly then he'd have a real chance of spotting them halfway across the hardstanding and could radio for help. The plan really was madness, Jacob reflected, but Morris had hit the nail on the head—they had to try and make a difference. *Had to*.

They cleared the corner in a hail of scattered gravel, and caught sight of the postage stamp of light which marked out the location of the security office—

But there was already movement inside! A crisp black shadow turning against the frosted glass. Jacob's heart stuttered. Morris was still thirty paces away!

*No!*

Their reprieve was as swift as it was unexpected. The shadow paused, as if its owner had suddenly remembered something important, and then swung out of sight. As it did so, Morris cleared the final metres and caromed into the wall next to the door. He began scrabbling around feverishly in his sports bag. A beat later the door opened and the guard stepped out. Jacob was bang in the centre of his field of vision. The man's jaw fell clownishly open—

Morris lunged. He smothered the guard in a choking bear hug, bringing him down and clamping a gag over his mouth all in one movement. The cloth was impregnated with chloroform. The guard kicked and bucked, but the deed was done. Just in case, Jacob skidded over and threw himself across the man's thighs.

Eventually the guard's struggles dwindled, allowing Jacob and Morris to kneel up and whoop for breath. Liam, Trev and Bob skidded up, then between them they dragged the unconscious body back into the vacant cabin.

Most of the space inside was taken up with a bulky command deck, housing various CCTV screens showing multiple feeds from cams all around the complex. One screen was dark. Suddenly Jacob remembered the woman with the digital camera, pinning him with her lens, the zoom nosing in. He shook his head to clear the unwelcome memory.

Morris set about tying the guard to the radiator with Trev's rope, while the others wrecked the equipment as quickly and quietly as they could manage. From Liam and Trev's reconnaissance they knew that the other guard was stationed by the gate at the far end of the compound. Luckily, the dog pen was not far from the office. So, the plan was to rouse the remaining dogs and get them as excited as possible, then when the second guard came to investigate overpower him in the same manner.

Morris, Bob and Liam slipped out while Trev remained with Jacob, and at length they heard the dogs begin to howl.

Trev sat with his back propped up against the desk, relief spilling from every pore of his being. "*Jesus*, my heart!" he laughed, palm against his chest. "You gotta come on over here and feel it," he invited. "Man!"

At that moment the second guard—who had crept through the open door as they chatted—struck Trev full across the face with his nightstick. Trev went down in a falling shower of blood and lay still.

The guard rounded on Jacob.

He was a burly, lumpish thug with close-set eyes and bad teeth. The nightstick was clamped in his left fist, its dripping tip held menacingly low. He grinned wickedly before hurling himself across the narrow room.

*Bad move*, thought Jacob. Previously, the face of cruelty had merely been a blank for him. Rarely had the enemy been so focused, so easily distilled from a nebulous catalogue of unknown politicians, scientists and calculating exploiters into one tangible adversary. Now, this man served as an embodiment of all the things that Jacob hated in the world.

The rage came up out of him. A scalding cascade of terrible violence, dragging in its volcanic slipstream all the frustration he felt—over the break-up, over Maria, over his own failures and inadequacies. Everything. Everything he'd been suppressing erupting in one white-hot blast.

The guard caught him a heavy blow across the shoulder, but Jacob barely registered it. He cannoned through the attack as if it wasn't there, his whole weight thrown against his enemy. The sheer ferocity of Jacob's assault immediately drove the other man onto his back, his skull *thunking* sickeningly on the flooring tiles.

Soon, both men were screaming: the guard, because he being kicked in the head; Jacob, because he could not stop kicking him.

It took all of his companions' strength to tear Jacob away from the unconscious body, and another ten minutes after that to finally calm him down.

**

When Trev came to, he was groggy and nauseous, staring around the office with the astonishment of a newborn. The awful gash across the bridge of his nose pulsed weak sputters of blood whatever rudimentary attempts at first aid they made. Morris decided that Bob should escort Trev back so that Sondra could take a look at in the relative security of the van.

It was debated that they abort, but eventually the remaining team members voted to press on. Jacob abstained. He was terrified of what he might suggest.

Once they had removed the guards to the dog pen and secured them there, they sprinted, with their requisitioned keys, to the main entrance.

**

The reception area was a disappointment. Jacob wasn't sure what he'd expected, but certainly something more impressive than this cold, bare box.

A rank of scoopy moulded orange seats faced a single U-shaped desk, which was loaded down with a stack of pristine electronicana: silent PC; flatbed scanner; printer and fax machine; photocopier; a startling arsenal of phones. But, fundamentally, the same stark utilitarian aesthetic that made the exterior of the building so forbidding, also ruled the decor here. No carpet, bare walls, lots of scuffed plastic and stucco. Evidently no pampered CEOs or captains of industry were expected to tour the plant in the near future.

One door led off to the (unisex) toilets; a set of double swing doors was the only other route out of reception. Ideal for security. Once through the swing doors the saboteurs were confronted with a three-way choice, each corridor leading off to another single door and—seen through an inlaid porthole—a gallery of cages beyond that. Jacob led, looked about and sucked his lower lip.

"Right, once we get into the labs proper, the silent alarms get tripped. From then on in, we've got fifteen minutes before the cops arrive. Simple as that. Stay in any longer, boys, and go directly to jail. Do not pass go. Do not collect two hundred pounds."

"I still don't see why we can't release some of the animals," Morris snarled.

"I mean, that's what it's all about, isn't it? They're really why we're here in the first place. So, fifteen minutes is easily long enough to open the front gates and shoo as many of them out as possible. "

"You don't hurt international pharmaceutical companies by letting puppies out onto the streets to starve," Jacob answered. "You sting them by cutting their profit margins. You wreck millions of pounds worth of delicate monitoring equipment. Hit them in their wallet, not their heart. They haven't got a heart."

Liam hefted his jemmy and beamed. "Every boy's dream!"

They each chose a door.

Click. *Clock's ticking.*

Some of the puppies woke up as soon as Jacob opened his door, which was bad. They were held in tall rudimentary cages, wire cells with only the most basic amenities—bowl of water, concrete floor, handful of scattered sawdust for bedding. He could see that the dog nearest to him had been shitting blood, and another was heavily strapped with bandages around its shaved abdomen. Jacob's stomach rolled. The dogs that had woken wagged their tails excitedly, yapping, yapping. He couldn't believe the blindness of their trust; it brought tears to his eyes. It was a lengthy, harrowing walk to the procedural rooms beyond.

The first room was lit by banks of stuttering strip lights, and contained high benches with smooth glossy surfaces flush against every wall. On top of the benches sat all manner of equipment that he didn't recognise and didn't understand. Jacob allowed himself one grim smile before beginning.

He kicked the supporting leg away from the first bench, and imagined himself back in the argument with Maria, smashing shelves, crying. This didn't make things any easier, but somehow made the violence and destruction more satisfying, more justified. After a very short while he began to feel dizzy, but it was a sensation he enjoyed.

The second room was identical. The third room, however, was dominated by what appeared to be the glass-fronted cabinet of a large mainframe computer, and networking station. Three or four judicious crowbar blows opened it up for him, several more smashed the computer casing. Sparks flew everywhere, shards of delicate circuit boards swung down like ruptured guts. He checked his stopwatch: five minutes to go. Suddenly he heard Morris calling.

He froze. Footsteps were approaching. Morris appeared in the doorway, his expression indecipherable.

"You gotta come see this," he said very firmly.

"There isn't time!"

"For this, there is."

Cursing under his breath, Jacob tailed Morris back the way they'd come and into the second corridor. A clutter of stocky metal canisters plastered with ominous biohazard warning stickers stood just inside the door. The cages here were much the same as Jacob had just seen, but smaller—rabbits and cats. Thoroughly gruesome, but that wasn't what Morris wanted to show him. They ran on.

Past the cages, instead of procedural rooms there was only a dense warren of diminutive offices, most with their chipboard doors kicked in, jagged splinters strewn beside their burst locks. Morris led him to the centre of the labyrinth and a short, metal-panelled corridor. At the end was a recessed steel door with no porthole. It had one long vertical handle which Morris used to haul sideways. The door gasped on oiled grooves and slid into the wall with a pneumatic sigh.

Morris stomped through, but something brought Jacob up short and made him dawdle in the doorway, restless and confused. The atmosphere was wrong. Something about the room didn't scan and he couldn't pin down what it was. He thought maybe it was the aftershock suddenly hitting him.

The anger that Maria had warned him of—ultimately been driven away by—had been graphically exposed tonight. This terrifying lack of control had unseated his humanity. He couldn't avoid the fact that less than half an hour ago he had almost beaten a man to death. It was a crippling realisation, a dunk in artic waters. He thought of aggravated GBH and assault charges. Attempted murder. Maria. He found himself trembling with indecision.

"Whoa! Hold up, I'm n-not sure about this one." He stammered. His mouth was desert dry.

It was obviously some sort of conference room, but in marked contrast to the rest of the complex this area seemed luxuriously appointed. The phrase *nerve centre* came to mind as Jacob surveyed the interior. It looked like a presidential war room in some buried nuclear bunker.

A huge oak table stood beneath a crystal glow ball, which bathed the room in subdued, buttery light. The ceiling above was gently curved, black, and set with tiny fibre-optic lights, like a night sky glittering with stars. Morris went straight to the table and shoved a chair impatiently out of his way. It ran on coasters, skidding back towards Jacob.

Morris beckoned. At length, and with great reluctance, Jacob moved a short way into the room to stand at the foot of the table. His eyes strayed over the glazed wooden surface and snagged on a few of the most salient details: the fact that there were seven chairs and thus seven places set, plus each place had a fan of documents flared out in front of it and was provided with an inlaid electronic workstation. These were obviously PC terminals—state-of-the-art, multimedia—with combined video or DVD facilities, but by the looks of it slaved to a master unit at the head of the table.

Jacob looked closer at this pre-eminent place. A claw of ice closed around his heart. Beside the master terminal was a digital camera.

Seeing him stiffen, Morris plucked up a clear plastic wallet file and flicked it across the tabletop. With trepidation Jacob removed its contents.

Photographs. Black and white blow-ups. His face in close-up, replicated time after time. Shouting. Yelling. Features distorted with rage, smudged by motion and emotion. Jostled by the crowd. These were stills from the demonstration. But more than that, as he flicked further back through the sheaf he found other locations. Different scenes. Places he barely remembered, clothes he no longer possessed. Some of these pictures were ten years old!

His breath hitched. Comprehension dawned slowly, gathering from false light to eventual illumination.

"Oh. My. God," he breathed. There were duplicates of the photos by every workstation.

"More to come," said Morris quietly. He retrieved a high-density 3.5-inch diskette from the master terminal's "A" drive and pitched it over. Jacob snatched it from the air and examined the label. It read "File 10: Jan-Jun, 1984". Jacob looked up in bewilderment. There was a box full of identical disks next to the terminal.

"What were *you* doing in 1984?" Morris asked, not entirely joking. Jacob stared at him.

"What? Are you saying these are *surveillance* files on us? Dossiers they've been compiling all these years?"

Morris shrugged. "These days, man, who knows? I mean, really, who knows? They've got computers now, face-match mainframes that'll store you on file and pick you out of a crowd, on CCTV, anywhere in Britain. Anywhere you go. You get yourself classified as a dissident, a troublemaker, and you are going to be watched. And not just by the pigs, either. Private security networks got access to this stuff, plus less qualms over how to misuse it."

Jacob was dumbstruck. His whole world had fallen through a trapdoor into empty space. His grip on reality was becoming slippery.

"I don't believe it, any of it. I mean ... fuck, I don't know what I mean. Jesus, will you look at all this stuff." He flipped through the pile of glossies, becoming more and more agitated. Morris eyed him closely for a moment or two. Then—

"That's nothing. See here—" he held up a familiar-looking laminate tag with a bar code stencilled across it. Jacob couldn't quite place its significance at first, but Morris quickly plugged the gap for him.

"These are clipped to every one of the cages I've seen here. Guess it must be something to do with their drug admin."

Jacob merely frowned at him, even more puzzled. "Yeah, and so? Eyes on the clock, mate." He was still stunned by the photos. How widespread was this surveillance? And just how far back did it go?

Morris's expression darkened, and Jacob realised that the big man was scared. Not just nervous, or tense, or concerned. Properly, truly, terribly, *shit scared*. It was almost as if he didn't want to speak, in case voicing his terror would make it concrete, and bring it fully into being.

"I found this tag in here. Beside a very special cage."

He backed away to the far wall, where Jacob recognised the dim outline of another door, roughly analogous to the one by which they had entered. This door, however, had a porthole which was much wider and deeper than the others. The porthole was currently obscured by some segmented metal blind, but this was only half-drawn. From where he was standing—if the blind had been drawn back the whole way—Jacob would have an uninterrupted view into the room. Morris lifted his hand and tugged the blind aside.

And Jacob knew that his life would never be the same again.

The adjoining room contained another cage, larger than the puppy cages, but not as large as one might have hoped, considering. It was moderately clean, with a bare concrete floor and a jug of water in the far corner, a night soil bucket next to that.

A teenaged girl lay asleep on the floor.

Astonishment shoved at Jacob, nudging one of his feet forward so that he took an involuntary step towards her.

She was sixteen—seventeen at a pinch, but surely no older than that—and achingly thin. Her body, inside a wretched grey smock dress, resembled a collection of bamboo canes loosely gathered by string.

In spite of this she remained quite shockingly pretty, with magazine-cover cheekbones to offset the tear-stains and blurry bruises. She could have stepped straight off some Milanese catwalk. Her hair was black. True black, not some deep, dark mahogany. Midnight black. *Black* black. Her skin had turned sallow with the ravages of captivity, but its texture remained that of brushed velvet, unbearably smooth. A few freckles stood out in a diffuse band across her delicate retroussé nose.

There was a metal cuff around her left ankle, attached to a long snake of chain bolted to the wall. Her skin was chapped and split around the manacle, crispy with dried blood.

Jacob thought she had, perhaps, the look of an East European, and his mind immediately flew to refugees. The poor, shabby flood of war homeless, spilt willy-nilly out across the continent, dispersed by ethnic cleansing and starvation, winter and death. Shorn of nation or culture, identity or history. Their history was being rewritten by the victors, back in the country they once knew as home, under a different name. And now... Human vivisection? Snuff science? He gasped in horror.

The curious thing about the scene, though, was the single concession to decoration which had been made within the cell: a streaky, lopsided spiral of intricate, perhaps mathematical symbols, splashed in some luminous dye high up on the far wall. Glittering constellations. Perhaps it had even been daubed by the girl herself? Something alarmed him greatly about this whole scene, over and above its inherent cruelty.
There was something wrong here, hidden in plain view.

Morris stepped sideways to open the door.

"No," whispered Jacob.

Morris took hold of the handle—

"No!" Jacob shouted.

Morris tugged down hard.

The handle went *click*— a small, hard, mechanism sound—but the door didn't open. Instead there was a pneumatic rush and clank of gears from behind them.

The other door was closing.

Jacob spun around, the soles of his boots squeaking hysterically on the polished floor. But there was no hope of them making it in time. The door sprang across—

—and crushed the chair which Morris had shoved aside with a splintering crack, leaving a small space at floor level. Not for long, though: heartbeats at most. Already the chair was little more than a jagged sculpture of plastic and chrome petals. Machinery howled. A tang of burning singed the air.

Jacob dived for the gap. He felt Morris following close behind. They couldn't both fit through at the same time! The floor thumped the wind out of him and he landed half in, half out of the room. The chair gave way. Jacob screamed. And Morris shoved him the final distance through the gap.

The door crunched home, leaving one man on either side, with a sprout of shattered plastic leaves dangling rigidly from the join.

Jacob rolled immediately to his feet, gasping and retching fit to die. An alarm was chiming somewhere, a rhythmic drone from multiple speakers all throughout the complex.

He checked his watch: *sixteen minutes.* Somewhere far away he could hear Liam calling, but he couldn't detect the slightest sound from behind the steel door. Only a fool would beat or kick at a door like that. Jacob went slack with fear.

*Do not pass go. Do not collect two hundred pounds.*

*Go directly to jail.*

## 4. One Step Down

*The scream is pure terror. He glances left, trying to locate the figure in the soupy gloom, but the woman has left the spiral and become little more than a shade upon the shadows. Soon, even her scream is just the memory of an echo.*

*But the cacophony continues. Screeching explosions of timber whirl up into the night, while the ground vibrates like a vast drilling rig. He glances right and catches the eye of the young woman there, then wishes he had not. Fear is a great distorter of beauty: her mouth is a slack drooling flap, her eyes glistening oyster bubbles.*

*Suddenly, the precious cargo he bears is jolted from his hands and tumbles to the ground—he hears the impact even above the wailing chaos—and he feels the frightened, accusing eyes of his companions converge upon him. Quickly he gathers up the cool object again, holding the slippery cylinder so tightly that his knuckles turn a pearly white.*

*He has never felt such fear. Yet he senses that this is simply a precursor of what is to come, a prologue for the tale of terror which soon will be told into his own small soul. His heart is thumping hard, as if in an effort to escape the horror he has subjected it to; sweat deserts his body beneath the tight, warm clasp of his clothes; his balls have receded, hiding themselves away. He feels an instant of irrational hatred for his body, but then remembers that fear is the old ally of his species, and cowardice is not a word you can apply to the primal urge of self-preservation.*

*"Soon," the tall man shouts, his voice little more than a whisper above the riot. "Get ready!"*

*The line of trees explodes upwards, bursting like a wall of shattered glass. The falling black splinters seem to merge with what is being revealed behind: a darkness so profound, so harsh and fathomless, that it seems almost solid.*

*A voice from his left: "Oh God, oh God, oh fucking God!"*

*Ahead of him, the tall man: "Do it now! Now!"*

*For a split second, he thinks he's dropped the tube again. Then his hand finds the end, expertly twists it. His arm jerks backwards as its contents fly into the air.*

*There is a thump, and he is lifted into the air. He staggers back, disorientated by the impression that the ground itself has taken one step down. The cylinder rolls away from him, spilling spent gleams, but it no longer matters. It is done.*

*The spiral symbols have vanished, as has the trimmed grass and the moist soil. Instead he is sprawled on some strange surface, sinking slowly as he tries to lever himself to his feet. There is no pain, no feeling, just a scary sense of relaxation. He wonders if he will sink forever, descending until the porridge-like mess oozes into his nose, his mouth, clogging his lungs and damming up his blood ...*

*Then he realises why he feels so serene. He puts his hand to his chest and looks around to see the others doing the same. They are terri-*

*fied, but not surprised.*

*His heart has stopped.*

**

When Jacob woke up there was nothing. No feeling, no memory, no time. He didn't even feel like he owned a mind. He was merely a blank space where thoughts should play.

Tentative fingers of sunlight explored the curtains, and he opened the holes that — he guessed —must be his eyes. The sun dazzled him. For a few seconds he lay there as dream shadows gradually shook away. Then recollection flooded in, filling his brain with a million bright bits of thought that he no longer wished to claim. A lifetime that he wanted to disown. He was lying on a bed in the guest house.

He groaned, sat up and flexed his hand. His knuckles were bruised, swollen, his left foot bloodied from the split nail of his big toe. He wondered how the security guard was faring. He seized the little radio next to the bed, fiddled with the dials until he heard the burble of the local station. He glanced at his watch: ten minutes until the news.

Morris. Maria. The girl. Jacob could barely draw his thoughts into a coherent line, such were the shocks he had suffered over the last twenty-four hours. He began to tremble, even though the room was sweltering hot. Sweat soaked his sheets. A dog barked outside, a creature from another world. Jacob wondered if he could go back to sleep, dream some silly, ordinary dreams and then wake up to a more acceptable reality. One in which Maria was waiting for him at his flat, where Morris was ranting to anyone who would listen…

A reality in which teenaged girls weren't kept in cages like dogs.

"Oh Christ," Jacob muttered. The dog outside answered him with another volley of barks. Naked, he walked to the bathroom to piss, hoping that if he eased the pressure of his bladder his mind would clear as well. He stood there for minutes after he had finished, holding his flaccid penis in one hand and staring into the toilet bowl as if he could discern the truth of all things in his urine.

He was stirred from his reverie by the radio, the jingle for the morning bulletin. He dashed back into the bedroom, and dropped to the bed, grimacing as he stubbed his injured toe on the cupboard. The first story reported a traffic accident which had claimed the lives of three joy-riders. Nothing about Morris, or the lab.

He thought with relief that perhaps this was normality reasserting its grip. But the certainty of what he had seen still clawed at the back of his mind: there were surveillance files with photos of him from fifteen years ago; there was a fucking girl kept in a cage, for Christ's sake; Morris had been trapped. Fuck normality. It had taken a leave of absence the moment they'd cut the wire last night. And he had physical evidence to boot: an innocuous square of plastic—the stolen diskette—sitting on his bedside table.

As if in agreement, the newscaster moved on to the next story:

"An animal rights activist was killed and a security guard seriously injured last night during a break-in at the Hellier labs in Beckington. Details are still sketchy, but it is understood that the intruder was electrocuted during an attempt to damage the facility's power supply. Prior to the incident extensive damage had been caused to the building and a number of other individuals were observed fleeing the scene. The name of the dead man has not yet been released. A police spokesman has stated that this was a 'carefully orchestrated plan of sabotage and disruption which backfired with appalling consequences'.

"The Hellier labs have long been at the centre of controversy, forming a focus for animal rights protests due to their dependence on vivisection-based research. The secrecy surrounding their projects and funding has led to a number of large-scale demonstrations in recent years. The latest such disturbance occurred only yesterday, when heated confrontations between police and demonstrators led to violent scenes and several arrests. Police have not ruled out a connection between this demonstration and the break-in.

"The Dufuax Institute—owners of the Hellier complex—were approached by this program for a statement, but declined to comment. More coverage of this story on the twelve o'clock bulletin. And now, Carol Napier with our national round-up..."

Jacob let the radio burble on, but everything that followed blended into white noise. It was after seven o'clock, and the smell of frying breakfasts had begun to filter through the floorboards from below. However, Jacob could not even force himself to feel hungry. His stomach growled and his body screamed out for caffeine, but the thought of food—

Morris was dead.

Dead.

He would never rant again, never stand in the street and badger passers-by, railing at the perfume they wore or the meat they ate. One time, he had actually scrapped in the street with a woman wearing a fur coat, struggling to tear it from her so that he could "reinstate it to its rightful mink owner". Dead. *Killed.* An accident, they said.

Jacob barely reached the bathroom before he was sick, spurts of greenish-tinged vomit flecking the glossy tiles. He fell to his knees and puked again, almost relishing the agony in his stomach, wishing it hurt more, willing his muscles to tie him up in cruel tight knots. He retched again and again and again until there was nothing left to bring up, and then his tears took over. He used the shower-head to sluice the puke away, more in an attempt to dilute his tears than to clean up.

Morris had been fine when the door closed. Trapped, but fine. How far would an organisation like this go? Far enough to keep records concerning anyone who might be a threat? Videos? Surveillance photos? Far enough to track down saboteurs who had inadvertently nudged their secrets into the light? Far enough to *kill*? He had to warn the others.

"Morris, God, I'm so sorry, Morris," he muttered, the sound of his own voice providing some scant comfort. He hurriedly dressed and tossed his few belongings into his rucksack. The last thing he dropped into the bag was the diskette. He paused: some of Morris' skin particles—a smudge of his sweat—were still clinging to the plastic. Jacob pulled the rucksack's drawstring with a bitter snap, sat on the bed and began to shake uncontrollably.

How the hell could he tell the others? Had they heard already?

He remembered the sour, frightened journey back to town last night. Trev snorting blood, spitting great globs of the gory stuff onto the floor of the van, his nose a split plum which should have been stitched; Janey driving in silence, taking her anger out on the gearbox until Liam held her shoulder and murmured quiet, calming words. Sondra sitting up front, gnawing so hard on absent fingernails that blood trickled down her chin.

"Well, we've gotta go back," Dogstar Bob had said, scratching at his beard with one splintered drumstick. "Can't leave the man."

"Bob, for fuck's sake," Jacob had muttered wearily, leaving the rest unsaid because they'd been through it a dozen times already. Morris had been caught, and was probably banged up in the local nick already. There was sod all they could do about it. To the others, Morris's capture was paramount, Jacob's fevered comments concerning the caged girl virtually ignored. Morris was real, they knew him, and now he was in dead trouble. The spectre of the girl was something unknown, unquantifiable, and so, subconsciously, of far less import.

Jacob rested his hand on the door handle of his room and took one last look around. On the windowsill sat his watch, still synchronised with Morris's, no doubt. As he moved to claim it he wondered if Morris's watch was still on his wrist; whether it had been broken by whatever violence had killed him; whether one of the employees of the Hellier labs had kept it as a souvenir.

He wished he'd kicked that guard a bit harder. Caused some really serious damage.

The dog had stopped barking. There was a sudden stillness outside, an arrest in the natural rhythm. No birds sang. The rustle of trees moving in the breeze had died away.

Jacob brushed the net curtain to one side, and saw a car pull up in front of the Bed & Breakfast. It was big and black, the Mercedes hood badge catching the early morning sun, winking up at him. The windows were tinted as in all good gangster movies.

Three figures emerged from the car—two men wearing dark suits and ties and a woman who sported a black polo neck, black velvet hipsters and a bomber jacket. As they stepped into the daylight the two men drew out sunglasses and donned them with almost perfect synchronicity. Jacob would have sniggered had he not been paralysed with fear.

The woman glanced up at the building's facade, and Jacob recognised her from the day before. She had filmed him at the Hellier labs. His fears were confirmed. Here *they* were. The enemy. Maybe the ones who had done for Morris? Perhaps his body was even now stiffening in the boot of their Mercedes, shoved into one corner so that there was room for another corpse...

With their roles reversed—he the watcher, she the observed—Jacob could not help taking a few seconds to examine this woman. She *was* young, though not nearly as young as he'd thought at the demo, and possessed of a rawboned prettiness which flattered from afar. Her features were very sparse and contoured, like she'd bought her skin shrink-to-fit, tight around the wrists, sharp across the jaw. Her hair was a streaky strawberry blonde, scraped back into a stubby ponytail. Her bearing was militaristic, straight-backed with purpose, while her colouring seemed oddly toneless, like cloth bleached by the sun: a dash of caramel freckles; invisible eyelashes; zinc-coloured eyes.

She too put on shades —Ray-Bans—and then scanned the front of the guesthouse. Abruptly, she froze.

*She could see him.*

Jacob went cold. He tried to back away from the window, but her gaze held him pinned there, like a gopher in a cobra's stare. She pointed, mouthing silent words. The two men followed her lead and looked up. Jacob gasped, trying to suck down air which suddenly seemed thick as breeze blocks. The sensation conjured other dark memories, only adding to his terror.

The men were at the side door now, though they did not knock. One of them tried the handle, but the door didn't budge. Jacob could still hear the sizzle of frying bacon from below. He wanted to stamp on the floor, warn the cook, scream and raise the alarm. But he found that he could only stare into the dark glasses of the woman in the courtyard. His vision became hazy with fear, and a crawling sensation prickled across his back. He half-expected the woman's eyes to lift the shades and extend forward on black plastic stalks, zooming in on him as her camera had the previous day.

He wondered, with a feeling of dreadful dislocation, just what the fuck he had started.

The man at the door reached for the handle again, but this time he didn't actually touch it. There was a sound—almost too high-pitched to hear—more an irritation in the inner ear than a noise. Jacob cringed and the dog start barking again. Something jumped from the man's hand. It happened so quickly, and the distance was so great that it was difficult to see properly, *but…* But Jacob was sure that the air had *shimmered* for an instant, as if subjected to an intense burst of heat.

The door drifted open. The intruders swiftly entered.

There was no time to think. Fear still had its claws in him, but panic suddenly flushed his system with adrenaline. He tried to recall the layout of the building, but even that was wasting time. He reckoned it would take ten seconds for them to race up the stairs, break down (*"waft"* open?) his door, and then they'd have him. The thought of what they would do never entered his head; just the certainty that—unless he acted *now*—he'd be dead within twenty seconds. As dead as Morris.

The burst of anger was brief, but white hot while it lasted. He knew he would have no chance against them, but the notion of standing to fight was all he could think of for one idiotic second. Then his eyes flashed over the potential escape routes. The window was the only viable option. He reached for the latch and his heart skipped a beat—

The fucking window had been painted shut!

He tore the lamp from the plug next to the bed and hurled it at the grubby panes. The resulting crash fused with a scream from the landlady downstairs. He kicked out the remaining glass, feeling the skin ripping along his shin. *One of them will stay downstairs, stationed just inside the door, he thought. I would, if I were them.*

He threw his rucksack through the ragged mouth of the window and eased his legs outside. His hands were resting on the splintered frame, tiny slivers of glass piercing his palms.

"Fuck, oh you fucking bastards!" he hissed, and tried to swivel his body so that he could lower himself safely down the outside wall. The manoeuvre didn't work. Pain gnashed at his hands, and his grip failed. He was falling…

He hit the ground hard. Even over the confusion of his impact he could sense the high-pitched whistle again. The dog was frantic on its leash, visibly foaming at the mouth. Jacob half-crawled across the yard, trying to ignore the screams of pain from his ankles and knees. It took a good few stumbled attempts before he could finally haul himself to his feet again.

He hobbled to the Mercedes, keeping one eye on the guesthouse doorway. He jerked open the driver's door, knowing that they would never be so stupid, but *needing* to look anyway. He was right. The ignition was empty.

Terrified at what he might see, Jacob looked back up at the gaping window. It looked like an open wound in the pale face of the house, and the figures that suddenly appeared in the gash were like dark blood welling up. They still had their shades on, he saw. It was dark in the house, but they still wore their sunglasses. He barked a laugh that sounded more like a grunt of pain, and ran through the open gate to the main road.

Jacob ducked into an alley, then clambered over low fences to dodge his way through a brace of overgrown, tatty gardens. He encountered no one, though he couldn't shake the feeling of being observed. Fuck, he'd been watched for years. The photos proved that. Maybe he should always feel like this.

Jacob finally stopped running when he could barely walk. He heaved himself through a small gate into a secluded park, then slumped down onto a bench, feeling like a vagrant but hardly caring.

The day was warming up. The ground steamed lazily where the sun found its way through the trees. A cat slunk out of the bushes, startling him, and causing his heart to hammer once again. Images flickered through the morning haze, too quickly to discern, but as a whole they painted a grim portrait: the girl, curled like a foetus in a steel womb; a lawn, well-clipped and damp; a noise like thunder, and a throaty growl too loud to be possible.

He had to go to the police. He was a criminal, he was *hunted*, but there were worse things than breaking and entering, worse things than assault.

Just ask Morris.

## 5. Once Removed

Jacob left the park. It was peaceful there, comforting, but he couldn't hide forever. The world just didn't work like that anymore.

The huge iron gates, rusted open over the years, let out onto a quiet residential lane. Cars coughed away from driveways in clouds of exhaust fumes and blown kisses; their drivers were shadows, already hiding from the sun behind dark glasses and visors. Curtains twitched back as people took their first glimpses of the day. Further along the street a postman finished his round, and a raggedy stray cat sat staring into space.

Jacob walked quickly along parallel to the park wall, taking comfort in the shadows thrown by overhanging trees. Every time he heard the approach of a car he fell to his knees and ducked behind a parked vehicle or—when there wasn't one available—pressed himself flat against the stonework. But there were no Mercedes here, no black sunglasses scanning from darkened windows.

The noises of normal life increased as the road nosed into a main street. Cars in queues crawled by so slowly that Jacob easily outpaced them. Through the windows he seemed to see blank faces glancing up at him time and again, and abruptly wondered whether the people in black had only hypnotised him into believing he had escaped...

A tray of brightly coloured cakes tempted him from a bakery window. He realised with a slow shock how famished he was. But eating would feel all wrong while Morris was lying on some cold slab somewhere.

As soon as the post-mortem had been carried out, they would know how he died. How he'd been murdered. The police knew about the death —the radio report had made that obvious —so they would know of the lie, the misdirection.

He had to contact the others, it was the very next thing he had to do. The thought had been there all along, buried beneath the sands of his shifting fears, hidden by the primal urge to save his own hide. But now, alone and potentially safe, Jacob knew that he should be getting in touch with everyone else. Maybe they had heard about Morris, maybe not, but the time to mourn would come later. For now, he had to *warn* them.

They had all stayed in different guest houses, in a naive attempt to avoid detection should something go wrong. Well, something *had* gone wrong. Gone pear-shaped, fucking *pyramid*-shaped with their heads impaled on spikes at each corner. He turned from the bakery, hunger pangs scattered by a sudden desperation. Who first?

Janey, Saxon Guest-House. Right, first remembered, first approached. A new purpose in his stride he headed off toward the town centre. The hairs on his neck prickled with paranoia, but he thought himself safer in the bustling centre of Beckington than anywhere else. He felt his identity was subsumed by the myriad streets and busy alleys all ringing with the tones of early morning: car horns, coughs, tired sighs, shouts. He glanced behind him. He could see no obvious pursuers, certainly no black sunglasses, and the traffic had begun to flow steadily now. If a large black Mercedes did choose to hang back it would be easily visible, suspicious even to these innocents making their usual automatic journeys to work.

Jacob suddenly fiercely wished he was one of them. Lunch box under his arm, a twenty-minute stroll to work every day. Nodding hello to the same people, but never, *ever* speaking to them. Shirt and suit, colourful ties worn in a vain attempt to brighten the day. Sour MaxPax coffee, edgy computers causing grief, the most exciting event of any day the time when a typist brushed his leg, or when he realised it was an hour closer to home time than he'd thought. He wished for this, but at the same time there was a vile taste in his throat, a sense of condescension bordering on disgust for the life he had been yearning after. As if he knew he had something far more important to do. Now, he had to warn his friends.

A woman threw him a half-smile as he passed, but he didn't respond. He'd spied a telephone box. Fearing it was PhoneCards only Jacob jogged the last few steps and wrenched the door open. One side of the box had been kicked in, and shattered glass crunched underfoot like a million scattered diamonds. He lifted the receiver and heard the dialling tone, then fumbled a handful of change onto the shelf, losing most of it to the floor in the process. He whispered soothingly to calm himself down, closed his eyes to try to block out the red veil of rage.

He managed to slip thirty pence in the slot, then realised he didn't have the number for the guest house.

"Shit!" He dropped the receiver and kicked out at the wall, cringing as the rest of the shattered window sprayed across the pavement. Pedestrians jumped in surprise as glass tickled their heels. A few flashed sharp looks his way, but quickly thought better of confronting him when they caught sight of his expression. Others simply walked on, averting their eyes, unwilling to become involved in anything as nasty as this before work. Jacob giggled wildly, unable to hold it in. He was ready to knock out the rest of the windows and it took all of his restraint not to descend into hysteria right there and then.

He rang directory enquiries and memorised the number they gave him, then slid money into the slot once more and dialled. There was only one ring before the call was answered.

"Hello." Man's voice, neutral.

"Hello, Saxon Guest House?"

"Yes."

"I wonder, do you have someone staying there by the name of Janey Weeks? I really need to speak to her." He was almost tongue-tied with reluctance, dreading the next few seconds when he would have to tell Janey his terrible news, to beware of men in black.

*Why didn't they follow him?*

"Weeks?"

"Yes, Janey Weeks. Tall, dark, attractive." He bit his lip, frustrated at the silence, ready to shout into the void of crackles and static. He couldn't even hear the guy's breathing.

*Why didn't they get into their car and cruise around looking for him? It was early, not many people around.*

"No one here by that name." And the line was cut.

"What the fuck—" Jacob struck the phone with the receiver, anger and violence his retort. He hissed as ground glass from the guest-house window dug deeper into the wounds on his palms. Returning the receiver to his ear all he could hear was the dialling tone, droning out its burr of dismissal.

*Maybe they knew what he'd do? So they knew where to wait...*

Jacob shouldered the door open and stumbled into a woman wearing sunglasses and a dark jacket. He jerked backwards, and the reproach which had so obviously been on her lips faded when she saw the way he stared at her. He launched himself off down the street. In his mind he turned over the possible reasons why Janey had not been staying where they'd agreed. But his thoughts travelled the same road, and led back to the same destination. A place he didn't want to consider—the same place that Morris had been approaching last night when Jacob had left him behind the steel door. The place those thugs in black had come from.

And he was heading there now, unless he was very careful.

He sidestepped into a shop doorway, glancing back through the converging panes of glass which threw the street's image into a geometrical nightmare. He waited there for several minutes, ignoring the suspicious stare of the shopkeeper. In all that time he caught not a hint of pursuit.

*Surely they wouldn't have given in that easily, though? He'd had a twenty-second head start, little more. What had they done to the landlady?*

The thought was sudden, unbidden, chilling. Guilt mixed in with other emotions and coursed through his veins like acid. He closed his eyes and bit his tongue to try to recover. Eventually, he felt calm enough to carry on.

He stepped once more into the throng. He looked down at the pavement as much as possible, trying not to catch anyone's eye.

Suddenly there was a shout behind him, loud and commanding. He spun around, fists clenching even though the voice had come from a distance. Heads turned in his direction, eyes bored into him. He readied himself for whatever attack was to come. Something was dashing at him, something dark, accompanied by the rhythmic clatter of claws on concrete.

The crowd parted. The shape lunged.

"Cujo! Here!" The voice contained a hint of desperation. Certainly not the voice of pursuit.

The dog almost knocked him over. Its slavering jaws left a splash of froth on his trousers as it passed him by, accelerating through the gap formed for it, dodging the legs of those too slow to step aside.

Jacob breathed a sigh of relief and leaned against the front wall of a shop. Seconds later a little man ran by, the few fat strands of hair on his head flapping like worms as he chased after his escaping hound.

Jacob saw the train station signposted across the street. He could not see the distance but the direction was clear, so he continued on his way. Home was where he needed to be right now, comfortably cynical in his flat. He could ring the others from the station, see if he had any better luck than he'd had with Janey. The worry that they wouldn't be where they should be either ate at him. He tried to throw a blanket over his fears.

"None of this is happening. It's all okay… It's all okay…," he muttered to himself as he walked, under his breath, in time with his quickening stride.

He reached the station twenty minutes later. He was fairly certain that he was not being followed—twice he had ducked into shops and waited for black-suited figures to catch up, but both times had proved to be false alarms. Still, there was the continual prickly feeling that he was being watched, and he couldn't shake the fear that easily.

The main flow of people was coming out of the station, ready for the day's work in town. Jacob stood to one side for a while just watching faces, expecting at any moment to see a pair of dark sunglasses or a scarred female face. He wondered where she was now, back at the lab or off somewhere in pursuit of him? Was she looking at him right now? Running her cruel fingers across the matt-black of surveillance photos, staring into his absent eyes?

He shivered, forcing his way back into the crowd. He received a couple of disgruntled "tuts" as he shouldered his way through the exit doors, but ignored them. These people lived in a different world, now. A safe world, a cocoon. He was headed somewhere else entirely.

There was a bank of telephones against the far wall. Exposed, but they would have to do. Dogstar Bob was staying in a B&B called Wenderview House. Directory enquiries once more furnished him with the number, and Jacob rang directly. There was a tight knot of expectation in his stomach, twisting his guts into painful contortions. As he listened to the dialling tone he doodled random, twirly shapes in the dust on the perspex shell over his head.

"Hello, Wenderview House." More hopeful.

"Hello, yes, I wonder if you could help me?"

"That's what we're here for, mate." Sounded friendly.

"Good. I wonder if you have a guy staying there with you, name of Dog-er, Bob Hale?"

"Hale? Hale, Hale, Hale." Jacob imagined a finger running down a neat register. The knot in his stomach began to unwind slightly. He wasn't worried about what he'd say this time, he just wanted to hear Bob. He was desperate to hear a friendly voice.

"Dogstar Bob, you say?"

"Uh? Yeesss," Jacob answered hesitantly, trying to remember what he *had* said.

"Nope! No one here by the name of Dogstar Bob, I'm afraid," the voice said, jauntily. "'Fraid not."

"But he's staying there!" Jacob said, already realising the futility of his words.

"No, he isn't. Now—" But the voice was cut off. In the distance, through the crackle of interference, Jacob heard another voice, faint but strong. A woman's voice…

"Fade," it said. And the line was cut off.

Panic rising Jacob went through the motions one more time. He found out the number of the lodgings where Liam and Trev were staying. He dialled. The phone was picked up. He spoke. No answer. He sensed someone there—heard a faint whisper of movement, an almost undetectable breath. He spoke one more time, expecting no reply. He wasn't disappointed. He tried Sondra too, but much the same thing happened: the receiver was picked up but no one spoke, and Jacob had the overpowering sense of being *listened* to.

He slammed the phone down into its cradle with incredible force, willing it to break. It did not, and he was glad of it. The last thing he wanted now was to draw attention to himself.

He bought a train ticket, and spent the next hour sitting in a toilet cubicle, jumping every time someone came in, holding his breath until they'd left. When he heard his train announced he took a deep breath and opened the door. There was a man washing his hands; Jacob hadn't even known he was there. The man's eyes flickered over him in the mirror, then back down to his hands. Jacob left the toilet, starting violently when the door crashed shut behind him. Sink man stood with his back to him, drying his hands. The hand drier sounded like a jet engine taking off.

Jacob scuttled through the ticket lounge with his head lowered, feeling eyes upon him every step of the way. There was a woman reading a magazine in one of the scooped plastic seats. It was *Guns & Ammo*. She seemed to be turning the pages with unnatural haste.

By the time Jacob boarded his train he was sweating heavily, his roiling stomach grumbling with fear. As they trundled laboriously out of the station Jacob tried to peer back into the foyer. He thought he could still see the magazine woman sitting there, but he wasn't sure. He was not sure of anything anymore.

Morris. Janey, Sondra, Bob, Trev, Liam.

He needed Maria now, more than he had ever needed her while she was his lover. He had gained a clearer understanding now of why she had left, but even that seemed unimportant. She'd have to listen after what he'd been through.

The train sailed into countryside and rolling fields. Constant greenery and the occasional glimpse of scattered farmsteads calmed him, yet he spent the entire journey standing in a compartment between carriages. He tried to convince himself that he was not entertaining the thought of jumping should he be approached by someone suspicious—someone with dark glasses, for instance—but one hand was always resting on the window, ready to reach over and flip the latch.

He heard laughter from one of the carriages. He set his face to it, for it was a sound he was sure he would never make again.

He had moved one step down from reality.

## 6. Breath Takes Breathing

*The air is alive.*

*Everything here is alive. Every tiny component piece of this place is hideously, swarmingly living. He looks down at his feet and sees the evidence there, in the ground that at first he thought was wet ash; scribbles of motion play across its glistening surface… crawling tides… insectile migrations.*

*Instinctively, he tries to take a step, but it comes out all wrong, as if something unseen had kicked his ankle sharply to one side. He almost falls, staggers, rights himself, then fights the urge to scream. The feeling of being touched all over, all the time, threatens to drown his sanity. Dizziness spins inside his head. He gulps for breath…*

*But he only opens his mouth.*

*He gulps again. Mouth opens. Nothing.*

*He gasps, or tries to.*

*Gulps, gasps. Nothing.*

*A memory of saner times reminds him that this is all part of the plan. He thinks of the dropped tube, the luminous matter gushing out. His bodily functions are stalled—chest still, lungs empty, blood stagnant—but without any apparent loss of mobility. He is just one single surviving point of light, somewhere up inside himself, a bright pinprick of consciousness huddled away from the madness.*

*A milling cloud of mitelike things envelops him. The first mouthful of the swarm is understandably the worst—he gags and spits—but after that they still persist, flooding into his throat, exploring his every passage. This, he knows, is exactly why such drastic measures have been taken, why he is not even breathing. None of their team could face this otherwise. An artificial death is much preferable to a real one.*

*Around him his companions try to cope in their own desperate ways. He decides to walk, to orient himself if he can, and get used to this place where even gravity plays tricks with perception.*

*He senses no open air, no space between him and any other object, just density. It is like being submerged in some oozing, viscous medium, heavier than water, but not quite as thick as gelatine. Walking is nigh on impossible, like struggling through a sea of molten fudge, but after a while he finds that by hauling his arms back and forth—hands cupped like paddles—he can generate a rudimentary form of locomotion.*

*There is no direct light source here, just a general indirect glow. However, in spite of this, some curious trick of refraction enables him to see far into the distance. Though seeing and understanding are not the same thing. Not the same thing at all. He forces himself to gaze up, gaze out— and sees…*

*Boundless glossy black plains. Chitinous causeways. Moist constructions of glassy resin. Vast sprouting bulks, like mountains of leprous iron filings. Tiers of anthracite-coloured bone-stuff, flecked by bright silver. The whole sky seethes; a gaping maw infested by an infinite tide of squirming black maggots. And while the sky writhes, the earth breathes, literally, flaunting its terrible reluctance to settle, or remain in any one fixed state for more than a heartbeat. It is forever spilling and churning, collapsing and rearranging, endlessly animate.*

*Spider armies made from tar march, merge and march again. Locust volcanoes spout eruptions of black vomit, which transform into avalanches of rotting termites, which turn into slithering rivers of cockroaches that aren't actually cockroaches, which then evaporate.*

*The place reeks something like the sea: briny, pungent, but with other conflicting odours thrown in, as well: rubber, mint, formaldehyde. And the silence. That is the most eerie thing of all. No sound. Even if he wanted to, even if his body allowed him to, he could not scream. None of the noises he is familiar with could be transmitted through this lazy stuff. Not even the blood music of the inner ear can soothe him here.*

*The group quail. One or two fall—or drift to their knees.*

*Then, as if on cue, the real reason why their hearts are held silent suddenly brushes against them...*

*One quality of this air that is not quite air is that it conducts rumours of motion in the exact same way an ocean might: ripples of a far-off disturbance wash up against their bodies, while nearer tremors of displacement stir gently against their skin like faint tides. Or—as in this case—an immense wake which knocks them in every direction as something the size of a cruise liner plunges by—an invisible colossus which leaves them tumbling like corks in its terrible riptide.*

*They freeze as best they can. Their hearts are quiet and lungs empty, but who knows whether this will be sufficient to shield them from the attentions of the vast denizens of this world? A long time passes, but only the subtlest of vibrations carries back. They have escaped detection... For the moment.*

*He sees the fingertips of his nearest companion flick together, describing some elaborate pattern in the air. The man nods at the horizon, which is dominated by an inverted cone hundreds of metres high; it resembles a Cornetto, but one formed of igneous rock and filthy gum. It revolves majestically, and he imagines that if there was noise here, they would be able to hear the screech of protesting rock for miles around. About its jagged crown even darker shadows flare, exhale and scatter away like chasms in the sky.*

*"The Citadel," the man signs at him.*

*"Quickly," he signs back, then points meaningfully at his chest, his throat.*

*They make to move in the direction of the Citadel, when—abruptly—disasters strikes.*

*One of their team goes berserk.*

*A tall, wild-eyed man on the edge of the group suddenly begins to thrash. His whole body convulses, throwing out distorted bow-waves in every direction, dwarfing the minimal currents caused by their earlier movements.*

*Without pause the woman directly behind him draws her combat knife and thrusts the blade into the back of his neck.*

*Time stretches, blood corkscrews through the sludge, and though the man's panic dies with him, something has changed.*

*They all go stiff in unison. Tighten in horror as they sense a mighty swell coming their way. Something huge and dark and endlessly flowing is headed directly for them...*

**

"—you go, mate."

Jacob clutched at the seat and glanced around in panic, eyes wide, heart jumping. He was alone in the back of a taxi, but then he should have known that...

"There you go, mate. Akeley Street," repeated the driver. Jacob's neck ached terribly from the awkward angle at which he'd succumbed to exhaustion, but he quickly paid the fare and dived out into the dying afternoon.

**

At first Maria wouldn't even let him into the flat, so he was forced to tell her there on the doorstep.

"Morris is dead," he confessed numbly, staring at the floor.

She let him in.

Luckily, today was a "work-at-home" day for Maria. A "pyjama day", as she liked to call it. Not that she ever wore pyjamas. A T-shirt generally, or in the summer, nothing. Thinking of her naked scattered Jacob's thoughts in every direction as if they were marbles spilled from a box—

*—Maria stretching exquisitely on the sheets in the morning, the arch of her back lifting her breasts slightly off the delicate bow of her ribcage; the lean tan line of her thigh as she stepped from the bath—*

They were intimacies he could no longer treasure, though his throat still tightened with desire. He closed his eyes, shook his head and followed her through to the living room.

Maria was wearing an olive terry-towelling robe scrunched closed with a fist at the front. *A Little Miss Bossy* T-shirt under that, extra large, down to the knees, and damp hair, tied back in a lopsided ponytail to keep it off her face. No make-up. Truth is, she didn't need it. The absence made her look very young, though, even with the slimline specs she wore for reading.

She regarded him with one hand steepled over her face, index finger pressing against the bridge of the glasses, thumb-tip in mouth, chewing on the nail. She snatched off the glasses and angrily flipped them closed. Rubbed her eyes. Blinked at him.

"Fuck," she said, then sighed. Without the glasses she squinted a little, her vision readjusting after a long day spent in front of the VDU.

Jacob stepped towards her. She leapt back as if scalded.

"*Don't*. You can't be near me. Sit. Sit over there," she stabbed fiercely at the sofa. "Let me think."

It was obvious to Jacob that she had already consolidated the break-up in her mind—shored up the sandbags of her emotions—and his unexpected reappearance was a sore test of her defences. He felt obscurely moved by this recognition, and then angry at himself that he couldn't even *begin* to let go, that he begrudged her happiness so much.

He did as she asked. After a pause, she lowered herself into the wicker chair by the television, scowling and rearranging its fat hillock of cushions to get more comfortable, using the delay, Jacob knew, to work out an angle on this scene.

A sudden, vivid insight into her emotions flared out inside him: he understood how distressed she was that her hard-won composure was being compromised; he saw her resentment at the realisation that perhaps she still loved him, and how that was making her weak; he perceived her dismay and crumbling confidence over her inability to deal with him as she might one of her patients. And he felt her rage that he had returned at all.

And somewhere in there too, he hoped, she felt sadness and shock at the news about Morris.

"So," she said, her voice flint-edged.

So Jacob told her his story. Everything, from start to finish, in every particular, with each minor detail dug out, polished, and held up to the light for her inspection. He related it all in the same low, dead voice, like clockwork winding down.

To her credit, Maria didn't gasp or shake her head in disbelief or say "None of this makes any sense" or "I just can't *believe* it". When he'd finished his story, however, she did fix him with a steady gaze and said: "You absolutely and completely have to go to the police, Jacob. Straight away. And there isn't a single argument in the world you can use to change that fact, so deal with it."

"But Morris is dead," he whispered, holding on to the idea as if it were a cliff face; hanging on might be scary, but to fall would be worse.

"All the more reason."

"No. They're after me. I just can't," he said. It occurred to him that, perhaps, he was in shock. That his mind had been bumped out of gear and was now freewheeling toward madness.

"*Jacob!*" Maria snapped, furious.

Suddenly he was crying. He heard the thick, dreadful sound of someone sobbing and thought for a moment that it must be a TV nearby. A bellow of sorrow and frustration exploded outwards and the sound shoved him to his feet. He lurched towards the door but somehow his feet became tangled in the rug and he went down in a howling heap.

*... His whole body convulses, throwing out deep tidal waves. Something huge and dark heading their way...*

Tears coursed down his cheeks as his body coiled up, drawing itself into a foetal curl as the grief wrung him in its fists. His eyes were burning, his chest was. The girl in the cage. The poor girl. How could they save the girl? How could they save Morris? Maria? The puppies? Jacob? Anyone or anything?

Somehow he'd knocked over an occasional table in his anguish, and now the floor was littered with broken china, pot-pourri and upended textbooks. Maria appeared above him and, kneeling, put her arms around his body.

"Hush," she breathed as she rocked him. "Shhhh, shhhh. There, there."

Finally, he was quiet. Weak and trembling, but quiet nonetheless. He stared at his shaking hands, the scabs and the bruises, the visible traces of the landslide that his life had been crushed beneath. So here he was, searching through the rubble as best he could, looking for the survivors he knew they would never find.

A soft silence grew between them, interrupted only by the steady low murmur of the traffic outside. Something occurred to Jacob and he turned his face to ask it. He had to lick his lips a few times to get it out, though.

"Maria, look, if something terrible happens to you, and you … forget it, *repress* it, well, can it come back? I mean, surface unexpectedly? *Haunt* you?"

She clucked at him, frowning.

"Don't be silly. All that recovered memory stuff is just so much bullshit, Jake."

"In your dreams, I mean. The unconscious-"

"No, Jake. Look, that simply isn't how memory works. If something awful happens to you—if you're abused or in an accident—then you remember it all too vividly. You might well dream about it, too, but you'd have it there just as clearly when you woke up, believe me. Things that terrible don't go away simply because you can't bear them. Life isn't that forgiving."

Jacob became aware that they'd come to rest in such a way that his hand was lying on her thigh, while his other arm was looped up and around her body, underneath the T-shirt which had ridden up slightly. The waistband of her knickers was scratching his elbow. The bare silk of her lower back slid along the underside of his forearm. He sensed his cock stir in his jeans, his breath stiffen… Even here, even now. He felt dizzy. He felt sick. Then he clutched onto her like he'd clutched onto the taxi's upholstery—panic swimming up from the depths, that same blur of terror smearing behind his eyes.

"What's that got to do with Morris?" she asked, slicing through his terror.

"I just need you back, M—You've got to help me," he spluttered.

Maria shook her head sorrowfully. She gently disentangled herself from him and returned to her chair, picking her way across the cluttered carpet. With a shudder Jacob returned to the sofa.

"Will they come here?" Maria asked, too swiftly to hide the tremor in her voice. Jacob clenched his fists very tightly, relishing the sprinkles of pain.

"No." He hesitated. "I don't know." There hadn't been any photos of her in amongst the sheaf, none that he could remember, at any rate. Well, there hadn't been any, had there? *Had* there?

Then, quietly, reluctantly: "Maybe."

"You've *got* to go to the police. Right now," she said tightly, and he could see from the unnatural stiffness of her neck that she was very afraid. "Jesus fuck, Jacob. What if they followed you here?"

"But how can we go to the police? I'm a criminal. I'm on the run. And where's the proof, M?"

"Don't call me that," she said automatically, and shrugged when she caught herself. "Sorry."

"It's all just hearsay. Their word against mine." His voice was still husky from grief. He felt like a dry husk of himself. A brittle, desiccated shell, empty of ideas, emotions. Of hope. *Oh, Morris.*

Maria stared at the floor, frightened. Then her face changed. It was like a cartoon light bulb had suddenly popped into existence above her forehead.

"The disk," she said.

"What?"

"The disk you took. There has to be something on there. Proof." She turned smoothly to look across the room at the PC on her desk, its screensaver enthusiastically throwing pixellated stars in their direction. After a moment Jacob understood. He unzipped his jacket pocket and passed the flat plastic panel over to her...

## 7. Thunder Rising

12th Jan '84.
They found a body today. By some place called Tarbet, near Loch Morar, east coast. Farmer, I think. Remains in same condition as the animals. Very disturbing. Inner Council concurs: steps must be taken, top priority. F going to oversee pm in person, will return with corpse. Not to HQ, but to facility. All will congregate there tomorrow. Highest security in place. Watertight, a Black Veil operation. V instructs restraint, but none of this augurs well. V figures it could still be down to human agencies. Anyway, full investigation *must* follow. If necessary will use veto to ensure it does. Still, V's wait-and-see policy= sensible. Tomorrow will tell.

13th Jan.
At facility F showed video first, recording of the scene. *Not* pleasant viewing. There was a dog with the farmer, treated in same manner. Mutilation follows identical pattern as previous livestock carcasses. Is it a ritual thing? (Note: check archives for cross match). Details: both corpses disarticulated. Multiple sharp force injuries, of sorts. *Not* from blows. Wounds surgical in nature. Neat dissection. Dismemberment. Bodies carefully dismantled, drained of blood (exsanguination) and arranged on the grass like engine parts. The fanciful metaphor is F's, of course.

pm added little to visual evidence. Pathologist couldn't determine exact cause of death i.e., which of wounds was fatal. Thinks both were still alive when dismemberment began. Meeting of Inner Council convened immediately to debate implications. Result: wait and see (of course). Inner Council members to tour Highlands, etc, placing Fifth Circle wards wherever practicable. Next time we will be ready.

19th Feb.
No further developments. Still, charged by V with researching matter in athenaeum at HQ. The tiresome duties of high office.

27th Feb.
Am utterly sick. Had to trawl through all that rot shipped from Miskatonic. Unbelievable froth-at-the-mouth stuff: Prinn's *De Vermis Mysteriis*, von Junzt's *Unaussprechlchen Kulten*, Vaschimone's *Cyclical Cantata and Rhythmic Stigmata,* Comte d'Erlette's *Cultes des Goules*, Kayle's *Scarlet Shedding, Book of Dzyan, Book of Eibon, Revelations of Glaaki* (Order's own copy—great toppling photocopied pile of complete 12-volume edition. Gah!), *Liber Ivonis*. Abdul Alhazred? Famously mad, infamously tedious! "Cthulhu fhtagn, Cthulhu fhtagn ba-blah blah blah blah blah." *Jesus*. Poetry too, ye Gods! Derby's *Azathoth* garbage, and T*he People of the Monolith*—Justin Geoffrey? Whatever. All becomes a blur after a while. Had to cast seven Shapes of Focus just to get through the whole lot without dropping off. Never been much of a scholar at best of times. Action is always best policy. B understands. Came to see me again last

night. Not sure whether V knows or approves of relationship. F would fucking lose it, if knew. To hell with them. We are happy.

Still, some hints in *Glaaki*, but inconclusive. More in *Dyzan* and the Kayle. One striking phrase keeps repeating: The Multitude. Hmm. Who are "The Multitude"? Find this curiously unsettling, but then hints always are. Give me the whole truth, straight-down-the-barrel every time. One other thing, not actually an entry. Marginal note scribbled by one of my predecessors beside passage in *Scarlet Shedding* which mentions, "The Multitude". Note simply reads *Some day they will notice us*, and is underscored several times.

Afterwards, had to resort to our own research material, dangerous though that is. Exhausted after visit to Lower Archive. Strength severely depleted. V demanding full presentation tomorrow.

28th Feb.
My précis of the relevant details, as presented for V:
All texts that I can definitively class as pertinent to the case refer to it only in the broadest, briefest fashion. Elsewhere, can't be sure about anything. Snatches, fragments, vague signs and frightened hints. Even in core texts all is allusion, run-around and hearsay, marginal ravings at best. It is almost as if the relevant material has been intentionally excised. Maybe no one dared to write anything down in first place? Nothing concrete to go on. But what I *have* gleaned: veiled suggestions of enormous physical size, but also a certain incohesion of corporeality. A manifold of dark impressions, like living shadows. Periods of nervous, agitated motion and/ or the possession of actual human bodies by multiple entities. Additionally, something like storm clouds, and peculiar deep-sea descriptions seem to be associated with historical occurrences of these manifestations. Plus, of course, that phrase "The Multitude", with its attendant suggestive imagery and discomforting associations. Equally, and curiously, some references to a female figure. Tall, dressed in red. Not sure of significance, though, if any.

All supposition, truth be told. V not pleased, but understood. Think my visit to the Lower Archive was the deciding factor. Not a matter to be undertaken lightly. Even so, *am* genuinely worried. Can't see any way this could be actions of a human agency. Is unarguably Order business, an incursion of some kind. Is V too hesitant? Is it time we "elected" a new suzerain? Should I be preserving my energies for a coming contest with F?

Ho hum.

B has been a great comfort in many ways of the night!

5th April.
No doubt now. Three more deaths, just as terrible. The Wards failed completely, but at least we were alerted promptly. A team was already there, dealing with other bodies. More animals. Excessively grisly: a sizeable herd of deer "attacked" (if that is the right word?). After death the remains had apparently been graded by size, and arranged in neat columns on the

rough grass. No one could offer any theories as to this new behaviour. The three people, however—this is bad. They were campers. Tourists. Canadians, from Vancouver. Devil to cover up. Most curiously, though, their car had been stripped down as well (showing up F's earlier "engine parts" allusion in a more literal and disturbing light), and the vehicle components incorporated with the human remains to form some rudimentary, hybrid *collage*. Terribly gruesome. Most troubling.

*What* are we dealing with? No sightings yet, no physical manifestations. Only evidence. Only corpses.

Might it be invisible, or capable of invisibility? Whatever. Something from *outside* has been well and truly unleashed.

Extraordinary general meeting convened at HQ. Posting of Inner Council members to strategic towns around murder sites debated and passed. Naturally, F will co-ordinate. B volunteered to second the task force—wants to be in the thick of things. Am in two minds about this. Will be dangerous. Can't even go to help, V instructed me to stay at HQ and develop defensive strategy. Do I detect F's hand in this? Politicking already? Hmmm.

13th May.
Becoming more and more diff. to maintain covert status of operation. Leaks slip out regardless. Even some references in the press to "serial killer". Something is definitely trying to break through. Are these the first sorties of an *invasion force* (???). Ye Gods! What if this is a full-scale war with something from *outside*? How could we even hope to defend the whole population? And our defences less than half ready! Still no one, none of the Order or the public has witnessed any physical manifestations. Why?!? All those hints from the research. Was I so wrong? Barking up all the wrong trees in a completely different fucking forest? Hope so. Hope I'm wrong.

25th May.
Can *they* take on human form— the Outsiders? V thinks so, as does F. If this *is* true, our options in event of a full-scale invasion= drastically reduced.
More murders. Corpses mount up. Cover-up nigh on impossible, there must be a cover story soon. Only vaguely heartening note is that murders are confined to isolated, outlying communities. No strikes at the population centres, as of yet.
The towns are safe.

1st June.
F has been talking about using the Weapon. This worries me as much as the threat from outside. So dangerous, so foolish … talk about last stand! But facts speak for themselves: peculiar sightings have begun, in abandoned areas. The hills, the Highlands. People report actually seeing *her*—

tall, dressed in red, so it must be true, what V and F think.

2nd June.
Is this what some have feared all along? *Can* they cross the barrier unaided? So easily? The very heart of our Order under threat. It *is* the threat. A traitor in our midst. Our own power—the only strength we possess in the face of the enemy—will be our undoing! All these years have we just been standing in a dark room shouting, "Look at me! Look at what I can do! Look over here!"?

*Some day they will notice us.*

The Multitude?

Can barely write for shaking. Gods save us all. What *can* we do?

3rd June.
At end of tonight's Inner Council Meeting V launched into a great, grand speech about how we are the "custodians of the human race". But all I could think of was how terrified I was. Throughout, B simply watched me, and F watched B.

7th June.
F and I almost fought last night. Not blows, but came close. Saw his hatred, could taste it. All started after an extended row over use of the Weapon, once again. A brief struggle, but inconclusive (think F saw sense pretty soon into it). But I was encouraged by how closely we were matched in strength. Even so, this is madness. In the midst of a silent, unknown war that might destroy us all, we are fighting *each other*!!!

Madness.

The cracks beginning to show. To widen.

9th June.
A dark, dark day. Terrible, terrible day. *A whole village*! The name? Hell, can't even remember the name. Where? Where? F knows. Ask F. Well away from anywhere. Just a little spot of life near the hills, miles from anywhere. But. Dead. All dead. In the morning. A bright, still day by all accounts. And silent. Absolutely.

The Wards warned us. They didn't help, but they warned F and team, who went straight away. But even F wouldn't film what they found there, will barely talk about it. Gods! The horror!

It had been to every house, *every single house in the whole village*! Men, women, children, goldfish, livestock, cats, spiders, cars, even some of the buildings themselves. Taken from every circumstance: at the breakfast table, in bed, in the bath, even taking a shit, for God's sake!

Dismantled. Dismembered. Very, very carefully trimmed, sliced into neat, bloodless pieces and then rearranged into all manner of unnatural patterns. The *whole* village. Every single occupant of that doomed place.

But worse still (or better, in a terrible way), *IT* was still there. It, the thing, the murderer was still lurking in the houses. Finishing off? Waiting to be transported back? Who knows. F and the others *saw* it. Drove two of them mad straight off—Inner Council members at that—just to lay eyes on it. They tried to send it back, but it *wouldn't go*. They used all the castings they knew, but still it wouldn't go, and they couldn't make it. So they had to fight.

F is guarded, says little of the thing, but was in conference with V for over two hours just trying to describe it. Later, V dropped hints—flakes of blackness, like living, pulsing ink; blades and feelers and tentacles, moving like maggots in the hot belly of week-old road kill. And one particular detail that won't leave me, about its presence. When it attacked there was a dreadful hush that was stiller and denser and deadlier than normal silence.

Don't want to know any more.

One other thing. F said they couldn't even be sure whether entity was actually a creature at all—an actual Outsider—or some *tool* of theirs. Like a living, organic instrument. A remote blade. A living *surgical* implement, say? A scalpel with a mind of its own?

Twelve adepts entered the village with F.

Only F survived. Scarred inside. And the Thing finally left of its own accord, after its curiosity had been sated.

Is this the end of our Order? End of our world?

11th June.
Visited the Lower Archive once more. Almost didn't survive. Heart stopped. B there to revive me just in time. However, think have a plan. Very dangerous—stupidly fucking dangerous—but possible. Last chance. Only chance. Will put it to the Inner Council tonight, at midnight muster.

12th June.
Scheme was passed, unanimously. Am to compose my team post-haste. V wishes to proceed as soon as possible (the element of surprise?). No time to wonder why F changed allegiances so dramatically, now supporting me. Maybe his experience in the dead village? Seeing it?

28th June.
Tonight is the last chance. No other options, no other choices. If we fail then they will come through and there will be nothing we can do to stop them. They might destroy us all in one blow, or hide amongst us, dressed in our skins, for years, waiting and watching, toying with us. Playing. Experimenting, while we carry on dreaming of safety and sleepwalking to our doom.

Tonight. B will be with me. I pray. I pray for us all. The night, the darkness presses at my windows.

Time. No time to write any more. They have come for me. I go.

**

There were no further entries.

The gloom hummed with the gentle breathing of the PC, its fan. Jacob had his hand on the screen. "Fifteen years ago," he said, almost inaudibly. His fingers were trembling. *What happened*? No answer, only fear. The screen's light daubed his face with powder-blue highlights, scraped out sickle shadows beneath his eyes.

"The police," Maria told him firmly.

"'Some day they will notice us…'"

"Come *on*, let the police figure it, Jake," she sounded a bit desperate.

Jacob felt dazed. "Uh, yeah. Yeah. Police."

*... hidden amongst us, dressed in our skins ...*

"We go together, M," he said. "We stay together." He meant that he needed her now, and he knew that she knew. It didn't matter.

Maria looked undecided in the gloom, gnawing on her lip. "Okay," she finally said. "Yes, yes. Just let's go. "

## 8. Way, Shape or Form

"I'll drive." Jacob thought Maria would argue, but she seemed almost relieved to drop the keys into his hand. She looked pale, drawn.

"You okay?" he asked, trying to grin. But his face creased the wrong way. He felt about as bad as he ever had about anything. His life has been tossed up into a hurricane, and spun around and around while he gasped and prayed not to fall. And now he had drawn Maria into the storm with him.

"No," she replied, but accompanied her answer with a pained smile that lightened her face a little.

"Maria," he said softly, but he could already sense her recoiling from his tenderness. He opened the car door for her, then hurried around to the driver's side, risking a glance in through the back window to spy on her. He'd seen some crummy film once where the main tag was, if the girl reached over to open the driver's door for her guy, they were each other's forever.

Jacob opened his own door. Maria was picking at her lower lip and staring blankly at—not through—the windscreen.

"That disk—," Jacob began.

Maria shivered. "The police, Jake. Leave it for them. It's their job, after all."

"But it was ... disturbed. I mean, terrible, horrible. *Jesus*. 'Some day they will notice us'- what *is* that shit?"

"Jake, will you just leave it!" She stared at him and he saw a sheen of pity clouding her gaze. He didn't like it, not one bit. "You fall apart if you want, Jake, I'm getting out of it. Right now."

Jacob cursed and twisted the key sharply, stalling the car immediately. Trying to rest his foot gently on the clutch only made his ankle twitch spastically, as if the car was transmitting a minor shock to him. He started over again and the vehicle jerked forward with a crunch: he'd left it in gear.

"Here, I'll drive." Maria already had the door open as Jacob jerked the key for the third time and nosed the car along the pavement. She slammed it shut and scowled at him, but he was concentrating too hard to be distracted.

He aimed the car towards the big police HQ on the outskirts of town. It was rush hour and they were travelling with the flow, cars pressing all around like uninvited escorts. Somehow Jacob nursed the car through the throng, his instincts taking over in spite of his thoughts being miles and hours away.

He watched the rear-view mirror, searching for the gleaming black Mercedes, even though he knew it couldn't possibly be there. He saw a dark-coloured car and his hands tightened to claws on the steering wheel. After an instant of terror, then he identified it as a Mondeo. Even so he kept looking back, sure he could see three black figures behind the Mondeo's windscreen, sunglasses glinting in the strobing bars of evening light.

"You should have turned off back there." Maria's voice was flat, quiet—qualities he recognised all too well. She was fuming, storing up her anger like a giant capacitor, ready to unleash it in a flash if he gave her half a chance. That was the crucial difference between them, the one that had finally infected the waters of their love beyond any hope of purification. If he was mad, he let it out. Maria kept her temper bottled up like some dangerous culture, a killer virus only ever to be employed in the direst of circumstances. Like now, when she was terrified.

"Just nipping to my place," he said as he swung into another side street.

"What?" she almost shouted.

"A few things I want to pick up, that's all."

She shifted to glare at him. He didn't turn. He locked his gaze onto the asphalt, though all he could think of were her beautiful eyes—how wide they were, how dark, how the dipping sun caught the moisture there and on her cheeks. He had hurt her again, hurt her and scared her and dragged her into all this ....

He hated himself even more. Why couldn't he start to heal like she had? Why couldn't he let go?

"M, really, I need some stuff. Some clothes. Money." *And my pictures of you, he thought.*

"Then we'll go to the police, tell them what's happening. Show them the disk. I'll copy it while I'm home, just in case—"

Maria didn't answer but resumed her pose of silent reproach, glaring straight ahead, jaw set, eyes hard. Jacob drove on.

**

"What is it?"

Jacob had stopped the car at the end of his street, hidden behind the high park wall that dripped with banal graffiti: *Dave 4 Clare 4 ever; I fucked Sally here; I see the end and it's gloppy*. He'd always wondered about that last one, had the unsettling notion that the handwriting mimicked his own.

"Something's wrong," he murmured, unease prickling the hairs on the back of his neck.

He eased the car forward, riding the clutch until he could see past the end of the wall. The street was alive with the usual gangs of children playing football, and larking about. Ragged trees stood stoically on either side, their trunks scored and ravaged by decades of love-struck kids, bad parking and dog piss. Smashed glass winked from the gutters, and several young women perched on a doorstep passing round a roll-up.

There was a black Mercedes parked in front of his apartment block.

"They're here. They're here, M... Waiting for me... They know where I live."

He could see someone lounging on the bonnet of the Mercedes, facing the opposite end of the street. His posture was very casual, exuding a faint boredom, his hair a silver-grey buzz cut, smooth suede buff close across the scalp. He was short but neatly made, evidently quite trim and rather fit. Wide through the shoulders, snake-hipped.

Jacob felt a tingle of fear. The man was holding something he couldn't quite make out, and was manipulating it with blasé twists of his wrist. At first Jacob thought it was a flick knife, catching the late rays of the sun as it described circles around the man's hand. Then, peering closer, he had to think again. The Mercedes was in shadow. The tower block hid this intruder from the sun, yet his hand glowed with a queasy luminescence.

At every flicker of the light, Jacob winced as if his eardrums were being pricked with tiny needles. Dogs up and down the street were barking in an agitated cacophony.

Maria leaned forward in the passenger seat, stared at the Mercedes and the man for two minutes. She didn't speak. At last, she turned slowly back to Jacob. He could almost see the threads of disbelief intertwining in her mind. "Police, Jake."

"M, let's just see if—"

"*Now*, Jacob."

"Wait, what if—"

"I'm scared." She didn't raise her voice—her tone remained the same—but the force of her words hit him like a body blow. What the fuck was he dragging her into? What right did he have to expose her to this?

"M, I'm so sorry. Oh, Christ..." He trailed off when he realised that mere words were inadequate.

"Police, Jake."

He nodded. Went to knock the car into gear. Stopped. "No need."

A police Range Rover—painted with that gaudy Battenberg design which stood out so clearly on wet grey motorways—was cruising down the street from the other end. Jacob nodded and Maria followed his gaze. Her hand shot out and flattened against the dash, as if to secure herself against an impact. She choked back a surprised gasp.

Silver Hair must have seen the Range Rover; something that big and colourful couldn't escape notice. Jacob waited for him to dash to the front door, call his goons and make good his escape. But he remained where he was, spinning the glowing thing around his hand, head casually on one side, shoulders low.

"Now what?" Maria spoke as if things weren't over, and the inference dragged up a spray of old fears for Jacob, terrors that he couldn't name or properly identify. It was as if he had written messages to himself long ago and now found he could no longer read his own writing.

"Now," he said. "We'll see what these bastards have to say for themselves."

"No. Jake, why isn't that guy running? What's he up to?" Silver Hair had stopped his hand twirling and quenched the dancing brightness of the object with a complex gesture.

The Range Rover double-parked next to the Mercedes and two

policemen climbed out. The driver spun his baton in a poor imitation of Silver Hair's dexterity, then slipped it into his belt. Jacob had a fleeting memory of Trev, smiling with relief a split-second before the guard's nightstick pulverised his nose. The Rover's passenger was huge, at least six-foot-six even without his cap, but as he approached Silver Hair, Jacob still felt a twinge of doubt. This seemed all wrong. None of the body language made sense. It didn't feel right.

Someone appeared at the entrance to the apartment block. It was one of the thugs from the guest house. He slipped his sunglasses on as he saw the policemen. He looked to Silver Hair, who, despite his curiously laid-back air, seemed to be in charge. Silver Hair raised a palm to him: an "I'll take care of this" gesture.

The big policeman reached Silver Hair, who swung round easily. He appeared younger than his silvery thatch might suggest, though possessed of one of those curiously indeterminate faces that was difficult to date with much accuracy. Sharply handsome, thirtyish, fortyish, maybe. He raised his hand to the policeman. Jacob subconsciously waited for some shrill scream. A vibration of his eardrums too high to actually hear, but low enough to cause piercing discomfort. None came.

"What the hell?" Maria's hand slumped from the dash into her lap like a landed fish.

Silver Hair shook the tall policeman's hand with a flourish and greeted the driver with a nod, then waved airily back at the house. The man in the doorway strolled down the path, closely followed by two others. The last in line was the woman from the raid, the one who had filmed him at the demo. Perhaps the woman who had been tracking him for years, compiling a dossier of his movements and habits and contacts? He tried to remember the colour of her eyes behind those damn glasses. They made her face look as though it had been blacked out for confidentiality on a late-night TV exposé.

"This is just not fucking happening," Jacob hissed.

"But they're the police." Maria gaped, stunned.

"One of those guys might have killed Morris."

"But they're the ..." Shock had stolen her vocabulary.

Jacob went to start the car, but Maria grabbed his leg and squeezed. "Wait. Let's see. We need to know what's going on."

Silver Hair nodded at Jacob's building, shrugged, flicked a cigarette into his mouth. Everything he did was like that shrug: langorous, underpowered, calm. The policeman he was talking to doffed his cap and ran a hand through his hair, shaking out a mist of sweat droplets. The three others, dressed in black and wearing dark scowls to match, slipped into the Mercedes. Silver Hair was the last to embark, exchanging a final few words with the policemen before he slammed the door. A puff of exhaust smoke marked their departure.

"Follow them," Maria said. "Let's find out where they're staying. Maybe they'll even lead us to Trev and the others."

"What about my flat? I need to check what they've done!" Jacob exclaimed.

Maria glared at him. "What do you own that's valuable?"

Jacob shrugged.

"You value your life?" Maria pressed.

He felt like shrugging again, but nodded instead.

"If I were you, then, I wouldn't worry too much about your flat. Doubtless these people you've got us mixed up with will be keeping an eye on it until you get back."

Jacob felt a surge of guilt as she talked of "us" being mixed up with these killers. He had dragged Maria into something deadly, and as the minutes went by, he realised there was less and less of a chance of her easily shaking free of it. She'd been trapped by his anger, caught by his misdirected, fucked-up rage.

Once again, he realised why she had left him. And once again he found himself loving her all the more.

"Yes. We'll follow the bastards."

The Mercedes was already at the other end of the street, left indicator winking. The police Rover cruised past their car, and for a few prickly seconds they were exposed. But the men inside were talking, the driver's attention pinned on the road, so Jacob was certain that they hadn't been spotted.

If there were others watching his house, then so be it.

**

Jacob had seen it done in the movies countless times. Keep a few cars back; drive casual; slip through gaps in the traffic. But now, forced to trail a car himself, he found it far more difficult than he ever could have imagined.

Maria was little help. Every time it looked as though they had lost sight of the Mercedes she became agitated, squirming constantly on the car's upholstery as if the stress was discharging mild electric shocks. Speed conspired against them, too. The Mercedes ate the road, while Maria's old Metro took slow bites like a dozy heifer. Jacob kept knocking down a gear or two to try to coax more power from the old engine, but the grating reports from under the bonnet only earned him a stern reprimand from Maria. In the end, though, the car didn't matter. Nothing mattered. He was still living with the certain guilt of Morris's death, and the vicarious pain suffered by his fellow eco-warriors, whatever they may be at that moment: alive or dead.

He never thought it would take so long. An hour after tagging onto the Mercedes, they were still shadowing it. They had left the town and headed off into the countryside, Jacob began to worry that they would be noticed. While the sparser traffic made the pursuit easier, so the chances of their being spotted increased a hundredfold.

As the sun hit the hillsides, the Mercedes turned off the main road onto a narrower lane. Jacob held back and knocked off his headlights, trusting the fading light to keep them out of ditches. Maria sat upright, peering hard so that she would be able to tell as soon as the Mercedes left the lane.

They needn't have worried. Jacob put his foot down as they saw the bloody glow of brake-lights, and when they passed the gate a mansion loomed out of the darkness like a giant's gravestone. Lights twinkled across its brooding façade, yet still it seemed strangely barren.

Jacob drove further on along the lane, coasting to a slow halt before performing a nervous U-turn. He crept back up the road, letting the clutch pull them along rather than risking the throttle. Not far from the mansion another rough track opened into a ploughed field on the opposite side. Maria jumped out and hauled the gate open. Jacob grimaced as the old hinges squealed in protest.

Minutes later they were safely ensconced behind a row of low conifers. Starlight glinted off the Mercedes in front of the mansion, though they couldn't tell whether its occupants remained inside.

"I'm sorry, M," Jacob said quietly. He felt like one big apology.

She reached across, and for a moment he thought she was going to take his hand. But she patted his shoulder, the gesture distant and impersonal enough to draw stinging tears to his eyes.

"It's all right Jake," she said, but he knew from her tone that no, it really wasn't. Not now. Not ever.

## 9. Waves and Wounds

*He cannot tear his gaze from the dead man.*

*Even though terror is bearing down inexorably upon them, still the body grips his attention. The corpse has fallen to the crawling ground, and has started to disintegrate. Darting shapes—ant-like things, big as scorpions, made of blood—nip at the exposed flesh. They burrow into the wound at the back of the cadaver's neck and bear away gory morsels. The body's cells seem possessed of a sudden repulsive energy, their binding properties reversed by this perverse domain until their very molecules rip apart in a cloudy red haze. In a matter of seconds the dead man has ceased to be an individual. Now, he is a swarm.*

*He turns away from the sight as something brushes his arm. He spins around, but the movement is instantly transmuted into a dive by the unnatural geomotries of this place. He thrusts out his hands, certain that they will be seized by the swarm and undone in a bloody frenzy.*
*Above him—if one can use such a term in a place such as this—"up" where darkness pirouettes endlessly, something is stirring.*

*A hand catches his arm and jerks him upright. The woman with the knife passes her hand in front of his face, disturbing a shimmer of motes in the air and casting black rainbows across his vision.*

*"He's gone," she signals. "It is coming... Priorities."*

*He nods, feeling as if his brain is a loose ball-bearing rebounding off the inner planes of his skull. He yearns for the luxury of a scream, a cathartic bellow of rage and madness, but if he opens his mouth all that seething life will flood in unchecked. Besides, he has no breath.*

*Something appalling is almost upon them, something terrifyingly awesomely malevolent. Without a heart to beat faster or flowing blood to run cold, his body stiffens into a parody of terror: hands hooked as claws before his chest, eyes bulging.*

*The woman tries to sign to him but she too is gripped by the icy vice of dread. Her hand springs open and the knife falls away, or descends at least, and is immediately lost to sight.*

*The whole group stare fearfully in the same direction, the Citadel at their back the only reference point. They can see nothing but the gluey darting thickness surrounding them. They can sense the pressure building, though. A gentle shove comes first, rocking them on their feet; then a kick, a full-force explosion that sends them hurtling backwards.*

*From out of the corner of his eye—his vision distorted by the tricks played by this realm's skewed light—he sees one of the men calmly gutting himself as they tumble back, repelled by the bow-wave of the approaching terror. The man's innards snake out, blood pluming into the dense air like strands of dead sperm.*

*Then the entity arrives, looming—or maybe gathering—out of the seething air. The gigantic thing surges on, and with every blink he thinks it is upon them. But it takes an age to arrive. An age in which the woman beside him opens her mouth to scream and swallows a thrashing shape studded with glistening barbs and grappling hook-like shapes. She gags, her eyeballs bulge—then erupt from their sockets, to be followed by twisting spumes of flowing mucus which themselves seem to be swimming with lidless, black eyes.*

*He tries to look away before the creature—or swarm of creatures—reverses its journey, but still he witnesses the cascade of red and purple and pink as she is turned inside out.*

*Her body bumps the ground ("Down"? Where is "down"? What is "down"?) and quickly dissolves away, though her innards remain hanging grotesquely in the air. Seconds later, they slap across the surface of the approaching terror and remain where they strike, like smashed flies on a black, reflective windscreen.*

*He catches a full glimpse of the terror then, a wall of blackness on which colours play like oil across water, endlessly flowing. Some of the colours he knows, yet others are so alien as to register only blankness in the visual centres of his cortex. The thing fills all the angles of his vision, expanding up and around the remains of the team, a giant bubble enveloping them, changing and billowing. For an instant before it hits they see their reflections along its shiny, living, dreadfully sentient surface.*

*The thing sweeps unstoppably over them, driving a man and a woman into each other's arms, blending them as they are driven beneath the surface before they burst asunder in a gush of red. He is still trying to scream, still trying to expunge the filth and the pain from his convulsing body. The entity scrapes his skin, tearing chunks of his flesh away with barbed hooks, ripping his clothes and shredding them from his body. He tries to force his hands down to protect his genitals, but feels them grabbed and held by something slippery and cold.*

*He bounces. His rucksack absorbs some of the impact, flinging him up again into backward flight and forcing him clear of the passing mountain of madness. He looks down and sees a man grabbing onto his lower legs, eyes wide and teeth locked into an insane grimace.*

*He is still tumbling, distance and direction exchanging places, spinning his senses all around. The ground grasps at him with greedy claws, but the great wake left by the horror drags him from its tearing hands. He bounces again and reaches down, trying to grasp onto whatever he has bounced from, eager to feel anything solid in this maelstrom.*

*His hand closes around a shape and draws it to his face: it is a rat-faced, offal-limbed obscenity, its multifaceted eyes glimmering with cool intelligence. Its fangs are enormous, chipped, newly reddened.*

*He flings the creature away from him and it explodes into a cloud of tiny bat-things before disappearing altogether in the haze. He feels his momentum slowing. The rucksack is tugging him down, recognising gravity as, perhaps, an animate being cannot.*

*At last, a halt. The surface beneath him is a transluscent black mirror, like volcanic glass. He sees his own shadow, looks away quickly. Too unsettling. He examines his body, noting the slashes in his skin that do not bleed. He grabs for his genitals, glad at least to feel them whole.*

*To his left, the man with the manic grin is rolling across the black glass. He comes to a stop and kneels quickly.*

*"Rush? Rush? Rushing? Where's my head? Have you seen my head? I ate it, so it went well." The man is signalling frantically, words and phrases tangling together.*

*He crawls to the madman and grabs the sides of his head, trying to stare some sense into him. Eventually, the man calms himself slightly. He has lost a layer of skin from his face, and looks grotesquely sunburned.*

*He signals to Sunburn: "The Citadel. There."Pointing at the slowly turning mile-high spectacle. "We go there, now. You and me. Okay?"*

*Sunburn nods, fingers twisting at his side. "But my head!"*

*"You're fine. You still have your head. Anyone else left?"*

*They peer around together and see... no one.*

*Nothing.*

**

"Jake. Wake up."

For a moment his mind was full of reflections and fangs. Then: "Maria?" Jacob felt her hand on his leg, but she quickly withdrew it, perhaps realising the ambiguous implications of the touch.

"I'm right here, Jake... Something's happening."

He could just about make out the glitter of her eyes and vague outline of her face silhouetted against the starlit night.

"God!" He sighed and rubbed his face, shifted to stretch and immediately felt the tight weight of his swollen bladder. He had a vivid memory of pissing in the bathroom while Maria stood on the threshold ready to leave him, the laws of nature overriding the ineffectual rules that govern relationships. "Wassup?"

Maria didn't answer directly, but he sensed more than saw her nodding towards the mansion. The gates had been opened while he slept and now they stood like two outstretched arms, pointing back towards the old building. A splayed spider inviting flies to enter.

The sound of engines was approaching.

"I didn't want to wake you, but the Mercedes went off somewhere about an hour ago," Maria murmured. "Couldn't see who was in it, though."

Abruptly the night was lit up by a crowd of headlights: there was a police car, then a vehicle which looked like a cross between an armoured personnel carrier and a transit van. The Mercedes came next, and following that a gunmetal-grey Jaguar.

"And aren't we getting cosier and cosier?" Jacob mused.

He looked to Maria as light splashed across the car, and they both instinctively ducked. However the cars passed without pause, turning smoothly into the mansion gates and crunching their way up the gravel driveway. They finally fetched up before the building in a rough semicircle.

"Every time I see these people, there seems to be more and more of them."

"Maybe they like parties."

"Well, I don't know anyone who'd invite them—"

"Shhh!" Maria hissed, reaching over to grab his arm in the gloom. He liked the feel of her fingers; it reminded him of the way she used to grab him when they made love, as if she thought he would buck her off unless she held on tight. He was about to touch her hand, but then he noticed what she'd seen.

"The girl!"

Maria squeezed his arm tighter. "I never really believed..."

The van doors were open and the girl stood there, tall and blinking in the cool night air. Even through the fencing and shrubs Jacob could clearly see how she was shivering.

"The bastards!" He moved to open the car door, but Maria wouldn't let him.

"Jake, no! Jacob! You'll only get yourself hurt. Let's just wait a minute, see what happens."

Acknowledging the futility of his rage, Jacob let go of the door handle. They stared back at the mansion.

Silver Hair came out of the entrance and leaned beside the door, one knee up, foot braced against the gothic architrave so that he looked like a dancer at rest. Jacob could see the ruby spark of his cigarette bobbing like a firefly.

The driver's door of the Jaguar popped free, and the young woman from the guest house launched herself out. She stomped over to the security van where the girl was being held. The black-clad guards stepped aside to let her near.

The woman snatched hold of the girl's chin, digging her fingernails in to force the younger woman's mouth open. She jerked the girl's head back to inspect the inside of her mouth, then, once satisfied, moved her hands to search through her hair, which splayed around those questing fingers like greasy spaghetti; Jacob wondered when she'd last been allowed to wash. The brutal woman felt meticulously all around the girl's neck, scalp, shoulders and then— when she reached the collar of her dress— simply tore it down the front, right to the hem. Maria gasped, Jacob's breath caught. Beneath the dress the girl was naked.

The woman took equal care in checking the girl's body, patting her down, hugging round to check her back, her flanks, her sides; it was like watching some intimate medical examination, or an elaborate S&M role-play. She tugged off the remaining streamers of material and tossed them aside.

Maria made a small noise, her fist in her mouth, and Jacob noticed she was crying. There was nothing they could do other than bear witness to this gross humiliation. What a terrible thing it was for one woman to do to another, he thought, to expose her so completely and with such callous disregard. This casual disdain for another human being's dignity was chilling, almost more so than any atrocity these people had yet committed. The deed spoke of scorn and contempt and a horrifying, blank-faced arrogance.

Afterwards, the woman shepherded the girl towards the building with a series of bullying knocks and shoves. There was real cruelty in her attitude, in the way her body swung, following through with her kicks and punches.

The girl's head hung low, her long hair falling past her face to mask it completely. One particularly savage push caused her to stumble. She went down onto her knees and—unable to extend her chained hands—swayed forward and landed heavily on her face.

Another black-clad shape darted in from behind, lifted his foot and planted a kick in her side. The brutal woman bent to the girl and began clawing violently at her shoulder, trying to drag her up, while every now and then one of the other guards stole his chance to jab in a boot or lash a fist at the fallen teenager.

"Bastards," Maria gasped.

"Fuckers!" Jacob was incandescent with rage, but still he managed to prevent Maria from throwing open the door and running over to help the girl. The victim's back was trembling now, shaking as she cried and cried—lost and abandoned in a dark place.

Silver Hair dropped his cigarette and stamped it out, used his shoulders to shove himself off the wall and wandered over to the huddle of figures. He put a gentle hand on the brutal woman's shoulder. She paused and turned and the two of them wandered off a few paces to talk. After they'd expended a few moments' in intense conference she spun on a heel and stalked off in disgust.

Silver Hair stooped beside the sobbing girl. He put his face next to hers and Jacob imagined his expression to be very compassionate. His pose suggested it. He paid no attention to the other guards, neither reprimanding them nor favouring them with a glance.

He took the girl's chained hands in his and lifted her to her feet. As he did so another one of the black-clad men approached and casually kicked her between the buttocks. She almost fell again, but Silver Hair encircled her with his right arm and held her up.

"What's going on?" Jacob asked. Maria only shook her head, but Jacob thought it was more from disgust than bafflement.

"In the doorway," she said quietly. "Do you see? Isn't that the woman you described?"

Jacob squinted past the main action, and tried to make out the entrance to the mansion. It stood in darkness, but the stars were out in force tonight, and they dusted the frail sheen of distant suns over the scene.

"Yes, it's her," he said quietly. He could see the shading of her scarred skin even from this distance as the stars' undecided luminescence played across her face. He detected a hint of her long flowing robe and recognised again how tall she was, how stately in bearing. The red of her garb seemed to merge with the bloody hue of the stone behind her.

Silver Hair and the girl neared the steps, his hand fixed benevolently to her shoulder. After their final act of disobedience all the guards had hung back, cowed by Silver Hair's restrained authority. The brutal woman glowered beside her Jag.

"She's very beautiful—the girl—you never mentioned that."

Jacob frowned. He hadn't mentioned it because he hadn't thought about it. The girl was beautiful, so what? It hadn't even occurred to him to think of her in that way. All he'd felt for her so far was tenderness. Outrage at her treatment. There was something about her that repelled his desire. But now he tried to see her as a young, naked, beautiful girl, to test out those other emotions.

It didn't work. He noticed how tall she was—at least three, four inches taller than Silver Hair, almost as tall as the scarred woman—and the fact that, despite her maltreatment, she still managed to move with a certain weary grace. He remembered how, when he'd first seen her, he'd thought that she looked like a fashion model. For a beat he imagined her in the future— if she survived all this—saw her prowling down a catwalk; swish of the hip, high poised chin on the turn. Then her physical condition—the ugly taint of bruises and the trails of drying blood —brought him back down to earth with a jolt. He tried to imagine what the lustre of her skin had been like up close, but he felt nothing, nothing more than a father might feel for someone else's abused daughter. A paternal outrage.

He wondered what the girl liked: did she have a favourite band, or a boy-friend? Posters on her bedroom wall at home? Immaculate rugs and scatter cushions? Maybe she still shared a room with her sister?

Maybe her parents had kept her room exactly as it had been the day she went missing.

Jacob knew that he had to *save* this girl from whatever fate her captors intended. For Morris. For the puppies. For Maria… For *himself*. It was the only way he could make any kind of amends.

The girl reached the door with Silver Hair, and the scarred woman stood to one side. The girl didn't look up as she passed, nor did the woman glance down at the wretched figure. After the rest of the group had filed obediently inside, the woman in red remained there, alone, regarding the night with a straight back and stiffly crossed arms, her face obscured by shade. Jacob imagined her gaze beaming through the darkness, searching for them with X-ray penetration. He shuddered, felt his face prickle as her head turned their way.

"We've got to do something," he whispered in frustration.

"The police—" Maria began uncertainly.

"The police? The *police*! Take a good look- *there* are your police!" He flung his arm out for emphasis, an all-embracing sweep. They both heard his elbow click, such was the force of the gesture. The three officers who had come in with the convoy stood in plain view, the polished buttons of their uniforms glinting from across the mansion's driveway.

Maria said nothing. The coppers—their special duties evidently discharged—climbed back into their car and swiftly pulled away. The tall woman watched them go, then closed the heavy door behind her.

The forecourt stood once more in darkness. The house, too. Darkness and silence.

**

Jacob and Maria spent some long, cold while waiting for something else to happen, but nothing did. It was helplessness that kept them there—and fear—and an excruciating sense of impotence. As they waited they puzzled over where they could go for help, now even the police had turned traitor? When things finally livened up, though, they did so with alarming speed:

At about midnight five police cars roared along the road, spraying plumes of gravel as they hastily drew up in front of the house. Their occupants remained inside while a black snake of figures emerged from the mansion, and then scattered as people proceeded to clamber into the assembled civilian vehicles. Jacob and Maria were able to make out Silver Hair and the woman in red, the brutal woman, too, and others who'd been involved in the search of Jacob's flat. The forecourt was flooded with harsh security lighting, but hardly any sound crept back to them, with the whole operation being concluded in grim, stealthy silence.

As they all departed, birds fluttered from treetops and mysterious rustlings came from the hedgerows. Afterwards, the heavy silence reigned once more.

Jacob and Maria stirred in their seats, unable to decide whether to follow the convoy or not.

"The girl's still in there," Maria ventured.

"I know. How many guarding her, you think?"

"What?"

"Just wondering."

"Jesus, you numb skull! What are you thinking? Have you gone insane?"

*Maybe*, thought Jacob. *Nothing else could explain this.*

Maria sighed. "Sorry," she muttered. But her words were already out there, causing harm. They sat on in silence, only it was a silence which curdled in the space between them, stinking and putrefying. Neither one looked at the other. The minutes slunk by.

Then came the light.

Abrupt flashes at first, brighter than flashbulbs and shorter-lived. They strobed through every window in the mansion, scorching the impression of the window-frames onto Jacob's retinas, slicing the night into pieces. It was as if an alien sun was flashing into existence inside the old building, struggling for purchase on the slippery walls of our reality before slipping back into dark oblivion.

Maria leapt from the car the instant the flashes ignited, heading for the mansion, quite ignorant of her own advice. Jacob followed at a run. He wanted to shout, to tell her to wait, but fear rendered him dumb.

They reached the open mansion gates together, and that's when whatever was inside the mansion found its rhythm.

# Hush

The whole night exploded.

## 10. The Only

As they sprinted along the gravel driveway a new sensation met their advance head on. It started as a rumbling, flesh-crawling vibration, part sound, part feeling, then became a wall of incredible pressure which detonated against their bodies. Maria stumbled to a halt and rubbed her ears as if they were ready to pop; Jacob kept on running, swallowing hard to pop his.

They witnessed strange animate shadows rolling around the base of the mansion—as if darkness flowed in waves to fill the absence left by the eruption of light—but when they finally arrived at the great Gothic entrance everything had fallen still. No security lighting came on, no dogs came running, no voices shouted.

The main doors were slightly ajar. Jacob nudged them open with his boot and peered inside.

Many years of exposure to Hammer films and English heritage documentaries had schooled Jacob in what he should expect to discover behind a mansion's front door, so it came as a slight shock for him to find himself confronted with a narrow panelled corridor not a draughty arching hallway. He aimed a quizzical look at Maria, but she only shrugged, so he crept gingerly inside.

A thick stew of odours met him as he entered. Foremost was a pungent chemical stench that he couldn't quite place. Some sort of preservative, perhaps? Underneath that he could distinguish other tangs: mint, urine, rubber. There was one naked lightbulb above the door, but its light was very weak, a dusky glow that only intensified Jacob's sense of claustrophobia and unease.

The panelling was dark glazed oak to match the outer doors, oddly rough-grained to the eye. Under such feeble radiance the varnish seemed to glisten, like a coating of saliva. Jacob ran his fingertips across the nearest panel and frowned, detecting a very definite pattern of ridges beneath his touch. Leaning closer he realised his initial mistake: the wood wasn't rough, it was *engraved.*

Fluted onto the corridor walls was an elaborate scroll of tiny runes, a little like Egyptian hieroglyphics but more abstract, less individualised—a sinuous spool of insignia creeping in every direction.

Jacob paced slowly along, following the patterns with his eyes and fingers. The tortuous scoring was so dense, so convoluted that it was difficult to make out any overall scheme, but he *did* detect certain motifs repeated in amongst the cross hatched jungle of helixes, pips and crescents. The general cast of these marks seemed more *mathematical* than mystical, as if they comprised an elongated stream of mad equations.

The clicking of his heels on the wood rang out in the unearthly stillness, followed by the more cautious scrape of Maria's feet. "God!" she breathed in awe as she noticed what he'd seen. The ceiling was decorated as well, and the floor. They were standing in a whole *tunnel* of runes; surrounded on every side.

The corridor wasn't long. The final panels approaching the single inner door held the added curiosity of symbols inlaid with bright strips of silver.

Jacob moved to the door and put his hand to it. The wood was warm. He could feel intense heat radiating from the handle, and knew that it would scald him if he touched it. What was behind the door? No noise slid through. He found he was holding his breath, so let it out as one long uninterrupted hiss.

He turned to Maria, who had drawn close. Their eyes met and she nodded tersely. He shucked off his jacket, wrapped it around his fist and reached for the handle.

It took quite an effort to work the action of the doorknob—which had seized up somehow—and even then Jacob still had to force the door open with his shoulder. It was warped in its frame. When he saw the main hall beyond, he realised why.

Every exposed surface had been burnt to blackened ruin.

Gusts of heat still hung in the air like clingy drapes which fluttered against them. Sweat instantly prickled on Jacob's brow and his eyes began to water, but he moved forward all the same, blinking tears away. Maria stood at his shoulder, her sweater tugged up to protect her mouth and nose. They surveyed the destruction together.

Although the ceiling vaulted much higher in this room than in the corridor, it still wasn't the vast swooping space Jacob had anticipated. The chamber had a cramped, boxy feel to it, a sense that was exaggerated by the fire damage.

It was like being in a forest directly after a snow storm; everything remained slightly in motion. Soft brittle collapses, settling cracks and nervous gunshot pops. Showers of ash, like clumps of leprous snow, fell repeatedly from the toasted beams above. A constant shiver of rearrangement, as if the room kept adjusting its clothes in a mirror.

The floor was a uniform crispy black, carpet and wood transformed into the same grizzled wad. If the panelled walls here had borne any markings then their secrets were irretrievably lost—blank as fire could make them—but somehow the modest chandelier had escaped mainly intact and lit up the devastation with a stubborn milky glare.

No fewer than eight doors opened out from this chamber. All were closed, seared, burnt tight into their warped and splintered frames. A tolerably impressive staircase stamped directly up to the first floor before branching out left and right into a landing which afforded access to yet more doorways and passages.

What did confuse Jacob, though, was the amalgam of scents he had detected upon entering the building; it was actually stronger in here. The stench of cooked wood merely played a supporting role. He sniffed around experimentally, to see if he could gauge the source, but couldn't.

He sucked noisily on his lips as he pondered, opening and closing his mouth in little contemplative air kisses. Something didn't quite add up. Wouldn't an explosion have left a blast centre? A gradation of damage radiating outwards, not this even charring of all exposed planes?

He looked at Maria, puzzled. "So. Where?" he asked. She shrugged and peered around. Craned her neck.

"Do you think that staircase might still hold our weight?"

"Yeah. I think it was just the tops of everything that caught the brunt. Can't figure on why, though." He shrugged. "Structurally it looks sound enough. Upstairs, you reckon?"

"Well, there's a door open there. Look."

She was right. A pair of double doors stood ominously agape, right at the limit of the landing. With scrupulous care they began to climb, cautiously testing every step with their weight. Though scorched boards squealed all throughout their ascent they managed to make the summit without serious incident.

They reached the open doorway and Jacob was amazed to see that, miraculously, the room beyond had barely been brushed by the flames. However, the distinctive stench was even more pronounced in there, and emblazoned on the plush carpet was something that froze Jacob to his bowels: across the floor someone had splashed out a hasty spiral of intricate symbols in luminous paint.

The geometric whorl was conspicuously unfinished, and terminated in an arcing splatter, as if a can of the stuff had been kicked violently against the wall.

"Aren't magical circles meant to protect people from summoned evil?" Maria asked quietly.

"Is that what you think?"

"Frankly, I think I want my mummy."

Jacob smiled, heartened that she could still joke in the midst of all this.

"Me too," he returned, but could only manage to keep up the smile for a moment. Maria looked pale and gaunt, a smut of transient ash soiling her cheek.

Suddenly there was an explosive crash, as if something had collapsed back in the hallway, and they both jumped.

"Is this wise?" Maria blurted into the eggshell silence that followed.

"No."

"They could be back at any time, and what if there are people left in the house?"

There was another door in the room, leading further into the mansion. Jacob moved towards it. It was closed, but a key protruded from the lock. Maria tugged at him. He shrugged free of her and flicked the key, throwing the door wide open.

He wished she had tried harder to stop him. Much, *much* harder.

Patterns. Interpreting patterns is what the human brain is good at. We wander through a world of sleeting information, bombarded by a ceaseless storm of pictures, scents and tactile impressions of every kind. From that maelstrom we wrestle significance. We decode. Our brains pin together all the random bits of readout from our senses, then assiduously arrange them into coherent patterns. Millions of years of focused evolution have forced us to impose order onto chaos. The world just happens; *we* give it meaning.

The passage they stared into was full of dead bodies, though Jacob couldn't understand it that way at first. His brain wasn't able to decode these images in those stark terms, not straightaway at least. The bare boards had buckled and strange wooden ruptures were all he was seeing; the mounds were just mountains of discarded clothing; it was all an elementary trick of the light, a symptom of the weary illumination lighting the corridor.

The evidence of his eyes simply didn't make any sense. If these shapes on the floor— these random scatterings of meat—were dead bodies, then where was the blood?

This new world he had opened the door onto defied reason. He'd plunged headfirst into lunacy; the patterns escaped him, slid through his fingers like streams of water. Streams of blood. A great white something was rising up inside his mind. An all-consuming blankness that ate into the edges of his rationality…

Those terrible lines from the diary came back to him:
*Corpses disarticulated... carefully dismantled, drained of all blood and arranged on the grass like engine parts.*

At the end of the passageway stood another door, and beyond that he could hear someone crying.

Maria clapped her hands to her face and began to shake. Instinctively, he knew she wouldn't be able to accompany him. This was his duty. He had opened the door and everything spun out from that act. *He* was responsible, and he alone would have to follow this sequence of events through to its conclusion.

"No," Maria whispered. "Nonononono." She fell onto her knees and hid her face.

Jacob noticed with detached curiosity that her nail polish was exactly the same hue as the blood would have been, had it been present. The only true red he could see in amongst all this death.

In the decryption centres of his brain the struggle continued. He was being told something important through these patterns, if only he could get at it. There was a story written in the engravings, in the arrangement of the bodies, in the colour of Maria's fingernails. A truth was being told.

The only way to solve the mystery was to move on. He couldn't turn back now. All that was needed were footsteps, though for Jacob footsteps had become the hardest thing in the world to muster. His legs were lead, his body stone. Panic welled up but he clenched it down, gazed at his feet in the hope that the very act of observation would somehow force them to obey. Against all the dictates of reason this strategy seemed to pay off. A pronounced shudder passed through his body, and he began to walk.

He reasoned that, if he wanted to know how many people had died here, all he would have to do was count any one class of body part: eyes, forearms, fingers, genitals.

*Wounds surgical in nature... Neat dissection... Dismembered... Dismantled.*

He also knew that if he paused to meditate on the carnage he was finished. The white gulf in his mind would swallow his sanity, leave him gibbering and playing with his own drool. But if he locked his gaze onto the door handle ahead, then those pale shapes out on the periphery could easily be mistaken for broken shop window dummies.

*Very, very carefully trimmed, sliced into neat, even bloodless pieces... Still alive when dismemberment began.*

Jacob tried to swallow, but couldn't quite manage it. The membranes in his throat seemed to rasp. The floor felt faintly sticky, slimy, with a slight adhesion which hung on jealously to his soles.

He proceeded with infinite patience, his hands raised up at hip level like a tightrope walker. The tunnel seemed to stretch on interminably, then deflated around his field of vision until he was staring down a dark-veined, revolving tube. His consciousness ebbed, threatening to fade altogether. The door retreated as he stubbornly trudged towards it.

Eventually, though, he reached his destination. The door was engraved and inlaid with silver. He rested his forehead against the neatly scored wood and just breathed, deeply, evenly for a while. He became very aware of the shape of his lips, their distinctive texture. He wondered, absently, what colour they were now. Then, without any more thought or ceremony, he opened the door.

What waited for him in there wasn't terrible simply because it resembled a collision between some of the wetter installations in a Damien Hirst exhibition and one of Bosch's more outré visions of hell. No, the room he stared into was horrifying because of its simple tidiness.

A stupefying array of body parts had apparently been graded by size, shape and function, then carefully arranged into long tapering columns. Jacob visualised some mad alien professor, complete with white lab coat, squatting over the bodies, eagerly inspecting every item, the light glinting off his skew-whiff spectacles, manic gleam in his eyes.

The effect of this collage was disconcerting, and not a little beautiful. All those pale, bloodless fragments resembled a collection of rare deep-sea fish, calcified like pastel-tinted coral. At the centre of the gruesome clutter was a ring of luminous symbols, one that had been completed.

Within the circle sat the girl.

She was still naked, and her skin shone in the cone of soft light located above the spiral, bright motes waltzing in the slow air. Astonished at how serene he actually felt, Jacob picked his way calmly across the ranks of human shards to the outer limits of the ring.

He was aware that dotted about the room were various arcane appliances, apparently unscathed— perhaps they were the remnants of some black rite gone horribly wrong? Wrought iron-braziers —complete with fatty candles—described a five-point star round the edges of the spiral, while pushed against the north wall there sat a low onyx altar. Atop the altar were strewn a number of strangely hinged metallic devices. From this distance the mechanisms resembled some terrifying bastard three-way wedding between an outsized set of compasses, a multi-bladed scalpel and a set of birthing callipers.

Nervously, Jacob glanced back to the girl. He stood very still while he watched her. She didn't appear to be moving, and her sobs had fallen silent. Was she even aware of him? Some atonal note of unease, whirring high up in the dusky clouds of his awareness, prevented him from stepping over into the ring. Breaking its sanctuary.

Steeling himself he lifted his left foot, wobbled on one leg for an instant, then eased gingerly forward. As his toes crossed into the invisible exclusion zone he anticipated the slight tingle of static electricity, but nothing disturbed his composure. The ball of his foot bumped the floor, settled tentatively and then finally spread out, relaxing into the tread. Breathing a sigh of relief, he stepped over to the girl.

She was curled up into a tight hedgehog ball, head tucked between her knees, the cobbles of her spine poking painfully through the gauze of her skin. As gently as he could Jacob put his palm to her shoulder.

She uncoiled in one fluid motion, skittered fearfully back to the far edge of the spiral. She stared at him through wide, rapidly blinking eyes. Her breath was hoarse, terrified, audibly racing. A long moan escaped her lips, barely a human sound.

She looked as if she had been scrubbed down with wire wool. Wounds spangled her body, a veritable galaxy of nicks, slits and grazes. Her tautly splayed fingers displayed smashed and crushed cuticles, dark crescents of filth buried beneath those nails that had survived. Dried blood caked the scratches on her legs, while half-moon bite indents stood out across the pristine skin of her shoulders. Around her eyes were mottled purple ovals—evidence of earlier abuse—and her rat-tail hair flopped greasily in every direction.

Jacob stooped to try and lift her up, but he was suddenly overwhelmed by a wave of *deja vu*. The sensation was strong enough to make him dizzy. He needed to take a moment to steady himself, while nausea danced in his gut, cold waves rippling across his scalp.

Finally, he felt sufficiently composed to reach for her again. His arms went under hers, round her back. As his right shoulder nudged her collarbone, however, he caught the flash of unreasoning panic in her eyes. She screeched in terror and struck him as hard as she could, a puny pat across the side of the face which made his ear sting. She proceeded to beat him back with all her might, in a frantic whirl of narrow elbows and knees, kicking and scratching.

Jacob smothered her pathetic blows with his chest and arms, careful not to brush any of her wounds. She continued to fight, but her initial hysteria began to fade. He felt hot tears dampen his collar. As her terror cooled her eyes lost their previous brilliance and dulled to a horrifying, blank insensibility, lost to the world. Jacob scowled, his rage crackling.

What home-made hell had she been forced to endure? Little wonder that she had fought him so hard, expecting only more of the same. Jacob hugged her very fiercely, determined that no more harm should come to this pitiful innocent.

The realisation that this was the first time he had held another woman since the break-up with Maria caused a fresh burst of emotions to flare up inside his chest. A conclusion of some kind had been achieved, a step upon some new road. He felt the minute flick of her eyelashes, the fragile intimacy of her blink on his cheek.

He moved towards the door, the girl cradled in the hammock of his arms. Her face flopped limply against the crook of his neck, but the warmth of her cheek encouraged him. She stirred suddenly and croaked a phrase. Jacob bent his head to hear her better.

"Some day they will notice us," she whispered, and an icy chill pierced his heart. Her voice sounded like a quill scratching on parchment. Dry, brittle, aged beyond its years.

After that confession she refused to utter another sound. So he bore her quickly away from that place of slaughter and revelation.

Beyond the corridor Maria had regained some of her equilibrium. She bowed her head as they passed by, then quietly turned to follow.

Jacob carried the girl all the way to the car without breaking into a sweat, then placed her gently in the back seat. He slid into the driver's seat, his purpose now unflinchingly clear. Maria climbed in back to comfort the girl

The engine turned over on cue and they sped off into the night without another word.

## 11. Night Duties

Jacob stood in the bathroom doorway and watched Maria bathe the girl. In a way he felt he should leave, but equally he knew that he *couldn't* go. He felt bonded to the girl now, through ties of grief and atonement, and personally responsible for her safety. He didn't watch her being bathed; he had carried this girl naked from the fire and now he *watched over* her. For Morris. For the puppies. For Maria. The girl was his charge from here on in, and if all else failed then that must remain. So he didn't feel awkward anymore. He watched Maria wash the girl's hair with a clean conscience. It felt right. This was his duty.

Maria's bathroom was very small, barely larger than a closet with little enough room for its bath, sink and toilet, let alone three adults as well. This was probably why most of the bath water had ended up on the floor. The sheet of ancient lino beneath Jacob's soles—already curled like dead leaves on its outlying edges—shone with standing pools. Maria's best efforts at washing were hampered even further by the girl herself, who refused to touch her own body, just sat hunched and shivering in the suds.

Maria finished rinsing the last soapy medallions from the girl's neck and reached past her glistening flank for the plug. She gathered the girl's hair into a single slick cable—wrapping it tightly round her own wrist in order to squeeze out the last dregs—then used her grip on the topknot to get the girl to stand. Sluggishly the teenager complied, but almost came to grief on the tub's slippery slopes. Maria had to steady her with a hand on her elbow. The filthy water coursed away, glugging mournfully over the plug-hole lip, and Maria went to fetch a clean towel.

As the girl stood there shivering Jacob found something indecently sad in the sight her unshaven legs and the damp dark curls beneath her arms. She hadn't declined to depilate out of choice; like everything else this had been *forced* upon her, her self-determination crushed beneath a careless black heel. Her thighs puckered with gooseflesh. Suddenly embarrassed, Jacob averted his gaze.

Maria returned and unravelled the new towel with a smart *crack*. Upon arriving back at the flat she had launched herself into the girl's care with a shocking single-mindedness, and despite his own pledge Jacob had found himself buffeted clumsily along in her irresistible slipstream. Truth be told, Maria's behaviour had become positively school-marmish. Was this the sort of mother she would turn out to be? Clipped, crisp, relentlessly capable? He wondered whether the whole episode simply represented some sort of displacement activity, and if so whether she recognised it. He shook his head.

"Not sure exactly what I've got to fit Beanpole here," Maria said, patting the girl tenderly. Even this honest gesture of affection caused the teenager to flinch, however, and Maria's face darkened. Jacob saw the rage glow behind her irises, like dirty fire. It had been obvious that although the girl was scratched, bruised and emaciated, the principal damage she had suffered was psychological. Her mind had been scarred, very deeply—perhaps permanently. The only thing they had been able to coax out of her on the return journey was her name, Lila. Fortunately her visible wounds were not serious—though some of the cuts were old and likely to scar—but what they could do to soothe these more profound mental injuries Jacob didn't know. Incandescent rage against the girl's former captors consumed them both at regular intervals, but it didn't do any good. They could only console themselves by helping the girl.

Maria guided Lila gently through to the bedroom. There she began to rub the teenager down, gently towelling the moisture off, leaving splotchy pink tracks on the girl's alabaster skin. Jacob sat on the bed and stared at the wall. Even that used more strength than he had left.

Maria threw open the wardrobe's louvred doors and chewed on her lip as she reviewed its contents. Quickly, she selected a floaty summer dress in glowing strawberry: chiffon, high-waisted and sleeveless. She draped it across the bed, found some appropriate underwear in one of the bedside drawers, and beckoned to Lila.

She held the knickers splayed out and managed by some minor miracle to get the girl to step into them without toppling over. It was exactly like dressing a two-year-old. Maria yanked them briskly up to her waist with an audible snap of elastic, then went to grab the dress off the bed.

"Arms up," she urged brightly. The girl just stared. Maria sighed softly, and placed the dress back on the bed so that she could arrange the girl the way she wanted to, then removed the towel and slid the bunched material over Lila's drooping head.

The dress flared rather too much around the hips, swung and billowed in clumsy folds, and tugged down to mid-thigh only reluctantly, but still it mostly did the job, and now Lila was at least fully clothed. Maria crouched beside the girl's knees, trying to fix a fiddly thread on the hem.

"I never wear it, truth be told. Bargain, see," she chuntered on cheerfully, ostensibly to the girl but in reality to herself. "Got it in Knightsbridge, last summer. Wish I hadn't bothered now. The colour's all too savage. But you make it work." She settled back onto her haunches and smiled encouragingly up at her lanky ward. The girl blinked, a slightly less dazed expression gradually illuminating her features. She looked rather fabulous wearing the dress, after a demure, baffled sort of fashion.

Pleased with her accomplishment Maria flashed Jacob a rueful grin. Though he knew this was hardly the time or the place, he felt a silly splash of joy spray through his chest. Maria, smiling for him once more! This bizarre surrogacy had managed to bridge the gap between them. Made them allies again.

"One more detail and we're done," Maria announced, and pounced over the bed to scrabble around inside one of her bedside cabinets.

Lila actually looked a bit startled when Maria went to work on her moist hair, freeing up the black tangles with an electric-blue brush. Her eyes stretched with amazement that this could even be happening. Jacob noticed her cheeks were still wet, in stripes. Ribbons of moisture bled away. Water, not tears. She was all cried out.

"There," said Maria finally, and as she spoke the girl fell on her in an impulsive, wholly unexpected embrace.

A volley of emotions—confusion, affection, shock—burst across Maria's face as the girl hung on tightly, her face buried in Maria's hair. The hug was very awkward, and Maria almost overbalanced when she attempted to return the squeeze, but she did manage to pat the girl's back and smile uncertainly across at Jacob.

However, before they broke off the embrace something odd happened. Lila suddenly turned her face and seemed to *kiss* the older woman's ear. Maria frowned, looking slightly at a loss.

But then the girl stood quickly—albeit a tad unsteadily—and skipped over to the bed where she flung herself down and slithered round into a foetal position, thumb in mouth. Her neatly combed tresses smeared across her features, blurring them. After a short interval they heard the rhythm of her breath change, and realised that she was asleep.

Jacob exchanged a puzzled look with Maria, who just shrugged. She dug out a spare duvet to cover the girl, since the bed's own was crumpled up beneath her, and Jacob knocked off the light. The two of them retired, bemused, to the living room.

**

"Magic," breathed Jacob, as Maria lowered herself wearily onto the sofa. She scowled.

"I can't think of any better way to explain it," he continued. "Can you?"

She let her arm fall down by the side of the sofa and clutched at the carpet in a momentary spasm of frustration.

"I don't know," she finally admitted in a tone verging on the venomous.

Jacob sat and rubbed his face. He was exhausted and didn't really know what else he could do. Maria hugged her knees and rocked gently. He adored her. He couldn't stop himself.

"So, what do we do now?" he asked levelly.

"You tell me."

She regarded him with a fixed expression of mistrust. Now that the subject had been broached the old barriers were slamming back down. Even by initiating this conversation he knew he had caused their fragile comradeship to erode. Without Lila's needs to hide behind, the reality of these events was left exposed. Jacob knew that Maria wouldn't be able to discuss anything they'd seen at the mansion, and certainly none of the ramifications of what they'd experienced.

This in itself was a blow. He'd always thought she was more durable than that, more open-minded. How could *he* be the strong one, the still point?

"What?" she demanded.

"What help is there? Who can we go to?"

"Don't keep asking questions," she snapped.

"But M, we have to talk about this, about what happened, what we saw—"

Maria shook her head in mute dissent, her brows meshing with frustration. Panic stirred Jacob's innards. It felt like being wet all over. A sheet of ice beneath his clothes, heartbeats thrown against his ribs. There really was nowhere they could turn, no one they could trust. No way out.

Couldn't go home; they already knew where he lived. Couldn't go to police; they'd just be handed over to the kidnappers straightaway. Couldn't tell anybody about the diary, the strange explosion in the mansion or the dismembered bodies; who would believe them?

If the police were involved, then who knew how far up the chain of command it went? He had been watched, recorded and monitored for years. *His* name, at least, must be on all manner of digital registers. Was it safe to use credit cards? Ride local transport? Book tickets? Go into a department store?

What organisation had they come up against? All those people in suits with the scarlet woman at their head. An *intelligence* agency that kidnapped teenagers and held pagan rites in rune-engraved mansions? Hardly. Mocking him, the diary's words came back on instant recall.

*If we fail then they will come through and there will be nothing we can do to stop them. They might destroy us all in one blow, or hide amongst us, dressed in our skins, for years, waiting and watching, toying with us. Playing. Experimenting, while we carry on dreaming of safety and sleep-walking to our doom.*

He could see the appeal of Maria's denial. For him, who knew her so well, it was easy to appreciate what had finally broken her spirit. When the police drove up to the mansion ... when order had turned to chaos ... she was lost.

In part it was what had set them at loggerheads for so long. Maria trusted authority implicitly, always had. Got a problem? Don't worry—off you pop to the police! It'll be all right, write to your MP! Start lobbying, collect signatures for a petition, contact the council. Follow the correct procedure and—in the end—it's *bound* to turn out okay!

This was a cruel time to be proved right, he reflected bitterly. This belief in authority was an article of faith for her. A pure, inviolate gem at the very centre of her personality. He could see it visibly crumbling before him. He hated to see her expression as she felt the hope slip away.

"Maybe it's only some of them," she speculated. "A splinter group within the local force. Masons. Or perhaps they're not even real police? Stolen uniforms, I don't know ..." She trailed off, realising how desperate her excuses sounded.

Suddenly she sat up straight on the settee. "Jacob, the diary! That's it. It *proves* that there's a resistance, someone fighting these bastards! Don't you see? We've got someone we can turn to! If only we can find them... Scotland, the diary said..."

Jacob had to admit this was a good idea, and in one sense it lifted his heart: if Maria was able to accept that there was truth in the diary's account, then perhaps in time she could bend her mind around all the other impossibilities.

He nodded, then frowned. "Let's think it through, though. If these other guys are such a success, then why does the diary just stop? The narrator said they were on the verge of defeat, and also that the Outsiders might hide amongst us once they'd invaded. Disguised." He shook his head and sighed. "Anyway, look, what do we do about the girl?" he asked, in an attempt to guide her to firmer emotional ground.

Maria looked utterly dejected. She picked up a cushion and clasped it to her chest.

"Jacob, I don't know what was done to her, what else she saw in that house, but I think it may have truly pushed her over the edge. She's almost functionally catatonic as it is. And she whispered the oddest thing before, when she hugged me."

Jacob looked up sharply. "What?" he demanded, his voice flaking with alarm.

"She said, 'Now we are one'."

## 12. A Special Blend of Darkness

*His eyesight is failing.*

*Baleful specks of gray germinate across his vision. They are fuzzy at the edges, blank in the middle, and it's that blankness that terrifies. He imagines the dots as dust particles collecting on the insides of his corneas, furring around the pinprick of his consciousness until they choke out that last brilliant point of light. One by one they pop open, like the first spots of rain on a clear window.*

*He is afraid; his blood would run cold if it hadn't already curdled in his veins. His breath would race if only it were able. He is frightened that his lifeforce is finally beginning to fade...*

*Come on, come on. Before it's too late. Work to do, duties to settle. Run, dammit, run!*

*He and Sunburn hurry across an enormous space roughly the size of Brixton Academy. In spite of its extraordinary proportions, this is only one of several curious tubular structures which combine to form the Citadel's interior. Tapering, yawning chimney-like shafts, monstrous in diameter, fused together to form that singular Cornetto outline they had spied from afar. If someone were to observe the edifice from above, he speculates, it would look like an ice cream cone filled with macaroni.*

*Furthermore, there is something unpleasantly organic about the tower. The inner slopes of each funnel resemble countless whale spines lashed together by a tangle of spars, barbs and ebony buttresses. Everything seems lextruded or grown rather then built.*

*In contrast to the writhing terrain outside the Citadel, its interior is mercifully solid—stable, coherent, concrete—but none the less alien. Although not churning like the atmosphere outside, the air in here is still alive. The sensation of being submerged has lessened but not abated entirely. The pressures are different—it's like shouldering through a sea of muslin drapes, though it is just about possible to run.*

*The chamber is a confusion of nooks and vents and fissures of fibrous black armour. Fetid sheets of alien gristle buckle upwards to cup nests of mutant alveoli. Running through the funnels you could imagine you were inside Satan's very own glistening viscera; seen from inside the structures could easily be mistaken for nightmare heart ventricles or gargantuan lung cavities, and this illusion is only exacerbated by the Citadel's most disconcerting feature.*

*Its pulse.*

*He watches as the walls give another shiver and begin to bulge out at the roots. Their base distends vastly before the repellent peristaltic energy migrates upwards, oozing in one long undulation all the way to the top, a thousand metres in a lazy instant. A beat later the sequence repeats.*

*The world around them shivers in concert with the process, swells, expels and deflates. Swells, expels and deflates. For every pulse discharged the floor seems to tighten and stretch in sympathy beneath their feet.*

*Desperately, he keeps on running, but his legs feel very far away.*

*His feet are another continent, across oceans of anaesthesia and paralysis. He stumbles. Sunburn doesn't notice at first, then spins round like a dancer—keeps on backpedalling—to stare at his predicament.*

*Sunburn signs at him, "Look. Look at God's heartbeat." He means the pulse of the Citadel. "In the belly of God, in the belly of God. Come on! Come on!"*

*Somehow he manages to right himself as Sunburn disappears through a rent in the wall. The gash resembles a fresh knife wound, but with puckered, sphincter-like edges that quiver repulsively every time there is a pulse ... or when something passes through them.*

*He suppresses a shudder as he between the lips of the gash, his skin crawling as they contract reflexively above him. A new, marginally smaller chamber unfolds before his withering vision. Sunburn is already fifty metres on, pounding across the scabby, oil-dark floor. Only one more funnel to go after this, and they should reach their goal: the core.*

*However, the meagre distance is abruptly transformed into a double marathon as the erosion affecting his sight suddenly transfers itself to the rest of his body. A tremor passes through his muscles, building, shaking, leeching his strength away. Weakness spreads. The cords in his neck and behind his knees begin to tremble: the rumour of a fit which will never arrive. A body readying itself to collapse.*

*The scalloped ground trips him—once, twice—but remarkably he manages to lurch on. Unseen and unexpected depressions bewilder his feet at every turn. He knows that each next step might be his last, and the only comfort he can take is the belief that Sunburn, at least, will survive to complete their mission.*

*His arrival in the penultimate chamber detonates even that conviction. On the far side of the chamber Sunburn is sprawled face down, a short distance from the wall. Obviously, it was only the dynamism of madness that powered him this far.*

*Plodding stubbornly onwards, he watches as Sunburn rolls himself painfully onto his back, shimmies his way round until he finds the wall and tries to lever himself to his feet. The effort defeats him, though. He looks like a spider thrown onto a fire, limbs instantly hooking into his body, death rolling him up into a ball. He just lies there, waiting to expire. But the wall has other ideas...*

*Nearing his companion he sees that Sunburn has somehow become bonded with the surface behind him. The back of his head is gradually altering its shape, seeming to spread out, soften and relax, spilling its colours in lazy stabs across the wall. Loose, porous filaments something like coral mingle with his hair and worm their way beneath his skin. Then Sunburn starts moving upwards.*

*A first the corpse appears to levitate—in a spooky, frictionless glide—but then the logic hits him and he realises that it is the wall itself which is lifting the body. Sunburn dissolves into a swarming crowd of multicoloured clumps. Mobs of these clumps disperse and stream in every direction. As Sunburn's head crumbles the rest of his body follows suit, unravelling as if a zip had been undone along his spine. His constituent parts spread across the wall, crawling along in defiance of whatever strange gravity governs this place.*

*He shakes his head, appalled, astonished, understanding none of it. But then another pulse distends the wall and immediately everything becomes clear:*

*Sunburn's residue is caught on the crest of this rising pulse, and is instantly propelled upwards at the same speed. The dead man's colours finally reach the top, where they vent out into the malevolent corona around the cone's upper rim.*

*The Citadel is voiding itself.*

*This must be why the ground flexes in time with each heartbeat. The floor—the whole base of the structure—is constantly being renewed from below, and then discharged upwards, out into the sky where it becomes part of the external ecosphere once more.*

*The base is seamlessly transferred to the top of the funnel. Not inside the walls, but of the walls. The method of conveyance is total. Entire swathes of wall tissue are being transported during each pulse, and instantly replaced. As the tissue reaches the top it loses integrity and dissolves, scatters, falls, presumably going back to the protean state this world revels in. Sunburn has become one with their domain. Maybe this is filtration, renewal or rebirth. Who knows? But the sheer scale is terrifying.*

*No time to pause, to meditate. Just time to keep on running, staggering. He's the last man alive now, trying to make sure all the other deaths haven't been in vain. The final chamber is ahead. The core, his goal.*

*On that urgent threshold he pauses, peers into the dingy space beyond. Uncertainty gnaws at him. Surely such a sacred zone would deserve an equally auspicious stage to frame it? The chamber inside feels inadequately meagre. Where are the cathedral expanses he anticipated? The horrifying guardians?*

*Expecting death at any moment he dismisses these misgivings, and enters.*

*Soft warm lights pop on. The air is immediately clean and clear and thin, the arrangement of the chamber simple, if ultimately as puzzling as anything he has seen before.*

*In the middle of the chamber, slightly off-centre, is a ten-metre high truncated bulb-shape, contained within a cage of deceptively slender black struts which curve up from the glossy finish of the floor. The bulb's surface is very strange. At first glance it appears translucent and cloudy, yet filled with an intense white light. Then he starts to wonder. Maybe it isn't white? Maybe it isn't cloudy? He squints painfully, conscious of the ever-present grease spots staining his vision. He can't focus properly on the structure. Whatever is inside the bulb, it concentrates his blindness. It is as if the bulb itself were somehow manufactured from the same stuff that his blindness is made of.*

*Despite this setback he can still detect motion inside, within the light. Slow but steady, wedded to spiralling smudges of dirty colour: deep reds, cinnamons, sepias, cherry hues. A breath of familiarity strokes him: the bulb is a womb.*

*Unlike the rest of the Citadel this chamber is enclosed, with a modest domed ceiling arching twenty feet above. The ceiling sparkles like a black mirror, generating random splays of solar flecks which only serve to confuse him further.*

*A palisade of glassy spears mounted on long knuckles of anthracite bone radiates out from the womb, itself raised up on what resembles a giant dorsal ridge. Multiple rills of topaz fringe the bulb and occasionally chase each other across the chamber like electrical discharges in a Van de Graaff generator. He approaches the enigma, screws his eyes up to try to discern the secrets turning ponderously at the centre of light.*

*In the blindness at the core, a red figure stirs.*

*For the first time he is aware of a presence in the chamber, an awareness that brushes him with its outermost skirts—*

*Suddenly he is ejected from the tiny globe of his consciousness, and sent shooting out across thousands upon billions of kilometers, entire galaxies of space and time whooshing away. He is tossed through supernovae, spun round black holes, punched screaming through the ghostly rings of gas giants and the coronae of gravid swollen stars. He hangs on the backcloth of the universe, insignificant as a colourless speck on the back of a colourless speck, less than a single electron, less than one quark.*

*His mind is vacuum-frozen by the indifference of eternity. But even when opened up to the scrutiny of the infinite, he is still conscious of the awareness inside the Citadel. On the scale of everything it is still huge. Then the presence lets go—withdrawing as swiftly as it came—and he is dropped unceremoniously back into his body.*

*Death breathes on him, licks the surface of his brain. Determined, damned, he stoops. His hands grope forward, fingernails glancing off the smooth surface as he scratches after his goal, skin prickling as he passes through the tassels of light. He touches something soft, something that yields.*

*And on that instant his eyesight fails.*

**

A blanket had been tossed over Jacob's face while he slept. He rolled irritably onto his side in an attempt to dislodge it. Nothing happened. The darkness continued to cling. He could feel it on his cheeks, his mouth—

Confusion swamped him. He was on his side on Maria's sofa, where presumably he had drifted off after their discussion ended. Had she fetched the quilt for him? He couldn't recall. He remembered her leaving for the kitchen with their dirty cups, but after that, nothing.

The atmosphere was different now. His skin felt strange, tingling, its hairs standing to attention. He brought his hands up to his face. No blanket.

He sat up, breathing rapidly. Swallowed hard. The sound seemed to fill his skull. A toadish, sandpaper croak. There was no other noise in the room. All he could hear was the gurgling orchestra of his body rushing through his inner ear.

He might just as well have not bothered opening his eyes. The darkness was absolute, a shroud of tar moulded to his features, breathing with him. It wasn't difficult to see how he had mistaken it for a real blanket.

He forced himself not to panic, sitting very still with his palms down flat, occasionally scrunching up his fingertips to feel the puffy texture of the sofa. He waited patiently for his night vision to tune in, reflecting on the exact physiological processes that this entailed in order to calm himself. He had no idea how long this would take, so he started to count in his head.

By the time he reached one hundred and no shapes had resolved themselves, Jacob began to panic.

A terrible suspicion gripped him. What if he had been struck blind in his sleep? Such things did happen. Exotic neurological disorders, malevolent inheritances that only showed their hand reluctantly, perhaps after extended bouts of stress ...

Trembling, he brought his fingertips up in front of his face, waved them deliberately back and forth, mere centimetres from his eyes. He could just about feel the slight displacement of air, but saw nothing. Something brushed his fingertips... *Eyelids.* It was a shock to realise how fast he was blinking. This reminded him of an interview he had once read. In it a blind artist had talked about the potential embarrassment of emotions flaring out into unchecked, inappropriate expressions. *Blindisms*, he'd called them. If you could never see your own face, then how could you train it for discretion?

Jacob imagined how he might look to someone standing in front of him with a pair of infra-red goggles: his jaw shaking, his lips slack with fear, his eyes blank, searching desperately, blinking, blinking.

He closed his eyes and pressed his fingertips against his eyelids, gently working the silky wrinkle of flesh in each direction. He saw splotches of photo negative colour bloom where the lids were tugged, ultra violets, sickly neon greens. His *eyes* were working. He wasn't blind.

The relief was sharp enough to push him to his feet. He took a step, collided with the coffee table and plummeted to the floor. Luckily he managed to twist aside and avoid the table as he fell, but the drop still smashed the breath from him. He heard the reports of dislodged objects knocking into each other as they hit the carpet and rolled away. Feeling like an idiot, Jacob paused to take stock.

Carpet burns on his palms, bruised knees and his pride grazed... nothing more.

Then he realised that there was something wrong with the air in the room. It felt thick on his face, drowsy, slow. The noise of items falling off the table had seemed odd, too. He recognised how the muffled air was conspiring with the dark to increase his sense of isolation, making it impossible to judge distances in the room. The atmosphere flattened his awareness, drew him down into the tiny box of his mind. External stimuli peeled away as if he was being subjected to some elaborate form of sensory deprivation. It became increasingly difficult to concentrate on anything outside. He could vividly taste his own mouth, gummy and sour with post-waking clag, and the liquid mutter of his bowels seemed loud enough to shake the floor. A sandstorm swept around inside his skull.

Jacob shook his head to dispel the trance, an angry growl low in his throat. It might not be prudent to call out for Maria, but at least he could go and wake her. The camper bed she'd set up for herself was only a few feet away, adjacent to the hall door.

He stood purposefully, but once vertical his resolve again began to crumble, trickling away in the dark. The blackness was like a second eyelid.

More than anything he felt incredibly *exposed*, vulnerable from every direction. And his senses were playing tricks on him. He found himself flinching as he continually imagined fists or claws flying at his unprotected face. The urge to crouch became unbearable. It was lunacy to be standing out in the open like this when he could roll himself up into a ball and hide.

He cursed his earlier fantasies. Now he found he couldn't rid himself of the conviction that there actually *was* someone with infra-red goggles stood in front of him, waiting patiently, grinning.

"Fuck this," he whispered. Morris would never have let himself be paralysed this way. Jacob began to move. He used the settee as a guide at first, feeding it across the backs of his thighs as he executed a crabways shuffle. Then, with a deep breath, he stepped into space.

*There's no problem here*, he scolded himself. *I've walked about in the dark before, thousands of times, and in this flat too. Going to the kitchen for a glass of water, trip to the loo in the middle of the night. Easy.* Maria's camp bed was probably all of five end-to-end steps in front of him. He decided to count them just to prove it, to illustrate how straightforward this would be if he just remained calm. It was only a darkened room, after all.

Ten steps later, with no sign of Maria or the hall door, he began to worry.

Eventually he must hit a wall, and then he could simply feel his way around until he located a definite landmark. This demonstration of cool, unflustered logic left him far less relieved than it ought to. He carried on. Ten steps later again his questing fingertips found a wall.

He scowled, highly unnerved. Twenty steps? From the *sofa*? So which fucking wall was this? He rested his head against the surface to think, out of redundant habit closed his eyes.

There was a slight noise behind him, the rumour of motion. Maria? He turned sharply, smashed his elbow into the wall and doubled up with pain. By the time he'd recovered, the room was silent again. The movement had ceased.

Jacob began to sweat in earnest. With supreme caution he turned around. All he needed to do was establish a schematic of the flat in his head—a simple task of spatial abstraction—and then he could exit this stupid nightmare without further mishap.

So, first question. Which wall *was* it? Well it seemed preposterous, but somehow he must have traced a diagonal away from the sofa, missed the camper bed altogether, and ended up in the offshoot corridor which led to the kitchen. This wall was the bedroom wall, one side of that corridor, and behind him was the other wall, the bathroom. Excellent. He could use the corridor as his trail, track it back along to the main room and make a beeline for the sofa. Then he would start all over again.

He slithered along left to locate the corner, pivoted awkwardly until the junction of the walls was at his back. He launched himself off again and counted his steps.

Twenty-five. He must have strayed. Somehow, regardless of all his precautions, he had veered away from true and managed to bypass the sofa. How lost could you get in a room fifteen feet by ten? Frustration clutched at him, tears prickling in his useless eyes. Why couldn't he *fucking* see anything? The gloom was dense as stone. He felt like screaming, but he was too scared to make a noise.

Suddenly, more movement—directly behind! He gasped, but forced himself not to turn. There *was* a wall in front of him. It wasn't possible that it had simply disappeared. If he plowed on he had to find something, *had* to. Breath hitched painfully in his chest. He flailed ahead, plunging forward, hands flapping in a lunatic's game of blind man's buff.

He'd lost all sense of direction now, and he gradually became aware that he was sobbing. There was furtive motion all around, scuttling and fidgeting. Then his hands brushed up against something and he almost screeched with relief. He whirled back and grabbed for it with all his might. A low-hanging length of softness fell between his fingers. A curtain!

At last he had found the outside wall. This was the main window. Rip back the curtain and starlight would pour in. He'd be able to see again. He was saved.

He was just about to triumphantly jerk the material back when the curtain moved. It billowed around his hands and gave vent to a filthy-sounding gurgle.

*... blades and feelers and tentacles, moving like maggots in the hot belly of week-old road kill...*

Jacob screamed.

## 13. If the Stars Go Out

Something hit Jacob across the chest and suddenly he was flying. Not staggering — as if he'd been shoved by a strong man —his feet actually left the ground. No time to duck or dodge or wonder which direction the blow had come from, just a moment of speed around his ears and the sharp lurch of vertigo. Then gravity had him again and he was hurled at the ground.

He struck the camper bed full on—which probably saved his life—and was then pitched heels over head until he fetched up in a crooked heap, legs hooked over the upturned bed, back against the wall. A lurid confusion of after-images blinded him, spastic pinks and blues, churning yellows. He started to cough. An attempt to lift his head sent jabs of agony down through his spine. Similarly, when he shifted his legs, he was only rewarded with pain.

Beats passed, deep breaths. He tried to focus. Flexed his fingers, wriggled toes. Both complied. Relief swooned through his chest. It wasn't paralysis then, merely pain, and pain could be endured.

Finally convinced that he wasn't dead or dying, two new thoughts arrived in Jacob's mind: if this was the camper bed beneath him, then where was Maria? And why couldn't he hear the thing over on the far side of the room? To that second puzzle his memory offered an awful solution: a line of glowing text clicked open behind his eyes—

*When it attacked, though, there was a dreadful hush that was stiller and denser and deadlier than normal silence.*

He moaned and rolled stiffly onto his side. Terrorist explosions of pain detonated throughout his body, obliterating his sight momentarily; starspots, magnesium flashes. He gasped, but fought it down. On hands and knees he groped around frantically, scrabbling after Maria. Where *was* she? Where could she have gone?

His palm encountered something wet. And mushy. He caught his breath, died for a second inside. This whole stretch of carpet was soaking. Terrible understanding bloomed in his mind, but he flinched away from it, whimpering.

*Still alive when dismemberment began...*

His heart beat red behind his eyes, heavy as a strobe. His throat was desert-dry. Jacob thought he must faint or simply drop away into the void. He thought he could hear oblivion calling. His knees were wet, his hands were. Sopping wet. *Maria.*

Maria's blood.

Just then he heard the toilet flush, and the doorway a mere five feet from his face lit up as Maria stepped out of the bathroom into the corridor. He saw immediately the broken water jug centimetres from his fingertips.

Then the bathroom bulb exploded with a hot *crack* and darkness descended like a guillotine.

That momentary blast of light had ruined whatever night vision he'd developed, reducing his sight to an incoherent static. Somewhere nearby Maria shouted. It sounded like she was screaming in a cardboard box.

He didn't need his eyes or ears to feel the tsunami of force crashing in behind them, driving its vile bulk across the room. Another phrase from the diary stabbed at him: *monstrous plasticity*.

He could sense Maria blundering about in the corridor, searching for the doorway, a light switch, anything. Jacob gathered himself together; this would require every fibre of his courage, every atom of strength he owned.

Jacob leapt to his feet and threw himself at the spot where he'd decided his ex-girlfriend must be. Scorching twinges coursed through him, but he didn't lose control. His body still obeyed his commands, however deranged they might seem. He heard a constipated thump from behind, which might have been the sofa upending or being demolished. Maria's right elbow took him hard in the chest, but it was the sweetest sensation he had ever experienced. Momentum drove him on. He collided with her soft flank, his arms stretched around as if it was a zombie's embrace, and they both went down, heavily.

"Don't talk don't move don't cry out," he hissed into her ear. She struggled against him, bewildered and angry.

Something the size of Maria's Mini Metro cannoned into the plasterboard above them. She yelped against his fingers, and in a moment of pure human irrationality Jacob felt unbearably resentful. He'd just saved her life, but all she could do was fight against his embrace! He held her tight, felt her heart thudding against his side. A stinging puff of plaster fragments sprayed across them. One piece struck Jacob's cheek, another grazed his eyelid.

Then, a pause.

In the depths of his earlier ordeal with the living darkness, Jacob had thought there could be nothing worse than not knowing whether a psychotic killer stood in front of you, unseen, leering. But there was. *Knowing* was worse.

The thing simply hung there, looming over them.

Of course, neither he nor Maria could actually see it, but this close there was no mistaking its presence. Jacob's vision had been reduced to a milling tide of ashen freckles, but he wondered: if he *had* been able to see, would the view have been much different? The air gurgled slowly, boiling, slithering in on itself. Maria trembled in his arms, her soft animal warmth his only solace. He had exhausted fear, how else should he react?

He kept expecting globules of the ghastly stuff to drip down onto them, a waterfall of caustic saliva, black as molasses, sticky as pitch. The fetor took him back to the mansion, that distinctive, cloying smell rising in his memory. He imagined the surface of the thing bubbling, glistening with temporary eyes and organs—but who knew? Who dared to wonder?

Then he heard the coiling slap of tentacles oozing along the wall. There was a strange new modulation to the sounds, and an instant later he realised what this meant: astonishingly, the creature was withdrawing.

He heard it retreat back across the room, folding its clotted abundance over and over, melting and flowing. He was too confused to rejoice in this stay of execution.

"What is this?" demanded Maria, close to panic, and he didn't know whether she meant the entity or the darkness or the embrace.

"I don't know. It was here when I woke. Something they sent? Don't know… God…"

"It didn't kill us it didn't kill us it didn't kill us," she began muttering. Her breath smelled of toothpaste. "Why didn't it kill us? Whywhywhywhy?" she sang quietly.

"I don't know," Jacob groaned. "Perhaps it's attracted to vibration, or movement, or noise? God, I don't know."

What to do next? How to escape? They had to get out as quickly as possible. But would it try to follow them? It wasn't that far to the front door. How fast could the thing move? What was its acceleration like? He heard it heave and slide at the rear of the flat, bumping into the flimsy walls. It made a hollow, sullen *thunk* when it knocked against one door.

"The bedroom," Maria said flatly.

Jacob couldn't move his mouth at first, had to work his tongue to unglue it. His stomach turned in snaky loops.

"*Lila*," he croaked.

Oiled by fear Jacob's mind hastily thrust options in his direction. None of them were appealing. Most were suicidal, but that didn't really matter. There couldn't be any debate over this. The girl's safety was his prime concern now; Morris's life for his, his life for the girl's.

As if his own thoughts had actually roused her, he suddenly heard Lila scream, a single drawn-out wail, eloquent in its primal inarticulacy. He heard the bedroom door splinter, split, *shatter—*

He shoved Maria towards the second door into the bedroom. "Go, go! Get the other door. When I distract its attention, grab her, and run, *run—*"

Maria didn't question or pause, her empathy uncanny. She scrambled up swiftly and was away along the corridor. Jacob fumbled round the door jamb, stooped to haul up the camper bed, and then, without another moment's pause, he charged towards the far side of the room. He bellowed as he ran, the camper bed jutting out in front of him like an impromptu lance or vaulting pole, hoping that the noise would draw the thing straight to him. He knew there was nothing to trip on, so if he didn't slip in the gloom he'd assured himself an uninterrupted run-up. He also knew that if he missed the creature he'd slam slap-bang into the wall directly behind it. Carrying a camper bed. Welcome to the Marx Brothers school of supernatural death!

His war cry became a demented cackle.

An instant later he tripped over the new rug by the window.

Lila's shrieking filled his head as he plunged. There wasn't even time to shout before his fall launched him into the enemy, camper bed first.

He tried to roll aside, but the pliant tides of the entity caught him, billowing up and out like the wings of a manta ray. The reeking stuff was all around, he was drowning in it. It enveloped his head, methodically drawing him deeper into its mush, draping countless rolls of skin over his shoulders, suffocating him. Fluid meat boiled against his cheeks. Pulses of vagrant phosphorescence skittered by, mocking him, revealing the seething horror for instants at a time. Revulsion gave him strength and he began to thrash about, without discipline or sanity. A pure, bestial, back-brain fit.

Suddenly, surprisingly, he was free. He stood—disorientation rocking him unsteadily on his feet——and fought to find his bearings in the gloom. He heard voices, the sound of a door, a gurgling scream.

Then terrible impacts began to rain down.

At first the barrage didn't seem too bad. It felt like he was being beaten with strips of foam rubber. It was only when half of his left ear fell away that he realised the truth: the strips were blades. He'd be dead in seconds.

He tried to step back—to fend it off with the camp bed—but it drove relentlessly forwards. There was an explosion of agony in his shoulder, the aftershocks of which plunged him into overwhelming nausea. He almost fainted, losing hold of the camper bed, but this only precipitated more pain. The bed hung spookily in the air before him. Jacob gasped like a moron. It took several dull seconds to understand why: he'd been impaled.

The thing had pierced both the bed and his shoulder with one of its razor-tipped tentacles. A perverse umbilical cord now connected the two of them, the bed slung in between. Not for long, though. The enemy wrenched its blade free but the bed went with it, bobbing backwards into the smothering dark. Jacob recoiled violently, weak-kneed and gasping, and cracked his head against the wall behind. But it was not a wall, he realised; the echo of his collision was wrong. It was a door. The *bedroom* door.

Their lunatic grapple had managed to swing him round to exactly the spot where he wanted to be. Barely able to believe his luck, he groped for the handle, but the beast came after him again, squelching and roaring, the size of a falling wall. The door opened easily, though it was a futile measure. Even as he fell away to momentary safety, he knew this was the end. The thing would just pile its bloated body through the doorway and crush him. There was no time to flinch aside. No last opportunity for escape. His muscle tension dissolved.

He heard the resounding *crump* of the beast ramming the door frame ... and the 'thunk' of the camper bed lodging across the narrow entrance. Unexpectedly thwarted—and presumably as perplexed as a cluster of protoplasmic bubbles and seething luminescent pustules could ever be—the creature froze.

Maybe there is a God, thought Jacob.

He hurtled across the bedroom on his hands and knees, retaining just enough forethought to skirt the looming spectre of the bed. At the opposite door he leapt up painfully, just as the entity made its second attempt to shove a six-foot bed through a two-and-a-half-foot doorway. Perhaps it did not even understand the nature of the impediment?

This was something he'd not considered. How intelligent was it? As bright as a dog, a chimp, a child? Could its powers of reasoning even be measured in conventional terms? Jacob thought he heard the bed's struts begin to buckle. One way or another it was going to get in, and this wasn't the time to wonder just how many GCSEs it had.

He hobbled down the hallway, expecting the beast to spew forth and envelop him at any moment. He could hear Maria and Lila dawdling at the end of the corridor. Had one of them fallen?

"*Run!*" he screamed. Maria yelled something incomprehensible back at him. Lila was whimpering.

The creature broke through the bedroom door.

Jacob all but long-jumped the final stretch, tumbling clumsily into the waiting women and the front door, which burst open explosively. They tumbled out onto the darkened street.

Then juddered to a halt.

Arrayed in front of them—standing in silent ranks before a semicircle of waiting cars—stood the Outsiders. The woman in red was at the fore. A few moments sluiced by while everyone stared at each other in surprise.

Then the woman slowly shook her head.

## 14. Breathing in Fire

Maria clutched at Jacob's shoulder. He hissed as her fingers compressed the fresh wound there, and at the same time felt the blood flowing from his ruined ear. Lila had fallen to her knees before them, and now she was sprawled there, gazing helplessly up at the woman in red. Any semblance of beauty she had once displayed was extinguished by her fear. Her whole body jerked with each breath, her face pinched with terror.

The sense of dislocation was intense. The pell-mell panic of the flat had left Jacob trembling but lucid. Unbidden, his mind dredged up a chilling comparison. He recalled a natural history programme in which an antelope was being chased by a cheetah. In flight, the victim's system was flooded with adrenaline to give it speed, but if the pursuit went on for too long the animal would eventually collapse from exhaustion. It was only a brief defence, not accounting for the persistence of a hunter. But then, nature was hardly fair.

Jacob took the scene in with a glance, heard the scarlet woman's sigh of impatience as she shook her head, saw the brutal woman and the Silver Haired man standing among the fifteen other immaculate weirdos. Silver Hair was smiling faintly. Brutal's expression was so rancorous that it wrapped an invisible hand around Jacob's throat. The car headlights illuminated their faces with a macabre chiaroscuro. The monotone thrum of engines idled out on the edges of his concentration.

A fleeting image from last night flashed through his mind. Lila, lacerated and bruised, lashing out at him as he bent down to help her. Imagining, perhaps, that he was one of these fuckers, here to assault her yet again. The look in her eyes, when he recalled it, still terrified him. A look burned there by her treatment at the hands of these ... *creatures.*

"You—," Jacob snarled, but then his senses were assailed from all sides.

Jacob had seen the Outsiders waiting for them in the street, but he had forgotten about the thing in Maria's flat. Now, like a petulant child outraged that it was no longer the focus of attention, it announced its presence again.

Maria's house exploded.

The downstairs windows spat outwards like ice struck with a pick axe, a horizontal splash of glass fragments which sliced through the air, shredding the back of Jacob's shirt. He cried out but his voice was lost, a sigh within a tornado. He heard a high-pitched scream and thought it might be Lila, but then he realised that she was at his feet, curled into a protective ball. Maria went down over her, arms wrapped round the girl's head, her hands and back taking the brunt of the glass shower, shielding Lila from the splintered needles.

There was a crash of splitting masonry, then bricks came sleeting down all around them. Jacob threw himself forward, stretching out to shield Maria and Lila. A smashed brick caught him behind the left ear. He clenched his eyes shut, in anticipation of further pain as much as to protect them from the flying dust and glass. A stench made him gag—mint and blood mingled with the insides of a fish gone bad. For an instant the inner surfaces of his eyelids were crawling with a million spiralling particles. Then the noise stopped.

It didn't dwindle. It simply *halted*, as if swallowed whole by some vast maw of silence. Jacob glanced back over his shoulder... And saw what was happening to the house.

It was being consumed. Shrunken and ingested. The downstairs windows were shattered, their brick surrounds demolished, raw holes gaping in the facade like busted mouths. Jacob was certain he saw a terrified face at one of the upstairs panes as the frenetic blackness blocked out his view and kept expanding, spreading out a fog of deeper darkness.

"Up!" he shouted, grabbing Maria under her armpits and hauling her unceremoniously to her feet. "Up! Up!" She and the girl stood, Maria grunting with the pain of her lacerated hands and back. Jacob looked back at the Outsiders, and froze. The tall woman was holding something in her hand, an orb of sickly effulgence. It threw out deep-sea shades in every direction, indigos and putrescent pale greens, which danced with darkness over her skin, making it appear as if it were being eaten and spat out in ghostly chunks. The woman seemed to heft the ball, testing its weight. She did not remove her eyes from Jacob.

"What?" Maria gasped. "What? What?"

Jacob touched her arm. He turned to look once again at the thing behind them, the tool sent to destroy them. It looked, he thought, exactly like the pulsing perversion in the scarlet woman's hands. The stink was the same, as well, dredged up from Hell's own sewer.

Their vision was obliterated by a sudden explosion of light. Voices cried out in agony as retinas were scorched, spears of agony driven into brains. Jacob realised that one of those voices was his own. The air seemed to heat up ten degrees instantaneously. His skin stretched and tightened across his scalp. He fell.

"Here." It was a shout, but the tone was soft, firm. It was not Maria's voice. Jacob felt a hand clamp around his wrist, fingers strong and cool. The world around him appeared to consist of little more than vague, smudged negatives, like amoeba shadows. But after-images of the explosion also remained, stark uprights of figures set against a blazing white background.

Someone's bound to call the police, Jacob thought, but he realised that the authorities could never get here fast enough.

The air sizzled with the discharge of static. His eardrums were singing with the constant drum-drum-drum of aftershocks, buzzing as if an electrical current were being passed through his head. His temples throbbed; a migraine tightness sat behind his eyes. A briny stench seemed to emanate from his clothes, hanging in the violent air, waves of it following on from each fresh thunderclap. He was sure his eyes were open, but light erased everything. It was like staring into the sun, trying to see the dark spots, finding only blindness.

Lila tugged at his wrist. Jacob didn't move. *Maria.* He reached back and splayed his fingers wide, feeling for her. A sense of dread seized him, thrusting horrors into his mind. He imagined his fingers being sliced off as he stretched them out; his wrist clutched by something inhuman; his blood deserting him in hot, dark spurts.

There! Something soft bumped his fingertips. Something wet. Warm.

"Jake?" The name was screamed, but barely audible above the cacophony. The voice was full of panic and terrible desperation.

"Maria!" Jacob lunged, hauling Lila with him, and caught a fistful of Maria's hair. It was slick and soapy with blood, but still it felt wonderful, real.

Something detonated in the air above them: a thick, liquid report. Its warm contents rained down, and for an instant Jacob's damaged vision reddened. Then, another concussion-wave struck, buffeting them all around. He heard Maria groan, and once more Lila cried her imperative:

"Here! Come on!" She hauled on Jacob's wrist, and he winced.

His skin crawled. As Lila dragged them back across the pavement, it felt as though a bucket of heated insects was being emptied across his back. They scurried and crawled into his clothing, pinching his skin between savage mandibles, transforming his whole dermis into an acid-bathed landscape of pain. He cried out and thought he detected similar exclamations, before and behind him. He wanted to turn and protect Maria, soothe her and tell her how sorry he was that he ever got her involved in this. Still Lila drew them on through the chaos.

Something bit his hand. He jerked back, but then realised that this pain was different. It was sharp and fresh, and welcome for all that. He felt around cautiously, found the shattered panel of wood that had dug splinters into his palm. How many times had he knocked at this wood? How many times had he and Maria leant against it, kissing as she tried to ease her key into the lock? It was the decimated front door.

A warm mouth breathed into his ear. Lila. "Inside, and out the back." He nodded against her lips, squeezed Maria's hand. She squeezed back.

Lila led them through the remains of the doorframe and across the torn carpet inside. For an instant the tumult lessened, but then Jacob heard the unmistakable sound of running footsteps, barked orders.

They were coming.

Jacob concentrated on his own panicked breathing, the reassuring thump of his heart.

The squeals of pain from behind as Maria struggled to keep up.

The white-vision, obscuring everything.

"Here, now!" Lila urged. Her voice sounded very strange, very bright and clear with authority.

Then the noise of an eruption—louder, harder, hotter than any before-rolled over them. Jacob gagged as the stench of death coated his mouth and nose, spilling down into his throat. The noise dropped a few decibels, but persisted in the form of a scream. Jacob realised with a terrible icy certainty that he knew that voice.

Maria.

As the realisation hit him, his arm was violently shaken, Maria's hand clasping his painfully hard. Up, down, left, right, up again, as though his ex-girlfriend was caught in the jaws of some huge beast. Opposing forces wrenched at her, and consequently at him. The shriek continued, too highly pitched to be anything other than the sound of insanity, calling his name with an intensity and passion that he never thought he would hear again.

"Maria!" he screamed. "Lila!" he shouted, thinking that perhaps she could help. But the girl merely tugged at his left arm, while Maria heaved on his right.

Something happened then: another explosion flexed the ground he stood on. The floor seemed to drop several inches, and his knees juddered with the impact of the shock wave. His hand clutching Maria suddenly jerked up, higher, actually lifting him off the ground.

And then, weightless, still holding onto Maria's palm, he fell once more. Maria's screaming had ceased. Her hand was wet and warm, the fingers locked around his, lifeless, and beyond that only a ragged mess where the arm had been torn from her body.

A bellow of rage escaped him; he let go of Maria's hand and felt it slip to the ground. He reached back into the light, but his fingers closed on hot air.

"NO!"

Lila hauled him into the hallway. Waves of force broke against the house, melting brick, dissolving wood.

"Maria!"

He smelled fire. Seconds later he felt the scalding lick of flames around his ankles. The carpet was ablaze.

"Maria! MARIA!"

But however loud he shouted, and however much he thrashed his hand in empty space, he knew that Maria was gone.

## 15. The Curse of Memory

Jacob remembered only snippets of their flight through the house. Impossibilities wrecked the air around them, great coughs of power that burst out in all directions. The din was louder than ever, a white noise of hatred directed against him and him alone. Sight returned, but registered only the most fleeting of impressions:

A glistening smear of blood splashed on the back of his hand in the shape of a question mark, as if Maria were begging him to change one last time—

The air was clouded with plaster dust. Shimmering grey-green light drooped from ceilings and banisters like grotesque Christmas decorations—

But Jacob's thoughts were really elsewhere.

He was in Maria's flat two years ago. They had been out for a romantic meal, there was wine spilled on the carpet, and he had his face pressed between her silky thighs. Then the phone rang. It was Morris. There was trouble up the road, at the Traveller's Rest. The fuckwit of a publican had rented out the back room to some sloganeering Nazi band. Word had gotten round and there was already a seething face-off in the Lounge Bar between Morris's Socialist Worker mates and a mob of NF C-18 boot boys. Jacob was out the door within minutes, muttering excuses, hardly even glancing at Maria as she covered herself with the duvet.

Five hours later she came to the police station to see them and it was only then—when he saw her pinched and furious face—that it even occurred to Jacob that he may have made the wrong choice.

His mind flew on, diving back through time—

He was with Maria for the first of his several birthdays they had celebrated together. They had been to the cinema that afternoon, making out in the back row even though they had both wanted to see the film. Kissing, then, was still a new and wonderful experience for them, something to revel in, bathing in each other's warmth and the tang of each other's breath. By the time the credits had begun to roll their hands had already strayed further than either of them had intended.

But on the bus home Jacob had taken exception to some lads spouting drunken post-pub pre-club bullshit about "disease-ridden, AIDs-spreading fuck-boy homos" and decided to re-educate them himself—an encounter which finally resolved itself in the local Casualty department with seven stitches and Maria in the waiting room, worried half to death, furious beyond words.

Now she was no longer with him. Now she was dead.

Lila hurried him through the chaos, her thin fingers still clamped around his wrist. Her floating summer dress seemed out of place in these preternatural surroundings. It was Maria's dress—and Maria was gone—so how could it still exist?

"Hey!" There was a face in front of him. Thin, gaunt, eyes glittering with something that could have been fear, or hate. "Listen!"

The noise had mostly ceased—mostly, apart from the sounds of crumbling masonry and the crackle of greedy fire. An olive tinge lit the night, a clinging green nimbus which flowed across the ground like marsh gas. Behind them he could hear the sound of feet, picking their way through the debris of Maria's home. Glass crunched, a door slipped from its heat-twisted hinges and hit the floor.

"Come on!" Lila hissed. She tore Jacob away from the back door and sprinted down the long, narrow garden. Nettles and brambles scratched at her legs but she paid them no heed. There was no concern for personal safety in her flight. Her sure-footedness was more the product of luck than design. She was simply obeying the urge to flee, to escape, to get away at any cost.

For a moment—as this terrified waif dragged him in a desperate, patently futile escape bid—Jacob tasted the lust for vengeance. It was a frightening feeling, a dehumanising rush of fury that threatened to hobble him in his tracks, wrench him round to confront whatever *thing* might be pursuing them through the ruins.

They reached the garden gate, gummed shut after years of untended advance by brambles and honeysuckle. Lila grabbed the rusty handle and yanked, grunting as her knuckles turned pearly white. Maria's loaned dress had come away at her shoulder, and Jacob watched the burning light from the flats glaze her skin with gangrenous highlights. He wanted to reach out and touch her, brush away the stain, because Lila was innocent, blameless, the very image of perfection.

"Maria," he said. It had been only minutes, but already he felt like she had died decades ago. His mind was a torrent of memories of their time together. It was as though he were reliving her whole life, because she had been killed too quickly for it to flash before her own eyes. Even his thoughts of the time before they met felt as rich and deeply textured as his memories of the days they shared, because her tales of her early years mingled with his own recollections.

"Maria," he said again. His voice sounded—to him at least—devoid of inflection or emotion. Lila struggled with the gate, releasing his hand so that she could work on the stiff handle. Thorns cut her arms. Blood glistened in the acidic half-light.

Footsteps. They crunched over glass, then the tempo changed as heavy boots impacted with concrete. Rage flaring, hands raised and knees bent in the universal stance of aggression, Jacob spun around.

At the back door, silhouetted by the dirty fire from within, stood the woman in red. Now, though, she was monochrome, an enemy out of time.

Nearer, running across the garden, came the woman from the lab, the one with the camera who had led the raid on the guest house and beaten Lila outside the mansion. Brutal. Her arms pumped at her sides, flinging scraps of luminescence into the air behind her. The green light persisted for a beat or two, defying physics, before it finally faded back into darkness.

She reached him. Her face was rich with contradictions: high, attractive, cheekbones pasted by the scars of old battles; a frown of consternation; hard, dead eyes. She paused several steps from them. Smiled. Jade fire rippled momentarily across her lips.

Behind him Jacob could hear Lila's ongoing battle with the gate. Wood splintered— rotten. Metal whined and snapped—rusted through.

Jacob flew at the woman, this thing from beyond or whatever she—*it* —was, dressed in human skin. He thought she said something, but didn't catch the words. Even as he lunged he expected unearthly flames to leap out and devour him. Instead, she simply stepped to one side and he was sent sprawling.

He regained his footing, rage making him agile—then was suddenly reminded of the horror he'd felt after beating the guard at the lab. He quickly quashed these traitorous recollections, though: this fight was justified. Even if his opponent was a woman, half his weight and size. She had helped kill Maria. In a very real way, this was self-defence. And if not that, it was certainly sweet vengeance.

He made to pummel her with a flurry of blows, but she blocked every one, her hands moving faster than he could follow. She kicked him in the side of the head and he went down. He hadn't even seen it coming. From the ground he stared up and cringed. She seemed as tall as the sky itself, malevolence incarnate. He couldn't see her face, but he could feel the crackle of energy on his skin, rooting through the tiny hairs like a stinging breeze. Death stared down.

Then abruptly she was gone, and in her place stood Lila, swaying slightly, a three-foot-long shank of fence clutched in one fist. The wood was studded with a necklace of crooked nails.

"Come on!" Lila hissed. She dragged him up and they staggered for the gate, leaving the brutal woman on the ground, in the shadows, stirring unseen. Green fire sparkled there.

The tall woman came after them in a red flash.

They ran.

Lila was astonishingly fast. The darkness cowled their surroundings, only the soft face of the moon providing a low-grade illumination, but Lila seemed instinctively to know where they were going. She weaved nimbly through twisting alleys, and stinking, refuse-stacked lanes.

Jacob's senses retreated from reality and he let his lower motor functions control him. In the deepest black morass of grief Jacob had placed his life in the hands of this child. This tortured victim.

"Hurry," she said. Her fingers were still locked around his, even though their route took ever more violent twists and turns. Soon they would be lost, and the Outsiders would catch them. Perhaps they would give him back to the brutal woman so that she could dispense her own vile justice. Maybe they would make him watch as they raped and murdered Lila.

Hope glimmered. Lila turned and grinned at him, her teeth flashing slivery in the moonlight. Her look filled him with an enormous sense of relief. The sounds of pursuit seemed to vanish at that instant, as if driven back into the maze of alleys and gardens just by her smile. Jacob glanced over his shoulder and saw a glow in the sky above the remains of Maria's flat. Above the place where Maria's remains must lie, also. A green glow, spreading like a virus through the atmosphere, infecting the heavens. Searching for them. Casting fingers out across the night.

He knew that their escape could never be assured.

But Lila was still smiling.

## 16. Treading Violent Waters

The car was parked on a rough concrete slab. Rundown garages crouched at either side, one wearing a sturdy timber trough around its base like a skirt, sprouting wild blossoms; they looked like some forgotten tribute laid against a huge gravestone. The timber sidings were rotten, shedding bits of themselves across the concrete like dead skin. Dirty pipes held the decomposing remains of a decade's worth of wind-blown leaves.

There was a smell hanging in the air here, a mixture of spoiled meat and heavy spices. It was a bad smell, one which did not belong in the land of the living. It scratched at Jacob's nostrils; he sneezed once, and gagged.

More surprise, then, when he saw the car. It was a beautifully restored Aston Martin DB5, the moonlight emphasising all the elegant curves and dips of its bodywork. It sat there between the dilapidated garages, as sad as bright flowers tied to a dented roadside telegraph pole.

Jacob saw no way in which this strategy would work, though Lila approached the car, tried the driver's door, and opened it easily with a compliant squeak. Jacob stared, amazed. In spite of himself, he began to laugh.

"I can't drive," Lila said. "Will you drive me?" The change in her manner was astounding. To Jacob she appeared to be the same abandoned, unresponsive waif whom Maria had bathed and dressed last night. Yet seconds previous—in the garden, in the alleys—Lila had been strong, their roles reversed. Perhaps it had been a strength borne of righteous anger, rage at her former tormentors. But now it had burned itself out.

"Maria's dead," he said flatly. In the distance—mingling with the night songs of cats and the secret music of the city shadows—he could still hear the occasional calls from their pursuers.

Lila nodded. "I'm frightened," she said, her voice wavering. "I know she's dead, but I'm frightened. Will you drive me?"

"Keys," Jacob said. "We don't have any keys."

Lila reached into the car, fiddled with the sun visor and produced a jangling key ring. They dangled from her grip, catching the thin light like a cheap glitterball.

Inside, the car smelled of new leather and loving attention. The seats felt fresh, unbowed by the weight of years. Lila shrank into the passenger seat and drew up her long legs, somehow resting her feet on the seat. She locked her fingers around her shins, lowered her chin to her knees. Jacob patted her shoulder, but she didn't look at him, and for a terrible moment he was certain that she was going to lash out again, descend into unreasoning mania as she had done in the mansion. Jacob started the car. It purred.

His grief at losing Maria—restrained for the moment by shock—had translated itself into a protective feeling for the girl. Duty again. Such terrible wrongs had been done her, and since he couldn't approach the police, it was his responsibility to shield her from any further threat. Morris would be proud.

She sat next to him, an enigma, unfathomable, unreachable. He knew her from the pores on up, the bare skin, but nothing from beneath that shell. Not a clue, never a whisper. She had led him from the fire; saved him from himself when anger had tried to hold him back; guided them to this car, with its unlocked doors and poorly hidden keys. Now, though, it was as if someone had switched her off at the mains. Her eyes glittered, but it was with borrowed light rather than at angry memories. She hadn't put her seat belt on. Jacob wondered if such a mundane attempt at protection was even appropriate for someone who had suffered so badly. He leaned across and clicked it in place for her.

Maybe he was lucky to have this distraction. Perhaps, while he struggled to keep this vulnerable girl alive, the process of grief would continue inside, unnoticed. It could linger at the edges, and at times—while he was asleep or in hiding—it might find the route to his heart. For now it swam at the periphery, while Jacob treaded water in the centre of this terrible lake.

But he couldn't fool himself that easily. He knew that one day he would have to push to the banks again, in order to rest. No one could tread water forever, in the end you could only drown or get out. One day, probably soon, he would have to face Maria's loss, naked and alone. Sink or swim. Nothing, not even duty, could last forever.

"How do you feel?" Lila asked almost inaudibly. He'd been about to ask her the same question. She didn't move, her dim gaze hardly faltered.

Jacob sat with his hands at ten-to-two on the steering wheel, feeling the eager vibration of the engine through the leather. The car wanted to be off. So did he.

How do you reply to a question whose meaning you don't fully understand? Words were not adequate to describe his current state of mind, he couldn't hem his feelings in with language.

"I don't know," he whispered, feeling weak, but glad that he was honest enough to say it.

"Why?"

"I can't allow myself…" He trailed off, rallied. "I want to help you. That helps me. Maria's gone. But I don't think I really understand that part yet." He shook his head in the dark, glanced sideways at Lila's unchanging pose. "I can't understand it… don't feel it yet… She had a mole on her left breast. She liked crisp and HP sauce sandwiches. She drank coffee with a spoonful of powdered chocolate in it. She liked to watch rain, loved to get caught in it… Said it made her feel safe." He turned to look at Lila fully, and she shifted her head fractionally. Her eyes had stopped sparkling; a cloud had covered the moon.

Jacob shook his head. "How can she be dead?" Then he engaged the gears, and slid the car out between the garages.

He drove along the lane at several miles per hour, unwilling to put the headlights on until they reached a road and a genuine route to freedom.

They emerged onto a lit street where streetlamps flashed out a jittery Morse code as the soft breeze whirled stray leaves around their bulbs. The avenue was deserted. Jacob turned right, heading out of town. He flipped on the headlights and gradually ramped up the speed, not wishing to attract any undue attention by accelerating too quickly. Lila was quiet once again, as if digesting the answer he'd given her. He hoped that he hadn't made her feel guilty.

At the junction a low, wine-dark lump in the road marked out the demise of another unfortunate cat. It was smeared rather than crushed, pasted onto the tarmac like a grotesque brushstroke. Jacob had suffered the sudden conviction that it was the wheels of a black Mercedes that had done the deed. He powered away from the scene, glancing in the mirror, expecting at any moment to see the shark's outline of a trailing black car.

"Where to?" he said. For now, he was just driving, but they would soon need a destination. A stolen car would be noticed and reported sooner rather than later. Equally, a destination implied purpose, which in turn kept the mind busy. He did not want to dwell on what had happened. Not yet.

Lila turned in the passenger seat and worked her shoulders back against the leather, as if readying herself for a long journey. Her eyes were wide and surrounded by bruised skin; tired of life.

"I don't know everything. But those people back there, they were sorcerers. Once." She stopped. "Now I don't know if they are even human."

"No longer human?" Jacob asked, awed.

"Since the coming of the woman in red."

"The Multitude," whispered Jacob, remembering the diary.

Lila nodded, very deliberately. "They wear our faces, dress in our skins."

"Fifteen years," said Jacob.

Unreality washed over him again, but with it came a comforting sense of corroboration. He was not the only one thinking impossible thoughts. Unlike Maria, Lila had no choice but to accept.

"They have been using me," Lila said. "For tests. And other things."

Jacob nodded. He did not ask what other things. Perhaps he should have, because his imagination did a grotesque job of filling in the unspoken details.

"In a way, they still are," the girl continued. "I'm an ongoing experiment. Even all this—" She waved her right hand over the dashboard, indicating the whole world, "—could be a part of it. I'm not in control. They are. It's all part of some kind of ritual," she paused and frowned, then continued, "but maybe there is someone who can help us. There was a village near where I come from—and where they kidnapped me. Another place that they'd destroyed many years before."

Jacob scowled. Loose ends twirled in his mind, then knotted together. "Is this place in Scotland?"

Lila nodded. Not as surprised as she should have been.

"A ruin now?"

Again, the nod. "Abandoned. Save for one man. I met him when I was little, investigating the ruins with my friends. But I was the only one he talked to. The only one he appeared to... The only one he *befriended*," she paused then, as if dredging up the memories of this strange hermit. "He is the only one who can help."

"I'm helping," Jacob said, unreasonably slighted by her words.

Her face betrayed no emotion. "I know you are. And I am grateful. But you aren't an adept."

Jacob snorted. "A sorcerer?"

Lila nodded.

"So who is he?"

"He is known as Fenton."

"Strange bloody name for a sorcerer." But as he said it the name tickled at the back of his mind, threatening recognition. Fenton?

"And what should sorcerers be called?"

"How should I know?" He felt aggrieved that, after all his deeds and the dangers he had suffered, the girl needed someone else so suddenly. A sense of rejection needled him sharply.

"Look, this guy—this Fenton—one man on his own?" He paused. Fenton, Fenton? Where did he know that name from? "How the hell do you think he can help against all this? We got away back there—somehow—but that isn't the end of it. I think we should go east. Head for London. Get to someone in authority, I don't know, MI5 or someone."

"Those in authority started this," Lila said. "They sanctioned it. Commissioned it. It was because of them that the Outsiders came through in the first place."

"The village?" Jacob said. "Your home?"

A nod from Lila.

"They allowed it? But why?" But he thought he knew. He could smell the unbelievable twists and deceits of a far-fetched sci-fi story in the air. But it worked, all the edges fit.

"Oh shit, I've seen *Alien*," Jacob said. "Special Directive. Crew expendable. Is that it? Are we expendable to the plan?"

"Not just you and me. Everyone."

"One day, we were going to be noticed," Jacob paraphrased.

Lila nodded again. "Except that day has been and gone."

Jacob recalled the dreadful images from the diary, the vain attempt of the writer and his long-gone comrades to hold off whatever was "coming through". How their attempts had culminated in some unwritten mission, a frantic endeavour to win back some ground. After that, nothing.

He should have realised how wrong it had gone. "Oh, God." Despair. Defeat. A sense of time slipping away, laughing at their meaningless struggles. All too late, and after the fact.

"As for Fenton," Lila said. "He's the last of his kind. A revenant. How they haven't found him yet, I don't know. He's kind, considerate, strong. And he knows them—the things inside them—very intimately."

Memory suddenly slid into gear. Its cogs meshed, began ponderously to revolve. One of the characters mentioned in the diary had been called "F".

Fenton?

The narrator had been in conflict with this mysterious F. They had argued, fought, and the narrator had been especially frightened by F's final method of defence, an item alluded to merely as, "the Weapon". Was that what Lila was now proposing? To find this Fenton, and use his Weapon to try to oust the Outsiders? Jacob frowned, confused.

"I'll get us there," Jacob said. "We'll go together. That's the important thing. That we go together. We've both lost ..." He could not finish the sentence. Not yet—

Maria's final shriek as her hand went limp in his, the wet end of her severed arm striking the ground just out of sight. Her scream, rising in pitch and altitude, volume dropping as the thing had torn her from his grasp. His hand. His weak, pathetic hand, unable to save her, unable, at the last, to drag her back.

Lila watched him with her head on one side, her expression curiously empty. "I know," she said, a little tonelessly. "Don't worry. I want it to be us. You are with me the whole way." And with that curious statement she turned away.

The road unrolled ahead of them, dark and smooth and deadly. Soon they were speeding through the city limits. Within minutes the street lamps disappeared, as if they'd shrugged and given up on anyone foolish enough to travel this far. Lila curled into a ball and slept. Jacob listened to her steady breathing, smiled as she murmured something in her sleep, then frowned as he wondered what she was dreaming of.

In the gloom, he couldn't make out her face properly. He tried to imagine that it was Maria sleeping next to him, but the image would not come. She was lost to him, and it seemed that his memories of her were as tenuous as his grip on reality had become.

**

Jacob had no idea he was going to be sick.

He shut the cubicle door. Stared at the grubby ceramic tiles without really seeing them, sat down. Then he puked, in one great fountaining spurt. It hit the cubicle wall and splattered onto the floor. His stomach heaved. More came up.

In this state of distress it seemed that his memories had been freed to parade themselves throughout his mind: Maria's face pressed itself up to the window of his mind while his stomach muscles clenched and released, pumping up stinging bile from his empty guts. Her voice sounded clear and loud in his ears, her hands mopped his sweaty brow. Puke dribbled from his nose, between his face and the toilet seat. He swept the disgusting streamers aside with a wad of toilet paper, and rested his head against the wall, relishing the cool touch on his skin. Maria—her face already dimming again in the fog of memory—berated him softly, but he wanted the pain. He wanted to remember.

An immense wailing madness was buffeting him, but in spite of its howling his composure endured. Grief was held back, even now, by a sense of duty.

If Maria had never taken a shine to Lila, then perhaps he wouldn't feel like this. If she had shunned the girl, maybe he would be under sedation in a hospital somewhere, mumbling mysteries in his sleep, screaming when he woke. Or would he be caged? In a cold metal box, strange signs splattered on every wall, cold grey eyes peering in at him. A flash of scarlet in the viewing porthole as the scarlet woman turned on her heel to leave.

The muscles in his gut clutched with another spasm. Nothing came up this time, but he flexed his throat and this encouraged another flash of pain. He welcomed it.

**

Once he'd finished in the Gents—straightened his clothes and swilled his mouth out with cold water—he went outside to stand by the main exit. He cast his eyes over the milling crowds passing through. Even now, early in the morning, the place was busy. It was as if there was another clock at work here—one without a.m. or p.m—turning its way endlessly towards some mythical hour when the place could finally rest; close up for just a little while, shutter down.

Lorry drivers mixed with couples; kids held the hands of tired parents and gazed in wonder at every colourful toy display; a party of nuns shuffled through the foyer like a crowd of extras. In a small alcove next to the automatic doors, fruit machines gobbled pocket money and free time. The hypnotic dirge of plastic pop issued from ceiling speakers, while next to the Photo-Me booth a fat man in a cheap suit was programming the business-card machine with a hunted look imprinted on his face. A couple dressed in black passed through the doors and immediately snagged at Jacob's attention. His breath stuttered, but they were only goths, sad and sullen and pale.

Without warning a fresh wave of nausea hit him. Dizziness meddled with his balance. He blinked and stumbled. For a moment the steel and glass and posters vanished. The hallway seemed to dissolve into a billion individual specks, each of them visible like a glowing grain or a firefly. The ceiling parted like a waterfall. A great beating cloud of swarming creatures swept down, dive-bombing the ground with their own vile bodies, splitting and falling, before being consumed by the floor and reabsorbed by the walls.

The shifting ground rose in great billows, each as tall as a house, washing back and forth, transforming into great tapering cones of agitation. Some of these restless columns split from the main mass and rose so high into the sky, that they receded into a distant haze. The very fabric of reality was playing tricks on him; heaven and earth were changing places.

Then it was just the service station again.

Jacob shook and trembled, had to go and lean heavily against a telephone kiosk for long minutes, fearful that his guts might rebel explosively once more. One pure crystalline thought cut through his disorientation, though: protect Lila. All else was meaningless static. Forget hallucinations, forget sorcery, forget nausea.

Protect Lila.

**

After collecting the girl from the restaurant Jacob discovered that he was a nobody. Mr Nothing. Little more than a face glimpsed by strangers, and instantly forgotten.

They needed cash, but the service tills spat his card back out. He tried again, this time losing the card completely. He had the sudden urge to ring for help. Someone, anyone. But events had trapped him outside the normal mechanics of life, the everyday clockwork of events. Because of Lila, what had been done to her. What he had seen.

These people rubbing shoulders with him were no more his kind anymore than the Outsiders were. He was a different race now, a breed apart. He caught sight of their reflection in a shop window—the wan skinny girl and the shabby, trampy guy—and he realised that these images did not belong there. The normal world had disowned them. They slipped from its surface like water off glass.

Mr Nobody. A revenant. He was someone who would not be missed when the time came.

They were doomed. His determination did not waver with this realisation, but his confidence flinched, took a fearful glimpse down at the rocks below. The drop that he had already committed himself to.

He snatched hold of Lila's elbow and steered her towards the exit. They had to pause momentarily before the automatic doors responded, as if even mindless mechanics had started to doubt the truth of their existence.

"When will we get there?" Lila asked. Her eyes were heavy, tired.

"It'll take hours," Jacob replied.

"We will get there," Lila said.

It was not a question. Nor was it really a statement. Perhaps it was merely an utterance of personal reassurance.

Somehow, it was not a comfort.

## 17. Empty of All but Echoes

The road was long, but like most roads travelled in the company of grief, time barely registered. Beneath Jacob's robot stare hundreds of miles of Tarmac unrolled blankly. His pain couldn't be denied, but it could be fooled. Lila was his armour. He was her knight-protector. She was the most important thing to him in the world.

As they left the city far behind—where presumably evil still sniffed at their cooling trail—she began to open up.

"How do you feel?" she asked.

Jacob shrugged. "Like death."

"How is that?"

He glanced at her, but she was not mocking him.

"Maria and I had ... well, we'd broken up. Not long ago. Day before yesterday. She left me. It was a long time in coming... not that I could see it. I was always so angry that I couldn't see. Wrapped up in myself... My obsessions—direct action, animal rights..." He trailed off, conscious but not resentful of how his priorities had changed.

It was Lila he thought of today. She was his single cause, the only one left worth fighting for. He tried to imagine what he would do if he was faced with taking a bullet—or a gobbet of green fire—for her. Then he steered away from this line of reasoning. It was just too morbid, too self-indulgent. A romanticised death wish on his part would help no one.

"When she went, I was lost. I knew, you see. I knew that it was for real, this time. Maria's a serious girl. She doesn't just up and off at the first sign of trouble. Some people run their relationships like that, knowing that the other person will always come running after them, begging for forgiveness. It's a defence mechanism, I suppose, like having a gun to your head. 'Misbehave, and I pull the trigger.' But not Maria. She'll put the work in. Tuck her head down and go for it if there's even half a chance. She'll really work through it if she can. She must have thought it over for a long time."

Jacob fell silent, truly absorbing the truth for the first time. How long had she been considering leaving him? Had she been thinking of it last month, when they made love in the park? Staring over his shoulder as she sat astride him, staring into the dark with sad, contemplative eyes?

"You talk about her as though she's still here," Lila said.

Jacob looked in the rear-view mirror. There was only blacktop unravelling behind. "My defence mechanism," he said. Tears smirched his vision and he had to blink them rapidly away.

It was now fully light in the car, revealing to him the injuries Lila had sustained during their escape. Her dress was torn across one hip, a scrape of pink flesh showing beneath. For an insane moment Jacob wanted to reach out and touch it, to see if she was actually real and not some flimsy guardian angel. Really there. Scabby bulbs of dried blood had strung themselves along the scratch as though ready to sprout.

"You believe you are to blame," she said. "But there's no logic to that. It was them, not you. They destroyed her. They took her from you. Maybe you'll be able to get back at them one day. Someday soon."

Jacob's lips pressed into a thin slit as he imagined a fitting vengeance.

"I didn't kill her," he said. "I know that. But if it hadn't been for me—"

"If not for you and Maria I would still be trapped in that place. They'd be hurting me. Testing me. And that one … that one … he would be…"

Jacob did not look at her. He couldn't. He didn't think he could bear to witness the pain her voice implied.

He slammed his hand furiously into the steering wheel, sending the car veering across the white lines into the oncoming lane. Tight with anger he guided the bonnet back to true and accelerated over the brow of a small hill.

"Bastards! Bastards!"

He had felt this fury before. The flailing hand of rage which tore free of all the moral straps he tried to bind it with. It had almost killed the security guard back at the Hellier labs, and in the past it had raised more than a few bruises on people he called friends. But now, burning through his veins like a quick-acting poison, the anger had nowhere to escape. Boxed in, constrained, he couldn't vent the rage properly. Lila seemed to shrink down in her seat, though she still watched him. Her cheeks were dry, her eyes wide and observant, but Jacob saw only a tortured, wretched young girl, cowering from his rage because it terrified her, just as she had been terrified by those who had abused her. Which just enraged Jacob all the more.

He nailed the accelerator to the floor. The car leapt in his hands, darting over an old stone bridge and heading up a steep incline, the first of the Scottish hills. Farmland flashed by on either side, startled cows staring after the growling vehicle. Great stone mounds stood high and weather-beaten in their ancient bays.

Gradually, his fury bled away into the road, drawn through the hot wheels, sucked down into the engine and spat from the exhaust. He slowed, the car slowed, and soon they were parked in a lay-by and Jacob was crying into his crossed arms.

Lila reached out and touched the back of his head, just the once, very lightly. Then she just sat there and waited for him to finish.

**

As the day wore on they wound their way further into Scotland, mist dusting the windscreen with ghostly breath.

Finally, near evening, Lila began to recognise signs. First, a turn of her head. Then, a finger pointing to where her suffering had begun.

"They must know where we're heading," Jacob said, quietly voicing a doubt that had been niggling at him for hours.

"They know of Fenton," she said. "But not where he is hiding. He's in the last place they would ever think to look—the place they have already destroyed. Also, we have a head start. They may be sorcerers, but they are not birds. Next left," she indicated. "There will be gates. Maybe road signs. It stands to reason that they wouldn't want just anyone stumbling onto the site. Remember, everyone is involved."

**

ARMY TEST RANGE - KEEP OUT.

The board was badly weathered, spots of rust spiralling out from the screw-holes like a metallic cancer. Lila seemed to have little trouble forcing the padlock and opening the gate.

Jacob shook his head to clear the ringing in his ears. Tired, exhausted, his body was severely fucked. He still had on the same shirt he'd donned that fateful morning in the bed and breakfast, though now it was caked stiff with gouts of fallen blood. An assortment of minor cuts and bruises had nagged at him throughout the journey, and his shoulder was aflame. Looking in the mirror, he could hardly believe that he was still able to see through eyes so bloodshot, so haunted. Surely he would only see ghosts with eyes like that? Gingerly, he raised his fingers to the gnarled tangle of gristle that had once been his left ear. That needed attention. A tetanus shot, a clean dressing. He touched the wound and winced. The intensity of the pain made him nauseous. He really was one sorry sack of shit.

"Jacob!" Lila called.

Jacob looked up. The girl stood at the open gate, motioning him to drive through, looking tall and invigorated, vivid in the dying sunshine. A stray gust of wind lifted her raven hair from her shoulders, sent it questing back and forth in the air behind her. She shivered deliciously and laughed. So beautiful. Tortured, beaten, abused beyond belief, yet still able to giggle at the caress of the breeze. Jacob marvelled at the resilience of the human spirit, shook his head and smiled. She waved him on. He drove through.

Lila jumped back into the car, grinning, enlivened both by her break in the bracing air and by their destination. He glanced in his mirror as he pulled away, and started as he saw the gate swing shut: reversed, the metal bars of the gate swirled and parted and kissed in a complex sigil. It's all done with mirrors, he thought.

Jacob returned his gaze to the road ahead. Some things, he just didn't want to see. They were magicians. Sorcerers. The diary had mentioned something about "wards" ... so perhaps Fenton had them, too?
Or maybe they had been seeded by the Outsiders themselves? An unsettling prospect, but logical. Keep Out, in fuck-off monochrome splashed across a range of supernatural media.

The road curved down into a valley cut through the hillside at an angle to ease the steepness of the descent. To his right, Jacob could just make out a huddle of buildings crouching beneath a broad canopy of trees. The closer to the valley floor they came, the more buildings he could see, until he realised that a whole village lay spread across the heavily wooded plane.

"They planted the trees to hide the village," Lila said, suddenly. "I'm surprised they didn't do more. Flood the place to make a reservoir, or something."

"Planted them, when? Those trees are huge. They're at least a hundred—"

"Magic, remember?"

"I don't understand any of this," Jacob said.

Lila reached out and touched his face. She smiled, but her eyes… There was something about her eyes, something hooded, hidden far down in the dark. An emotion he couldn't divine. Fear? Worry? Pain?

Jacob suddenly asked: "Did you have posters on your walls?"

"Posters?" She offered him a blank look, didn't seem to understand. He wasn't sure himself what he was trying to ask. It was just an underlying itch he needed to scratch, that was all he knew.

"What was your house like, before?"

"Small."

"Did it have a garden?"

"A garden? Yes. But small. There were bushes round the border, a wood behind us, all around."

"And your sister?" he asked, with a rising sense of alarm.

"I never had a sister."

"You never had to share a bedroom?"

"No."

"No brothers, no sisters."

"No."

"But posters? Did you have a favourite band? I don't know, I don't get much time to fathom pop these days. Travis—is that right? Steps? Robbie? Moody picture of James Dean on Forty-Second Street? Marley in psychedelic wipeout with a king-size spliff?"

For some reason he found himself near desperate with these questions.

"No. No, I never listened to music. I read a bit. Talked with my mother."

Jacob felt like he was drowning in this conversation, choked by the horror of the girl's dead-eyed testimony, but he couldn't help himself. He had to press on.

"What was she like?" he breathed.

"Tall, sad, worried. She wore red a lot in the summer."

She regarded him closely, answering politely but simply, as if only waiting for him to finish and get this nonsense over with.

They had reached the graceful belly of the glaciated valley, and now the car was rumbling over millennia-old deposits from hundreds of miles north. A part of everywhere is here, Jacob thought. Everything is one.

"Fenton is through the village. On the other side. There is an old stone bridge, at least there used to be. He lives in a coal bunker just near there."

"A bunker?"

She smiled. "Fugitives do that. They hide. Or if they can, they escape. Fenton never had the chance."

The gloom was beginning to gather in earnest, fumbling at the car windows. The trees were swaying and whispering together in the quickening breeze. Lila nodded ahead. Jacob drove towards the village.

The landscape changed in an instant, from the bleak and beautiful countryside of Scotland to something subtly different. For a moment Jacob couldn't figure out what the change was. Then, with startling clarity, he knew.

His senses had been amplified, enhanced. He could see in more detail than he had ever thought possible: the scars of old wounds where buildings had been hurriedly rebuilt; one house remade piece by shattered piece, each constituent part held together by a clear gummy paste; the shades of age where new paint tried to weather in with old …

Then the myriad smells of nature crowded in. Jacob stretched his neck like a dog, taking his nose nearer to the open window. He could smell death here, but it was a comfortable old scent, a natural undercurrent: death was a natural part of life—an old friend—and it encouraged rebirth.

He could smell the fear of a stag hunted on a distant hillside, the sweat of the men hunting it.

He could smell Maria on every part of him.

A thick mist was riding in, softening and thickening the air until it felt like clotted cream smeared across his face. The road bore around to the right, and then passed over a stone bridge. They crawled along the main street and down into the village square.

Cosy family stores passed by, a post office, a butcher's, a grocer's and dozens of quaint, coy little semi-detached cottages. But however enticing this place might look, it was dead. Just an absence—an enormous graveyard with headstones the size of buildings. Dark rectangles delineated the skull's-eye windows, yawning black and silent and open to the elements. Dusk was upon them. The silence was almost reverential.

They pulled up in front of a demolished church. Pews and fragments of stained glass lay scattered amongst the rubble. The cross from the church tower was still intact and protruded awkwardly from the building's ruins. Its edges seemed to quiver in and out of focus.

Lila sat forward in her seat and placed her hands against the windscreen. She opened her mouth slowly, turned to look at Jacob, then opened the door and stepped from the car. One pace away and already the mist blurred her shape—like muslin drapes wreathed around her shoulders—but she swung back and beckoned to him.

"Come on," she invited. "Come on," she repeated. Hastily, Jacob followed.

Lila walked towards the ruined church, her hands stretched out in front of her to ward off the mist, moisture moulding Maria's dress to her body. Without looking back she vanished round the side of the shattered building.

Left behind, Jacob called her name and broke into a half-run. He skidded into the garden behind the church, only to find that she was already nearing the looming shadow of the tree line. He tried to catch up, but the overgrown lawn interfered with his stride, and despite his best efforts he couldn't seem to gain on her at all. She disappeared into the forest.

After what seemed like an eternity he reached the edge, and paused. The matrix of limbs and branches looked virtually impenetrable. Hesitantly, he stepped between the ragged trunks. He saw a twist of brilliant red some way ahead.

"Lila!" he called. "Is Fenton in here? Is this where he lives?" But the girl did not turn around, and he heard no reply. He began to follow. He struggled to catch up, but always seemed ten steps behind. He picked up the pace, and soon found himself running. Everything was gloomy, everything was cool. He felt like he was running through the very substance of sleep, the light slowly ebbing from blue, to purple-dark, to black.

He only noticed the silence around them when it was broken. The sounds were gentle at first—the chuckle of leaves rasping together, the trickle of a stream running nearby —but then the new sound arrived, and it was like nothing he had ever heard before. Something was coming, or he was going towards it. An eruption, but not like an explosion. A rumble, but not like an earthquake or a tidal wave. Jacob couldn't picture it as an avalanche in the distance, or a whispering crowd approaching. It had elements of all these things, and yet it was none of them.

The rising breeze carried a stink he had encountered many times before—a minty, vaguely marine taint, crawling with the promise of rotting things, shells burst open, entrails laid out bare for the sun to cook...

The undergrowth around him started to churn. Something was moving through the trees, shoving the great boughs aside, cracking trunks asunder.

With a low moan Jacob turned to run. Guilt clutched at his heart. He had betrayed Maria completely by leading her into an unearthly death, and now he had failed Lila as well. She had not only gained his trust, but warranted it merely by being what she was, a pathetic waif, starved of humanity by the Outsiders. Not for the first time Jacob wondered just how inhuman they could be. It looked as though he was about to discover the answer.

Memory was pursuing him now, too, annoyingly evasive, a recollection allied to what he could see, smell, hear. Allied, too, to the taste of fear in his mouth.

"Fuck," he exclaimed. "Fuckers!" Terror and rage combined to raise his hackles and shrivel his balls. "Lila!" As he dashed across the forest floor he prayed he wouldn't stumble. His lungs felt as if they might spontaneously combust inside his chest.

Tree trunks detonated behind him. Every nightmare he had ever had was chasing him.

"Lila! Lila!"

Then she was there before him. Facing away, head down, hands clasped casually behind her back. She was standing beside the stream he had heard.

"LILA!"

She turned around. She'd heard him that time. But the girl merely watched him sprint over, an ambiguous smile curving her narrow lips.

"Almost there," she called.

"Lila! Look out!" Jacob cried. "Behind me, it's coming."

He could barely breathe. Great serrated shards of timber blasted past his shins and buried themselves in the soft earth. Trees screamed. Trees exploded.

"What do we do?" he shrieked. He realised that not so long ago he had vowed that he would protect the girl. Now he was asking her what they should do.

"Come here, Jacob," Lila said. She held out her hands. "I'm going now."

"What? Call to Fenton! He can help us!"

She smiled again. "I've learnt so much in recent years. Even more in the brief time we spent together."
Somehow her voice carried effortlessly over the storm. "But it is not enough. I don't think it ever will be." She sounded sad.

"Lila, come on!"

She closed her eyes.

"Now we are one," she whispered.

There was a sound in counterpoint now, a soft rustling, as if a billion tonnes of sand were making their way across a sea of broken glass. He felt an unnatural heat caress the hairs of his arms, and he had to blink his eyes rapidly to keep them moist. He glanced to one side.

The stream flowed red.

Red.

My God.

The stream flowed red, then raised itself like a cloth banner and began to twist and turn on the banks. Fish fell from the unsupported waterway, growing transparent wings and fluttering away before they could strike the stony stream bed. Their mouths grew beaks, and birdsong scratched at the wailing air. Something vibrated beneath the ground, under the gorse, strange creaks and groans as if a troop of giants were waking from some centuries-old slumber.

Jacob turned and Maria kissed him full on the mouth. He stumbled backwards, but she clung on to his face with clawed fingers. She was immensely strong.

Strangely, with that kiss, there was a pause. Everything stopped. Then—

A bursting green fire-flash exploded about his head. The noise was so loud that it literally pounded at his eardrums, shaking his eyeballs until they felt ready to burst. He had the sudden sensation of falling—but only briefly—before striking a surface entirely different to that he had been standing on mere moments before.

Silence. Stillness. Except for the thunderous roar of his heart.

Lila began to change. First she blurred, then her features seemed to flow into a shifting, strobing blossom-shape. Her face was made up of countless squirming parts, each of them whole and clear and well-defined. Her hair danced and flailed at the air, parting from her head and disintegrating into a cloud which billowed around her. From the corner of his eye he saw that the stream had turned to ash.

Somehow Jacob managed to tear himself away from Lila's gruesome metamorphosis. He stepped back, stumbled, fell… and then saw that she was unknitting.

Ties formed of ligament and gristle simply let go in one dreadful explosive instant. The Lila he had known ceased to exist. In her place there appeared a tumbling, swirling ribbon of skin colours, like an Escher print manifested in three dimensions. The impossibilities hurt his eyes, as he experienced up close the horrifying new physics which ruled this preternatural domain.

Everything here was alive. The ground crawled around and over his knees, parted, fell away, scrabbling to and fro like insects or reptiles or the bastard mutant children of both. The sky was a hundred shades of grey, streaked with grey and blurred with grey. Giant things swooped up there, dissolving into clouds, then forming again as entirely different entities. Falling, thrashing, they struck the ground and were swallowed back into the mass of the living plain. The plateau appeared infinite to his eyes, a slick oily sea of ceaseless agitation. Feeding, rebuilding, birthing, shitting endlessly back into itself. Perpetual, eternal, incessant. Vile beyond belief.

The thunder of his heart continued. Louder… louder...

Clouds of milling specks formed a barrier before him, too quickly to be retained as anything other than a subliminal image: a remember-by-numbers idea of what Lila had been. She was smiling, but not as she had before. There had been an innocence then, underlying all the pain and suffering, but now her smile said nothing. It spoke an alien language, a tongue that Jacob could never fathom.

His breath came short and fast and shallow, but he knew that he was not breathing the air here, couldn't be. All the sensations were wrong: he felt like he was submerged at the bottom of some oceanic trench, miles from land and light. All he could sense was pressure, pressure and the incessant, unbearable seething of the swarm around him. The scant oxygen he breathed seemed drawn from the scraps of saliva Lila had deposited inside his mouth with her kiss. He tried to groan, but no sound came.

Then something grabbed him—a claw of green fire—and snatched him bodily from the ground. Some of the flesh tore from his legs and was sucked into the vortex, as though this stinking pit had always been its home.

Sound came back from nowhere, increasing until it finally drowned out the panicked speed of his heart. His chest ached. He was dying. Everything was green now, everything.

**

Jacob shook his head. Trees emerged from the lime-green glare of his vision. A starlit night surrounded him once more, blessedly cold and wet. He put his forehead against the forest floor and sobbed.

Voices. Footsteps. He glanced up, finding that even now he was not beyond terror.

The black figures were standing in a perfect circle, with him as its hub. The Outsiders, murderers of Maria and Morris.

The woman in red stood before him. Her face, where it was not marred by plastic-pink scar tissue, was deathly pale in the moonlight.

"Congratulations," she said quietly. "You've just annihilated the human race."

# Part Two:
# Shades Against the Storm

## 18. Pushing Stones

When Jacob was a little boy he loved to yell at the dark.

His dad would carry him upstairs to bed, Jacob's head resting against his shoulder. Once in the bedroom his father would leave the light turned off and feel about in the dark, walking carefully and slowly, leading with his clever toes so that Jacob felt like he was being carried across a carpet of slumbering lions. He could recall with absolute clarity his dad's wheezy breaths as he stooped to deposit him on the cool, straight sheets. He remembered the ticklish scratch of the counterpane against his chin.

Though not, clinically speaking, a hyperactive child, Jacob probably only escaped the diagnosis by a twitching whisker. Consequently, it was always a blessing to his parents when he finally wore himself down at night, and it was why — every time he tucked him in — his dad would hiss, "Don't *dare* stick your feet out. I'm letting the monsters out of their cage now, and they'll have 'em off in seconds. Grrrr."

As soon as he heard the door click shut, however, Jacob would jump up and begin to yell. It wasn't that he didn't believe in the monsters, all the demons of childish imagination; he did. He believed in everything that he couldn't see in the dark, but it simply didn't matter. He would yell and scream, whirl around and around in a giggling fit precisely *because* he believed in the monsters.

He loved to run screaming through the rain, trying to catch all the long droplets that looked like thin knives slicing the air. "Daddy!" he would cry. "Look at the knives, Daddy! Daddy, the knives! Look at me! Look, look!"

Time after time he would be sent home from school for fighting. Angry parents rang his house to complain every week in term time. Teachers perpetually found themselves stood over him, shaking their heads at his bruised face and bloodied mouth.

But after Jacob started at the Comprehensive the pastime of bullying soon dried up across the school. In part, it was because it was so easy to draw his retribution. The littlest things could do it: a bigger boy standing over a smaller child, fear glimpsed in the corner of someone's eye. But in reality, it was his righteous anger they feared. It never mattered if the aggressor was twice Jacob's size, the frenzied blows would come pummelling down whatever the cause or slight. No mere school kid could ever match—or even appreciate—the depths of his fury.

On his knees in that forest, far from childhood and all those poorly grasped, belligerently articulated ideals Jacob understood—perhaps for the first time—how his anger had always made him stupid. He understood that he had never been of any real help in the struggle against apartheid or during the miners' strike; that no corrupt magnate had ever opened the morning paper and shuddered at his photo on the front page; that—in reality—he had never influenced one single bill travelling through any parliament, anywhere, ever.

He realised, finally, that he should have thought more and fought less. That he should have listened to Maria and seen the wisdom of what she tried to teach him.

*Maria.*

"*This is exactly what I mean*," she had said. "*These...* spasms *of unfocused rage. You spit in every direction at once, Jake, but the only person you ever hit is...*"

"Me," Jacob whispered.

The woman in red cold-eyed him for a slow-burning second, then made an emphatic gesture with her head. The brutal younger woman detached herself from the anonymity of shadows and dragged Jacob to his feet. Silver Hair stood a few steps back, a faintly mocking smirk tugging at his thin lips.

"You," agreed Brutal in a low voice. Her face was very close to his and her breath reeked of almonds; her eyes were feline, like green fire in the gloom. "Don't struggle and don't run. I don't want to have to kill you."

Something suddenly tugged her attention away so that he was afforded a glimpse of her shocking profile, all lines and bones and predator's poise. Then she released his lapels and shoved him back contemptuously.

All the other Outsiders had swivelled to follow Brutal's gaze, all except the woman in red, whose eyes remained pinned on Jacob. Eventually she made a small noise of disgust before spinning away and striding off across the clearing. Obediently, her entourage followed. Only Silver Hair loitered, grinning at Jacob. Was he being left behind as guard? Or executioner?

A sound was coming through the trees. But this wasn't any dread preternatural siren: it was a man-made klaxon, a particularly human visitation. The forest was throbbing. There was movement everywhere. The sound of chainsaws startled him, car doors slamming. Trucks and cars and at least a pair of articulated lorries were drawing near. Jacob didn't know where to look, what to do. Despite the brutal woman's lingering threat, he wondered whether he shouldn't try to make a break for it amidst the confusion.

Instead, he stammered, "W-what's happening?"

Silver Hair deigned to answer. "You don't fight a war without mobilising your army." He glanced around very casually, brushing a speck of lint from his sleeve before returning his attention to Jacob. "Come on," he said with a sigh and indicated the nearest Mercedes. "You ride with me." He actually sounded bored.

"Not until I know what's going on," Jacob blustered back. "Where's Fenton?"

At this the man started to laugh.

"Tell me!" Jacob demanded, but he knew he sounded frightened and shrill. "What have you done with him?"

Silver Hair was still chuckling. He put a hand to his chest and smiled. "Fenton," he managed, "is a dog."

"A *what*?"

"Come on, I'll explain everything in the car. That's what she wants me to do, at least." He glanced across the clearing to where the woman in red and her retinue were readying to depart. More doors slamming, engines being revved.

The din was deafening and the ruddy glow of brake lights cast a satanic pall over the whole scene. Silver Hair's eyes gleamed red. He beckoned.

Shell-shocked, Jacob acceded. They climbed into the cavern of the Mercedes' rear compartment and slid across the soft leather. Silver Hair spoke softly to the driver, and immediately they were off.

"We're going to the hotel," he drawled by way of an explanation. "Don't worry, they won't attack yet. It'll take a good few hours to redistribute the energy contained within the Lila nexus."

The conviction that he might have made a mistake — a terrible, godawful error — began to steal over Jacob. The red woman's words spun inside his head. Meanwhile, Silver Hair had fished out a cigarette and was proceeding to pat down his pockets in the futile quest for a lighter.

In this light it was obvious that his suit wasn't even black, but a very deep shade of claret, and gorgeous with it. A Cerrutti, perhaps? On his lapel he had a pin that Jacob half-recognised: a stylised Egyptian eye in white gold. With the unlit cigarette tucked dismissively in the crook of his lips he reminded Jacob of nothing so much as a slightly aloof public school prefect, from a Lindsay Anderson film.

Abruptly, Silver Hair abandoned his search and made a quick gesture in the air—like a fold or tuck—as if he were signing. But he definitely wasn't signing. There was a small fizz, a pop. Jacob felt a burst of heat ripple across his cheeks, and then the cigarette was alight. The man's eyes twinkled.

He cracked his near-side window a sliver and directed the first jet of sweet-smelling smoke through the gap. His cigarettes were something exotic and expensive, with a burgundy emblem on a very dark barrel. He pursed his lips to discharge the remainder of this initial mouthful of smoke and closed his eyes. He looked exhausted. Jacob could detect a web of fine blue veins ringing his eyes, like ghostly racoon markings.

"*Magic*," breathed Jacob.

Now that the introductory nicotine rush was gone the man smoked with lazy, listless abandon, as if he wanted the experience to be over as swiftly as possible— as if it had failed to live up to his expectations and had begun to bore him. He opened his eyes again, but only to languorous slits, and shrugged.

"No. Not really. At least, not in the traditional way."

There was a pause.

"You aren't planning to kill me," Jacob said. He didn't know whether it was a question or not.

Silver Hair offered him a jaded stare and sighed. He turned away to watch the red woman's car in front.

"*I'm* not," he replied finally, disinterested. It seemed as though they were heading back towards civilisation. The roads were getting progressively wider and less roughly-hewn, perilous gravel giving way to tarmac. "You'll have to excuse all that business before—" said Silver Hair. Jacob realised he was talking about the red woman. "She has the unfortunate tendency to lapse into Gothic melodrama under pressure. You're lucky she didn't throw her cloak over one shoulder and stalk off cackling."

Jacob couldn't deal with this right now. He felt like he'd been buried by events. The speed of this reversal had all but suffocated his wits. He just stared at the man uncomprehendingly. He was favoured with a weary glance in return. "That was a joke," Silver Hair scolded softly.

"Oh," Jacob mumbled by way of a reply. He remained bewildered.

"Apologies," the man relented. "It's been one of those lives."

"Yes. Lila told me all about *you*," Jacob spat, with a venom he was no longer sure he felt. Silver Hair's response, however, surprised him.

"She spoke?" He seemed shocked.

"What?"

"She hasn't spoken for years," he mused. "Not a word. To any of us."

Jacob shook his head moronically. "I don't understand—"

Silver Hair shrugged. "You don't keep something like that under lock and key forever. It isn't possible— I told them. It's almost as dangerous as the alternative. Bought us some breathing space, though, I suppose. There are all manner of fail-safes in place now. There are... battle plans." He smiled tightly.

"Who *are* you?"

"Think of us as..." The man searched, smiled to himself. "Ah. Think of us as a branch of the MOD. Yes," he seemed very pleased with this analogy, chuckling dustily.

He appeared friendly enough though, and far moreso than any of the scarlet-clad woman's other minions. Jacob recalled Silver Hair's surprising kindness towards Lila. In spite of himself, he felt safer now than he had at any time during the last three days.

"You're sorcerers?" he asked. "Magicians. Pagans and Satanists like ... like those Golden Dawn guys, Alastair Crowley or—"

Silver Hair cut in hotly. "Don't even fucking mention Crowley. The amount of grief that bastard caused us. The Order really had to pull out all the stops over that one." It was the first time he'd raised his voice since they had met. His anger soon subsided, however, and he smoothed a hand across his hair, smiling ruefully. He apologised for the second time that evening.

"But magic...?" Jacob persisted.

Silver Hair regarded Jacob thoughtfully for a while, as if trying to decide something.

"No. It's simple. Not magic, but cause and effect. And you can't get more basic than that, my friend. You push a stone — cause — and the stone moves— effect. A hypothesis supported by empirical evidence. Scientific method pared down to the bone.

"But what if I were to tell you that there are other ways to push a stone? Ways no one has even considered because, in the end, everybody knows — or *thinks* they know — how to push a stone. The powers we possess, this supposed *magic*—" (here, he curled his lip distastefully) "— are simply the consequence of the more extreme possibilities offered by cause and effect. The science of the unexpected, the ignored, the outrageous and the mad. An arcane branch of mathematics, with a close relationship to Platonic philosophy and Gnosticism."

Very gradually, as Silver Hair talked, the landscape became more industrialised, then residential: lone houses with lemon-lit windows, outriders for some major conurbation up ahead.

"See, what you have to understand is how everything is connected. The preternatural is holistic. In the same way that Sefer Yetzirah teaches cosmology, or numerology tries to mesh the universe together with calculations, so our Order braids together all the traditions that have come before us— hedgerow magic, tribal juju, whatever. From out of this babble we have forged a new science, gathered in all the threads to form the Mathematics of Non-linear Causality."

There were buildings on either side now, cliffs of towering blackness. The place was deserted, stark in frozen concrete. Jacob couldn't remember the name of the town. He'd known it as a road sign for ten minutes on the motorway, but lost it somewhere with the coming night. Narrow claustrophobic streets. *Easily defensible*, another part of his mind suggested and he shivered, trying to concentrate on what Silver Hair was saying.

"How come you're here? Why Britain, why now?"

Silver Hair waved a hand dismissively, as if Jacob had missed the point entirely. Perhaps he had.

"It's merely an accident of history that we're based here. Personally, I'd much rather be on the Continent, Vienna maybe. Godawful piss-ant little country, this. Forests of red tape, bully-boy bureaucracy, and a fuck-dreadful climate to boot. But we came across with the last shards of the Knights Templar, when they fled to Scotland. It was simply a propitious time to gain possession of their incunabula—fragments of Hermetica copied straight off the Emerald Tablet, no less—after King Philip IV and Pope Clement V shattered their order."

"I'm not sure you're making much sense," Jacob said, frowning. All he really wanted to do was sleep— a numbing tide, a soft downy coverlet to draw down over this terrible day.

Silver Hair laughed out loud, delighted, as if this were a very fine joke indeed.

Shop windows flashed by, angular plates of reflection, and it had started to rain, but softly; a mist of silver needles drifted through sodium-charged air. The drizzle made the light beneath the streetlamps look frothy and metallic.

As they progressed towards the town centre they found themselves travelling through an ever-more complex warren of streets. Finally they ended up barrelling along one road that eventually opened out into a surprisingly generous hexagonal square.

"There we go," murmured Silver Hair, almost to himself.

The Order had opted for a hotel in a square with only one access point, Jacob noted. This was in preparation, presumably, for the attack they said was coming. Their driver took them in a too-fast parabola round the central monument — some war memorial that reminded Jacob of the monolith from *2001: A Space Odyssey* — and skidded towards the hotel. A fleet of expensive cars already clogged up the square's parking bays. They were all abandoned, sitting there sweating, glittery with rain-dash. The hotel itself was a very grand edifice, gratifyingly solid and regal in the amber streetlights.

"That dog—," said Jacob suddenly.

Silver Hair wrinkled his brow. "Pardon?"

"About the dog—" Jacob began, but they had already coasted to a halt on the hotel forecourt, and it appeared that any more Fenton revelations would have to wait. Silver Hair was out of the car immediately.

"Inside," he called back to Jacob. "Come on, we have an audience with the Suzerain and I doubt she'll be in a better mood than before— though hopefully a tad more restrained."

Jacob hauled himself out and dutifully followed. The drizzle soaked his face, his hair, his skin. It felt like he was walking into a storm cloud.

## 19. The Truth Will Find Its Own Level

The lobby was silent, deserted. Behind them the revolving doors went *tick-tick-tick* on the gleaming marble floor. Silver Hair swept through the cold space like visiting royalty, moving so lightly, so happy with his suit and steps and his own airy grace, that Jacob almost expected him to break into a soft-shoe shuffle. Where *were* all the staff? Maybe it didn't bear thinking about. He hurried to keep up.

They reached gleaming brass doors on the far side of the lobby and waited for a lift to arrive. Beside them feathery spurs of fern erupted from a row of ornamental pots. Jacob could smell the loam where the plants were bedded and it suddenly reminded him of the forest floor where he'd knelt, which in turn made him think of dead things. Worms and maggots squirming under the leaf mulch. Everything dead composting down and starting to stink, to decay.

He thought of Morris, his eyes like rotten grapes weeping away into the soil. He thought of Maria. He wondered where her body was now.

Silver Hair hummed quietly, some aria or other, while Jacob stared down at his mud-caked boots. He had shed a trail of wet brown crumbs across the lobby floor behind him. It didn't seem to matter. More than anything he wanted his dad to come and carry him upstairs to bed.

The lift arrived with a bright "ping!" and the doors parted. Jacob glanced up to find himself eye to eye with Brutal.

"Hi, Sis, mom home?" chirped Silver Hair. Brutal just stared at him. She held the door open impassively. Chuckling, Silver Hair breezed inside. Jacob could only follow. As he passed he noticed that Brutal wore a necklace with a pendant identical to Silver Hair's lapel button: the Egyptian eye.

"Menswear, please," Silver Hair quipped. There was a small wall seat and he lounged there, feet up against the opposite wall. Brutal stabbed at the button for the thirteenth floor. The cage juddered and began to ascend.

Jacob shuffled himself into the corner that was farthest from either of his captors, though both ignored him anyway. He clenched and unclenched his fists nervously. Twinges of pain from his ragged nails and torn ear prevented him from concentrating too hard. Fatigue had soaked into his every cell, dragging down his eyelids with a terrible weight, settling through his bones.

Gears wheezed softly, like an asthmatic climbing stairs. The ancient lift seemed to tremble with exertion. At the thirteenth floor there was an almost resentful delay, before it consented to open the doors.

The floor contained a whole series of interconnected luxury apartments and penthouses, and one mammoth function room-cum-dancehall which gave off from the lift vestibule. This was where Jacob was immediately herded by Brutal. Silver Hair mooched along behind, though he gave the impression this was only because the world had exhausted every other means of amusing him. It seemed to Jacob that Silver Hair always conducted himself with this same air, as if everything he did was merely his least worst option, whereas Brutal, by contrast, shoved and bullied him along with vicious dedication.

The double doors to the function room were already propped open, framing the awesome sights displayed within.

"Welcome to the War Room," said Silver Hair with an ironic little flourish.

Miracles were only supposed to happen at night, Jacob knew that. They were meant to be confined to the shadows and the gloom, half-seen and never understood. But here the miracles were on display— full-frontal, exposed, daring you to deny them.

The banquet hall was filled with so many impossibilities that it made Jacob dizzy. His head whipped too fast from side to side as he tried to take them all in. Then they stepped into the room and the peripheries of his vision became clogged with wonders.

A screaming man ran towards them.

Jacob tried to side step, but before any collision could occur the man was snatched off the ground and jerked up into the air, as though he had been yanked back by a gigantic strap of elastic. But Jacob could see nothing attached to his back, no tug of support wires at his shoulders as he was reeled inexorably upwards, kicking and flailing, into the centre of the room. Whatever force had seized him was quite invisible.

During the first moments of that "flight" the victim's face had been revoltingly slack—with fear or pain, Jacob couldn't tell—but now a look of intense concentration gripped him. He threw his weight to one side and pivoted through a clumsy about-face until his spine faced them. Then he flung out his hands in a stretching, clawing motion, shouting something incomprehensible...

A detonation of enormous pressure blasted out from the centre of the room, causing Jacob to take several stumbling steps back. A stabbing pain punched through his inner ear. He swallowed and the discomfort dispersed. Queasy green highlights and wriggling ellipses lingered momentarily at the edges of his vision.

The man plummeted, but his impact was arrested by an invisible cushion of the same force which had freed him. This cushion gradually deflated, slowly lowering him to the floor. He rolled to his feet, looking rather pleased with himself. A grinning crowd of black-clad colleagues surrounded him to slap his back and shake his hand. Someone even ruffled his hair. Thoroughly mystified, Jacob's gaze swept on to examine the rest of the pageant.

To his left another man sat inside a glass-fronted tank. He was naked save for a swarm of locusts, which clung to him like a second skin and swarmed ceaselessly inside the confined space. His eyes tracked every step of Jacob's slow entrance. Though his skin was virtually coated in insects, what visible flesh there was sported the oddest silvery sheen, like fish scales.

Elsewhere, a stocky woman paced warily around five seeming

clones, men with raven hair and gunmetal eyes. She lashed out and struck one of the clones on the shoulder. The other figures instantly shattered into emerald showers. The remaining man smiled, and Jacob noticed for the first time that the woman's eyes were glowing with a fierce, golden effulgence, as if she wore contact lenses made from sunlight.

More sights, more sounds, more impossibilities danced like casual partygoers in this huge banqueting room: whips of green fire performed backflips through floor and ceiling; ribbons of living darkness boiled beneath the skin of grimacing volunteers; underwater light effects crawled incongruously across mirrored surfaces; noiseless, invisible detonations blew momentary craters in the air.

Here, there and everywhere Outsiders grappled with the various phenomena, analysing, correlating, recording. In fact the banquet hall reminded Jacob of nothing so much as Q's lab from a Bond movie. He recalled the Hellier labs and all the equipment that he had smashed there, so long ago and so far away... God, had it really only been three days? Jesus.

The banqueting tables had been shoved roughly out to the margins of the room, but this didn't mean they had been abandoned. On the contrary, forty or fifty people sat at these tables tapping away at matte-black PC terminals, staring intently at VDUs, constantly murmuring into bead microphones.

People continually dashed by, Outsiders busy with mysterious-but-urgent errands, weaving in and out of the tightly marshalled chaos. In fact, there was a distinctly martial cast to all this activity, as if they had walked in upon a tense military operation on the eve of war. As Jacob moved further into the room, this impression was heightened by the presence of so many crates of conventional ordnance: rows of rocket launchers stacked against the walls alongside pyramid stacks of assault rifles, hand grenades and mortars. There were enough arms here to prop up a South American banana republic.

Jacob could detect an underlying edge to the proceedings, a tangible note of stress, like a tight wire strumming through the centre of the room. On a table in the far corner sat a huge stainless steel coffee drum, beside which another trestle table bore serried ranks of plastic cups, some upturned, some smashed, some still half-full, and plates of the kind of biscuits they give you after you've donated blood. A few Outsiders sat there chatting, their bodies eloquent, apprehension evident in every gesture, their shoulders rounded as they bent in close to whisper. Others, though, simply sat motionless, blank-eyed, gazing at the walls.

Near the back of the room stood the tyrannical woman in red. She was consulting with an aide as they pored over a laptop VDU.

Now that the shock had subsided, Jacob's anger was sizzling once more. The instant he saw *her*, it all came flooding back. He found himself doubting everything he'd been told. Throughout the whole of this affair he'd been lied to, deceived on every side by every party. They all knew so much more than him: Silver Hair, Lila, the scarlet woman. He was the only one in the dark. Used and abused, manipulated and disdained. He would welcome the chance to confront one of his chief tormentors, regardless of where her allegiances might finally prove to lie.

"HEY!" he snarled and broke away from his captors. Scarlet turned. Her eyes blazed. Jacob didn't care. He was going to get some proper answers if it killed him.

"I WANT A FUCKING WORD WITH YOU!"

He ran.

An arm's throw from his goal Brutal grabbed his elbow and flung him around. He tried to throw a punch at her, but somehow she was too quick and managed to snap him into a body lock before he could move. Scarlet beckoned for two more strong-arm types, and while they forcibly restrained him Brutal proceeded with a body search.

She was very rough, *slapping* his sides as much as patting him down, her own rancour overwhelming her military discipline. It should have reminded him of the terrible treatment she had meted out to Lila. It should have stoked his outrage, or coaxed him into formulating some mad scheme for using her malice to his own advantage. It should have ... but his actual reaction was appallingly different: he became aroused.

It was the unexpected softness of her breasts which caught him first. He'd not imagined there was a single soft curve on this woman's body, which had seemed to him to be carved from soapstone. But her chest bumped him as she reached around to check his back, and her equally unexpected warmth seemed to transmit itself directly to his groin. She straightened, but neglected to step back so that her breasts compressed and slid against him. She was left standing barely centimetres away.

Jacob's erection tightened and he bit his lip. He could feel the soft pulse of her breath on his chin, easing in and out as she regarded him without expression. She smelled very sweet—of almonds and pine cones—and he willed himself not to betray his arousal, fighting to expunge every flicker of emotion from his face. He knew that she *couldn't* know, and yet something seemed to register deep within her metallic gaze. She cocked her head and pursed her lips fractionally.

Jacob despised himself, his genetic imperative, all those hard-wired biological responses. He wanted to cry. When was the last time he had been this close to a woman? Lila, two days ago, in that strange, stolen moment of intimacy when her terrified eyelashes had scratched across his cheek. When was the last time he had made love? Two weeks ago, with Maria, whom this woman had helped to execute. This woman who now made his cock beat and twang and sing with desire.

Plagued by visions of sex, Jacob raged. But equally he knew how good it would feel to put himself inside this woman and fuck her, and have her fuck him back. And if she bit his shoulder when she came, he could no more try to throttle her than he could tear off one of his own arms. Instead, he would tenderly kiss the hollow of her neck. His cock knew no conscience and no morality, nothing of vengeance or evil. Sex was all.

Betrayed by his own body, he dug his teeth into his lower lip and tasted blood.

Brutal placed her palms flat against his chest and stroked downwards, rolling out long, slow, systematic circles as she continued with her search, the same mild note of enquiry wrinkling her brow. Her eyes remained locked on his.

Jacob could barely breathe for anticipation. Suddenly, her eyes narrowed and she slipped her hand inside his jacket. His shirt was torn and the sensation of her fingertips grazing his skin was almost unendurably sensual. He ached to lash out at her, furious at how she was making him feel. His hatred soared. It was making him feel physically sick.

"Got it," Brutal reported and drew out the stolen diskette. Then she stepped back briskly and Jacob thought he might faint from the loss. Instead, he was left facing the woman in scarlet.

Her attention was fixed elsewhere, however. "Why did you not retrieve that?" she demanded of Silver Hair.

Silver Hair shrugged. "In case you haven't noticed, I've had other things on my mind. Anyway, what does it matter? He was in my custody and you have it now. We only talked about cause and effect. It hardly seemed dangerous—"

But Scarlet had already begun to shake her head. She closed her eyes, rather theatrically, and held up a palm to stop him.

"I thought I gave orders that a Bond of Submission was to be cast over him. I know I did not give you leave to *talk* to him, nor discuss our plans. He needed to be restrained until *I* could deal with him, here, employing all the appropriate countermeasures."

Silver Hair looked mildly startled, as if he hadn't even considered such a reprimand was possible. "Surely we're beyond all that now?"

"Beyond rules, beyond the sacred hierarchy?"

"Hmmno—" said Silver Hair cautiously. "Not exactly. Still—"

"Here, in extremis, more than ever before, the rule of law *must* apply. I will not have my authority undermined, by you or anyone. My concentration needs to be absolute, else all will fail. We dance on the brink of oblivion. The fate of the human race rests upon our shoulders."

Though she remained a forbidding presence, she sounded hoarse. Like Silver Hair had been in the car, she seemed close to exhaustion. "Do. You. Under. Stand?" she demanded.

The ambient noise level plummeted. People stopped what they were doing to turn and stare. Jacob sensed that note of stress again, thrumming amongst the strained, uneasy faces. So here was friction in the highest ranks. To Jacob it seemed very unwise for Scarlet to chew Silver Hair out in front of the troops. In fact, it was a command decision that bordered on lunacy, to let a personal antagonism run out of control on the eve of war. It suggested minds and nerves fraying.

Silver Hair inclined his head with icy deference, "My Suzerain."

All in all, it was a marvellous performance, but Jacob saw anger coil deep within his eyes.

Jacob began to applaud. "Oh, bravo. *Bravo*! Is this little show for my benefit?"

"Be quiet," Scarlet snapped without looking. "You've caused enough trouble already."

"Murderer!" Jacob spat.

"You haven't even got a clue what you're saying," Brutal sneered from the sidelines.

"Fucking cold-hearted *killers*!"

Scarlet finally pivoted to glare at Jacob. "What are you talking about?"

"You can cut all this Masterpiece Theatre crap right now. You're a bunch of manipulative butchers with a penchant for mind games and emotional torture, simple as that. Ergo, you're trying to mess my mind up because I know where the bodies are buried."

"Jacob, all we do is watch and protect," Silver Hair said. "We can't interfere like that, we have our own laws, protocols. Never the aggressors, never *pro*-active. We have one guiding principle— defence."

"No. No, I don't believe any of this. You're fucking with my head, the lot of you. You… are ... killers. I know that for sure. You killed her…" He advanced, unable to say Maria's name out loud, shaking with outrage and terror. "You butchered *her*!" Nobody tried to stop him. He could have just reached out to touch Scarlet, though he didn't. "Morris is gone as well, and all the others, too. And Lila, I've no idea what you've done with her, what fucking foul experiment that was!"

"Save it," muttered Silver Hair, but Jacob was too far gone, steeped in a grief so deep that all he could do was plough on through to the other side. The bodies were clawing their way up out of the graveyard of his mind, their maggot-softened fingers squirming through mulch to clutch at him.

Images of Maria shredded his concentration. She rolled towards him in bed and her breath smelled of morning. He licked her back and her skin tasted of sex. He stared into her eyes and they glowed with life. And the storm dragged her away one more time, so she screamed...

Screamed again...

…again ...

"The diary proves it," he yelled and flailed wildly in the direction of the diskette. "And that's why you want it back. The figure in red—you, you bitch! Whoever wrote the diary *knew* they were doomed. They didn't win, they didn't write any more. It just *ends*!"

Scarlet's stare transfixed him like an arrow. "Don't be a fool. It's *your* diary."

There was a silence, devoid even of heartbeats. It lingered forever.

"We should, perhaps, introduce ourselves more formally," said Silver Hair gently.

"That might help," Jacob whispered, barely audible. He was sure he was going to faint. He couldn't feel his fingertips properly.

"Fade," the man with silver hair offered, hand outstretched, rolling over into an easy handshake.

"*Fade*?" echoed Jacob on a rising note of incredulity. The walls of his world were toppling away like theatrical flats.

Fade shrugged. "It's a title, not a name. Hereditary. You have one, too... or you *did* have. Now I wouldn't care to guess." He shrugged again and looked to Scarlet for guidance.

She declaimed imperiously, "I am Vanguard. This is Battalion." She indicated Brutal.

Jacob shook as head, as if trying to clear his senses after a heavy blow. "Look, this is fucking preposterous, how can that be *my* diary?"

"Because fifteen years ago, in another life, you were… Hush. A member of the Order and one of our senior adepts from the Inner Council," Vanguard replied.

"Look, it can't be my diary. And Hush, what kind of a name is that? I know who I am. Jacob Alistair Naylor, forty-two, only child. Unmarried. Convictions for Unlawful Assembly, Disturbing the Peace and Criminal Damage. Member of Greenpeace, CND and Sustrans, Friends of the Earth..."

"For fifteen years, yes. But before that, let me assure you, you *were* Hush. Employed, as we all are here, to guard against aggressive incursion from transcorporeal realms."

"Transcorporeal *bullshit!* I don't remember any of that. No Order, no defensive strategies, no cult, no *Hush*. Do you not think that if any of this were true, then I'd have at least the whisper of a shred of a recollection of it? One tell-tale scrap?... Jacob Naylor, geddit?"

"You're missing the point, Hush—"

"Don't fucking call me that."

"You're missing the point," Vanguard insisted. "The life you're leading now is a false identity. A *new* identity. Your second identity, the one which we crafted for you fifteen years ago. And that's how old the life you remember is. Fifteen years."

"I've got memories. I've got proof. I remember all about my childhood. My father, you want to hear about my father? My father used to—"

"Carry you upstairs to bed?"

Jacob went cold.

"And he would never turn on the light, but instead feel around in the dark like he was creeping across a carpetful of slumbering lions," Vanguard continued evenly, a humourless smile resting against her lips. "And the bed's counterpane would rasp against your chin with a ticklish scratch. Then your dad would hiss, 'Don't *dare* stick your feet out. I'm letting the monsters out of their cage now.' But you wouldn't care; the moment you heard the door click you would always jump up and down on the bed, because you used to love to yell in the dark."

"How could you know that?" Jacob stammered.

"Because I created those memories for you myself."

A wave of vertigo dived through Jacob's chest, riding his breath down into the void where no words are and life gutters and sputters and falls forever.

"But I have proof," he whimpered. "Keepsakes..."

"Really? But isn't it true that one of your greatest regrets is that you don't have any photos of your mother and father, or yourself growing up?"

"My dad—"

"But that didn't matter, you felt, because your memories of childhood were so vivid. Strangely pure and clear."

"No, no..."

"Look at the knives, Daddy," she crooned. "Daddy, the knives. Look at me. Look, look."

"Dad used to carry me upstairs to bed…"

"Jacob, I'm sorry, but no one knows who your parents were. You were brought to us as an orphan."

Into Jacob's mind flashed a sudden image of himself as a cartoon Egyptian mummy—from Count Duckula or some other kiddies' show—and someone had got hold of his trailing bandages. They pulled *hard* so that he went into a Tazmanian Devil spin, unravelling in every direction until, instead of a wizened corpse, only an empty space remained. What was Jacob Naylor now, revealed inside his flimsy bandages? Nothing. A fiction. An absence. Twists of guilt and rage weaved from thin air.

He lowered his head, shattered, "What happened?"

"Fifteen years ago you were involved in a cataclysmic supernatural event that almost destroyed our Order. Had you not done what you did, all human life would have been exterminated. In saving the world, however, you suffered horrific injuries, both physical and mental. Wounds of the body we were well able to treat, but your mind was so badly damaged that it was no longer viable for you to remain part of the Order. You might have needed years of conventional therapy to recover, even to rebuild the basic components of your personality... So, instead, we simply wiped the slate clean, and started over again.

"Didn't you ever wonder about all the surveillance pictures, how comprehensive they were? That would have been impossible unless we *already knew* everything about your life. Where you lived, where you ate, what cinema you went to and who all your friends were. Your daily routine, down to the slightest variant. We couldn't have a former high adept wandering around unchecked, however comprehensive his new identity."

"This is a fairy tale," Jacob gasped. "A fantasy." The glue that held his sanity in place was dissolving.

"You already know what links to conventional government we have, how far our influence stretches. In fact, the night you made your somewhat untimely visit to our mansion headquarters, I had been summoned to London to deliver an interim report to the Home Secretary. You can understand, I'm sure, how the mundane details of assigning you a new identity were child's play... and after that, *we* saw to the rest."

"You didn't. You couldn't have provided a whole lifetime of made-up recollections. It's madness."

"Of course we didn't. We merely provided new building blocks. A *basis* for your substitute memories to take root. Cause and effect, remember. Your brain did all the rest. Bridged the gaps, filled in the holes, tied off the frayed ends. In many ways you were as much the architect of your new identity as we were. Even so, no conditioning is perfect. Side effects abound. Restlessness, instability, unfocused rage. In the end our treatment had engendered exactly the symptoms we hoped to avoid." She paused and sighed, then added, "Think of what we did as like sewing on a memory *patch*, if that helps— masking what was underneath. And tonight we need to unpick that stitching."

"You're not trying anything else on me, you bitch," Jacob warned, though he could feel his heart jerking in his chest like a frog caught on a hotplate.

"It's not a question of choice, Jacob. Very soon, if we don't act, you'll become functionally psychotic. The stress is causing your mind to reject the transplant... Let me remove the patch now, then your old memories can return and you will see. You'll understand everything."

"It's a trick," Jacob babbled. "It could be you'll actually be inserting *those* memories, which would make *them* the patch."

"No. When it happens, the side effects will clear and everything will slot into place. Your pain, your rage, will have a context. You will know that you have become whole again."

"I won't." Jacob was more panicked now than anything.

"Too late. We may need you for the coming struggle, so this discussion is academic." Vanguard stepped towards him.

"Stay back!" he shouted, backpedalling desperately. If he were to believe Vanguard's story then he hadn't stood among these people for fifteen years. Many of them might even have been his friends.

No, it couldn't be true.

It couldn't be.

*Jacob Naylor, aged forty-two…*

"Jacob," Vanguard whispered. "Goodbye, Jacob."

She made a complex ravelling gesture in the air, and Jacob's mind yawned on its hinges like a barn door to let the past flood in...

## 20. Drops in the Ocean.

*Hush coughed once into the mike and the dictaphone whirred to life. He spoke in a clear, steady tone at dictation speed:*

*"Tonight is the last chance. No other options, no other choices. If we fail then they will come through and there will be nothing we can do to stop them. They might destroy us all in one blow, or hide amongst us, dressed in our skins, for years, waiting and watching, toying with us. Playing. Experimenting, while we carry on dreaming of safety and sleep-walking to our doom."*

*He paused and rested his forehead against the machine. He held his other hand out to check for tremors. There were none. He could almost believe he was ready for all of this.*

*Hush slumped back, settling into the sagging embrace of the old armchair, where he'd thrown himself after returning from the final London run an hour before. He'd been hungry and exhausted then, but now he was too distracted to eat and wired to sleep. All he could do was mutter into the dictaphone, updating his desultory diary as he conserved what strength he had left for the coming storm. Fear had consumed all his appetites.*

*He surveyed the room through gritty, bloodshot eyes. In truth the farmhouse had altered little since the original owners had vacated it and the Order had converted it into an early-warning station. It was Hush's understanding that the family had been urged to relocate abroad, with the Ministry of Defence footing the bill. Not that dumb distance would save them from this particular enemy.*

*The rough-weave throw rugs were all worn and faded, the furniture balding, the wallpaper mundane. The room was decorated with a ragtag collage of agricultural clutter: sacks of feed, rolls of wire mesh, brace of shotguns in a wall-mounted case. Still, the huge plate glass window provided an excellent vantage point, looking out onto the garden and driveway, the undulating carpet of hills beyond that. Furthermore, the seat where he lounged was located directly above the confluence of three major ley alignments: a fierce knot of energies for him to draw upon.*

*The whole house stank of dog, a smell that reminded him of the guard hounds back at the facility. Despite their fearsome dispositions, he'd always found them to be surprisingly affectionate creatures. Hush liked animals. It made the Order's experiments at the facility even harder to bear. He rubbed at his eyes. Ah well, needs must…*

*He raised the dictaphone to his lips. "Tonight," he tried to say confidently, but he heard the crack in his voice and winced. What was confidence now? Where was hope? All the Order's defences lay in tatters. The enemy broke tenth circle wards as if they were twigs, kicked holes in the transdimensional medium as easily as if it were crêpe paper. Surely, invasion was inevitable? And an unpleasant death the only consolation afterwards. Fat lot of good the Order had proved to be when it actually came down to the crunch. Defence as their one guiding principle? Ha!*

*Unless…*

*No. He couldn't allow hope. There was no point.*

*"B will be with me. I pray. I pray for us all. The night, the darkness presses at my windows." He croaked and regarded the black prospect dourly.*

*Hush became aware of a distant drone drifting in from the higher ground, and looking through the window he could see motile sparks of light beetling around the far hills. Someone was approaching.*

*So the time had come at last. At least there remained a short interval in which to compose himself, so he flicked off the lamp and breathed deeply. The darkened room swelled around him like a gaping maw. He shivered and stood, joints creaking, then moved to the sideboard. Searching by touch, he found the catch to the drawer and removed the heavy London package.*

*The item was wrapped in a curious bandage of raw silk, which he carefully unwound. Revealed inside was a hand-turned metal cylinder about the length of his forearm and roughly the weight of a champagne bottle. It had an immaculately sealed end-cap, and had been engineered to fit snugly along his palm. The whole surface had been etched with row upon row of serpentine symbols, like maths equations for the demented. One section had been left smooth to serve as a handhold.*

*He hefted the cylinder experimentally to judge its weight, then exhaled gently on the metal to test the potency of his cantrips one last time. The engravings shivered for an instant with lime fire, then dulled back to grey once more. Satisfied, Hush rewrapped the cylinder and went back to the chair to await his doom.*

*What the hell, he ruminated. This was his plan, and as the prime architect he needed to be there, in the thick of the action. Anyway, it was how he preferred to confront events, direct and unflinching, upfront, resolute. Surely the fear must fade soon?*

*But it didn't. Time dawdled, the lights drew nearer, but the terror wouldn't go. If anything, it increased.*

*He stood purposefully and made his way into the hall, still whispering to the dictaphone as he went, like a war correspondent lost behind enemy lines, recording his last words for the benefit of eternity.*

*"Time. No time to write any more. They have come for me. I must go."*

*He placed the machine carefully on the table by the phone, stroked it with his forefinger and let himself out. He stood for a moment on the porch and felt the night squeeze sweat from his cheeks and forehead. In the undergrowth insects snickered to themselves. The darkness hummed with the day's heat, and Hush fantasised that he could see it glowing, a malevolent throb of infra-red.*

*He stepped off the porch to meet the purring BMW on the grass, a sleek and silver shadow beneath the starlight. At his back he heard the locks slam home, independent of any human agency. He turned to watch the door's metal slats flex through an elaborate sequence of contortions as the ward pulled tight, and the farmhouse sealed itself.*

*Rationally, he knew that the trick didn't require his gaze to make it work, and furthermore, that these precautions would be as so much chaff in the wind if their real enemy came calling. Still, like patting down your pockets for keys, this had become a soothing custom for him. Once satisfied that the steel had clotted shut again, he smiled tightly and walked to the car.*

*The driver was standing waiting for him, the car door propped open against his thigh. He made a stiff greeting to Hush, who immediately saw the terror gnashing behind his eyes. A snail's trail of sweat silvered his upper lip. He rubbed at it with the side of his palm and loosened his black collar nervously.*

*The driver's distress made it easier for Hush to centre himself. He had two duties tonight: the first was to calm the troops; the second... well, that was little more than suicide and not worth dwelling upon.*

*"Easy, lad," he whispered, and placed a comforting hand on the driver's shoulder. The driver was blond and barely out of his teens, freckled and slightly plump with damp eyes. Obviously all the senior adepts were caught up in the fray, so only the children were left to see to minor chores.*

*Hush hooked his thumb against his palm to cast a very subtle Shape of Focus. The boy's breathing softened and he looked ridiculously grateful... and then utterly mortified that he'd let his fear show so nakedly. Hush shook his head to show him that it was okay, then indicated the car.*

*Inside, as they pulled away from the house, he reflected on his role within the Order: Hush, the steady hand; the comfort blanket; the hard, brave heart at the centre of the nightmare. Fearless and bold, prepared to face any menace head-on and triumph whatever the odds. Playing this role had always been easy for him to banish his own insecurities that way. People might think he was a take-no-shit type, gruff as a troll at times, but everyone knew he was the best person to have at your back in a firefight.*

*He wound the window down. The bumpy lane from the farmhouse opened out into the road proper, and Hush closed his eyes as gusts of cool air flowed inside the car.*

*"I'm not worried for myself," said the boy after a few minutes. "I mean—"*

*"Shhhh, it doesn't matter."*

*"No. It's only, well, my wife..."*

*Hush arched an eyebrow. "You're married?"*

*The boy grinned ruefully. "Six months come July." His expression darkened. "If any of us live to see July..."*

*Hush cut him off and, to keep the boy from drowning in his fears, launched into a deft interrogation of his life. He asked him about the wedding, the honeymoon, their house, what plans they had for the future and whether they wanted kids. He was pleased when he succeeded in shifting the boy's concentration away from the hopeless here and now. If the driver could talk about his future, then he would be convinced that there* was *one for them all. For a short while, as he talked, the lad forgot his fear.*

*The drive was taking them higher and higher, through a rising series of jagged inclines. It wouldn't be long before they caught sight of their destination. The boy kept throwing embarrassed sideways glances at Hush, until finally he brought himself to admit, "You know, I've always admired you."*

*Hush put a hand to his chest and chuckled with mock relief. "Thank God for that. I thought for a second you were going to tell me you loved me."*

*The boy looked bemused.*

*"You never seen The Blues Brothers?"*

*The reference clicked home and the boy smiled, relaxing a little. Then they topped the last ridge, and Hell itself was revealed below.*

**

As the memory left him Jacob collapsed, his legs buckling like rubber splints.

"The enemy," he gasped, and began to sob.

Vanguard seemed not to register his breakdown. She stood erect and proud with her palms against her thighs and her face tilted upwards. Her eyes appeared fixed on some faraway point. In the glow from the chandelier her scars resembled moulded plastic, glossy webs of pink wrenched tight across her sunken cheeks. No one else in the room would look at her, or at Jacob. Most just gazed at their feet.

"We are the custodians of the human race," Vanguard said. "All the other hoarders of arcana have failed, crumbled beneath the weight of centuries. Sects scatter and fall by the wayside, secret societies rip themselves apart with internal divisions, cabals simply fade away. Rosicrucians, Templars, Alhazrites, Order of the Golden Dawn. All gone. But *we* persist. *We* endure. And we have survived precisely because we have never craved learning for its own sake. Never searched for greater knowledge of the universe, or spiritual enlightenment, transcendence or power over others. No one will ask us to die for false prophets or cruel gods. We have survived precisely because our research has only one practical application— vigilance. We stand at the gate. We say unto the dark, 'This far—but no more.'"

Vanguard paused, breathing heavily now, suffused with emotion. She looked down at Jacob but her eyes were glassy and unfocused. She shook her head, then locked onto him with renewed clarity.

"All potential, all possibility, call it power if you will, comes from the same place," she crackled, her voice like the stroking of dry leaves. "Our abilities issue from that wellspring. A source, as it were. All worlds, all dimensions, are connected by this source — like islands in a vast ocean — and every time we employ our powers tiny ripples are discharged into that sea... Disturbances that — if you looked long enough — might be visible from the other islands..."

"Some day they will notice us," whispered Jacob.

Vanguard nodded gravely. "Yes."

"And now they're on their way… Across the ocean."

Another nod.

"The Multitude."

Again, the affirmative, but more tightly this time. More tension in the gesture. So it all made sense: the fear clogging the air; the blank drinking coffee stares; the preparations in the forest. An army readying for war.

However, before Jacob could fully understand what was happening—and what he had done—his thoughts were sluiced away by another dark tide of memory.

**

*They had designated it Village Zero, the primary incursion point. An isolated huddle of homes cradled in the hands of an unremarkable Scottish valley. One among a fan of untidy troughs gouged out by glacial stabs from the north. Its rocky slopes were scabbed by residual tufts of gorse and heather, stubbly grey grass. Bleak, spartan, dead...*

*Everyone who had lived there was dead too, but tonight the village lived again. In fact, to Hush it looked as though the very stones of Village Zero were alive. Seething and thrashing and squirming. The nervous agitation reminded him of spiders running, that spooky splindly locomotion, legs all a-skitter, flickering relentlessly onwards, under, over.*

*The boy had pulled up by a fang-like promontory so that they could watch the show for a while. With all the activity below it was difficult to fathom exactly what was going on. The light made it hard, too. A strange oceanic glow saturated the whole basin, clinging to hollows and roofs alike. It flared green and blue, blurring and smearing across the whole scene. Everything inside the margins of the light was distorted, like reflections in a funfair mirror seen through a fish tank.*

*The unsettling illumination appeared to emanate from an eerie bank of stromclouds massing directly above the village. Actually, the clouds — coiled, wine-dark, throbbing — resembled bloated internal organs far more so than meterological phenomena, and they seemed to reach higher and deeper than any eye could follow. Hush craned his back to observe what looked like tiers of tumorous viscera heaped up and up: black-meat mountains hanging in the air.*

*Still, he got the distinct impression that somehow the clouds weren't quite right — weren't quite real — that they were almost two-dimensional, and if you only knew how, you might tear them off the hardboard of the sky to reveal what vast and unknown horrors waited behind.*

*For a terrible, vertiginous moment, he felt the full awareness behind the clouds turn its attention upon him. The sensation lingered only for an instant, but it made him feel sick all over. It was like the universe peeping at you through a keyhole.*

*Light fell through the cracks which crazed the murky surface of the pseudo-clouds, descending in syrupy shafts congested by swirling particles. It looked as if angry locusts were dancing in the light. Everything was silent, but this only focussed the attention and made the scene seem even worse. It was like watching a war on TV with the sound turned down.*

*On the ground near the centre of town Hush thought he could make out a squat chitinous spire, besieged on every side by flecks of ghoul-light; retinal ghosts in sapphire and turquoise, sparkling so rapidly they made the spire itself appear to quiver. Overhead, darker whorls had begun to gather in the thunderhead, inky squirts pumping up from its unfathomable depths. As Hush watched, they coalesced into a single incursion point which bulged downwards.*

*The bulge proceeded to distend grotesquely, stretching and palpitating, until it finally yanked free and transformed into an elongated teardrop shape. The teardrop fell so terribly slowly that it was difficult to imagine it was descending through air at all, and not some denser medium. As it fell gobbets of oily blackness stripped away to reveal a resinous material beneath. The material was identical in composition to that of the spire below. A frenzy of cobalt sparks migrated from the ground to meet the teardrop's descent, artillery from the Order's front-line defences.*

*"They've been trying to establish a beachhead for about an hour now," said the boy. He'd come to sound resigned rather than scared. Hush wasn't sure if this was an improvement, but he certainly felt responsible. Sometimes the pressure of sympathy was a greater burden than any fears he himself might hold.*

*Beneath the black teardrop implosions boiled and percolated; to Hush they looked for all the world like acid holes being eaten through the fabric of reality. A moment later this impression seemed validated, as the corrosion leapt upwards and engulfed the teardrop, sucking it backwards into oblivion. Soundlessly, it disappeared.*

*"We're just about managing to hold them off," the boy continued tersely. "But our people are starting to weaken, and it's not like the enemy will ever tire. If even one of their sentient clusters gets through, then we're fighting them all. You know how it is with them, what they're like. My God—" He gulped down on the fear. "Vanguard wants your team ready to go ASAP," he paused, a tremble of greater uncertainty passing across his face. "She's about to launch our counterstrike..."*

*Another five incursion points had started to spike out amidst the pseudo-clouds.*

*"Come on," said Hush softly. "I'm ready."*

**

"—over the next few hours," Vanguard said.

Jacob blinked. "What?"

"The patch is dissolving, but the breakdown is gradual. Your original identity — and memories — will return piecemeal, over the next hour or so. Like flashbacks. This may sound disconcerting, but once the reintegration has occurred you'll feel better. Though whether you regain your old personality, or an amalgam of that and the man you have subsequently become, I can only guess."

"How could you do this to me?" Jacob appealed, ashen-faced. "Who *am* I? What have you made me into? How could you?"

Vanguard's look was compassionate, but behind it lay the steel of her certainty— the wall on which all of her emotions were pasted. She was absolutely convinced that she was right, and that her every action could be justified. "Casualties of war, Jacob," she answered at length.

"What?"

"You were a casualty of war. It was unavoidable."

The others gathered in the room watched silently. No one had moved while he lay suffering on the carpet, but despite their passivity, fields of intense emotion beat at him: waves of distaste and disquiet; awe and anticipation. Hate... and love. That he could evoke such wildly contrasting emotions startled Jacob.

"Don't worry," said Vanguard. "You won't be left to face this alone. Someone will be assigned to help you." She flicked an airy look in Fade's direction.

"You want *me* to continue babysitting?" Fade scoffed.

"What of it?"

"Haven't I got slightly more important duties to attend to? Like an invasion, maybe?"

"Are you questioning my orders?" Vanguard asked with deadly emphasis.

Fade snorted, though whether out of amusement or contempt Jacob couldn't tell. Vanguard fixed him with a hard stare. Fade shrugged, nonplussed, then moved to lead Jacob away.

"No. No, let go," Jacob started to fret, squirming against Fade's grip. "Who … is Lila? You have to tell me," he pleaded. "What has been unleashed? What have I done?"

Vanguard had already begun to pivot away, riding ever onwards along the laser line of her obsession. She scowled at this latest obstacle and favoured him with a wintry backward glance. "It will all come back. For now, though, we can't afford the luxury of expert counselling. Consider this field surgery. When the enemy is repelled you can have all the soothing psychobabble you want. Until then, if you don't mind, the Order has greater priorities to attend to."

Then she swung away again, and Jacob was reminded of Fade's quip about her throwing a cloak over one shoulder.

"The floor show has ended," she called as she marched off, her voice a clarion bell, pitch-perfect. "Hush has returned to us, that is all. And he will join us on the front line. But if we don't move, there will *be* no front line. No defences, no war, no human race. We don't have much time left, so get back to work. I don't intend on repeating myself."

She clapped her hands above her head like an impatient major-domo, and the adepts leapt back to their duties.

**

Walking along the corridor, Jacob began to question every assumption he'd made about Lila. The teenager's emotionless mien—which he'd previously attributed to the spectre of her abuse—took on a terrifying new aspect.

Fade sauntered ahead. "There's a room set aside for you. Somewhere you can shower, change. Don't worry, we'll provide a new set of clothes, we have your measurements already. Naturally."

Since Vanguard's rebuke Fade had become increasingly aloof. His teeth emerged more regularly from his smiles, making him look cunning and predatory. A mood of mercenary deliberation had stolen over him. The change worried Jacob. He tried to burn through the frost with idle banter.

"These names still confuse me. Battalion, I see. Vanguard, logical. But Fade? What do you do with a title like that?"

Fade halted and slowly cranked round to face him. "We are a *very* old organisation," he purred. "Our duties are sometimes very *distasteful*. Think of me as… Minister Without Portfolio." His perpetual half-smile became a curve scoured in ice.

Jacob swallowed and thought of Morris. Shivered. He was suddenly very afraid. To think that he had taken this man as his saviour, his only friend in amidst the terror.

"Tut, tut, tut," Fade scolded softly, wagging his finger. His bonhomie was very sinister now, and he knew it. He *used* it that way. Jacob decided to bluster through his unease, taking the game to his opponent:

"Well, you seem pretty damn calm, considering this spells the end of the world," he sneered.

"Yes, well, I learned to stop worrying and love the bomb. See, sometimes even long shots don't come off."

"What?"

"If all else fails—and I personally suspect that it might—there is still a way to run this out. If our battle plans crumble, we have a final endgame to play. One last Weapon to deploy."

With that, some stub of memory got stirred deep down in the ganglionic tangles of Jacob's brain.

*F has been talking about using the Weapon again.*

Jacob gasped. "You're F," he said, astonished. "From the diary. *My* diary."

"Yeesss," Fade breathed, and leered. He smoothed a palm across the nap of his silver-white crop.

The past took Jacob like a hammer blow to the back of the head...

**

*"Here comes Hush, bringing peace to all, laying on hands. Everybody's favourite uncle," Fade crooned.*

*He stroked a hand across his jet-black crop and chuckled slyly. He was perched on the bonnet of his Saab, smirking and smoking, looking for all the world like a malevolent pixie.*

*Hush kept his expression neutral as he threaded his way through the pulsing fortifications. Base camp was established at the head of the valley, where a moon-lens had been erected to focus the efforts of the troops. He touched shoulders and elbows as he went, whispering soft words of encouragement or gentle reassurances, cracking the odd joke. He even cast the occasional Shape of Focus to steady shell-shocked nerves.*

*Beyond the glittering arch of the moon-lens viperish stabs of jade fire crackled as the enemy tirelessly probed their defences. The air within the compass of the valley was bloated with electricity from the repeated detonations, and the air reeked of ozone. Two divisions of adepts stood their ground before the lens, meshing the span with deadly energies, sweating and shaking with the effort. The lens absorbed this primeval tangle of power and braided it together to form one united thrust.*

*Hush leant against the Saab and the car squatted down a little under his weight.*

*"For the greatest scholar this Order has ever produced, you have the mentality of a jackal," he told Fade, conversationally, though his eyes were cold.*

*Fade remained unflustered. "Tush. You and I both know this is all just so much hand-waving. We cannot win."*

*He looked at the sky above them, and Hush followed his gaze: the thunderhead now looked like an upside-down pine forest, it was punctured by so many incursion points. They could both see it was only a matter of hours—maybe even minutes—before the enemy breached their line.*

*"The Weapon gives us another chance, possibilities beyond imagination," hissed Fade. "It is the future, the past, the world itself. It grants us absolution."*

*"You're rambling."*

*Fade's grin was almost feral. His teeth looked very sharp in the febrile light. "Maybe. Though we'll find out soon enough, won't we? When your team fails—"*

*"We won't fail," Hush shouted. But they both knew this was a lie; of course they would fail. However, if he'd ever needed a greater reason to prevail, then preventing Fade from implementing his insane contingency plan proved an overpowering incentive. Had he actually brought the Weapon with him? Hush wondered. Was the Saab's boot spacious enough to hold it? He thought not, but still...*

*"Shouldn't you be preparing for the counterstrike?" he demanded.*

*Fade twisted his thumbs together, forming a sigil of savage power, which instantly drew a Mace of Puissance into existence. He manipulated the flickering mass across his knuckles and around his wrist, then coaxed it into a livid green ball which he nudged calmly from palm to palm.*

*It was an exemplary piece of casting, Hush had to admit. The calculations were point-perfect. Perhaps it was wise that he had not pressed Fade into a contest all those weeks ago. If it did come down to a stand-up fight, it certainly was not clear-cut who the winner would be.*

*"No need to worry about me. I'll fulfil my duty," Fade asserted. "You'd better go find her quick as you can...before the levee breaks."*

*His eyes hadn't left the splintering thunderhead.*

*Hush shook his head despairingly and moved off towards the centre of the encampment. All the vehicles surrounding him were daubed with numerous casting spirals, their streaky, phosphorescent digits glittering like the unseen stars. He found Vanguard in amongst the trucks that housed the Cray mainframe and the other number-crunching computers being used to navigate those big non-linear calculations— the calculations which were essential to launch the counterattack she was planning, and propel Jacob and his team on their mission.*

*"Are you ready to deploy?" was the first thing she wanted to know.*

*Hush considered this. "Have we pinpointed its location?"*

*"In their Citadel, co-ordinating the assault."*

*"Hmmm, not good... but only what we expected. Yes, once in position we can deploy immediately."*

*Vanguard allowed herself one curt bob of her head, then she placed a surprisingly companionable hand on his shoulder. Hush had always been fascinated by her hands. He used to watch them as she roused the troops, or ferociously rebuked a subordinate; in contrast to her brusque manner they had an almost swanlike quality. And then there was her face. Despite her age, her skin was beautiful and sleek and unlined. Her cheeks were like freshly laid snow. Untrampled. But her eyes when she looked upon him trapped him with their awful intensity.*

*"Faith, Hush. Faith is all. You know that our cause is right. Now go. I'll spare no more words. Faith is all that is left." And with that she shoved —actually pushed him — him in the direction of the muster, where his team awaited him.*

*Never had such a weight settled upon his shoulders.*

*Then, above, another explosion detonated.*

## 21. Shhhhh

The room was large and pastel-coloured, smelling faintly of roses. Fade stood behind him. Jacob blinked. Hadn't they just been in the corridor?

It was an ordinary, if rather tasteless, hotel suite. The carpet was fluffy, the wallpaper faun flock. Chintz ruled the décor, while all the furniture seemed to be padded, or gave the impression that it should be. Jacob felt like he'd been ushered into a special cell where he "wouldn't be a danger to himself". All they needed now was a floral-print straitjacket to complete the effect.

"Clothes, shower, enjoy," Fade said, encompassing the room with a gesture. Then he was gone.

Jacob stood for a while, trying to breathe evenly, then sat on the bed instead.

"Dad," he said out loud. "Mum," he tried. But the words tasted like ashes on his tongue. His parents were thumbnail sketches, backstory for an American telemovie. His childhood was the result of a script conference.

He knew that he should probably rouse himself to shower, but he was frightened that the water might wash his body away. Melting him back into the background radiation of the universe, a flurry of lost particles, dispersing now that they had been disabused of the ridiculous delusion that they somehow comprised a man. Maybe he should welcome such a fate; perhaps oblivion was better than what was to come?

"Who is this?" he asked the air, for it was no more substantial than his own sense of self. Am I Jacob? Am I Hush? Am I words written on a lake? "Who am I?"

But the air carried no answers, and dumb silence was its only eloquence. Shortly, Jacob stood and shambled to the bathroom, turned on the shower and listened to it rush. *Shhhhh*, said the water. He stripped, fumbling like a zombie, and stepped under the scalding jet. He didn't wash himself. He simply stared at his feet and began to weep.

And somewhere else in the endless dance of possible pasts and phantom futures, his dad carried Jacob upstairs to bed, while Hush lay alone, shivering, in an orphanage dormitory at midnight.

**

As Jacob towelled himself dry beside the bath, the door burst open and Battalion charged in. Without losing a step she barrelled straight at him.

He tried to fend her off, but she was too quick. She smashed into his chest… and proceeded to smother his face in kisses.

**

*"Hey, soldier, this ain't in the regs," Hush murmured.*

*Battalion was in his arms, trembling with excitement and sex and fear. He stumbled back unsteadily, knocked off-balance by her steam-roller embrace. They leaned against the side of a van to kiss. The vehicle was berthed under a sagging canvas awning, affording them a little privacy.*

*"There's been so much fighting!" she hissed, and her eyes were wild. "You wouldn't believe how hard we've fought. You'd be so proud of us!"*

*Her hair was a mess. He could smell the sweat and smoke on her clothes, the musk of her skin. His cock stirred, and Battalion squeezed her crotch against his. He smiled mirthlessly. This, in all likelihood, would be their last moment of shared intimacy.*

*Ever.*

*He kissed her again, but fleetingly. There wasn't much time, and they could only steal moments here. Neither of them could afford to be distracted later on. He rested his forehead against hers. Closed his eyes tight.*

*"We have to go," he whispered. "I'm so sorry. There's no time."*

*"Don't worry," she said before he could break down. "Never worry. We* will *make it. I know that... I have faith in you, whatever else happens, remember that."*

*She stood back and held him at arm's length, regarding him as if for the first time. Her face seemed unnaturally vivid to him, somehow more in focus than her surroundings, as if her very* being *was more concentrated by that electrified instant.*

*"Our time doesn't end here. I'll taste you again, I will!" the fiery woman asserted. It was difficult sometimes to remember that she was only nineteen. She had an instinctive gift for casting, a calculator's mind. Hush knew that he could count on her resilience, her constancy from one heartbeat to the next.*

*So he said in a level voice, "Let's go face them... shades against the storm."*

**

Battalion slipped from his unresponsive arms. She blinked, turned, unzipped her trousers at the hip. Dazed, Jacob could only stare at her.

*B has been a great comfort in many ways of the night*, whispered the diary at the back of his mind.

Battalion knocked up the toilet lid and sat to piss, indifferent to his presence, or perhaps simply recalling the intimacy they had once shared? Jacob could barely believe in such a thing, the two of them together. *Lovers*? It made no sense. The world was surely turned on its head. Battalion put her face in her hands, suddenly looking as desperately bone-weary as all the other members of the Order this night. Her shoulders drooped and she surrendered to a cat-like yawn.

A beat later she roused herself, briskly wiping and flushing, then kicked the hipsters from around her ankles and stood in one swift motion.

As he'd noted before, her demeanour was martial, her bearing rigid. There was a smart snap to all her movements that reminded him of military drill. It made the fact that she was avoiding his gaze while she unbuttoned her shirt all the more mystifying.

Battalion's hug had been like some passionate reflex, and now she didn't know how to deal with the lapse. Awkwardness had inflated to fill the gap between them. This was the first time they had been alone together in fifteen years. Obviously the memories were still unbearably vivid for her, but she didn't have any idea what *he* remembered, or how he felt. She, at least, had been forewarned of the reunion; he hadn't even been forewarned of the *relationship*!

In a few beats Battalion was naked, her clothes sloughed into an unruly heap beside the sink.

"Shift over," she instructed gruffly, still evading eye contact as she stepped to the shower. "I need to clean up, too."

He noticed the scars first. Maria had possessed exactly two and a half scars: one under her chin from a childhood fall; one on her hip from a riding accident; and a BCG scar gracing her left bicep (the half). This woman was covered in them.

The evidence of old wounds was hatched and cross-hatched across her body, as if her flesh were a poor artist's sketchpad, showing all the blurry evidence of earlier, partially erased drafts; displayed there were glimmery slashes and commas and notches, violet blemishes, scorch marks, puckered puncture blisters. One particularly savage gash ran from just beneath her left breast, diagonally over her flat-toned stomach, down to an uncertain termination in the fuzz of her bikini line. Barely survivable, Jacob thought.

In spite of this, she looked very fit. Her legs were long, lean and athletic, as was her torso. Her shoulders were wide and her hips narrow like a sprinter's. Her breasts were small and high, though the first pinches of age were evident, wrinkling round her dark sloping nipples. Jacob did the math: nineteen, fifteen years… Thirty-four. Her neck was very elegant, and there her relentless martial poise was transformed into true grace. She tipped up her chin with particular delicacy.

She was an ascetic's version of a warrior woman, Spartan, vulpine, grim. She was the colour of blonde wood or bone, spangled by faint chestnut dapples. She flicked her hair free of its tie and proceeded to rake her fingers through its length, freeing up the tangles. She glanced up and caught him appraising her body. An uncertain smile played across her lips.

Very pointedly Jacob turned away and walked through to the bedroom. He heard the shower door slam behind him.

*Shhhhh*, went the water.

He moved to the wardrobe and made an unsettling discovery: it was full of women's clothing. These were Battalion's quarters.

There *was* a suit for him, however, (a Nicole Fahri!) and clean underwear in a bag from French Connection. But the shirt was something else again. On the breast pocket had been embroidered — with particularly fine needlework — the stylised Egyptian eye that every member of the Order bore. He fingered the pattern, savouring the texture of its expensive thread, tracing the intricate design. The iris was sewn with delicate whorls of blue and gold, rimmed by a pearly corona.

"The Eye of Horus."

Jacob turned, startled. Battalion stood naked in the doorway, a towel slung around her neck. Her hair was slicked back, sleek dark-blonde spikes sharp against the creamy material. Her eyes looked like silver marbles. She studied him intently. An overpowering sense of unresolved emotion crackled in the air between them, sexual, powerful. It seemed like an eternity before Jacob could return his attention to the shirt. Battalion crossed behind him to a chair by the bed; he heard it creak as she sat. The shirt's material felt like ice sliding between his palms.

"It's also sometimes called the *udjat*, or *utchat* eye," she added. "The Egyptians used to use it as a funerary amulet, for protection against evil beyond this world, and to signify rebirth. It invariably decorated mummies, coffins and tombs.

"Horus was the son of Osiris and Isis, and according to legend he lost his eye to his evil brother, Seth, whom he fought to avenge Seth's murder of Osiris. The eye was reassembled by Thoth, the god of writing and magic, after which Horus presented the eye to Osiris, who was granted rebirth in the underworld. The eye is always assembled in fractional parts, with one sixty-fourth missing— a piece which was added by Thoth using sorcery.

"It is also known as the 'all-seeing eye'. That's the symbolism we invoke for ourselves." Battalion fell silent. Jacob did not look at her.

An irrational urge gripped him: he didn't want the eye staring at him. He wanted it hidden, blind. He needed his privacy again more than anything else, wanted to rid himself of all these grubby fingers rifling through the cupboards of his mind. He wanted control, seclusion. All the eye represented to him was violation.

On a shelf near the back of the wardrobe lay the perfect solution. A brand-new Swiss Army knife.

Selecting the largest blade, he began to rip vengefully at the offending threads. In his manic enthusiasm he managed to cut himself more than once, and the material quickly grew slippery. In frustration he started to tear at the loose threads with his teeth. Soon the shirt was soaked with spit and blood, damp-dark and horribly creased. He glanced over at Battalion.

She was regarding him with her head on one side, her expression unreadable. He watched her prop a leg up casually, bent at the knee, foot braced against the bed. It struck Jacob as an intensely masculine gesture. But then again the motion had parted her thighs slightly, revealing the shy tuck of her labia, pink conch delicate beneath the brisk stripe of her pubic hair. His throat tightened.

"If thine right eye offend thee, then pluck it out." She stood and moved over very close to him.

He was painfully aware of her nudity, and the effect it was having upon him. Revulsion and desire thrummed through his body, two equally matched but contrary forces. She took the shirt and knife from his grip, frowning at the mess he'd made.

"This is all wrong. You're not holding it right." She discarded the shirt and drew a new one out from the cupboard. Using the very tip of the slimmest blade, she proceeded to pluck away the threads with nimble precision.

"You taught me how to use a blade," she said quietly.

Jacob watched her without moving, without feeling anything as simple as hate or love.

"And you taught me to shoot... firearms, self-defence... higher casting. All down to you... I can kill because of you. I *have* killed because of you. I am what I am today because Hush came into my life, and changed me forever. Set me on a different path."

Jacob said, "I'm not sure I can be with you... not yet. Not here. I thought you were a murderer... I'm not convinced you *aren't* a murderer. Until a quarter of an hour ago I believed you hated me, and, frankly, I *did* hate you."

He saw his words strike home. Saw them hurt. She lowered her face nearer to the shirt to hide her wet eyes. She was breathing a little faster, and Jacob could feel the tension riding through her. The air was oily with emotion. She started to fumble with the knife, losing her dexterity as the dejection bit deeper. Then she let the shirt tumble from her nerveless fingers, straightened, and stared directly at him, tears standing in her steel-coloured eyes.

Jacob was wearing one of the hotel's bathrobes. Without ceremony she shoved it roughly off his shoulders, exposing his chest. He didn't try to stop her. She blinked rapidly three, four times, licked her lips, then placed a fingertip very deliberately on the snake's-head tip of the scar hooped over his ribs, as if enthralled by the geometry of its arc.

Jacob watched her eyelids twitching minutely while she traced the scar. Though she seemed in control, he kept catching reflex spasms of feeling: flickers of grief from beneath the crust of her restraint, like flames glimpsed through the eyes of a Halloween mask.

"I was with you when this happened," she whispered huskily, her fingertips still resting lightly on the scar. "We were storming a temple of Deep Ones off the coast of Peru. It was when I caught this—" She touched a shiny livid mark on her shoulder. "You were stabbed by one of their Elders."

"I got that when I fell from a tree when I was a boy," Jacob said weakly, remembering the fall, the impact, the pain.

She ignored him, touched a patch of grizzled flesh on his bicep. "This, this here, is the result of a failed ward when we were trying to ford the transdimensional medium in '82." A hand fluttered to her hairline, and she shrugged a little sheepishly. "You can't see my scars from that one, but I was nigh-on bald for months."

She carried on. "This and this we can attribute to the battle with the *shoggoth* at the South Pole. We all had cause to curse the name of Yog-Sothoth that night… Your repeated numbskull visits to the Lower Archive resulted in all these lesions, plus any niggling circulatory problems you may have. If only you knew how many times I had to jump-start your heart after *those* excursions…"

One by one she named his aged scars, ticking them off, pairing them with her own in a sufferer's symmetry. And when she had finished, she let her hands fall to her side in an attitude of sincerity, almost of pleading. She remained very near to him, deep within his personal space. He felt her heat on his chest.

"We're twinned by our wounds. You know it. You know it to be true… in your flesh."

Then she stepped quickly through those final inches to kiss him, lips on lips, skin against skin. *Her* skin was smooth and damp, still slightly tacky from the shower. She smelled of apple conditioner. Jacob thought that, if he was nothing but a rough cohesion of particles — infinitely malleable — then why couldn't he adapt to this? Everyone must blow where the storm scatters them — like puffs of dandelion seeds — and take what consolations they can.

Jacob gripped the nape of her neck very tenderly, but simultaneously bit into her shoulder with barely restrained venom. He heard her hiss, pain and pleasure mingling. She hooked a leg over his hip, lending her whole weight to the embrace, driving him backwards, desire boiling over. He shifted his balance to hold her up, felt her slip — already slick — along his thigh. Her eyes were very bright.

He manoeuvred them crabways towards the bed, passion making them clumsy so that they barked knees on table edges, rebounded painfully off the wall. He realised that she was crying: hot, furious tears, salt taste on her cheeks.

For her, this was the culmination of fifteen years of waiting, of *wanting*… And in mere hours it could be swept away again by the same enemy.

They fell backwards onto the bed. Old love reclaimed.

The sex was half like combat, half like love. Jacob wasn't sure if he wanted to win, or die.

**

*Before entering the village they had mustered in a gorge adjacent to the valley to review their preparations. There was already a major problem brewing: Smoke had been killed during an earlier assault, so their team was a body shy. The numbers were essential to success. Hush's calculations had left no margin for error; anything less than a full complement would surely doom them. As they debated the best way to improvise, a voice suddenly rang out from the head of the pathway.*

*"I'll go, Sir."*

*Hush turned, and wasn't sure whether to be elated or horrified: it was the boy who'd driven him from the farmhouse. Singer, his title. The newlywed. He rolled the possibilities around in his mind for a moment or two. There was no one else he could call upon at this short notice — it would take endless minutes to get word back to Vanguard — and the boy was right here, right now. Precious time had already been lost.*

*"You sure you're up for this, lad?" he demanded gruffly. The real question went unasked, but passed between them, nonetheless:* you know we'll all die? *The boy nodded. Hush grunted, then sighed, resigned. "Okay. Get Smoke's gear, you're in."*

*Once they'd kitted up they trudged to the end of the straggly trail which dog-legged from gorge to valley. Single file, Hush taking point, they stood on the final boundary between sanity and madness. The actual division was almost comically precise, a literal curtain of alien light drawn across the path. It glistened and seethed, vomiting squirts of frenzied shadow onto its sickly green surface. From this side, the motion looked like moths beating themselves to death against a translucent screen.*

*Staring into it gave one the same impression as looking into water of an enormous depth. Standing this close, Hush could feel a tension, a pressure shoving out at his temples, groping around inside his lungs.*

*"No time," he whispered to himself, then swivelled back to address his squad with a paradoxically devil-may-care grin. "Make the human race proud, boys and girls. Make 'em proud."*

*Then he stepped beyond the veil...*

**

The darkness was hot and fast and fragrant. Filtered light from the main room limned their skin with silver, but he couldn't see her face properly. All he could feel was the sweat and the sex sliding between them as they worked each other.

She rode him hard, arching high above, before dipping down low to kiss, gasping as the climax rose. He put a hand between her thighs, deep in the softness, and located the slippery bud of her clit, teased it lightly, then thumbed it with firmer purpose as her rhythm quickened. She moaned, her pace growing almost desperate as the orgasm threatened.

Every muscle in her body locked tight when she came, and Jacob thought his heart might explode…

**

*For a while they had made good progress. The village reeked, certainly: brine and rubber, mint and formaldehyde— the Multitude stench. Far above them the sky coiled in upon itself remorselessly, a vast pit of thrashing incursions amongst the meat and pincushion clouds. But direct at-*

*tacks were few, and righteous spears of white fire periodically stabbed out from the moon-lens to keep them safe from harm, scattering fans of pearly afterglow in their wakes. The air was hot with the residue of these blasts, and static crawled through their hair, irritating scalps and exciting exposed skin.*

*The assault on their senses grew increasingly difficult to bear. Tricks of vision were most common, and terribly disorientating. The region's oceanic glare caused them many unexpected problems with depth perception, producing actual nausea in some. Landmarks seemed to sway like kelp washing back and forth in a heavy swell. You needed to focus your attention down to a single tunnel of awareness, and follow it unerringly.*

*Similarly, they were besieged by auditory phantoms: niggling lower-range hums, and strident high-pitched trills which set the teeth on edge. Occasionally they would hear disgusting rending gurgles, like blankets being shredded in the middle of a bubbling mud pool. It made them squirm, almost causing a few of the younger adepts to turn and run. What was most unsettling was the impression that these sounds were being transmitted directly to their brains. It was even more terrifying than the entirely silent play of the attack that Hush had watched from the promontory with Singer. The concept of some malevolent agency insinuating itself directly into their neural pathways worried them all.*

*The squad advanced cautiously along wide grassy avenues, moving past the wrecks of countless homes, barely more than a few sad humps of brick and carbonised wooden stumps. Immaterial shades wheeled above them in agitated mobs, behaving more like darting shoals of fish than any birds Hush had ever seen. The evidence of the continued onslaught was displayed all around them. In the midst of one demolished building stood the remnants of a failed alien "bridgehead". It looked like a melted slag heap, but despite its apparent impotence they could detect slow tumbling sparks deep within its oily mass, still fuming with unspent malice. No one risked approaching it.*

*They followed the road as it curved to the right, climbing over an old stone bridge. From there they could see down into the centre of the village, and view the utter destruction wrought upon it. The only building left standing was the church.*

*Behind which the sky was on fire...*

*Vanguard's counterattack had punched a blazing corridor into the black dominance of the clouds. As a result it was possible to stare right up through the stacked layers of the thunderhead. Hush could see structures that resembled huge bone bridges and things which might have been cathedrals — or fortresses — composed of giant glistening tumours, and immense heart-like objects studded by maybe-cogs, surrounded by possible-pistons, drenched in the contents of a back-street abortionist's offal bucket. Galleries of gristle, battlements, causeways, weeping rectal birthing chambers, volcanic vents streaming smog.*

*It was dizzying trying to work out just what you were seeing.*

*Cobs of blazing matter fell all around like meteors, while cataracts of fire continually launched from deep within the louring mass. For a rare fanciful moment Hush imagined that this was what the war in heaven must have looked like seen from the ground.*

*The whole thunderhead seemed in danger of disintegrating, with splits the length of ocean liners riving its night-dark bulk. It was quaking and ponderously rotating, and its mass seemed to have slumped to the left, dangling inky plumes over the hilltops. The power of the Order's onslaught had even been strong enough to quench the vile green glow in the valley, producing instead a gaudy strawberry-coloured lustre to warm their upturned faces.*

*All of Hush's team were simply standing about, gawping stupidly.*

*"Let's go!" Hush roared, sweeping his arms round in the earthbound equivalent of a butterfly stroke: an urgent gestural imperative.*

*"But we're winning!" gasped a hulking adept, his face shining. "Look at it. Look! They're beaten!"*

*"NO!" Hush bellowed. "This will gain us fifteen minutes if we're extraordinarily lucky...That was just the first wave of their first exploratory foray."*

*Everyone took the hint. As one they sprinted for the church.*

*The church gardens were their destination: there, a dead zone had been maintained for them. They headed for the perimeter of the forest which scythed around the back of the plot, embracing the grounds in a dark, rustling arc. The lawns were neatly shorn and well tended, with polite little shrubs and rose bushes corralled into lonely islands here and there. Crossing the grass, Hush's team continued to be showered with brilliance from the celestial battlefield above, but when they reached their destination it instantly cut away, as if a fuse had blown. The dead zone was as black as any midnight, a velveteen pouch of spacetime tucked away from the real world so that they could perform their labours without disturbance.*

*The trees hulking behind them were vast ferns, brooding and dense, closely set, claustrophobic, brushed into gentle motion by the sly breeze. Smoothly, the team went to work. They knew by rote what was expected of them. Each member had a precise role, a task to perform. It was better that way. It meant that they could lose themselves in old rhythms, calming themselves with the familiarity of their tasks so that they didn't have time to anticipate what was coming next.*

*Ceremonial braziers were swiftly erected and lit, casting spirals outlined in phosphorescent paint on the stamped-down grass. Final cantrips were laid onto gear, wards braided into place, weapons locked and loaded. Then, their preparations complete, they took up their various stations round the ring. Hush stepped to the head of the group, hitting his mark behind the pre-eminent decal. He disinterred the cylinder, checked its seal.*

*"When the fording torque arrives," he began quietly, "I want you all to remember— you're safe within the spiral. Outside, the*

*transdimensional stresses could mince you to dog food, so remain absolutely still. Understood? When we arrive at their realm, communication will be severely restricted. We know... something of the conditions we might encounter there, but knowing theoretically... Well, be prepared to acclimatise on the hoof. Just tuck your head in and go for the Citadel. Always the Citadel. That's the goal.*

*"Surprise may be our one asset, but this period of grace will only last so long. Vanguard's attack may keep them busy for a bit, but not indefinitely. And they might not be fooled at all. The moment we pop through, whole armies could be waiting. If we encounter sustained resistance... Well, you know the drill. I'm killed, you head for the Citadel no matter what. After an attack, anybody left alive—"*

*"Hush," said Sun-Ray suddenly, his voice shivering with anticipation. "It's started."*

*Hush sensed it too, a thickening of the atmosphere; the air was obese with portent. Apprehension jabbed at him, so sharp and unexpected that it momentarily stole his breath. He swallowed painfully.*

*"That's it, kids. They're playing our song." In spite of his fear he managed to excavate a smile for them. He shifted his balance to try to ease the tension in his calves, which were even now threatening to cramp. Everything was dark; the light from the guttering braziers uncertain, revealing only stingy hints of the whole scene— the shoulders of his companions, a cheek or nervously blinking eye, the tips of branches bowing closer in the wind. From the ground, the non-linear calculus glittered up at them, luminous emblems frosty and pristine.*

*He gripped the cylinder even tighter and felt it slide in his grip. Speedily he scrubbed his hands on the cotton of his trousers, but to no avail. A beat later the sweat was back. He was not alone with his terror. They all radiated dread. The spiral stank of it:*

*Sun-Ray let out an involuntary whimper which segued into an embarrassed curse. On the heels of this slip came the unmistakable* ker-clack *of someone anxiously chambering a shotgun round.*

*Battalion coughed, and Hush stared at her, willing his own body to remain under control. He saw his unease mirrored in her eyes. Why wouldn't the terror go? Here they were, beyond all the limits, in the eye of the nightmare. There was no going back, no other choice. Surely there was no space left for fear, only duty...*

*Abruptly, he found it difficult to breathe. Pinpricks of light started to percolate on the meniscus of his eyes. He could sense his vision collapsing, caving in. Dizziness washed over him...Jesus, don't let me faint, he thought. Not now, not when so much depends on me. In the centre of his narrowing field of vision he could see Battalion, and she looked exactly like he felt: wobbly, horrified, verging on despair. Then, a breath: the stench of wet earth filled his nostrils, his mouth, and it tasted like revelation.*

*This is what we do it for, he thought. This is what's at stake here. Everything.*

*By that point they could hear the approach of the fording torque above the gnashing of the breeze: not really the growl of an earthquake, nor a tidal wave; it wasn't quite like an avalanche in the distance, nor even a whispering crowd. It felt somehow like all of those things, and yet it was none of them. Without warning the undergrowth thirty feet to their left exploded in a storm of wooden shards. Trees were bowing violently outwards, as if shoved to one side by the progress of some vast, invisible beast. The din was terrific, chunks of matter blasting in every direction, the wind shrieking and groaning and wailing. One more step and their true, terrible mission—the kidnapping—would be underway. The last gasp, Hush told himself.*

*But at that moment Battalion suddenly screamed, and stumbled back over the perimeter of the spiral...*

**

"*You* stepped out of the circle," said Jacob, astonished. "It was you. My God..." he trailed off, suddenly be aware of how accusatory his tone sounded.

They were lying on the bed together, sheets tousled beneath them. Battalion was smoking. She didn't reply for some time. Finally she said, "You were always the one."

"What?"

"You were always the one," she spat.

Jacob left a long pause before offering, weakly: "I don't understand."

"The calm one... the centre-point."

"*Calm?* I can't even remember a time when I wasn't angry!"

"You were the one, the guy whom everyone expected to save them, to look after them and keep the wolf from the door. The embodiment of faith, of... optimism. You were like everyone's favourite uncle. Kind, fair, quiet, but oh so strong when it mattered."

"The exact opposite of the man I became when my memory was taken away?"

She nodded. "You were the *heart* of the Order. Fade was no good, you couldn't imagine ever going to *him* with your problems. Nor Vanguard—far too fucking scary! But you, you were always there for us. You were always the one."

"So, now...?"

"You wonder why everyone seems to stare at you? They read the diary. They all found out what you were really thinking, all the fear and the horror and the doubt. It was like their dad had betrayed them by remortgaging the house to buy his mistress a flat. No one knew what to believe, even in the midst of victory.

"It was Fade who transcribed the diary over to disk, revealed the contents, released it to the troops. Vanguard just about had his head for that. He hated you even more for your admissions of weakness. You were meant to be his opposite, a standard of pure optimism to place against his Machiavellian example. I think he felt that you'd failed somehow, in your role as the anti-Fade. You made him seem… less well *defined*. Less himself. He didn't know quite how to be after that, what his role was. It was a blessing for many that Vanguard decided to wipe your personality and cast you out. It was part of our healing process. No one could believe in their champion any more."

Jacob shook his head, disbelieving.

"You're talking about someone else. I don't know this guy. All this, 'return of the prodigal' bullshit. That isn't me."

She watched him intently for a while, gnawing at her lip, and when she continued it was as if he hadn't spoken.

"For me it was the worst. You were my lover, my mentor. And I'd always tried so hard to live up to your example… But I failed. I let you down. Failed you. Failed the Order. Failed everyone… All the others on the team died, maybe because of me… And you came back… *shattered*. Changed… In all the years since, every night I've dreamed of stepping out of that damned circle. Again and again, over, over…" As she spoke she smoked aggressively, tracking angry little circles in the air with her fag tip.

"Why did I do it? I don't know. Because I was scared? Certainly, that's a part of it. Because I was too young? Because I was just a girl, really, and shouldn't have been there in the first place? Maybe. Because flesh is weak and life is precious, even to the point of choosing ten more minutes over three if we can? I guess. Because we're still the beasts we once were, and abstract ideals like faith, hope and even love can be overturned in a moment by hard-wired animal responses?" She looked down at her feet, callused and hardy.

"I've had so much to prove, so far to go, in those years without you. To win back their trust, erase the humiliation. I've needed to be a hundred times as fearless as any other adept. A hundred times as ruthless, too. You've seen it. You've even felt it, hard as that was for me. The girl that Hush once loved is gone, lost. She stepped into the darkness and disappeared. Hush couldn't rely on me then. *You* can now."

Jacob was overwhelmed by this declaration. To have caused all this, and not even remember it! To be responsible for this woman's dreadful reinvention. All those things he'd feared about her—the brutality, the iciness—they were *his* doing. It was too much, way too much. Frantically, he searched for some get-out, a way to diminish his responsibility.

"Have you… I dunno… I mean, have you been with other people since you were with me?"

Battalion sat up and tugged her feet beneath her, started to flex her thighs. More stretching, Jacob noted. Low-key exercise. Didn't this woman ever stop?

"Of course I have I knew you were going to. I knew about *her*-"

"Maria." Jacob went stiff as her name slid off his lips. His fingertips felt numb. The sounds in the room got fuzzy and distorted for a second.

"I was part of the surveillance team appointed to keep a watch over you," Battalion persisted bitterly. "One of Fade's little jokes, that, fucking white-haired freak. All those years of watching you together, you and her… But I knew. I told you I'd taste you again. You can't imagine how I've dreamt of this day." She glanced away, an embarrassed teenager again. She didn't notice how his mood had changed.

"Maria died because of you," he accused in a flat, deadly voice.

Battalion's eyes snapped back. "She died because of that *thing*. They sent a sentient cluster to retrieve it, the girl-thing— the Nexus. Or perhaps it summoned the cluster itself. But I will tell you this for sure— it claimed the lives of fifteen adepts before it was sent back again."

Jacob recalled the dark seething horror in Maria's flat. *Sentient cluster*? The appellation hardly did it justice.

"You abused the girl. I watched you beat her."

"The girl, the *girl*? Look, it wasn't a girl. It was a despicable, malevolent, evil *thing*. It was the reason we were parted. I beat it because it represents all the worst loss and pain in the world for me!"

Jacob digested this in silence. To hide his confusion he craned over to the bedside table for her Marlboro Lights. There was only one left. He flipped it out, then crushed the pack, accidentally drizzling tobacco dregs onto the bed. He swore and brushed them off as best he could. Deprived of a lighter he used a Minor Spark of Inception to get the fag going. Then he spoke again.

"But we won, we beat them back. We're still here so, we won the war. They didn't manage to cross over… and it has something to do with the girl, doesn't it?"

"You've seen your diary. You have all the information you need right there."

He frowned at her for a long moment. Then his eyes lit up with understanding. "The figure in red? Not Vanguard, but—"

"The girl. We think that somehow she forms the software to their hardware. That was Fade's supposition, at least."

"The Lila nexus," said Jacob sourly.

"Yes. All their previous incursions have been preceded by her manifestation. In folk myth and literature down the ages there has tended to be an unnatural focus on girls of that age — virgin sacrifice being merely the most obvious example — and many have speculated that this might be due to the influence of the Multitude on our culture. Previous fleeting incursions, perhaps for reconnaissance? We don't think that they perceive time in quite the same way as we do, so to them a century's gap might be like taking a few minutes to mull over strategy.

"They seem to operate like a hive organism — with every separate element forming a component of the unified whole — but the girl is an individual. She contains a great portion of their overall might. Vanguard claimed that she had been created to form an intellectual bridgehead for them. Employed to conquer realities that weren't dominated by hive species. She was used to decipher what they encountered. Once we established this, we used divination and the Lower Archive to learn about their native habitat, and its fundamental organisation. We knew that we couldn't beat them here, in direct warfare, so we needed an alternative contingency."

"So you went into their realm and captured the Nexus? Brought it back here?"

"Yes, *you* did."

"Holding the Multitude to *ransom*?"

"It was your plan in the first place."

"You don't say?" He cackled incredulously. "Well, that's lateral thinking for you, and then some. We kidnapped the *daughter* of a horde of invincible hive monsters… and they agreed to our terms!"

"Negotiations were, ah … oblique but conclusive."

"I'll bet." In spite of everything Jacob was mightily impressed.

"Without her they couldn't even *conceive* of how to make war on us. It was impossible. Like declaring war on an abstract notion: trying to attack jealousy with an axe, or dispatching helicopter gunships to hunt down self-esteem. We are simply too alien for them to fight."

"And now they're coming back for more? They get Lila back so that's it, roll up for round two? Full-on, full-scale war with the Beyond? Death or glory? You forget, I've been in your War Room. Christ, I even saw rocket launchers in there!"

"We've spent a long time planning for this eventuality. No one thought we could hold the hostage forever. The use of conventional ordnance may well be necessary, Hush."

"Don't call me that."

Her mouth was already open to reply, but instead she hesitated, pressed her lips together until they formed a pale bloodless seam. She closed her eyes and just breathed evenly for a while. After a sizeable interlude she opened her eyes and regarded him very honestly:

"I'm sorry. I have no more idea of how to deal with this than you. I can't work out what I should call you, or how I should be with you, or what we should do together, or …" She threw up her hands helplessly, furiously.

"You think *you're* confused. Two hours ago I was somebody else."

She glared at him for some time, as if searching his face for something hidden or lost. Eventually she gave a curt nod to her old comrade in arms. Truly, they were twinned by their wounds, as far as she was concerned. Something was still bothering Jacob, though.

"Tell me about the dog… Fenton? Who was Fenton?"

Battalion snorted with cold amusement, and rearranged herself on the bed to get more comfortable. She licked her lips carefully before replying.

"When you first brought it back, the Nexus started off by pretending it was a normal teenager. A little withdrawn perhaps, very odd, but a human nonetheless. Who knows what its motives were? Perhaps it was angling for escape? Hoping that maybe we would feel sorry for it and let our guard down? It asked endless questions, and it asked to see its family. It drew sketches, and kept a diary—in a jotter with those icky cartoon daisies on the front—and it tried to gossip with some of the female adepts about boys. And it cried itself to sleep sometimes. It was surreal. It was, frankly, very disturbing. To know you were holding an utterly malignant transcorporeal entity in the facility, and yet feel like you had one of your friends' kooky daughters banged up.

"Although our security never slackened I'm sure this camouflage moulded the way *we* responded to *it*. Infecting how we dealt with it and, more importantly, how we thought of it. The hours of interrogation, all the invasive procedures we performed — which, by the way, would have killed a real girl stone dead in a matter of days — well, we felt bad about it. No one voiced this out loud, of course. You couldn't. It would have been like saying Hitler had a really rough time in his bunker during the last days of the war. Yet after a few weeks, everybody began to develop this sort of *sick* look on days when it was to be experimented on. As a result, we did things we might have done were we looking after a real human.

"One of the ways we experimented on it was letting it interact with some of the on-site guard dogs. Only, as time went on, that stopped being a research procedure, and became like a treat. For it, the Nexus. And there was one dog in particular it spent time with— Fenton, an Alsation. Why it should have used that name to trick you, I haven't the faintest clue.

"However, I will say this, it was fascinated by the dogs. But not so much by the animals themselves, as by how *we* dealt with them— how we looked after them, tended to them, played with them. It's odd. I'd watch it some days and it was almost like it was trying to copy us. Like it was trying to *learn*. Like the whole invasion was just a crazy ruse so that they could come and watch us play with our dogs." She frowned and then snorted, half out of humour and half out of unease.

"In the end, after years went by in which it didn't grow old or change, it slowly phased out the deception, progressively becoming less and less animate, until finally, one day, it refused to communicate at all, just sat cross-legged in its cell, dumb, switched off, impervious to any stimuli."

"Yeah. Fade said something similar in the car over," Jacob remarked. "But, she talked to me, and Maria."

Battalion's face darkened. "Yes, I know, and this troubles Vanguard greatly. We have no idea what that might mean. Possibly, it was simply a ruse to gain your trust. And yet…" She looked worried. "Fade has speculated down the years that, since you were the one to kidnap the Nexus, some kind of non-linear bond has been forged between the two of you that we can't detect."

But Jacob had stopped listening. He was staring at his cigarette as if it were a lethal scorpion that he had somehow lit and tried to smoke, sucking at it for minutes without ever noticing.

"I don't smoke," he said shakily, ashen-faced. Battalion put a comforting hand on his forearm.

"That was Vanguard. Always deciding what's best for other people. She was very insistent that we build healthy habits into the scaffold of your new identity."

"And I lit it... *without a lighter*!"

"Minor Spark of Inception. I saw you."

"I did it without thinking."

"You did it on a reflex. Your skills are coming back. That's good. Shows that you're healing, your personality is integrating again."

Jacob started to feel faint. He'd begun to experience a strange noise — or a pressure, more like — a sort of low sonorous droning. He tried to focus on the conversation, but it was as if Battalion was being drawn away from him along an infinitely extendible corridor, her voice growing steadily fainter and fainter. Unable to stand it any longer, he surged to his feet. Rocked there unsteadily for a few beats.

"I think I need a glass of water. Hang tight, I'll—" he mumbled, weaving blearily towards the bathroom. His vision was tunnelling, black lace and filigree purling out on the periphery, spinning him remorselessly away from consciousness. He felt woozy. His knees were made of toffee.

"Hey, you okay?" Battalion called out, suddenly alarmed.

"Yeh, yeh— just cut me a minute here—" he slurred, tumbling into the bathroom.

**

Inside, he rested his forehead against the back of the door and spent a few moments trying to breathe clearly, to mash the panic down and stabilise his emotions. But the symptoms intensified. The unearthly hum continued to drill its way through his skull. Sweat poured off him.

He flung himself around to make for the sink, but what he saw slammed him back up against the door in horror.

Maria and Lila were sitting on the edge of the bath.

They seemed to be *wrestling* one another. Or more accurately, Lila was attempting to shove herself up against the older woman, straining nearer and nearer to her face, a determined almost clinical expression moulding her thin features. Maria, on the other hand, seemed to be filled with the same uncontrollable terror that gripped Jacob. It was obvious that she was using every particle of her strength just to keep the girl at bay, but even that wasn't enough. Jacob could see the tremors rippling along her forearms, painful tension stretching the cords of her neck.

But Maria did manage to wrench her head aside and stare directly at him. She mouthed something, repeated it, then suddenly he got the sense of what she was trying to say.

It was, *Now we are one.*

## 22. The End

They continued to wrestle, the two women in his life: Maria, who was gone, and Lila, whom he had once pledged his life to protect.

*Now we are one*, Maria mouthed again, but her eyes were stormy as she jawed the words from beyond the grave.

"No!" Jacob shouted, because he was truly Jacob now, not Hush: not some trumped-up magician who'd lost his cool and been conveniently pensioned off, but Jacob, confused and terrified and lost and alone, alone even though in the next room there was a wild, beautiful, determined woman who professed to love him.

"I love you!" he shouted at Maria as her image faded. "I love you," he said again, and he really meant it. At that moment love was all he could feel or think— love, unrequited and despoiled.

Gradually the image of the two women dissolved, vanishing in a heat-haze swirl, and all the while Lila fought to kiss Maria, while Maria simply fought. As Jacob stood there — staring at the normal bathroom with its ring of scum around the bath and the three new toilet rolls on the floor beside the loo — he wondered whether they were still fighting now, wherever they were… in death, or some place far stranger?

"Maria!" he cried. A worm of guilt squirmed through his chest as he pictured Battalion lying on the bed outside, anxiously waiting. The lingering taste of cigarette smoke made him want to retch. He had always hated smoking, a pointless bloody habit which made your breath and clothes stink. Jacob had hated it, but Hush—

Right now, he could imagine nothing sweeter in the world than a beautiful shrink-wrapped pack of Bennies. A chill for the nerves, oh yes. First nicotine rush of the morning, better than any high. He even found himself instinctively reaching for his pocket, only to realise he was naked. He looked down at his deflated cock, wondering what Maria had thought when she saw him, whether she'd realised that he'd just been screwing someone else. There seemed to be something wrong with his thoughts. He wasn't thinking straight.

"Hush!"

Battalion kicked at the door lock, nothing gentle or subtle about her concern. She started to shoulder the door and it leapt in the frame, architraves popping loose, old paint flaking to the vinyl floor.

"Hush, what is it? What, what?" she called out.

Hush slumped in the corner of the bathroom, and instead of lighting a cigarette he flicked his hands across his face and sighed down into a Flush of Calm. The door rocked on its hinges, but the action was stretched out, so much so that he percieved each movement like an individual movie frame, rocking forward one shutter at a time, beat by beat: the timber bowing in slightly as Battalion impacted from the other side; the paint drifting down in snowflake slowness. He closed his eyes and opened them weeks later. He was still in the bathroom, but no threat remained. No danger. He'd seen Maria, he thought, but who the hell was Maria anyway? Had he really ever loved her like he claimed, or was it all just another of Vanguard's fictions?

The door burst in and Battalion stumbled through, naked and flushed. Her shoulder was a vivid pink from the battering she had dealt the wood. She spun on the damp floor and came at Hush. He smiled stupidly up at her, trying to remember the taste of her skin, the texture of every scar as his memories drew a map of her body. She knelt before him and waved a palm in front of his face—

"Maria!" he shouted, shivering and quaking.

"No more casting," Battalion scolded. "You're not ready yet. You've not got the trick back."

"I saw Maria," Hush stammered. "And the girl, Lila, here and fighting… only Maria wanted to get away."

"The Nexus? Here?" Battalion reared and turned, bracing her legs into a defensive crouch. Ghoul-light danced across her fingertips, shivering through her hair: a beautiful Medusa. But all that confronted her was old talcum powder and lines of mould on the wall. "Where?"

Hush used the ledge of the bath to lever himself to his feet. Conflicting images fought for dominance in his mind: Maria slipping from his grip amidst the chaos of battle; Lila guiding him to Scotland, sadness hanging around her like a stench; Battalion astride his hips, riding hard, as if she thought she could bring love back into being by the sheer force of lust alone.

"I don't know what's going on," Hush said. He began to shake. As Battalion moved to him and hugged him tight, he shook even more. "I just don't know. I don't know. I don't know..." Bitter tears burned his cheeks.

There was a knocking from the bedroom. Without either of them answering, they heard the outer door swing open and footsteps march in. "Hush?" A voice called out.

"Fade," Battalion whispered. She looked at Hush with an expression that only served to confuse him more; there was love there, but also disappointment, doubt and fear. Most of all, fear.

She strode naked from the bathroom and Hush timidly followed. Fade's frank but dispassionate gaze took her in, then he brushed his hands through his hair before bringing a cigarette from nowhere and lighting it with a flick of his fingertips. He cocked his head quizzically, sardonic and sexless.

"The Nexus appeared to Hush," Battalion said, dressing as she spoke. "In the bathroom, to him and him alone. Didn't want me to see it." She frowned, pulling her sweater over her head. "Or maybe it was probing, testing the water. Trying to find a gap in the defence—"

"He's the gap," Fade said, nodding at Hush where he stood in the centre of the room. Fade glanced down at Hush's groin, then up again, a smirk twisting his features. "Look at him. All used up. A waste of space."

"We must tell Vanguard." Battalion sat on the bed to tie her laces.

"Tell her yourself," Fade said, throwing a mobile phone onto the ruffled sheets.

"I'll tell her," Hush whispered.

Fade frowned and leaned theatrically forward. "Huh? Speak up."

"I'll tell her. I saw them. I can best describe what they were like, what they were—"

"They?"

"Maria was with Lila."

"*Together*?" Fade looked genuinely shocked by this revelation, brought up short. He narrowed his eyes. "What does that mean?" He was evidently unsettled.

Hush looked down at his feet and closed his eyes for an instant. His head spun, but he cast another Flush of Calm, a subtle one this time to smooth off the edges of his panic rather than dousing it entirely. He looked up. Neither of them had noticed. He felt absurdly pleased … and Jacob faded into the background a little more.

Battalion handed him the cell phone. Hush pressed the memory pre-set for Vanguard.

"Yes? What?" The voice was crackly, as if the speaker had a mouth full of grit.

"It's me," Hush said. He tried to manage the hatred he still harboured for this woman. He considered a Veil of Forgiveness, but decided against it. Sometimes loathing sharpened the mind.

Static. An expectant silence. Then he told her what had happened.

**

Vanguard had taken over a small conference room as her Base of Operations. Flip charts were tagged to freestanding whiteboards, but left eloquently blank, as if no amount of planning could help them now.

"We must go," Vanguard said. "This manifestation of the Nexus can only mean one thing. They are almost upon us, in sight of our shores."

"I'm not sure," Fade began. "The portents are open to interpretation. If you just grant me access to the Lower Archive for one hour—"

"*No.* The time for interpretation is over. The time for action is at hand." Vanguard's face was pale, her burns standing out pink and raw. Her gnarled hands twitched restlessly in her lap.

Hush thought she looked scared, and that scared him. He thought of how graceful her hands had once been.

Vanguard glared across the desk at him, then sadly shook her head. "We could use you now, Hush."

"Then use me."

"I can't risk it, for a world full of reasons." She stood and surveyed her companions, then picked up a phone handset. "Quell," she barked into the mouthpiece. "Relay the order."

When she replaced the phone, Hush saw a terrible shadow pass across her face. "There it is," she said. "The end."

**

As soon as they exited the Conference Room they were engulfed by chaos. At least it *felt* like chaos, but beneath the surface Hush soon detected a merciless discipline, a backbone of methodical organisation. The hotel resounded to the stamp of booted feet, the clash of metal on metal, guns locking and loading, electronic whirrs, computers booting up… the occasional pluck on the inner ear as minor cantrips were cast, and non-linear calculus was checked.

An army was on the move. The corridors had become constant two-way streams, flowing with purpose and urgency. Vanguard's phone call had unleashed a maelstrom of activity, all of which Hush was sure had been planned for years.

"Battalion, with me," Vanguard barked, and she marched off along the corridor without a backward glance.

"Hush?" Battalion was torn two ways, the sacred draw of duty struggling with the pull of love. She threw herself into Hush's arms, buried her face in his neck, and kissed him there, sobbing and swearing and vowing to be strong. Her voice was barely audible above the cacophony, but Hush heard every word.

He looked at her and she was the most *real* thing in the corridor. All the light seemed to rush in to her, making her almost unendurably vivid and pristine, beyond life and time and history.

Vanguard turned and glared along the corridor at them, but then Hush saw a flash of something softer in her eyes. It was deeply submerged—nothing could truly disturb the calm surface of her resolve—but the sensation was like looking at his own face reflected in a bottomless lake: a pale ghost thrown upon the darkness.

She closed her eyes momentarily, as if feeling the moment. Then—

"Battalion, we have to leave. You and I must be there to guide the Order. You know that."

Battalion nodded against Hush's neck, but still she did not look up.

Vanguard said no more. Her impatience was obvious, and yet she waited for Battalion to make her choice, knowing all along that it would be the right one.

In the end, Hush chose for her. "Go," he said quietly. "I'll taste you again."

Battalion looked up sharply at him, her eyes glinting with tears of anger and defiance. "You will," she said. "No doubt. I love you."

Hush nodded. "I'll love you, too."

Battalion strode to Vanguard and in seconds they were lost to the storm. Neither of them looked back.

"How exquisitely 'Direct-to-Video'," scoffed Fade. "You really haven't changed, have you? The same B-movie clichés you smeared all over that wretched diary so many years ago. And yet she still swoons for it. How quaint."

Hush ignored him. He seemed to step back from events, felt the panic recede, as if he'd cast another Flush of Calm. But he'd done nothing, and Fade had done nothing; he'd simply found an icy coolness inside himself that he'd never felt before. More than a coolness— a *detachment*. Not from Battalion, but from everything else around him. It gave him strength, and he knew he could carry on, whatever else might assail him. But still, the numbness worried him.

"What now?" he asked.

"Now we watch the Multitude sweep aside our defences like the ocean crashing through a dam of feathers."

"Optimistic old you."

Fade shrugged and smiled his usual smile, an expression that would serve as a sneer on any other face. "*You* are going to lecture *me* on optimism? After that diary of yours? I've never read a finer example of snivelling despair."

Hush squared up to Fade, set his jaw. "I'm not despairing now, Fade. And Vanguard … She thinks we can beat them, otherwise why all this?"

Fade smiled, then laughed again. "Come on, baby," he said. "I'm still your babysitter. But don't expect for a minute that I'll protect you from the monsters. They get in here and believe me, you're on your own." He cooed, mockingly: "Daddy, the knives. The knives."

Chuckling, Fade led the way along the central corridor to a stairwell. His new-found clarity allowed Hush to follow, to push on through with a clear head, immune to the jibes. He sensed the building emptying around them, heard engines gunning in the square outside as cars and vans departed for Village Zero. By the time they had descended five floors to the basement, an eerie quiet had descended across the hotel.

"They've all gone?" Hush asked quietly.

"All gone. Soon, all dead," Fade said, sounding almost satisfied. "You'll never see Battalion again, or Vanguard, or any of them. No more girlish adoration for you, or needless pique for me to endure. All roads end here, my fucked-up friend." He raised his hand and ran fingers through his hair. "Cigarette?" The cigarette he offered was already lit.

Hush took it and sucked greedily, enjoying the brief lightheadedness. Fade had his eyes closed and was humming, idly conducting an orchestra playing in his head.

"What about the Weapon?" Hush asked.

"Ahhhh," Fade sighed. Without opening his eyes he flicked his left hand out in front of a recessed mirror-black panel.

A section of the wall gasped and slid smoothly to one side on oiled rails, allowing Hush a view of what lay beyond: a too-bright space, one small room jammed to bursting with technology, crawling with leads, humming with electricity. He looked questioningly back to Fade, and the silver-haired adept's expression shocked him to the marrow with its honesty and sincerity.

"The Weapon is apocalypse," Fade said simply.

There was no guile there, no ridicule, no cynicism. No edge. Here they were — in a basement — and Hush found himself unexpectedly peering into the pit at the heart of Fade's personality. And what he saw there terrified him more than the Multitude, more than the end of the world. A light was shining from inside Fade, a serenity.

Because Fade wasn't scared.

Unlike every other member of the Order who had overlaid their fear with mantles of discipline or duty or false bravado, Fade did not fear defeat. That would allow him to use the Weapon. And that *thrilled* him.

Hush was shaking. He could barely find the words.

"Tell me, Fade," he whispered. "What is the Weapon? What makes it so terrible?"

"It's the world new-minted. A second stab at paradise. You see, it makes everything *clean* again. Gives us a chance to start over. A new beginning!"

"But—"

"No."

"Fade, listen— "

"Shhhh," said Fade, placing his fingertips against Hush's lips to silence him. Then he did the oddest thing. With utter conviction — as if he'd planned the gesture for years — Fade leaned in gracefully to kiss Hush on the mouth. A benediction from the High Priest of the New Apocalypse.

Afterwards, all the emotion simply drained away. Hush felt it leave him in a rush, and he slumped against the wall.

Fade, utterly composed and serene, guided him gently through to the control room.

**

Inside, the walls were lined with banks of computers and monitors, exotic apparatus of all breeds, cables snaking away into ducting and through ceiling voids. The far wall was composed entirely of one composite screen which consisted of twenty-five separate monitors slotted together, their blank faces full of potential. And there were even more outré components to the control room: it was to these that Hush's attention quickly flew.

Casting sigils and glyphs had been daubed on the ceiling, and densely carpeted the floor as well. Each one caused a niggle in Hush's mind, a subtle nudge that, perhaps, he should be able to divine their intent. Perhaps he had even cast them himself once? Each had a different imprint, left a different impression on his senses— a clutter of cross-connections in his brain, like spontaneous synaesthesia. One sigil tasted of cinnamon, another sounded like soap drawn across sandpaper. All of them were potent.

Then Hush's attention shifted to the right-hand wall, where a hollowed out space had been left to house a curious flickering sculpture. It was fabricated from some strange semi-liquid alloy that Hush had never seen before. There were shapes forming beneath that molten surface that defied three-dimensional space, raspberries blown at spoilsport physics.

"What," he said, "is *that*?"

Fade glanced as if it were a familiar painting he barely noticed anymore. "That's for later... if needs' must. Come in, sit down, make yourself at home. There's a fridge in the corner with a few bottles of first-rate Chablis... my own little addition. The '84. An excellent year." He grinned. "What better way to toast the end of world?"

Fade splashed out an indulgent measure to sip, but left Hush to serve himself. They drank in silence. Fade closed his eyes, but when Hush followed suit all he could see was Battalion hanging in the blood-dark, clear-eyed and fierce. Seconds passed, then Maria's image intruded, and though Hush now knew the truth about his invented history, his thoughts of her remained razor-sharp. Poor Maria. She'd been used as badly as he. More so, really. And now she was dead.

Well, wasn't she?

After what seemed like hours Fade opened his eyes and straightened, suddenly infused with new purpose. "Right," he said crisply, as if talking to whomever he'd been dreaming of in his semi-doze. He looked at Hush. "Right."

Hush claimed a swivel chair and moved in next to Fade, whose hands were already dancing across an illuminated touchpad. An electronic chime sounded, and the whole room slowly came to life—monitors flickered, hard drives chugged, the gargantuan mainframe breathed through its fan. Wagner's "Ride of the Valkyries" blasted out from hidden speakers, its sensaround sound sheared into odd shapes by the room's jagged edges.

"The Kraken awakes," Fade proclaimed as the composite screen glowed into life, looking like the compound eye of a giant dragonfly. "Right," he continued. "Grandstand view. There are remote cameras mounted at three vantages to Village Zero. Here ... here ... and, ah, *here*—"

He toggled between the three views. Each feed showed lines of trucks and vans, black-clad figures hurrying across the hills like ants searching for a home. They also showed Village Zero — the most alien place on Earth — shrouded by morning mist, the hollow shells of dead homes peeping through the swirling cloak. The black swipe of the forest towered behind the church. Great swathes had been slashed out of it by the Order to make way for machine-gun posts and impromptu arms dumps.

"Lila took me there," Hush said, remembering the frantic drive upcountry, the supposed protection of Fenton, rogue sorcerer.

"The Nexus instinctively knew its way back to the primary incursion point. Knew that this was the only way back. Let's hope it's the only way through for them, as well. We can only pray we haven't missed anywhere ... somewhere in a desert, or the rainforests, maybe? Personally, Tunguska and Wabar still have me worried, but, well, our esteemed leader has made her decision." He shrugged and treated Hush to a wry look. "Comme ci, comme ça."

Hush was distracted by movement on the monitor. "What's that?" he queried. At first it had looked like static on the screen—they were still viewing the scene from one of the hilltop feeds—but as the viewpoint closed in on a huddle of nearby trucks the object gained definition. "Is that …?" Fade didn't give him time to finish.

"Hang on," he said, his voice suddenly professional, shedding its sarcastic veneer. He manipulated the touchpad and their view panned right. It appeared that the camera was mounted on some sort of articulated platform. Sound was added too, and Hush strained to hear what was happening above the Wagner.

It was as he'd thought. The man landed from his flight, a thousand transparent wings fading into the daylight.

"The medium is getting very heavy," the flier said. "Hectic. I think they're going to attempt a fording pretty soon."

"Any portents?" a disembodied voice asked.

The flying man looked just left of whatever camera was filming him. "No, not as such. The wards are still intact. There's no indication in the muscle of the grid. But… I can feel it. We all can."

"Then we trust our instincts," Vanguard said.

The camera swivelled and she came into view. It was only then that Hush realised that they were viewing the scene from a shoulder cam. Fade pecked out a few rapid keystrokes and the image flipped around to show Battalion standing on the left, another adept staring straight into the camera, this one on Vanguard's shoulder.

"You getting this?" Battalion asked.

"*Ay*-ffirmative," Fade drawled.

"Yes!" said Hush. At the sound of his voice Battalion turned his way, as if simply to hear him threatened her composure.

"What's that?" A voice off-screen.

Hush and Fade watched intently, but robbed of their other senses they couldn't properly divine what was going on, what sudden change had gripped the soldiers. Fade toggled impatiently from one feed to the next—at least five of the Order bore shoulder cams—and every expression was the same: tense, anxious, apprehensive.

There was nothing to see… Yet still Hush suffered a terrible sense of foreboding. It was all he could do to stop himself from jumping up and running until his lungs burst.

All eyes were turned skyward, waiting for the clouds to boil black and spit forth nightmarish needles. There *were* clouds, but they were fluffy and benign, as common and unassuming as clouds could be. Little else stirred the perfect calm of the sky, save for the careless spiralling of a kestrel, soaring on the heat currents, peering for its breakfast, blissfully oblivious to invasion or sorcery or fear. The miserly sunlight glinted off an array of moon-lenses ranked across the mouth of the valley. The day seemed to hold its breath. All was still.

But there was something wrong.

From one of the hilltop remotes Fade and Hush looked down upon the village. Fade used his touchpad to close in, the image blurring as the focus struggled to keep up with his rapid zoom. When it finally did sharpen, they divined a transformation which those on the ground simply hadn't the detachment to see: the buildings were *shimmering*.

Essentially the scene was exactly as it had been, but now the buildings seemed to be possessed of a stinging, shivering animation. The whole place had taken on an artificial sheen.

The village hadn't moved, but *something else* was taking its place.

"Something's happened to the village," Fade said. Microphones around the screen picked up his voice and sprang it, echoing, across the valley.

Vanguard answered instantly. "What?"

"Not sssuuure," Fade drawing out the word out with the thought. "Something we've missed? Nothing visible, and yet…"

"I don't detect anything. The sensor stacks show nothing, and the wards haven't been triggered. There's no sign of incursion at all." Hush imagined the red-clad tyrant narrowing her eyes.

"But we trust our instincts, right?" Fade's tone held a trace of cynicism, but perhaps translation through the com system would bleed it away.

"Of course," Vanguard said. "Vigilance is our guiding principle. First circle company, prepare to engage the enemy on my mark. Focus the lenses—"

Her voice cut off abruptly. In the control room Hush felt tension radiating from the speakers.

Fade switched to a shoulder cam. Its operator was looking down at her feet. There, the grass was alive, crawling and flailing, twisting in all directions, ignorant of breeze or weight or physics. Each individual blade was electrified with a shocking vitality.

Click. Another shoulder cam view showed a row of plants which seemed to be *stiffening* without altering their shape or texture. They became green knives. It was like watching a transparent bath fill up with water. But there was no discernible sign of what was actually happening, only a sixth-sense gooseflesh piss shiver to betray the silent invasion.

"What the hell?" Hush said.

"Exactly," Fade whispered.

"Last time they came from the sky. I was there. The sky fell in on us."

"Not this time."

"No!" Hush gasped. He leaned across and stabbed a key on Fade's touchpad. The view jumped three more times before he located Vanguard, doggedly glaring upward while all those around her stared at their feet, at the lawn and the flowers drizzled with traitorous dew.

"Vanguard," Hush said. "The incursion is different this time.

They're infiltrating via a different route. Not from the sky, but from *below*. Bridgeheads burrowing up from the core. The lenses may not work. The wards you've set might not even pick them up!"

"Something Lila told you?" Vanguard snapped, paranoid even *in extremis*.

"No! It's a trick. So obvious that I can't believe we never thought of it—"

Those were the last words Vanguard ever heard.

She had *changed*.

In her place was a shape that looked like Vanguard, a thing that possessed all of her physical attributes: the towering height; the plastic-pink scars; the sour matriarch's sneer. But her eyes had turned black, as if she'd been filled up with something that had drowned out the light once and for all. The night leaked from her pupils. It spilled down her cheeks and spider-webbed across her face, fingering into her mouth to prise apart her lips and manoeuvre her tongue, operate her voice box.

*Hush*, she croaked, and it was Maria's voice. *Now we are one.*

Vanguard had become a bridgehead for the enemy.

At that moment instinct took over for someone and a shotgun roared. The report through the speakers was deafening. On-screen, Vanguard's head detonated beneath the hail of pellets, but instead of brains and skull, only darkness spilled out. It splashed across the lens of the shoulder cam, and when Fade desperately switched to a more distant feed all they could see was a pool of blackness spewing from the shattered thing that had been Vanguard, the Suzerain of the Order, their mentor and mother. Spreading, spreading…

"And now it all goes dark," Fade said.

Off-screen, the screaming began.

## 23. A Multitude of Sins

It was Bosch and Géricault, Romero and King, Greenaway and snuff TV. Every nightmare Hush had ever suffered. It was each horrific memory from his new-found past. It was all of those things and more, balled together, sharpened to a point and stabbed through the back of his eyes to pierce his brain. It pinned him to his seat so that all he could do was stare in horror, unable to turn away or hide his eyes. He could only watch. He wasn't there, he couldn't help.

Hush sat in the basement control room of the empty hotel, Fade by his side, and watched the Multitude crush their defences like a giant kicking sandcastles aside. Slowly but surely, the valley cradling Village Zero was being transformed into the landscape that had haunted his dreams for so long: *Boundless glossy black plains. Chitinous causeways. Moist weeping constructions of glassy resin. An infinite tide of squirming maggots.*

A sky that seethed, a land that *breathed.*

Fade toggled feverishly from camera to camera, as if seeking to confuse the situation on purpose. Hush flashed him a sidelong glance and noted the set of his jaw. His wide eyes glimmered with satisfaction, his eternal cynicism proved right after all.

"Vanguard's dead!" One wild-eyed adept screamed, shaking the shoulders of whomever wore the camera and sending the image into queasy sea sick rolls. "She's dead. Gone. What do we do? What the fuck—" The adept's cheeks were speckled with blood.

"Calm down!" the camera-wearer shouted, and Hush recognised Battalion's voice. He leaned forward to talk to her, but before he could speak Fade had switched to another feed. Hush opened his mouth to berate his companion, then caught sight of the nightmare revealed by the camera's eye. His mouth remained open, his jaw slackened, a line of saliva swung down onto his chest.

"Out of the ground," he said, though the observation was redundant.

From the heights above Village Zero it was obvious what was happening. The sky was calm and unruffled, while the ground had turned black; here and there great glassy mounds rose into the air, like volcanoes formed over the space of seconds. The Multitude's poison bled from the summits of these mounds and poured down the sides, where it rooted itself then stretched out into vile gloom-flecked configurations.

Isolated members of the Order darted here and there, while one group of adepts made a determined stand against the boundary wall of the village cemetery. Their moon-lenses, previously directed skyward, were now focused on the ground. Pulses of blue light jumped and jerked, riding the black waves and then dissipating into impotent afterglows. Globular forms converged on the cemetery group, nudging their way closer and closer in spite of the combined efforts of the adepts. With seconds of life left two of the Order gave up on their cantrips and resorted to more traditional ordnance. The sound of their machine pistols over the speakers was like chunks of wood popping repeatedly in a fire grate. The bullets ricocheted into rainbow patterns as they glanced off the churning hides of the enemy.

The wall behind the group suddenly changed from grey to midnight black as another incursion point bloomed, and they were subsumed by the greedy void.

Other lenses still blazed at the sky, wasting energy. They succeeded only in scalding the clouds, which in turn drew down a steaming curtain of rain. Fade switched to a shoulder cam and Hush gasped at what it showed; even Fade was shocked, his swivel chair shunting back from the console as his legs jerked.

The view was skewed because the owner was lying prone, dead. Black shapes darted about on the screen, massing around the corpse, which was cloudy one moment, sharp and shining the next, throbbing with seams and braids of electric blue. Blood sprayed, and an arm was lifted very carefully, then laid to one side.

"We've got to help!" Hush shouted. "We can't just sit here, we can't..."

The camera lurched as another severed arm came into view, then the shimmering entity unzipped down the centre to allow more darting shapes egress. These smaller things — shadows within shadows, fluttering like black moths in a darkened room — went about flensing the flesh of the corpse's arms.

"Who is it?" Hush asked desperately. "Who is it?"

A sick submarine illumination vibrated over the action, shining in from some unseen source. Its acidic glow made events even harder to follow. The darting, cutting creatures — if creatures is what they were — flashed again, and a decapitated head came into view, mouth wide with shock, neck a ragged trailing root with several inches of spinal pegs hanging down below. Its long hair was clotted with blood and crawling with glittering things—

"Battalion!" Hush bellowed.

"No," said Fade, and switched their view again.

"It was, it was her. I'm sure—"

"No. Here. There she is, look."

The screen displayed the parked cars and vans which were being systematically dismantled by demented invisible mechanics. Bodywork was removed, shells gutted, engines stripped. With all the parts laid out on the grass swarms of minute cutters flickered in to sunder those parts down into yet smaller fractions.

"Now!" a voice said quietly, close by. *Battalion.*

The screen was flash-fried by a bolt of ghastly light, its afterimage burned onto Hush's eyes for long seconds. After his vision returned he discovered the image on the screen skittering and jerking madly. He thought for a terrible second that Battalion had been caught by invisible claws and was being held aloft, shredded by cutters right there in front of him. Then he realised that she was only running, the camera jarred by her frantic footfalls. There were others running with her, too; he could see their shadows on either side, hear their panting. They were headed for the vans — or what was left of them, at least — and the squirming, barely visible thing lying amidst the wreckage.

"Battalion, that's one of them," Hush said.

The image levelled as Battalion pulled up short. "I thought it was one of their probes," she panted through the speakers.

"No," Hush continued. Memory had scorched the truth into his mind. "I saw them. That's one. It's a small one, but it's one."

In the wreckage the clotted air flexed in upon itself, gaining weight again, regaining strength.

"Fuck." Battalion began to walk forward to confront the enemy, stare directly into its face — if face it had — before she and her team finished it, or sent it back, or did whatever they could to stop it. The ambient illumination lowered, green mould darkening, a sickness infecting the air.

Battalion reached the wreck.

The camera went dead.

Hush shouted, "Fade!"

"I know!" Fade's fingers rippled over the pad, pulling up view after view. There were only four cameras left now, two on the hillside, two down in the fray. Both of those latter feeds spun and shook incomprehensibly. The control room echoed to yells and piercing screams, hopeless wails from the heart of battle.

Explosions. Terrible roars as the air was ripped asunder by the Multitude; a crashing *whoomph* as a van burst into flame; the scream of a hand-held rocket launcher firing directly into the centre of the ruined church; a graceful arc of smoke and flame as a car was lifted and thrown three hundred feet into the air, a burning shape falling from it, arms still thrashing as the ground sucked it down.

One face in close-up. Silent tableau, audio pick-up all shot to hell. Open wounds bled across features made androgynous by fear and damage as he or she screamed, shouted, raged against what was happening.

"The end," Fade said tonelessly.

"Quell's dead!" a voice cried from the speakers. "All of them, all her crew gone. Gone!"

"What about Battalion?" someone else demanded.

"Battalion!" Hush hammered at the walls, maddened by his impotence. But no one answered him.

He flipped between images and the view shuffled in and out, back and forth between the two remaining remote cams. All the shoulder cams were gone, but there *was* still a sound feed issuing weakly from the speakers.

"Hush?" Battalion said suddenly. There were other screams around her, but her voice was surprisingly controlled. "Hush? Hush?"

"I'm here," he gasped, shocked by the depth of his relief. "I'm right here, B. Now look, there's—"

"Hush?" she said again.

"Battalion? I hear you. Get out, come back. Get away—"

"Hush, my love, if you can hear me, if you can—"

"Battalion! No, come back, don't fade away, fight, fight!"

Nothing more. No other sound. Just a single view from one of the remote cameras:

The whole valley was a reservoir of churning darkness now, nodes reaching up to mate with the black funnels that were coiling down from the pin cushion sky. One of the flat-bed trucks was making a valiant attempt to climb out of the morass, but sly tendrils of midnight swirled after it and wrapped themselves around its wheels, melting the rubber to the road. After that it only took a heartbeat for an incursion point to open beneath the stranded vehicle and devour it whole. Then the feed went black.

*Click.*

Only static endured, chuckling at them. There was no more.

"She's gone," Fade said without inflection.

"No!"

Fade looked at him directly for the first time since they had entered the control room. His face and his eyes were grey.

"Face it. The Order is finished. Vanguard is dead. Battalion is dead. There's only one option left."

"What?"

Fade glanced at the sculpture on the wall and darted his hand towards it. A blue spark jumped the gap, sending the sculpture into serpentine revolutions on its pedestal.

Hush felt a subharmonic vibration conducted through the stone to his heels. It set his teeth on edge. Fade looked at him again, and the light was back behind his face: the light at the end of everything. He grinned a rapturous smile.

"Brave new world," he said.

"Brave new *bullshit*. Battalion isn't dead. I know she isn't."

"Don't worry," Fade whispered with a secret smile. "You'll taste her again. I promise."

Hush despaired. Fade's mind had clearly snagged on the horror and been ripped clean away. His madness was palpable, burning up beneath the skin. Now, though, it hardly seemed to matter. Humanity was done for whether Fade was a loon or not.

Fade indicated the sculpture, which was even now throwing out feral shadows in direct contradiction to its apparent dimensions. "This is a portal to the Lower Archives. From there we can make our way straight back to the mansion."

"And there, the Weapon?"

"Ahhhh," Fade said. "Yes. You understand."

Hush chewed on his lip and the sour taste of despair for long seconds before making his decision. He still did not truly know what the

Weapon was, but when there was no other choice…

He nodded. "Let's get on with it."

**

The Lower Archive, the library beyond the veil, has as much in common with a common book depository as an abacus does with Einstein's brain.

If the Multiverse was a vast ocean — studded with universes like islands — then the Lower Archive existed somewhere beneath those waves, embedded in the silt and darkness of the transdimensional seabed. Its physical laws were the exact opposite of those in the light universe, and inimical to life. From a certain perspective the Lower Archive could almost be perceived as being *built* out of anti-life: galleries hewn from concentrated death, oubliettes, promontories, mansions, dungeons. Withered colours like time flaking away, graveyard textures, corpse-lamps.

It was fatal to visit the Archive unprepared, and perilous to use it even if you were. The Order had discovered its existence accidentally, through a fortuitous misreading of the Book of Eibon, and had both revered and feared it ever since.

The reason this zone was so important was simple: it formed a sink-hole for the Multiverse. Echoes and reverberations of all information — all learning, all the thoughts of the countless trillions of conscious beings who ever inhabited the infinite dimensions — all drained down, through long aeons, into the Archive world. The echoes collected there, like a vast sump tank of thought. They sank into the necrotic fabric of the Archive, and imprinted themselves. Though the experience of reading them was nightmarish, it was also priceless.

Still, even in the Order few dared to visit this most terrible of oracles, and then only during periods of direst necessity. The Archive left its mark on a person. If you lived at all, it *scarred.*

Remarkably, both Hush and Fade were veterans of the Archive. But this was no fleeting visit to snatch eldritch titbits. They were actually using the Archive to move from one location to another. Fade was navigating, so the burden was far harsher on him, but Hush suffered too. Oh how he suffered.

His eyes weren't working and his body felt like it was crumbling and drowning and being crushed all at once. The pressure was like an invisible vice the size of Chicago pressing down on him, and he seemed to be experiencing the bends whilst undergoing major stomach surgery without anaesthetic. Light made of screams buffeted him. His blood begged for relief, while his liquefied brain pumped sluggishly through his veins. His heart hid in his bowels, blackened and vitrified. Agony gushed and giggled, gushed and giggled…

Then his human senses returned, and he discovered a reasonably normal second-storey room sitting around him. Then he fainted.

**

When Hush eventually came to, he couldn't put a figure on how long he'd been unconscious. They were back in the Order's mansion, but inside one of the inner suites far from any natural light source. However, based on the stiffness in his side and back, he suspected he could have been out for many hours, perhaps even the whole day. He checked himself for other after-effects of his journey through the Lower Archive and found — *miraculously* — that he was unharmed.

Fade, though, had not been so lucky: he was supine a few feet off, his face drawn and pale, mottled with dark patches. He looked prematurely aged, haggard way beyond his years. His breathing came in feeble pulses. Hush dragged his unconscious companion across the tiled floor and sat him upright in an armchair. Abruptly, he felt eyes upon him and spun round.

Maria and Lila were standing in the corner. Lila hugged her close, but Maria was stiff as a board, as if she could barely stand the contact. She shook her head as Lila whispered something in her ear. She stared at Hush, a desperate plea in her eyes, even as she mouthed the familiar litany.

*Now we are one.*

Hush swayed backward and landed on his arse. Fade groaned in his sleep. Apart from that the room was silent. Nevertheless Hush's senses were under assault.

Lila ran her hand across Maria's breasts, apparently startling the woman, who turned to stare at her. The Nexus pounced on this advantage. Grabbing Maria's cheeks, she spoke slowly and gently into her face (although Hush couldn't hear a word). Hush saw Maria's eyes widen… realisation slotting into place… and then Lila kissed her full on the mouth. She cupped the older woman's head, fingers in her hair, and pressed her whole body into the embrace, soft curve fluted against curve.

The strangest thing was that Maria no longer resisted. It was as if she had fallen into a swoon or a trance.

Lila tilted her head, and moved her mouth with passion, obviously using her tongue, but gently. Only there was something wrong. Somehow, subtly, and despite all the surface implication, this was not a sexual act. Perhaps it was *intended* to be, but there was something missing, some essential component of living human vitality which was utterly absent from this act he was watching.

And then he had it: it was like watching someone who had learned to kiss from a diagram. Someone who had the moves down pat, but didn't understand any of the emotion that lay behind the gesture.

The girl broke off from Maria and turned slowly towards him, as if sensing his presence for the first time. Her eyeballs were entirely black. Her down-turned mouth and slack snarl spoke of something unspeakable: an appetite, monstrous and insatiable. A desire too alien for his small speck of consciousness to comprehend. A hunger that — given enough leash — might devour all eternity.

Hush let out a startled exclamation, he couldn't help it. Neither woman reacted, but he did succeed in bringing Fade around, just for a moment. As the silver-haired man woke, so the two women faded, dispersing into the air rather than simply vanishing— a silent puff of motes bursting into nothing.

"They're close," Hush said. "I can feel it." Fade attempted to haul himself to his feet, but then fell back into the chair, defeated. His eyes rolled up in his head, unconscious again.

Hush ran from the room, glancing back all the way. A part of him longed to see Maria again, but not like this. Never like this. Maybe Battalion would have joined them next time, in the foul embrace…

He shuddered to a halt, squeezed his eyes shut and stood panting in the corridor. He could smell the stench of old fires. The air was cold, slow and stale. Somewhere close by water was dripping, while a faint breeze blew through the dilapidated corridors.

He needed to know what was happening, how near the danger loomed. Should he try to contact the authorities? Get Scotland evacuated? He imagined a map of the world, with a malevolent whirl of darkness expanding out from Village Zero, wider and wider, faster and faster, until it engulfed the globe.

Was the Weapon their only hope? Did it crouch nearby, swathed in shadows?

Hush stepped through an open doorway to his left. He was confronted by a scene of such normality that it made him weak. He felt a swooning nostalgia for childhood times, even if those moments had been manufactured by sorcery. It was a bedroom.

A narrow shelf of books lined one wall, tattered Athena posters of whales and dolphins dotted another. Clothes were scattered across the bed, shoes tucked underneath. Washing hung from the radiator, dry and crusty like desiccated lizard skins. On a corner shelf sat a television. Hush switched it on and immediately began to cry.

An Australian soap flashed images of shiny teeth and tight bodies across the screen — all waiting to be extinguished. On another channel a group of volunteers frantically tried to whitewash someone's house before they came home from shopping — soon, everything would be black. All the shows were normal, usual, everyone carrying on in blissful ignorance, pacing around inside the white picket fences of their lives. Birds were singing outside, clouds drifting. All of it useless now, all redundant.

Tears rolled down Hush's cheeks but he barely felt them. Ten minutes passed, twenty? He cried intermittently. An autonomic response.

On Ceefax there was a vague news item about some freak weather system which had knocked out power and telephone lines in Scotland. Rumours brewing. The first storm warnings.

"Oh, the humanity," the snake suddenly hissed from the doorway. "Tears of a clown."

Hush didn't feel the need to answer. "Where's the Weapon?" he demanded, roughing away his tears. He clicked the television off.

Fade was leaning against the door jamb, shaking and sweating. Blood dripped from one eye. "Follow me."

"Lead the way."

"Better still, help me. I don't think I can walk."

"Yet you can still talk. Shame."

They stumbled slowly through the mansion, a cold arching tomb. Hush breathed shallowly and listened for any signs of disturbance from outside. When he realised he could not hear *anything*, he took this as a bad omen. He left Fade propped against a wall and dashed over to a window.

Everything appeared normal. Sparrows rooted beneath hedges for worms, a flock of starlings flitted from one bush to another. In the distance Hush could make out a row of hills, and he imagined the blackness washing up against their hidden flanks like a sea waiting to rush in and drown the world.

Then he heard the engine.

"Come on," Fade muttered, but Hush ignored him. A car was approaching, splitting the silence with its drone, crunching onto the driveway from the main road.

The motor sounded as if it were labouring desperately, and as the vehicle pulled into view Hush could see why. It was a big Mercedes, its bodywork mortally abused, black paint ferociously stripped and scorched. One wing had been completely ripped off. The windows, too, were all smashed, and the driver was squinting against the afternoon sun. Battalion!

"Oh, my God! Fade, Battalion's back. She made it, she's back!"

His relief was extraordinary and dazzling. He spun round to find that Fade had dragged himself off somewhere, like a cockroach with its hindquarters crushed. Hush didn't care. He scurried around like a trapped rat until he found a staircase, then descended quickly and ran to the entrance hall. He remembered the last time he had been here— the scorched walls throbbed with vile memories, hidden away in petrified depths. But all he cared about now was Battalion.

He sprinted down the engraved approach corridor to fling open the front door. "You're alive!"

Battalion pushed past him. "Where's Fade?"

"B, I thought you were dead. I saw, I heard you—"

"Hush, there's no time! There's no fucking time!" Tears stung clean paths down her filthy cheeks. Her eyes blazed. "It's all ending, dying," she said. "We couldn't hold them off. Couldn't make a dent. *Everyone's* gone. There's no time for anything now, but... The Weapon."

She turned and ran upstairs. Hush followed. He didn't know what else to do. Halfway up the stairway a painting was squirming in its frame, images of Lila and Maria leering out at him as they hugged each other, heads and lips together. *Now we are one.*

"Whatever," Hush said, and passed them by.

**

In the distance they could hear it. Silence. The erasure of everything. Tick-tock, tick-tock. The slow creeping clock.

Battalion and Hush stood at an open window, and he recognised for the first time how much background noise nature provided. It was an understanding which only truly hit home when you could no longer hear it. It was as if the landscape were being rubbed out, starting in the distance and then blurring inwards, closer and closer. No more engine sounds. Only a few birds still singing. No breeze, no wind, no hum of summer air. Nothing, save for the beating of their hearts.

"They're coming," Battalion said.

"Here? They know we're here?"

She would not catch his eye. Perhaps she thought it would erode her resolve. "No, everywhere. We're just in the way."

**

They found Fade hunched over a tea chest in the corner of a disused store-room. He appeared on the verge of death, but was still laughing, ragged shaking heaves, blood pulsing out onto his chin. His hair was falling out.

"Still here?" he asked as he saw Battalion.

"Fade, what needs to be done?"

"Needs?" he sighed wetly. "Done? Nothing."

"We have to prime it," she said.

More gurgled sobs as laughter.

"Maria tells me that they are one," Hush said suddenly. The two women were sitting in the corner of the room, whispering to him. Their voices appeared inside his head like unconscious memories, but they were definitely there.

"Nobody's won," Fade giggled. "Look—"

With great effort he slid from the tea chest and lifted the lid.

A green glow sprang from inside and set the room abuzz. Hush felt a sensation like locusts in the skull, skittering across the backs of your eyes. Brainpan timpani, desiccated carapaces, rustling forever.

"Huh?" Hush said.

"Vanguard," Battalion whispered. "She set it going anyway. She knew we'd never win, so she set it going anyway."

Hush understood at once, because he suddenly understood Vanguard. More wise than they ever could have imagined. Less human.

"Now we are one," he whispered as he gazed into the chest and the heart of the alien light.

## 24. And This, at Least, Is Hell

Jacob watched the television impassively.

On the screen, without much fuss, the Multitude was devouring Newcastle.

This was the first time he had watched the enemy work with anything approaching objectivity. He'd never been to the city, nor knew anyone who lived there. Sometime good football team, friendly accent, unemployment, Robson Green. He wished — with an unexpected stab of regret — that he'd bothered to find out more about this place when it was alive. Made a real attempt to know its ways, its people, its dirt and humour, its bars and beer and beauty. Maybe lived there for a year or two. Got close to as many of its diverse souls as possible, so he could properly mourn their passing.

He was dimly aware that he was romanticising the city's plight, and that the same lousy platitudes could have been regurgitated for any town. There was something wrong with him, and he couldn't blame it simply on television's aloofness. Millions of people were about to perish in frightful agony, and yet all he could feel was vaguely nostalgic. The *utchat* eye.

Is this how a sociopath felt, or only someone who knew that they were truly about to die? Throughout history, he wondered, how many observers had understood — with absolute and irrefutable certainty — that they were living in the end times? That their particular way of life — culture, empire and all — was about to be extinguished forever? Was he the first? It was a strange burden.

In the end, though, as hateful as it was, his detachment from Newcastle was useful: he could concentrate on the enemy in ways he never had before. It was a sobering experience. He watched human civilisation teeter on the precipice.

First, the alien thunderhead crawled into view. Over agonising minutes it ate up the sky, hovering on a slim rind of pale light, the gap between horizon and cloud stack. It resembled some vast spacecraft carved out of serpents' entrails, a mammoth ponderous chevron, blood-dark, convoluted like brain tissue. The great crescent of the Tyne Valley was laid out beneath it, a panoramic slice of the city in tiers. Streets dashed through that haphazard grid, while the stubby robot fingers of office blocks ruled the skyline. Here and there Gothic spears of older architecture — clock towers, churches — broke up the machine a little, and out on the western horizon squatted terraced houses, laid out as long diagonal slashes.

Now darkness hooded the city like a death shroud.

A scattering of lights came on in office windows as people mistook the coming of the Multitude for a summer squall, bright pixels spilling out ignorance across the metropolis. Vehicles braked and car horns hooted. Gradually, however, people began to detect that something was amiss. Drivers stood by their rides, necks craning back for a view. Windows opened. Small crowds formed.

The light over Newcastle changed as vents opened in the thunderhead, and the first aerial incursion points blossomed. Green effulgence crowded into the valley, travelling east to west, syrupy like sap. This was a revelation for Hush, a clue to the mind of the hive: he had always assumed that the Multitude groped after prey as a blind dumb beast might, devouring anything unlucky enough to find itself within those mindless jaws. But this new vantage point gave the lie to that. There was method to this assault, an orderly deployment. A warlike intelligence directed these forces.

Hush knew that, had he been on the ground, he could not have recognised this. He recalled with a sick thrill what it had been like to cower beneath that cloud bank, to be aware of the vast gaze which waited behind it: the consciousness he had brushed up against in their citadel, a thing so immense that it rivalled the universe. He could never have understood any of its strategies whilst exposed to that devastating cosmic indifference. He shuddered, but he felt a sombre sense of satisfaction, of vindication.

Now the invaders began to rain down. The elongated mouths of incursion points drooped free of the vortex, shivered, then spat forth their deadly teardrops. The resinous bridgeheads crushed everything below them, demolishing the gutted shell of the Baltic Flour Mill before it ever had the chance to reopen as an arts complex, pulverising the executive delights of the Malmaison Hotel.

Teal sparks skittered from alien spire to alien spire, like anarchistic ball lightning. It made the whole scene appear to be suffering from St Vitus's dance, and it was impossible to look at it without tempting a migraine. Minute figures were lit up by photo-negative bursts, arms outstretched, heads thrown back in terror. The palsied light made them seem to jig out a danse macabre. Hush thought of X-rays, Chemical Brothers' videos. The skull beneath the skin.

One by one the bridges spanning the river were engulfed: Redheugh, High Level, Swing, then the Tyne Bridge itself cracked in two, its arch falling to oblivion. Soon — as in Village Zero — incursion spikes began to stab upwards from the ground, ripping through flesh and soil, transforming the streets into a vista of black barbs and potholes.

In contrast to the battle for Village Zero, Newcastle's demise was mercifully swift. Already, multiple bridgeheads had rooted themselves in the ruins of the Quayside. One hunched among the smouldering wreck of the Law Courts, surrounded by heaps of scorched stick people scattered like fallen matches. Another glassy bulk had splashed into the river and was polluting the water with its seed; waves sloshed onto the riverside, drenching some of the remaining survivors with green-threaded acid. Invisible entities blew forth from the depths amidst detonations of foul spray. Tides of scrabbling insect things stirred up the riverbed, sending rotten tyres and shopping trolleys bobbing to the surface. The water boiled audibly, screams raped the air. All the while, the Multitude itself remained hideously dumb.

Panic had quickly gripped the city's populace, sparking off feeble escape bids, over bridges on foot or by wheels along the urban motorway. All were doomed. Hush knew it was best not to dwell on their fates; instead, he needed to focus on the other clues, the fresh observations that the nightmare was providing.

Most puzzling to Hush was the apparent *curiosity* of the enemy. In fact, the "mood" of their attack was all wrong. Time after time the invaders would pass up a chance at full-on destruction in favour of more morbid, yet delicate experiments. The behaviour of the sentient clusters, in particular, was marked by an almost pathological tidiness, as they used the cutters to perform procedures that were more akin to surgery than military strikes.

Not only humans and animals were being sampled. Everything from traffic lights to babies' buggies to hot dog stands was being examined, played with, tested to destruction, then filed away. Macabre hybrids were attempted: motorbikes combined with cats' heads; pub walls threaded with blood vessels; telegraph poles given human teeth.

It was as though they were *searching* for something, prospecting for gold, or carefully brushing away topsoil to try to reveal buried runes. The destruction of the human race seemed almost incidental, as if the world was just one big Petri dish for the Multitude. They were Nazi behaviourists, killing what they probed. In his mind Hush found himself transported back to the time when he had "rescued" Lila. He recalled all those fastidiously arranged body parts on the mansion's floorboards, graded like samples, lacking only name tags. Maybe he'd been right to imagine the mansion's assailant as a bespectacled professor, absent-mindedly rooting through the human ruins?

By this point in the proceedings the thunderhead itself had undergone new innovations, becoming translucent in sections along its flanks. These translucent regions were something like windows, veils of radiant smog behind which huge shadows toiled. Hush thought he could see vast mechanisms wheeling there, living cogs the size of city blocks, mysterious pylon-shapes that spun and spun forever, bloody pistons… He quickly averted his gaze lest the cosmic vertigo take him.

South of the river — if you could still call that stripe of swarming slag a river — Gateshead burned. To the north the decimated foundations of Newcastle lived again: the air *seethed*. Reality was being atomised before his eyes, scoured away, layer by layer. Flensed. But the individual particles were not destroyed— they were being liberated. Every lost crumb of Newcastle was swept up into that milling continuum — the infinite machine — and put to work again in its endless dance of renewal. The human universe was simply being transformed into one new annexe to their domain— that place which had haunted his dreams for fifteen years…

Roughly three hundred thousand people had lived in Newcastle Upon Tyne.

Incredibly, Hush thought that all of this seemed somehow familiar, like some hand-me-down story he'd once been told in a pub years ago. He thought that if he could just remember how the story ended, then he might be able to stop it from happening again.

Abruptly, he felt a shiver of *déjà vu.* Empires falling. Again. *Now we are one.* How apt. Out on the periphery of his vision he could see the spectres of Maria and Lila whispering together confidentially, throwing him the odd unreadable glance. He shifted his gaze a little to take them in more clearly, but suddenly they were gone — *snip* — as if time had stuttered. A clumsy jump-cut in reality. He blinked.

A second later he heard a scraping behind him as Battalion forced her way into the room; they were holed up in one of the fire-damaged regions of the mansion, and the door had warped grotesquely in its frame. In keeping with the inexplicable capriciousness of the forces ranged against them, however, the room itself was untouched save for a slight charring to the carpet. It crunched underfoot like cinder toffee.

Battalion dumped a haversack of grenades onto the floor. As she did so she caught sight of the screen.

"That live?"

Jacob didn't turn. "No. 'Bout an hour old. Sky just keeps on looping the footage like they don't know what else to do."

"Maybe they don't."

"No programmes, no announcements, just that… boom… boom… boom."

"Perhaps I should try to get through to the PM again?"

Jacob snorted. "Bit late. Saw the whole cabinet jet out of a private airfield a few minutes after Edinburgh bit the dust." He shrugged. "Well, the bastards don't know there's nowhere to run, let's at least be charitable. Maybe they've got good intentions. A war room somewhere to co-ordinate the resistance. Our plucky counterstrike."

He trailed off, and wondered if the ice around his heart was going to kill him before the Multitude did. Could you numb yourself to death? Would his heart valves get plugged with emotional cotton wool? And to think that mere days ago he had been almost uncontrollably ardent, willing to battle for any righteous cause. Starting brawls over the right to roam, for fuck's sake!

"Are we going to fight?"

Hush turned at the hip to look at Battalion directly for the first time since she had returned. Something flared behind the ice. He grinned.

"Hell, why not?"

**

In the disused storeroom Fade had his cheek on the filthy floor beside the tea chest. He was smiling weakly, his body slack like an empty grain sack. The gloom danced with gleeful shadows cast by the Weapon's sickly glory.

"Fade, we're going to mount a last stand," Hush said quietly from the doorway.

The silver-haired sorcerer chuckled, slugs of blood curled on his lower lip. His eyes gleamed with a terminal glaze.

"If that amuses you."

Hush tapped out a count of ten in his head before continuing.

"We could really use your help."

Fade didn't hesitate with his reply. "I think not."

Hush lowered his eyes. "Very well. Really, all I wanted to do was make my peace with you. Go well, Fade."

Amazingly, Fade seemed touched. He struggled into a pose where he could hold his old enemy within his gaze. A beat of understanding — of old wisdom — leapt the gap between them. Fade made a crisp salute.

"Go well, Hush."

**

Hush found Battalion in the conservatory, fortifying wards at the bay windows. She made flickering motions in the air with her darting fingertips, sketching air diagrams. A glance acknowledged her lover's return.

"I think I've worked out a way to hold them off— reflection glamours," she said with a narrowed gaze as she closed the loop on her final cantrip. A ward pulled tight and the window pane flashed. Next instant a mirrored glaze throbbed in the frame, sealed across the fragile glass. By now all the windows were protected by these slabs of compressed reality.

Hush smiled slowly, caught off guard by her outrageous invention *in extremis*. He barked out a laugh. "Clever. Use their own power against them. That's brilliant!"

She nodded curtly, pleased. But, a beat later, the doubt seemed to swamp her. "I feel like a shadow," she confessed, and shivered violently. "I don't feel like I'm really here any more, really alive." A whisper hissed from between her chapped lips. "Shades against the storm."

Hush put a hand on her shoulder. He tried to will his support down through his palm, causing it to radiate through her like waves of heat conducted along her veins. He didn't use sorcery; his simple touch seemed to calm her, as it had years ago, and she looked up at him, and to him. Her mouth was a grim, determined streak.

"Come on," Hush murmured. "We've got lots more to do before they arrive."

**

They worked in strict sequence, erecting a succession of defensive "shells", each tucked within the previous one, like Russian dolls.

This meant that they could collapse a new protective partition behind them each time they were forced to retreat — progressively deeper and deeper into the bowels of the mansion — thereby sealing off another layer for the Multitude to breech. These were not physical barriers, but intricately woven casements of sorcery: cantrips and wards and glamours, double-spun, threaded with counter-castings and reinforced by fearsome pan-dimensional booby-traps. Whole corridors were shifted out of phase with this universe, while some doors ported directly into the horrendous Lower Archive. Casting sigils glittered from every surface, every skirting board, every cornice— a fan of touch-smells and taste-colours when you walked by. At regular intervals they constructed foxholes, stocked with conventional arms and canisters of the necrotic dust Hush had concocted to enable adepts to survive in the Multitude universe. Cupboards, toilets and storage rooms became their hidey-holes.

Even before their preparations the mansion had been a distinctly creepy domain, scarred and blackened by fire damage, corridors crusted with mouldlike carbon. Now it felt positively macabre. The air was coated in magic, thick and slippery like sap.

Despite the fact that any conventional barricade would present little obstacle to their enemy, Hush and Battalion decided to pile all the ground floor furniture against the main hall doors. The hope was that the sheer brute heft of so much ordinary ballast might aid their conjurations a little. In reality, there was a far more primal impulse at work: they wanted to feel safe.

It was all very well to weave spells and moonbeams against the darkness, but if you couldn't *see* what protected you, then, as a species, old fears tickled. We have an age-old urge to find a warm, dry place, somewhere to hide from the night. If the windows are boarded up, and the hatches are battened down, then you can really feel that you are ready to weather the storm.

**

Hush stepped back from his work, mind whirling like the tumblers of a fruit machine with the effort of too many non-linear calculations. He wiped his eyes and looked over at Battalion. She was slaving still, ferocious and inexhaustible, hammering nails, kneading reality.

In a strange crystalline moment — outside of time and space and pain — he saw her as she had been fifteen years ago: a nineteen-year old spoke of lightning, laughing and dancing, hair flying and slicing around her shoulders, smile like summer, like sunlight and stars. She had transformed herself by force of will into this other thing, made herself into a living blade, ever-keen, never blunted. A sharp edge where a person used to be. It was a curious reflection, and yet somehow incredibly *human.* What she had decided to do for love… for him.

Why didn't they just lie down to die like Fade? What was so stubborn about humans that they wouldn't give up even when all hope was extinguished? They wasted energy, resources, courting only agony and a slow death. What hard dumb nub sat at their core and refused to be worn away? Animals didn't fight when there was nothing left to fight for, no young left to defend. Badgers didn't rage against the dying of the light, so why should they? Finally, it was all down to a handful of abstract ideals tied into the fleshy knots of their freakish, overgrown brains.

Abstract ideals had driven humans since the beginning of time. They were responsible for so much that was noble, weird and splendid in the world. Sure, humans had butchered each other, and oppressed each other, and cheated each other on behalf of those ideals. But still, those ideals had sent humans into space, allowed them to search the stars and planets. Forced them to scour the deepest nooks and crannies of the world, to peer back into history. Abstract ideals had forged beauties untold.

He thought about his friends, his comrades, the Order. He thought about Vanguard and Maria. He thought about Battalion— the fierce girl, the proud woman. He even thought about Fade.

A curious satisfaction settled around his heart. In the end, after all was said and done, the human race had not made such a bad fist of its tenure on Earth.

"Battalion?" he hollered across the ruined hallway.

Battalion worked the slide on her 9mm. "Ready," she confirmed. Her left eyelid twitched.

"Let's go take some air, then," Hush said mildly. They walked together towards the last daylight streaming in.

**

Outside, the day was beautiful enough to make the heart falter. The sky was an unblemished sheet of sapphire, the sun an orb of molten gold. Flowers provided starbursts of every hue, while the sweet wind whispered through the branches of picture-perfect trees. In fact, even the trees' bark seemed more lavishly brown, more exquisitely textured — more deliciously *barky* — than ever before.

Perhaps nature was rolling out one last encore, a glorious curtain call for this show called Earth. Insects chirruped quietly, while birds still paraded their songs and colours. Cascades of melody fell through the air. Dew sparkled on the grass about their feet, brilliant and unashamed. Hush and Battalion stood side by side at the edge of the garden, gazing out towards the moors and hills.

Hush felt fierce, good to be alive in this brief interval between one great dark and the next. So what if the light was passing? All things passed. Let them go, and rejoice. The air was balmy, blossom-scented. He breathed in deeply to savour its fragrance.

"Promise me we'll die together," Battalion said suddenly.

Hush turned to her, smiling. "Die?" he held out a palm. "We're living now together. That's all that matters."

She looked at him for a while with tears brimming in her eyes, then took his hand. Her grip was savage, biting into his skin.

In the distance the horizon began to boil.

## 25. Just Who Are the Gods?

"Shall I put a sigil on your cock?" Battalion asked. Her expression was so grave that Hush couldn't help but laugh.

"What, a Quill of Potency?"

"Stop it. I'm serious," she admonished, but he could see her brush tip was trembling as she fought not to giggle. She lost the struggle and dissolved into fits of helpless laughter.

They were both naked, cross-legged at the centre of an uneven casting spiral hastily splashed out in the least damaged corner of the hall. A plush green throw rug protected their skin from nails or splinters, and they were in the process of painting sigils on each other's bodies. For ink they used henna seeded with glittering thaumaturgical distillates, and their tools were delicate Phoenix feather brushes. In theory, the webwork of wards and glamours would serve as potent armour against any non-linear attack. In practise, the shapes were proving almost impossible to apply.

The bristles tickled like hellfire, and flesh was a desperately poor canvas for such precision draughtsmanship. Unrestrained larking about was more often than not the only result. Indeed, it was very difficult to square their jolly frolics with the spectre of their impending doom.

"You used to laugh a lot," Hush said, after they'd recovered from this most recent lapse.

"You remember?"

"I do now," he answered fondly. And it was true, he did remember. He held his past with her complete inside his mind, like a photograph lying against his hand. He could glance at it easily now, with acceptance and a new-found surge of emotions which had merely been hidden, never lost.

Yet, in reality, the photograph was more like a cheap hologram. If he tilted his past at another angle, then it flipped around to show him Maria instead, and *their* time together. Two lives beat inside him, two histories, each as real as the other, each as vivid. Hush and Jacob were entwined, a double helix, DNA strands kissing. But it was no longer a battle to see which reigned supreme. Both of his lives held equal weight in his heart. He felt centred and composed, finally at peace with his violated history. It was not often a man lived enough experiences for two.

Dingy afternoon light glinted off the arc of moon-lenses they had mounted along the landing overlooking the demolished hall. Battalion took a deep breath to compose herself, then reclaimed the brush and refreshed its tip on her tongue. Hush made an elaborate play of letting her get near him, then allowed a sly grin to spill across his features. With a filthy chuckle he lunged for her.

"Come here. If you let me shave your pubes, I can paint a tenth circle ward on your pussy and seal you up, so no one can get in and steal your honour!"

"Ouch! Get off!" she shrieked, twisting and thrashing as they both collapsed back onto the rug, which rode up in accordion ruffles beneath them. They wrestled together, Hush straining to tickle Battalion who giggled and begged for mercy, kicking out with her strong sprinter's legs, trying to throw him off. After a hectic few moments they tired, and gradually the battle died down into an affectionate embrace. Hush rested his cheek gently in the hollow of Battalion's shoulder, and they stayed that way for a while, chests heaving in time with one another, joyfully exhausted. Finally, Hush looked up at her.

"You dry yet?"

She touched her fingertips gingerly to her stomach, her breasts, tracing the symbols there. "Uh, yeh."

They sat up together and parted. Battalion frowned, dropping her gaze as if suddenly self-conscious.

"Look, Hush…," she began uncertainly. "I know you think I've changed… maybe beyond recognition—"

"I don't think you've changed at all," he contradicted softly.

She scowled, struggling with her unwieldy bundle of feelings. "But what I mean is, only… I always stayed young in here." She struck her sternum with a hollow clap. "The same person. The girl you knew. I held that part in here for you, safe from the storm… I mean, the thing is—"

She could say no more. They heard the drum-roll of thunder in the distance. The future had arrived too soon.

**

Outside the mansion, more hot rain.

A filthy, scalding torrent hurled up clots of dust to further congest their vision.

Hush and Battalion were watching the exterior through a Porthole of Scrying, which Hush had cast onto one of the larger gilt-inlaid mirrors in a first-storey bathroom. Although the image fidelity wasn't up to that of the feeds he had watched with Fade, it was adequate. They focused on the horizon.

The approach of the Multitude drove breakers of force before it. Chains of sentient clusters rolled like boulders across the chequerboard fields, an inexorable dark front sweeping in from the north. Hush and Battalion could see how the hills were being undone in the wake of this assault, scrubbed away just as the foundations of Newcastle had been, minced down smaller and smaller, shredded into garlands of living fog that fed the great vortex which followed. Funnels of teeming motes streamed backwards, upwards, venting cones of reality. From this distance the approach of the Armageddon machine looked almost sedate.

Then the tsunami struck the edge of the estate.

The effect was like the blast wave of an atomic bomb, a killing wind that tore trees, bushes, shrubs and hedges up by the roots, blasting them to burning chaff. A huge fiery hand slapped anything higher than the ground back down into the soil. In the blink of an eye, a blazing heartbeat, it drove a surf of destruction through the grounds, decimating everything in its path. Garden furniture shattered, outbuildings exploded, animals died without knowing what had hit them. A fence of fermenting blackness crowded in behind that first shock wave, flukes and tentacles groping at the house like the limbs of a monstrous squid.

Just as those feelers were about to graze the masonry, however, the image crumpled like cellophane thrown onto a fire. The porthole had ruptured.

"Hang on!" Hush bellowed. A beat later, the shock wave hit the building.

They were both pitched onto the floor, and the walls shook enough to shower them with broken glass and ceramic. But, in spite of the auxiliary damage, the integrity of the house seemed to hold.

Then the Multitude struck again.

Again.

And again…

The bathroom was being shaken apart around them. Each tooth-rattling impact added yet more chaos to the ceramic devastation.

Again and again they struck.

"They can't get in!" howled Hush exultantly. "The glamours worked!"

"But they're going to shake the mansion to pieces from under us, Hush! There's no way the structure can hold up to this battering. We'll have to let them in. It's a stand-up fight, or this is game over before it's even begun!"

Hush saw the logic of this instantly, understood how clever brute force could be. He shared a grim glance with Battalion. She looked like a warrior princess, bright sigils on her face, cheeks and brow, proud like war paint.

Hush grinned. "Then let's go make some noise."

**

The outer skin of the main hall was pierced in so many places it was like a sieve, holes stabbed repeatedly through the walls, ceiling, and floor. Puffs of ground masonry spat like talcum powder from the roof, while the floorboards had ruptured so violently it was like walking over crazy paving.

Hush and Battalion sprang to the rune-scored entrance corridor. There was a tangle of ley alignments at the foot of the inner door, and this is where they had installed their first command module. They could collapse all the external glamours from there. Hush dove down the narrow way to the barricade, while Battalion stayed by the inner door to initiate casting protocols. An intricate torque of corrugated shadows pulsed before her hands and she went to work, fingers flickering through the insubstantial convolutions, freeing up insubstantial bows and twines as quickly as she could.

At the main door Hush summoned up a Mace of Puissance, angling his face away from the fierce blaze as it flared into existence. The leprous flames whipped around furiously, licking up the walls and across the barricade, greedy for prey. The house quaked again, even more forcefully. Hush almost lost his footing.

"Come on!" he yelled.

"Done!" was the screamed reply. "Go! *Go*!"

Hush threw a globe of fringed energy at the barricade, which kicked a ragged hole straight through to the door, blasting flechettes of tinder in every direction. All the wards tied onto the barricade were broken at a swoop. Hush could sense them falling outside, too, domino-style, the glamours folding away like origami flowers.

He began to retreat. The air inside the corridor sucked in on itself, creating a pouch of intense pressure. Pain poked at Hush's inner ear. It felt like he was back-paddling underwater.

Something was eating noisily at the main door. The wood cracked, splintered, then disintegrated, giving entrance to a frenzied cloud of cutters. The tornado targeted Hush and flew for him. He made three precise signals with his left hand and triggered their first trap.

Wave fronts of lime fire *raced* along the walls, lapping into the grooves of the runes, spilling over as emerald sparks. In half a heartbeat the fire had overtaken the cutters and leapt ahead, transfixing them in a mesh of radiant threads. Hush only just managed to stumble back from the flames himself and escape, before the trap snapped shut over the mouth of the corridor. He regarded their results with savage amusement.

It was unlikely they would have been able to actually destroy any of the cutters, but this was far better. Now they were imprisoned in the midst of a matrix of reflection glamours, trapped like flies in amber. Furthermore, the web was woven in such a way that the more the cutters struggled, the tighter the net drew.

With no to time to dawdle and gloat, Hush back-peddled a few steps—

"Hush! Look out!" Battalion screamed from the landing, where she was readying the moon-lenses.

He skidded round clumsily, staggered, froze. A sentient cluster was laboriously unpacking itself out of a fording rift into the middle of the hallway. It was between him and the stairs, blocking his only escape route. The rift was a gash in space and time, leaking a misty halo of red-shifted light. Through the tear he glimpsed their teeming domain, mere feet away.

The cluster was emerging from the rift in slow peristaltic surges, unpleasantly like shit from a giant anus. Its filthy surface pulsated thickly, inky mercury squeezed into a throbbing black slug-shape. The air around the thing seemed to grow dimmer at its presence. It gurgled hungrily deep within its rolls of liquid meat. The "living blade" slopped out onto the floor, and started to singe the wood, but most of its vile bulk remained in their world, still waiting to pour through.

Regaining his wits, Hush tugged a grenade from his belt and bit away the pin. He lobbed it at the base of the rip where the transdimensional stresses were strongest. Then he ducked.

The resulting explosion visibly ballooned up through the rift, which for an instant expanded to twice its size, then dwindled at incredible velocity to a pinprick. Then, nothing. The sentient cluster was sucked down with it.

Though Hush had been squatting mere feet away, most of the blast was swallowed by the rift, and the cantrips on his body deflected the rest. A ward throbbed painfully on his cheek, stinging him as it protected him from greater danger. He sprinted for the staircase. The building shook with more reports of cosmic violence. He nearly fell. The floor was unhinging into widening jigsaw chasms, as if forced upwards by flows of lava. After much precarious leaping and teetering— bounding from one safe island to the next—Hush made it to the foot of the staircase and began climbing on his hands and knees.

At the top Battalion hauled him to his feet. They traded shaky smiles while activating the second command module together. Ribbons of eager shade slid around Hush's fingers as he took control of the serried rows of moon-lenses; they pivoted in unison. Below them new incursion points were already blossoming out of the wreckage.

To Hush and Battalion the next few minutes felt like Hades Uncut, a no-holds-barred, full-frontal exposé of what goes on in the deepest bowels of hell. Glistening bridgeheads shouldered their way up into the hallway, sending fissures spidering across the walls and floor; supple, vile bodies oozed through any juncture where two angles met; smoke hazed their sight like greasy muslin; and unseen explosions assaulted their senses to such an extent that Hush thought he might succumb to shell-shock.

It felt like reality was wearing thin, seared through by relentless discharges. The air reeked of ozone, and always that inevitable rank stink: mint, formaldehyde and brine. Out on the limits of perception translucent tendrils flapped, giants stirred.

Hush hurled orbs of energy at the moon-lenses, which magnified and redirected his blows, spearing the hallway with a crackling lattice. The air was chaotic with shapes and song, bleeding red and green in rolling flashes, convulsing, swarming, electric. Blobs of marine light illuminated their faces. Random temperature changes assailed them. Ephemeral moth shapes beat about their ears.

Hush was laughing, cackling really, but he could feel the pressure rising. The enemy's strength was unrelenting. The wards on his body smarted as they did their work, and his eyes watered, his muscles screamed.

"Hush, it's no good! We have to fall back!" Battalion hollered. Which was the moment the minefield at the foot of the stairs chose to detonate.

Hush was blinded and lifted simultaneously, sent soaring on gusts of heat, cocooned by fire. Everything seemed to be burning, the world was. Purely by instinct he went into a forward roll and came to his feet on the carpet... swayed... staggered. *Fell.*

His eyesight cleared after a second. Painfully he flipped onto his stomach and looked around for Battalion. He found her in an instant. He stood unsteadily, but screamed out loud as the tattered remnants of his clothing shifted. His top layer of skin had been scorched away, taking his armour of wards with it. Lymph fluid, melted fat and blood wept as a thin gruel down his flayed cheeks. He moaned weakly as he limped towards his lover.

Battalion appeared unhurt, though groggy. She was shaking her head, trying to throw off the confusion. Hush's heart leapt when he saw that she was uninjured. Everything would be okay. Already the blast had thrown them right up to the boundary of their first defensive "shell". They could seal themselves inside and let the Multitude fight its way through a whole new maze of booby traps. Rearm and regain strength. Their battle plans couldn't have worked out any better. He sighed thankfully.

An incursion point opened directly behind Battalion.

The black maw yawned across the whole landing, dilating massively to engulf her. She recognised the danger at once, hair-trigger reflexes swinging her round to meet it. She drew her 9mm with the same motion and managed to loose off five shots before the mouth even had time to properly unfurl. He could hear her screaming obscenities into its jaws.

The bullets merely ricocheted harmlessly into the vortex, and before she could fire again limbs of scintillating darkness leapt out to grasp her.

"NO!" Hush shrieked.

Battalion's gun arm was seized and snapped backwards until it cracked. Her torso was enveloped — its openings invaded — and then mashed like a straw doll against the carpet. Tentacles slithered around her legs and began to jerk her backwards into the pit. She seemed paralysed, but her eyes managed to lock onto his.

In those deep, calm pools he found a kamikaze's composure. Very deliberately Battalion lifted her good hand and traced out the design of a single rune on her chest. The shape immediately flared to life and began to pulse, a dazzling heartbeat of pure white light. Slowly the other sigils lit up, too, joining in the rhythm.

"*Goodbye*," she mouthed before the killer stems engulfed her face.

Feelers stretched out for Hush, too, and he knew he was about to die.

"Promise me we'll die together," she'd said. Near enough, he thought, as the darkness lunged. The pulsing of her runes blazed through the shade to leave magnesium arcs on the backs of his eyes.

Then hands closed beneath his armpits and he was being lifted, dragged back to safety. He wanted to fight against this unwanted Samaritan, but the fire had robbed him of his strength, and all he could do was hang limp. He couldn't even protest; no sounds came out.

The rune on Battalion's sternum flashed once through the gloom, brighter than a thousand suns, and then all the sigils on her body detonated at once. The effect was devastating.

Hush saw the bridgehead that had swallowed Battalion blasted to dusky shreds the instant before Fade closed the door. The waves of force from his love's final act of vengeance pounded up against the frame, but Fade had managed to accelerate the cantrips so that their partition held. Just.

This second explosion, following on so quickly from the minefield's detonation, was more than the hall could endure. They heard crash after deafening crash as the structure finally surrendered to gravity and slumped in upon itself.

Hush lay on the singed carpet trying to gather enough saliva to spit at Fade, but the ceiling of his mouth was charred. All his brain could do was snake round in hopeless loops.

He hadn't died, he hadn't died... Battalion was gone, and he lived on... He hadn't died, he hadn't died...

Suddenly he caught sight of Fade's cheek, and the momentary madness splintered. The adept's flesh was crawling with gold, streaming in motes of brilliant agitation. Hush recognised the symptoms at once: Fade had cast Icarus's Wing on himself.

"My God, what have you done?" Hush gasped.

Icarus's Wing was a truly terrifying glamour, which granted the subject enormous physical strength and vitality at the expense of their essential life force. Many adepts referred to it as Suicide Alley.

"You think I should be saving myself for a good marriage?"

"That'll burn you to a husk in minutes! What were you thinking?"

"I don't think either of us has enough time left to care." Without looking, he gestured to his left.

Hush followed his lead and saw that the door was already bulging inwards like slack elastic. He gagged in astonishment.

"No! That's not possible. We cast legions of wards on that barrier. It should have held for hours!"

Fade simply looked sad.

"We've always underestimated them, haven't we? Never truly understood what we were up against."

Hush refused to believe it, couldn't budge his gaze. Fade stooped to pull him up. He was incredibly strong, his flame flaring high this one last time. Hush tried to spit in his face, but only ended up rasping like a lizard.

"Let me be, you fucker. Let me die by her."

"Ah, ah," Fade admonished him with a finger. "You have to follow it through to the close. See out the end with me, Hush. Usher in the second Eden. Don't lose heart." He leaned in close and whispered. "You'll taste her again, don't worry. I promise."

Still Hush hadn't recovered enough to challenge him, particularly with Fade's enhanced strength. So what could he do? He lolled back, and Fade effortlessly bore him up in his arms.

For a second Hush was reminded of how he'd carried Lila. Two times, once from their own domain, and then more recently out of this dying house. Full circle. Everything is one.

They fled deeper into the labyrinth.

**

The Multitude harried them throughout the endless tangle of rooms and corridors. It was forever snapping at their heels, stripping away the house behind them, gulping down stone and wood and reality. All of their meticulously laid traps were brushed aside like paper, and Hush thought of the panic which had gripped the Order during their first invasion, fifteen years ago.

While Icarus's Wing lasted Fade held him up. When it began to ebb they supported each other.

They stumbled and ran, and hid, and tried all manner of clever pan-dimensional evasions. But finally there was only one place left for them to go…

**

The last retreat, the final bolt-hole, was the boxroom containing the activated Weapon.

Fade tumbled to the ground, spent, while Hush slammed and bolted the door, hastily refreshing the protection wards. They both sensed the Multitude ramming up against the perimeter.

It felt like they were buried beneath an avalanche, lost under hundreds of tonnes of snow in a cardboard box, its flimsy sides already buckling beneath the weight. Miraculously, though, their defences held. The cardboard box was secure for the moment.

Hush leant against the door and stared at his old adversary. Alien light from the tea chest jiggled fluid patterns across the ceiling, making the room seem even more claustrophobic.

"What does the Weapon do, Fade? No more run-around or bullshit. *Tell* me."

Fade sat by the open chest and spent some moments making himself comfortable. Hush was sure that he never intended to stand again in this life. Finally, he cleared his throat.

"You know all about cause and effect now. Non-linear mathematics. All our old disciplines. Your memories have returned sufficiently to understand." He paused, breathing raggedly. The effects of Icarus's Wing were biting deep, the effulgence sliding from his cheeks, tarnishing. He only had seconds to live, but then so had Hush.

Fade pursed his lips to continue. "Hush, the Weapon *undoes* cause. It unthreads the intricate interplay of cause and effect back through time, working to free the knots of causality. It rips up history by the roots, tears out the old pages as if they'd never been written. Casts them to the wind. All you have to do is choose how much you want to play again. How far to rewind."

There was a rumbling creak behind them, the sound of destiny pressing near. Tendrils of darkness waltzed across the walls, like animated veins in marble. Hush was aghast, struggling to come to terms with the enormity of the concept.

"You mean the Weapon reels in the past? *Rubs out* events?" Fade's messianic grin was all the proof he needed. Hush shook his head as the true horror of the Weapon settled upon him. "Madness. You maniac, it could end up undoing *everything*. Every cause, every effect throughout our whole timeline. It could erase it all!"

"Would that be so bad? After all the hurt and terror this world has had to endure? We could wipe the slate clean. Forge a new beginning."

The veins on the walls were moving faster now, vibrating. The bricks groaned in protest.

"*We*? There'd be no 'we'. There might be no anybody *ever* if we use that thing. It's madness, absolute derangement. If you've got your calculations wrong, then it could be like we never existed. You could rip out every cause of every event since the beginning of mankind! Stop our ancestors coming down from the trees, standing erect, evolving into humans at all!"

Fade grinned. "Exactly. But don't you relish the chance to start again? Build a kinder, better, brighter species?" He looked down. "One touch and I can do it. One touch, Hush."

"Fade, no—"

"See you in the New World!"

But before Hush could stop him their defences suddenly *tore*. The sides of the room fell away and the Multitude surged in, a babbling ocean of dark impressions, demon-frilled. Hush snarled, spun to face them. Someone whispered close to his ear.

*Now we are one.*

At the same instant, Fade triggered the Weapon.

# Part Three:
# Grey Areas in Time

## 26. Less Is More

Jacob awoke to disorientation. The bedroom was dusky, the curtains still closed, which lent the gloom a strangely granular quality. Early morning, he concluded. So what had woken him? Had he been dreaming? Uneasy speculations purled beneath the surface of his mind, like prehistoric worms stirring along the belly of a swamp. Lingering images niggled: something was coming towards him, or he was running away. A sound, like thunder...

Before he could unlock the clasp of memory, though, Maria turned over in her sleep and nudged his shoulder. She muttered muddy syllables, kissing on the words, REM-chattering. It was obvious he wasn't going to remember the dream, so he snuggled up against Maria's flank instead, trying to nuzzle his way back into slumber. However, his warmth roused her and she came to with a tiny shudder.

"Wha?"

"Shhh," whispered Jacob. "Go back to sleep."

"Mmmmno," she yawned daintily. "M'awake now."

"Okay, well, do you want to get up, then?"

She made a scrunched-up little-girl's face. "Eugh, no! Let's just lie here, malingering."

She stretched exquisitely against the sheets, yawned again and pouted. Some moments swam by dreamily as they languished in the shared heat.

"Love you," she said very suddenly, like it had slipped out unexpectedly and she wasn't sure quite how the sentiment would be received.

Instead of replying he reached round and gripped the nape of her neck very tenderly. He kissed her, long and deep and lingering. She hooked a thigh over his hip and drew him close. He felt her slip a little, already slick, ready for him, for this.

"I want you," she whispered, the definition of her features was lost to soft gloom. It made her seem even more beautiful, slightly mysterious. For the briefest of moments Jacob thought that her body was scarred. Just some fugitive fragment from his nightmare.

He stroked the velvet bowl of her stomach, teased her pubes with his fingers and the rough-soft pad of her *mons*, which he cupped. Found her clit and traced its Braille. She hissed with pleasure and arched her back, breasts lifting off the delicate bow of her ribcage.

She squirmed onto her front to find his mouth, compressing his busy hand between them. She giggled, licked him. On her breath, the scent of morning. He laughed and used his hands to position his cock instead, guiding it gently inside of her.

The sex was sweet and sweaty, hot and fast and fragrant. It brought them closer than they had been for months. But in the centre somewhere, Jacob shivered, felt a note of falling desperation which passed so quickly that he wasn't even sure the emotion was real.

When they came, they came together, muscles locked, hearts in time.

Afterwards, her face against his chest, she murmured, "To think, I was planning to leave you… and miss all this. Mmmm—" She chuckled, rubbed her nose through his chest hair. Sneezed. "Thank you for blowing out the demo, J. You did the right thing."

"I know," he said with conviction. "Yeah."

But when she'd gone to the bathroom he sat on the edge of the bed, scowling. Everything was tickling him with resonances today, half-remembered recollections, buried hints. It was like he'd woken up inside an echo chamber.

His eyes tracked over to Maria's side of the room and came to rest upon her nylon rucksack, which was sitting beside a mound of other day bags. She'd snatched the pile of them from the cupboard yesterday, when she was threatening to leave. After the crying, after the loving, they simply hadn't retained the energy to clear up. He was amazed that she'd consented to stay. He'd been terrified, so *sure* that she'd go. The last thing he wanted to do was to upset their delicate equilibrium today.

And yet…

**

Jacob entered the bathroom while Maria was in the shower.

He flipped up the toilet lid to piss, then moved over to the basin and started brushing his teeth. Abruptly he paused, oblivious of the toothpaste slime which ran down his chin. Though he'd tried to banish it from his mind, the echoes of his nightmare kept derailing him. He frowned at the mirror. *Shhhhh*, said the water over his shoulder. It fell silent as Maria killed the stream.

"Pass me a towel, J?" she called out.

She had twisted her hair into a dark slick rope to wring the water out of it, and was blinking to keep the shampoo residue from her eyes. Dazed, Jacob pressed a towel into her hands and watched as she patted her face dry, admired the clean line of her thigh when she stepped from the steamy cabinet.

He found himself staring at her body as she went about drying herself down. He couldn't work out why he'd expected her to be bigger when she emerged, leaner and more muscular. Maria was slight, with an elfin build, small feet and hands, willowy thighs. Her shoulders were narrow, hips a gentle flare. Her breasts were small and high, though at thirty-four the first pinches of age were evident, wrinkling round her dark sloping nipples. No, that wasn't right…

A moment of acute déjà vu swamped him. A sense of nauseous dislocation, as if he'd unexpectedly woken up in somebody else's house with a hangover and couldn't remember how he got there. Maria was actually very busty for her frame. It was something she'd never been comfortable with, and rarely wore tight tops, preferring to lose herself in sloppy shapeless sweaters instead. She hated all the unwanted attention. An ex-boyfriend once dubbed her his "page three stunna", and it had always grated. Maria was twenty-six.

What the hell was wrong with him today?

"This isn't right," he said out loud.

"Hmmm?" Maria inquired from beneath the hood of her towel. She was drying her hair.

"I can't stop thinking about the demo, the Hellier labs," he murmured. "I'm worried about Morris."

Maria snorted dismissively, she wasn't keen on the big Cornishman at the best of times. "The one person you don't need to worry about is that idiot. He can handle himself all right, violent sod."

She seemed pretty miffed. Jacob supposed he couldn't blame her, not after all yesterday's rows, and especially since he'd capitulated to staying with her instead of storming off to the demo.

"Still... Mind if I just phone him?"

She was drying her calves now, her face turned away from him. He watched her shoulders stiffen. Jacob knew he was on dangerous ice here, but the urge to check on Morris had come up so sharply it was almost like a physical ache. Finally she shrugged.

"He's your friend."

**

"Yo, mate, it's Jake."

"So?"

The big man's breath made the line crackle. It was obvious he wasn't happy, but despite the cool reception Jacob found himself filled with an unexpected joy just to be hearing his friend's voice. It was almost embarrassing how moved he was, and for the life of him he couldn't work out why. He was actually welling up. He blinked the tears away and laughed gruffly.

"I just phoned to…" he started then trailed off, feeling bewildered. "I mean, well, you're okay, aren't you? Everything's sound, yeah?"

"No thanks to you."

"I can appreciate you being mad at me, mate—"

"I'm not mad. If you've had a morality bypass and want to be a crack whore for the Man, that's your own business."

"You still going ahead with that other gubbins, Morris? After the demo, the spiky stuff?"

"That ain't none of your concern."

The conversation carried on for a few minutes in the same stilted fashion. Jacob had already tried to explain to Morris why he had to stay with Maria, but naturally Morris hadn't understood, only ranted about social responsibility and the poor puppies. Now, however, the only thing Jacob could think about was Morris' own safety. He found himself falling back on empty platitudes to convey his apprehension.

"Please look after yourself, Morris," he urged, frustrated. "And… And… Just don't do anything stupid, all right?"

But before the warning was even out Jacob heard the burr of the dialling tone. Morris had hung up. Sadly, he replaced the handset.

Meditatively, he scratched his ear. Somehow it felt wrong. With a sudden shock he realised that he'd been expecting to feel scar tissue there. He'd thought he only had half an ear! Jesus. He wiped his hand on his bathrobe in automatic revulsion. One, two; a deft, nimble motion, skin momentarily rasping across terry towelling.

He looked at the silent phone and shook his head.

**

Jacob scooped his porridge into a large wedge in the centre of the bowl and stared at it intently. He refined the peaks and troughs, trying to recapture something he couldn't *quite* visualise, a shard of nightmare memory.

The surface of his sculpture was glazed with a film of milk, and it glistened in a way that was almost resinous. Jacob put his chin on the breakfast bar to stare at it more closely. Behind him the toaster popped, disrupting his attention. He wiped his face with a hand and shivered, irritated by his constant abstraction.

Maria padded over to claim her toast. She was wrapped in an old sarong, frayed silk sagging off the hem. She hadn't noticed him playing with his breakfast.

"Do you ever wish you could go back and change things?" Jacob asked as he watched her. She paused in buttering the toast, put down her knife.

"I hate it when we fight, too, J. I'm sorry about what I said yesterday, but what's done is done. Let it go."

Was that what he had meant? Jacob wasn't quite sure.

"Yeah," he said sadly. "But I mess up all the time. And I just want to make things better. Go back and make amends… I wish time was like videotape, so we could go back and re-record all our bad takes. Shoot the happy ending instead."

"You only get one chance at paradise—"

"What? *Paradise*?"

Maria looked at him with amusement. "No," she smiled. "Don't interrupt. I said, you only get one chance at this life. So you just make up and make do. We all make mistakes. Wishing you could go back and change is dishonest, Jake."

"I suppose," said Jacob slowly. He could have sworn she'd said "paradise". "We never learn, though, do we? Sometimes life feels like it's just a bunch of old reruns, like I'm damned to mime the same lines forever. Never learning, always playing the same mistakes. An endless episode of *Men Behaving Badly*."

Maria's expression softened. She left off preparing the toast to join him at the breakfast bar, took his hand and squeezed it.

"Hey, honey, sshhh. It'll be okay. I'm here for you. We'll get through together."

He glanced up, and their eyes met. Jacob experienced a sensation of profound warmth in that contact, of peace. He reached out to stroke her cheek, gazing deep into her eyes. He knew then that he loved this person, unequivocally and without question.

Then his blood curdled. "Your eyes," he stammered.

"What about them?"

"They're *green*." He found himself shaking uncontrollably, as if in the grip of a *grand mal.*

"They *are* green, so what?"

"No, no. Your eyes are brown. They've always been brown."

The thread of unease he'd been dangling from all morning suddenly snapped, and his panic dropped into free-fall. He stood. The stool tumbled out from beneath him. Clattered to the tiles, ignored. Maria rose too, very distressed.

"Jake, stop it. You're frightening me! What are you talking about?"

He retreated from her in horror, trying to ward her off with his hands. "No! No! Stay away from me! Get the fuck back! DON'T TOUCH ME!" he screamed. She pursued him into the unlit hallway which led off to the rest of the flat.

"It's all different! Everything's changed. Wrong! I'm in the wrong life," he cried and stumbled backwards to the bedroom, pirouetting awkwardly inside.

Lila was sat on the bed.

Jacob's throat constricted. He couldn't breathe. There was a dry sound rushing through his ears, a taste in his mouth like metal.

The girl wore the scarlet summer dress from Knightsbridge, and ribbons in her hair, which had been tied back in bunches. She didn't blink, and her eyeballs were black sunless globes.

Maria sailed past Jacob into the room, a vision of serenity. She went to the bed and perched there. Jacob gawped, bug-eyed.

"I remember now. All of it...," he stuttered. "You're dead. *I'm* dead— where is this place?"

"Don't be afraid, Jake. It's okay, really. Come sit by us," Maria patted the sheet next to her as if this were the most natural thing in the world. Lila slid round to lean against her back, peering over her shoulder at Jacob. Her gaze never left him for an instant, depthless and alien and still. Maria kissed her on the cheek, a casual peck, as one would kiss a lover or child. She turned back.

"Come on!" she encouraged Jacob, as if he were a diffident toddler. "J, there's something I've got to explain to you..."

Jacob staggered away.

"Oh sweet Jesus, Jake, I think you've killed him," said Liam.

Jacob turned—

## 27. Too Many Finales

"I think you've killed him," Liam repeated in a horrified voice.

Jacob blinked, disorientated. He was standing over the guard in the poky little security booth at the Hellier labs. There was blood on his hands and tiny bits of broken bone in the man's hair. A sticky red pool leaked out around his boots.

He tried to catch his breath, but even that evaded him.

"But I didn't kill him. I didn't," he muttered. "He was only stunned." Below him the guard's face was ashen, scarlet-flecked. The rear of his skull was resting at a strangely flattened angle to the ground, like a broken egg. Jacob thought he might throw up, and bent over. His stomach rolled. Liam was staring at him, aghast, while across the room Dogstar Bob knelt beside Trev's prone body, examining his neck for a pulse.

"No no no," Bob hissed in panic. "Oh no, oh no. Shitshitshit-"

It seemed positively otherworldly how swiftly their mission had disintegrated into chaos. Barely a minute ago there had been two more living beings in this room. Empty vessels now, and their deaths were like twin black holes drawing everything in towards them. It was impossible not to stare at the bodies… the corpses.

Jacob felt that his life was like a video, and that someone had their finger locked over the fast-forward button. He shook his head confusedly. He couldn't keep up with the pace. He felt dizzy. He had just killed a man. Oh god. The black holes were dragging him in…

Liam was shivering uncontrollably. "We've gotta call the police," he whimpered. "Get this sorted out. It— it was a mistake. Just a mistake. No one meant any harm… I never— I ain't going to prison— I ain't. Come on, we gotta call them—"

Morris punched him in the mouth.

Liam didn't fall over. He simply stood there, blinking, like he'd had a custard pie shoved in his face. After a second, he turned round and ran out of the room. Bob followed him directly, the door slamming closed behind them.

"Come on," Morris growled. "We've got a job to finish."

Jacob goggled at him in shock. "Uh, yeah, man…"

He didn't dare look at the bodies again.

**

In the main complex they split up, the better to do more damage. By entering the labs without the proper codes they had automatically tripped the silent alarm, which meant they had barely fifteen minutes before the police arrived. Time was of the essence. Jacob sprinted through to the procedural rooms, willing himself not to glance at the puppies in the cages on either side. Once inside the laboratory, he began to smash as much equipment as possible.

As he went about his righteous vandalism, his mind skittered off in other directions, drawn irresistibly away by the gravity of events, the consequences of which were even now snaking away from him like the aftershocks of a mighty earthquake. He wasn't merely an agitant any more, a man with a Cause. He had crossed another line, a line few humans crossed. He was a murderer. A *killer*.

So why did he feel nothing? Why did none of this touch him like it should? Abruptly, his musings were interrupted. Morris had appeared in the doorway.

"You gotta come and look at this," he said firmly, face grim. Jacob paused mid-stroke, hung the crowbar over his shoulder.

"There isn't time."

"For this, there *is*."

"Okay, but we'll have to make it fucking quick."

**

Jacob stared at the teenaged girl asleep on the filthy mattress.

"That's obscene," he whispered, and without even realising it he reached out for the cell's door handle. "My God."

"*No*," said Morris. Then again, with more power, "No!"

But it was too late. Jacob had already tugged on the handle. It made a small hard mechanism sound, but it didn't open— only Jacob was already turning away. Instinctively, he *knew* what was coming: the pneumatic rush of gears from the other side of the room came as no surprise. The outer door leapt across as they leapt towards it.

But they managed to reach the gap in the nick of time. The door had jammed up against the office chair Morris had pushed out of his way when they entered. Gears howled. The plastic started to warp. Before the gap could narrow any further, Jacob rammed his crowbar into the space and they both began to squirm through.

The door wouldn't be denied, though. The crowbar began to buckle. Seconds seemed to swarm too fast, instants cramming in to get through the pinch. The mechanism vibrated, seemingly drawing in its strength for a final, decisive shove…

Then they were through. The crowbar snapped like a wooden toothpick and the door crashed home behind them, crushing the chair to plastic shards like black petals. Morris rolled to his feet, and Jacob rose, too. He shook his head giddily, but not because of the fall, or the excitement.

"None of this makes any sense," he muttered, his mind spinning with past and future echoes. "You weren't meant to escape," he said to Morris. He didn't understand what was going on, why nothing seemed to fit.

There was an angry growl from further along the corridor, the snicker of claws across metal. Both men spun to discover an enormous Alsatian regarding them malevolently. It snarled — loops of hot saliva dripping off its jaw —and advanced a few paces.

Then Morris sat down.

Simple as that. He just tucked in his legs and casually plonked his arse down on the cold moulded flooring. Jacob stared at him with amazement.

"What the fuck are you doing?" he screamed. The dog barked, almost deafening them. An audible alarm was droning throughout the complex, too.

"Don't worry. It's okay," said Morris. There was an ominous click, and a volley of electric whirrs issued from the doorframe. Jacob glanced back to see the automatic door glide open, wheezing gently on compliant hinges. The teenaged girl stepped lightly through.

*Lila.*

Ignoring the men, she rocked down onto her haunches and beckoned to the dog instead. It padded obediently towards her, immediately docile. On its way past, Jacob caught a glimpse of its collar: FENTON, the name-tag said. Jacob quailed. Reality had turned on him, and its teeth were sharp.

"They come from a place which is all them, Jake," Morris said conversationally. "Nothing else exists there except them. It is *made* of them. The earth is them, the sky is them, the sun is, the air is. The *universe* is them— and only them. Has only *ever* been them… How could you expect entities like that to understand a house, say? Or a government? Giving birth, or physics, or…The human race. Think of it. How could they even comprehend us? A whole other universe where things *aren't them*!" He paused, and Jacob was held by his febrile gaze. "But individuality *fascinates*, mate. It does."

Lila was petting the dog, stroking its coat, scratching it behind the ears and suchlike. The brute panted happily, its tongue lolling like a flap of dark wet liver. The girl's expression was profoundly strange, though. The muscles of her face kept twitching, tugging violently at the edges of her mouth, kinking through the smooth line of her brow. It was like she were attempting to force emotions onto her emotionless mien. Testing them out. Trying to experience enjoyment as she "played". And she was utterly silent, as if her vocal chords had been surgically excised. Not a grunt, not a sound. It was highly unnerving.

Jacob watched the girl and the dog as if from a thousand miles away, as if through deep water. The shadows seemed to be growing all around him. Jacob's eyesight was dimming. He had so much to say, but he could squeeze none of it out.

"*Dark*," he managed to whisper.

"See, she's trying to be a human. Sweet, isn't it? Only she wouldn't see it that way. She isn't even a she. She isn't anything we could properly understand."

Suddenly Lila struck the dog. The attack was so swift and heavy that it was hard to believe that such a light frame could have delivered it. She didn't lash out in rage, though, this was an entirely calculated gesture, clinically executed.

The dog's head rocked sideways with the recoil, then slowly returned to regard its abuser. It blinked at her exactly as Liam had blinked at Morris when the Cornishman had struck him. A sort of dazed dreaminess. Otherwise it didn't react.

Lila hit Fenton again, a devastating roundhouse strike which knocked the dog off its feet. It made a sound like a medicine ball hitting concrete. The animal kicked and kicked for a few seconds, before lying still. A thread of muddy piss nosed out from beneath its prone body. Blood gradually mixed in with the urine, thickening the flow. Lila put her head on one side to examine her handiwork, black eyes darting with avian restlessness.

"They don't understand," said Morris sadly as he watched the girl, who was now prodding the dead dog, as if trying to coax it awake. Her expression was utterly immobile. Jacob shivered. The gathering shadows rubbed themselves against his calves, gently caressed his shoulders. It was getting dark.

"Is there something wrong with the lights?" was all he could ask.

"Vanguard," said a voice to his left. "It's started."

Jacob turned to look at Sun-Ray, who had spoken, but Sun-Ray only had eyes for Vanguard, poised at the head of their casting circle.

"That's it, people. That's the clarion call," Vanguard called out in an amazingly level voice. "You know that our cause is right! Let it keep you strong. The families of the world are relying on us! Keep faith for the children, friends! Keep faith and be strong!"

Jacob could hear an approaching roar. Something was coming through the trees. A sound, like thunder. Beside him Battalion looked terrified. A teenaged girl gripping her shotgun with dangerously unsteady hands. If she shakes too hard that's gonna go off, he thought distractedly.

Slender rills of silver crossed and back-crossed beneath his feet, bisecting each other in pell-mell squiggles as they mapped out shimmering constellations on the grass. The air felt flat and dusky, unnaturally still when compared to the thrashing branches mere centimetres away from his face. An envelope of stealthy spacetime had been folded over them for protection, because they were behind the church during that first battle with the Multitude. Only, somehow, Vanguard was in command of the mission this time. Jacob glanced around feverishly.

"No!" he raged. "This isn't how the story goes!"

"What?" yelped Battalion to his right.

"I'm in charge! The kidnapping was *my* idea. Vanguard should be back at the base camp co-ordinating the counterstrike! I should be here, not her."

"What are you talking about? You *are* here."

"No!" he screamed. "It's all going wrong!" He began to back away from Battalion. A ripple of alarm quickly spilled out along the line of adepts. Wide, scared eyes flashed his way. Outside the ring the undergrowth was shredding itself to pieces, churning and snarling, spitting out huge shards of bark as the fording torque closed in on them. In his confusion Jacob stumbled out of the hidden security of the spiral.

"Hush!" Vanguard bellowed after him.

Instantly, Jacob realised it had been a mistake to leave the circle. That was Battalion's role. All the characters were getting mixed up in his head. There was a ferocious gale pulling at him. Shorn of the spiral's protection, he was buffeted in every direction. Jacob fought to stay vertical, leaning into the wind. He found himself gazing at the adepts left in the ring: young faces contorted by fear, smeared with misty radiance, determined, pallid. Barely more than children themselves, some of them. Strong faces with vacant eyes.

They were all going to die, he thought sadly. Lost in the Multitude's domain for his — Hush's — folly. What could he do to save them? This had already happened once before. What penance could he offer up in exchange? His memory? His history? Not this time.

He stared regretfully at Singer, the young lad who had driven him to the battle. The lad whom he had condemned to death simply by allowing him to join his team. He'd said he was married, hadn't he? Yet he only looked about fifteen.

Surely that couldn't be right, though. Jacob wasn't leading the team, Vanguard was. So who had shared the car ride with Singer? He couldn't really imagine Vanguard cracking *Blues Brothers* jokes.

Had he dreamt that whole encounter? The boy's face — with its rounded cheeks, high colour, scrap of sandy hair with wet friendly eyes — seemed so familiar, like a treasured family photo, passed every day on the sideboard. Jacob squinted to see the boy's expression more clearly.

Battalion was shouting something at him through the veil, but the roar of the fording torque was overwhelming, and, anyway, everyone in the van was arguing too loudly.

Maria and Liam were bickering up front, while Morris, Trev and Bob rowed in the back, and Janey kept yelling, "Shut up! Shut up! I'm trying to drive!" at the top of her voice.

Sondra was attempting to comfort Lila, who had a filthy dog blanket wrapped around her skeletal shoulders. The van swung out sickeningly on its half-busted suspension as Janey took another roundabout in third. She accelerated recklessly away down the slip road onto the motorway, nailing the pedal to the floor.

Jacob's back was braced against the rear door, his knees pulled in tight to his chest. He could feel a rough edge sawing away at his spine as the van rocked from side to side, but he remained very quiet, waiting. It was strange that Maria had been included this time round, though she looked very fetching in her dog punk get-up: trailing white-girl dreads, silver chain dangling from her nose to an earring, beads and crystals, Celtic clasps and henna tattoos. Were they lovers in this version, he wondered?

Liam was saying, "We have to go to the police. Like, *gotta*. This is way beyond anything we're ready for, man. It's the real deal, no jesting."

"And how long do you think we'd survive if we did that?" demanded Morris. "How long before an MI5 clean-up team visited your family in the middle of the night?"

"You're fucking dreaming, man," Liam retorted. "You are, like, sooo paranoid it isn't true. Oliver Stone ain't got no flies on you, geezer!"

"The boy's right, this is bushwhacked. *Kidnapping*, kids. Major bad ju-ju," added Bob for typically pharmaceutical emphasis. He scratched behind his ear with a drumstick.

"Poor thing," whispered Sondra, and hugged Lila closer. "Where do you think she's from? Kosovo? Reckon she speaks any English?" The girl didn't react, merely stared straight ahead. Stared directly at Jacob.

Why couldn't any of them see her eyes properly? How come they didn't notice the impenetrable black holes where her human gaze should be? The van was painfully cramped, but Jacob tried to wriggle as far away from the teenager as possible. The vehicle's interior stank of animals, their hair and loose hides, and by now it was also musty with tension, stale deodorant and bad breath. Jacob felt faint.

"I swear, this is just what we've been waiting for," barked Maria passionately. "Think of the press coverage, think of the TV, the trials. Don't you see? This means the end of animal vivisection in the UK! This is bigger than McLibel, bigger than GM foods. This is the biggest ever!"

"This is a cunning trap for our righteous cause!" Morris angrily retorted.

Jacob cut across them. "What this is, is utter bullshit... We never rescued her from the Hellier labs! That comes later." He stabbed an accusing finger at the shivering teenager. "*She* stayed in the cage, and Morris was caught. That's the way it happened. I remember it all."

The eco-warriors fell silent. Seven sets of eyes turned in spooky unison to stare at him. He tried to shrink from their attention, as he had from the presence in the Multitude's citadel. The urge to curl up on himself like a frightened caterpillar was overpowering. Lila watched him, grinning like a corpse.

Maria reached out a comforting hand to Jacob's shoulder. He couldn't even summon the strength to shrug her off, though, in truth, her face was full of honest compassion.

"He still doesn't get it," growled Morris.

Maria frowned at him. "Course not. What do you expect? Look at how scared he is, poor thing."

"Try and calm down, Jake. You're amongst friends, you know," cooed Sondra. Everyone murmured soft words of support. Maria gave him an affectionate squeeze. None of it salved his fear, though.

"Now we are one, dude. Doesn't that make you happy?" Bob asked.

"You've got to get your head round this, mate," Morris chided him, good-naturedly.

"It's in their nature to wish for companionship," Trev chipped in with a generous grin.

"To *include*."

"To expand their margins!"

"To embrace everything."

"To consume," hissed Jacob. "To destroy!"

The atmosphere in the van changed instantly to one of social embarrassment, as if he'd farted at a Women's Institute dinner dance. Liam coughed uncomfortably. No one seemed to know quite where to look. One by one his former friends averted their eyes. Ludicrously, Jacob felt humiliated.

But Lila drew his attention back. *Her* eyes seemed enormous, too large for the space that contained them, caves of endless night rolling away into forever. The one thing he could focus on, the only thing in the world for him. Black holes drawing him down…

*Hush*, croaked Vanguard, but it was Maria's voice which spoke through her lips. *Now we are one*, the face mouthed. Jacob felt strands of grass squirming beneath his feet as he stared into those same ebony orbs.

Mere seconds earlier Vanguard had stood with grim nobility, directing this defence of their species. Now she had been invaded by the vile ink, and only her shell remained— a cipher filled to the brim with alien malevolence. Darkness spilled down the ropes of her neck, worming its way into her ears, too. Soon the invader would have complete control.

At that moment instinct took over. Jacob's shotgun jerked upwards and he unloaded both barrels into Vanguard's face. The results were spectacular:

Vanguard's skull shattered into a thousand fragments, which blew out in every direction, screaming as they went. In their wake they left what could only be described as a "gash in reality", hovering above the neck stump. The corpse refused to fall, though, remaining rigid and erect while a seething mass of cutters swarmed out of the rip and set about prising the gateway open further still.

Adepts scattered. Someone opened fire with light arms. Lances of curdled fire leapt from the nearest moon-lens. Jacob danced backwards, fleeing the killing zone as swiftly as possible.

"REFLECTION GLAMOURS!" he bellowed as he retreated. "Reflection glamours, you idiots! Use their own power against them! It's the only way you can match their power!" Then the ground gave an indifferent shrug, and he was thrown from his feet, landing heavily on his back.

He lay there gazing up at the once-peaceful sky, which was beginning to fill with sooty flowers, long necklaces of detonations that leaked evil smoke. He sighed. It verged on the surreal that this was being played out in broad daylight. The nearby buildings gleamed, pale stones blanched by years of sun. Their edges were weathered by exposure, blurred and softened, ivy-wreathed, colonised by fat droopy dog roses. If Jacob closed his eyes he could almost imagine that he was on a day out somewhere. A quiet family picnic? The sunlight gently warmed his face. He could lie undisturbed amongst the chaos of battle if he wanted, an oasis of calm.

Suddenly there was a thud to his right. He looked round to find himself face-to-face with a corpse. The grey face was spangled with streaky bright pressure haemorrhages, and the woman resembled Battalion; Jacob's mind locked for a slow-burning second, then urgency came flooding back on a wave of adrenaline— he had to let everyone know about the reflection glamours!

Fade would be in the control room at the hotel. He could pass on the word to the rest of the troops, broadcast it out across the valley... Maybe they could even win this time!

The corpse still had its shoulder cam intact, and apparently functional. If he could only... if he could just...

Over his shoulder he heard the distinctive shuddery *whoosh* of someone firing a rocket launcher into the heart of the melee. He started to grope his way towards the dead adept.

*His fingertips slid on the glassy surface of the Citadel's throne room as he strained towards the glowing womb. Only another few centimetres to go... But his eyesight was failing fast, almost entirely clogged by specks of deadly void. Behind him, Vigil and Smoke were already slumped where they had collapsed en route to the final prize. Lashes of topaz lightning rippled in low waves over their bodies, prowling back and forth.*

*They had made it this far, to the seat of the enemy's power: the core of their citadel, the Nexus. But only Jacob was left, the last of the troops. The lone soldier.*

*And if he failed then their world died.*

*He was no longer aware of the presence which had snatched him out of his body and thrown his mind across the universe, but he knew it gloated still. Only, its attention was elsewhere, concentrated on Vanguard's futile defences. The disadvantage of a mind that vast was that the tiniest things could fall between the cracks. The Multitude would never notice one human, even inside its Citadel. The Citadel was no more important than any other place. Everything, after all, was one.*

*His flesh tingled, but not unpleasantly, as he penetrated the outer curtain of the womb, in effect a simple veil of clotted radiance. Inside he discovered a teenaged girl in a red party dress. He took a foolish second to recover from the shock. Though he'd been well prepared for this moment, in his heart he had never truly believed that their invincible cosmic nemesis was, in fact, a rather ordinary-looking teenager.*

*She was coiled up in a foetal loop, asleep on top of a resinous hillock that seemed to have coagulated around her like candle wax. It formed an exact mould for her body, though the material itself was iron-hard. The girl frowned in her sleep, and rolled over. The mound flowed with her, instantly accommodating to this shift in position. When she had settled herself again, it froze back to metallic immobility. Beneath her lids the girl's eyes danced, her mind arching in a tenuous umbilical cord across to their own universe and the battles which raged there.*

*To his horror, the girl seemed to be reacting to his presence. Her lips parted, as if in surprise, and her eyes seemed to flicker even faster beneath their silky hoods. She swivelled her head in his direction, searching, jerking left and right, her malleable pillow pooling and solidifying uncertainly as it tried to work out where she wanted to settle. She stretched out an arm to him, squirmed onto her back. The signs were obvious: she was preparing to wake...*

*In panic, Jacob hastily activated his homing protocols by stroking a stud of beryl tagged to the inside of his ragged lapel. The stud began to vibrate in tune with a non-linear resonance pattern, which the Order could detect through the whirling static of the transdimensional medium. They would immediately dispatch a fording torque to this location. He stooped closer to grab hold of the girl—*

*Suddenly, he was overwhelmed by an alarming surge of feeling. The emotion was strong enough to actually make him stagger, his forehead diving through the womb's shield which flared out into brilliant waves across its surface.*

*His initial thought was that this was the end. On the verge of success, death had caught up with him. But, actually, the feeling was much too diffuse for that, an echo of something smaller. A slither of* déjà vu, *or jamais vu. He had done this before— or was going to do it. He* already *owned a memory of stooping to lift the Multitude's girl, and this realisation — swooping up at him from nowhere — had struck like a physical blow, wasting precious instants. He crushed those phantom doubts down and lifted her up.*

*Then death* did *arrive.*

*Jacob's strength dissolved. His knees buckled and his sight went out. He tried to hold onto the girl as he fell, but she tumbled out of his arms. His chin struck the smooth floor with a jarring impact. He scrabbled about blindly after his prize, desperate fingernails snapping on the impervious surface, but found nothing. An involuntary tremor quivered along his spine. His chest convulsed. He was beginning to breathe again! His old bodily functions were coming back to life. And that would be fatal in this domain. Panic blazed in his chest. He heard a dim noise away to his left.*

*A noise? Here, where no sound could live? In a realm where air was thicker than gel?*

*Yes...*

*A sound, like thunder.*

*Just before the thunder arrived his fingers brushed something soft. Joyfully, he reeled the supine figure back in to him. Her body was limp, limbs flailing bonelessly.*

*A vast "claw" grabbed him. He was yanked bodily into the air — the precious burden of the Nexus still hugged in tight to his chest — and then he was swung violently around. His sides screamed in agony as he was crushed in its merciless talons. Transdimensional stresses raked his body up and down. He felt clods of flesh being torn away by the invisible vortex.*

Then everything changed, like a TV channel casually flipped.

The air was *air* again, and it exploded into his lungs with such sweet force that he feared it might blow straight through the back of his ribcage. The pinprick of consciousness he'd nurtured in the sad hollows of skull suddenly shot spikes of golden light out through his being.

Jacob opened his eyes and looked up. Dim shapes sidled, almost reluctantly, out of the blankness. With agonising sluggishness his new surroundings revealed themselves. Textures scribbled across surfaces, blobs of pale light put on their proper masks. Faces soon stared down, the grizzled stones of Church Zero clearly visible in the background.

Strong hands gently prised open his grip on the girl, who had bolted awake and seemed terrified, her huge eyes darting around frantically. In strict violation of the natural human order, however, while his saviours treated Jacob with infinite tenderness, their brutality towards the girl was truly shocking. They all but broke her arms in order to drag her from Jacob's chest. Then, once she was on the ground, they set about beating her mercilessly with rifle butts. Sickening meaty thuds resounded throughout the garden.

"STOP!" bellowed a voice. The burly adepts froze. Fade's fury was incandescent, his authority absolute as he stamped towards them.

"Get that into containment now!" He pointed at the girl. "You haven't the faintest clue what powers this aspect might have! It could port itself straight back to their domain, burn us all where we stand. Why do you think we've been preparing this for months?"

A Mercedes van was reversing carefully in his wake, its back doors gaping. The selection of outré modifications which had been made to its interior were plainly visible within: necrotic alloy shielding, manacles fashioned from pure emerald, platinum surgical equipment, a lead isolation tank with reinforced waldos. Teams of adepts tramped along behind the van in the muddy troughs its wheels had gouged out of the grass.

Where previously the garden had been deathly silent, now it buzzed with activity. Booted feet chewed divots from the smooth nap of the lawn, transforming it into a slippery-dark morass of loose wet scars and sloughed turf. Dizzy torch beams carved the gloom into ghostly jigsaw patterns. Walkie-talkies crackled. Shouts rang out.

The adepts gingerly lifted Lila to her feet. Vivid purple flowers decorated her lily-white flesh. She shivered and sobbed, eyes scarlet-rimmed with tears. Faceless figures in plastic biohazard suits pressed forward to claim her, bustling her thin frame inside the waiting van. The doors slammed closed over the monster's mimicry of human terror. Jacob could muster no sympathy for its plight. Who was it trying to fool?

The survivors of Jacob's team had been returned to the forest clearing of their departure. Medics swarmed round them, bright scarlet crosses emblazoned on their stiff black collars. Jacob's wounds, though painful, weren't serious. A few judicious glamours staunched the bleeding, while butterfly stitches sealed the rest. Others were not so lucky.

Of the squad members who had been retrieved, Jacob, Vigil, Sun-Ray and Smoke were relatively unscathed; Glaive had been badly gored, but she would certainly survive; three others were touch-and-go, needing immediate field surgery… while all the rest had been delivered back as frigid bags of dead meat: Cabal, Frost, Shade, Shift, Parallel.

And Singer, the boy who had driven Jacob to the battle, the boy who had volunteered to join the company at the last moment… dead as well.

On his knees, amidst the Order's victory, Jacob stared at the six bodies. Guilt sawed at him like a garrotte.

"My God!" gasped Vigil as Fade turned towards them, out of the shadows beside the van. "Your hair's gone white!"

He was right. The sorcerer's jet-black crop had bleached to a shocking blaze of silver in the space of just a few hours. Fade treated him to a lofty glance.

"You should see what happened to Vanguard's hands. I think her alternate career as a concert pianist must now, alas, remain only as a fond dream. Mind, she'll have a doozy set of scars to show off at parties."

"Callous fuck," muttered Vigil, presumably feeling his recent suicide duty entitled him to a moment's insubordination. Fade snorted. Jacob couldn't tell whether it was out of amusement or disdain. It didn't matter. The only aspect of this scene which still held any significance for him was Singer. Singer's body.

He stared unwaveringly at the dead boy, as if trying to burn Singer's image onto the backs of his retinas, so that he might never forget the details of the moment: the vacant eyes, the corroded teeth, the wrecked web of burst capillaries meshing the face. He was directly responsible for the boy's death. If he hadn't allowed him to volunteer, then he would still be alive.

He had made the decision. Done it to save the human race, certainly, but that wasn't going to ease his sleep. Abstractions wouldn't hold back the night, or the nightmares. If only he could try the scene again, run it over one more time.

It would take so little to alter that single moment, and yet save the rest. Save the world *and* the boy.

Jacob sat very still, knees tucked painfully beneath him. The dew had soaked right through to his skin. *If only he could run the scene over—*

Jesus.

He waited until the garden had mostly cleared. The perimeter watch had pulled back, and the troop transports had growled off into the greying dawn. Fade was the last to leave, but before he could go Jacob's hand flashed out and snagged his ankle in a vicelike grip. Puzzled, the other high adept looked down. Jacob's expression was intense.

"Fade, don't say anything 'til I've finished," he hissed. "Don't wise-ass. Don't shoot me down. Just listen— this is crucial… I've done this all before. This *scene* is a replay for me— only there are changes, slight alterations… I can't work it out… But I'm pinging around in time! I'm being catapulted from one point in my life to another like I'm in some vast cosmic pinball machine. I was just in the future — *your* future — and we were fighting the Multitude there— in Village Zero fifteen years from now. Before that I was in a van with my saboteur mates, and we'd just broken into the facility. My memory had been wiped— I wasn't Hush anymore, I was someone called Jacob. Vanguard had given me a new personality to protect the Order from discovery… God…

"Help me, Fade, I don't know what's going on. In that future we lost. They broke through and you used the Weapon— I think that must have something to do with it, but I don't know what. I feel like I'm losing my mind. I don't think I can hold out any more. *Please*, Fade. Help me?"

Fade shook himself free of Jacob's grasp and twisted away. Jacob thought that his appeal had gone unheard; when Fade eventually replied his words seemed to be on a different track entirely.

"Did I ever tell you that my father's first wife was called Lila?" he asked, as he turned back from the observation window to face Jacob.

*The observation window*?

"She went mad," continued Fade, dryly. "Set herself on fire, threw herself into the sea. Very sad."

"It happened again," whispered Jacob.

"What did?"

"We just… jumped. We're back at the facility."

"Naturally. Where else would we have brought the Nexus? She needs to be contained while we carry out our negotiations. And we have experiments to perform. Tests to run… Questions to ask." His smile was very cold and sinister.

"No, no, you don't understand—" Jacob's words dried on his tongue as he struggled to cope with the disorientation the time jumps were causing.

They were standing together in a featureless concrete box with one plate-glass window that gave onto an almost identical room next door. In there they could see Battalion screaming questions at Lila, who had been shackled to a straight-backed steel chair beside a low metal table. Her head was trapped and held immobile by a complicated emerald neck brace which occasionally drizzled licks of bright jade fire. She had been stripped and every inch of her flesh — from palms to pudenda — had been scrawled with overlapping skeins of sigils.

As he watched her, though, the girl very deliberately pivoted to stare out at him. The rivets on the manacles popped free. The brace fell to pieces. She cranked round like a clockwork toy and transfixed Jacob with her gaze. All of the hairs along his arms prickled to attention.

"'Some day they will notice us'," said Fade on the periphery of Jacob's attention, just beyond his line of sight. "Many years ago someone wrote that in the margin of our copy of Kayle's *Scarlet Shedding*. Underlined it, too, the old ham. 'Some day they will notice us.' Pity whoever it was hadn't also thought to mention it to their suzerain. Not that the foreknowledge, ultimately, would have done us any good, but we might have been able to work out the truth about the Multitude—," he said, with a sigh, "—before all this business."

Through the plate window — supposedly a one-way mirror — Jacob could see Lila watching him. There was no question in his mind that she could see him. Battalion was still yelling questions at her, but the girl ignored all that. Her eyes were twin chips of expressionless jet. She put her head on one side and Jacob resisted the urge to read it as an inquisitive gesture. The *thing* that confronted him was an empty vessel. A cipher. Well, surely…?

Fade's voice interrupted his terrified musings. "The multiverse is like a vast archipelago set amidst an infinite ocean," he continued in a low, flat tone. Jacob thought he sounded a little melancholy. Ever so slightly regretful, in fact. This wasn't a lecture, or even a tale. This was a eulogy.

"Every time non-linear abilities are used on one of those islands, ripples spread out from the source. Unlike in a real ocean, those ripples never really diminish, they go on and on, forever. Eventually, the ripples wash up against the shores of every other island in the ocean. This is what we never realised. We blithely carried on using our powers, pretending we were policemen for the multiverse. Whereas, in fact, it was we who were drawing the Multitude to our dimension. Dreaming away… Making ripples," he shook his head, clucked in mild sorrow. "It is how *they* first became aware of us…

"They come from a universe — an island — which is all *them*, composed of the Multitude and nothing else. You might think of them as possessing a hive consciousness, but that doesn't really capture their essence very well. It'll suffice, though. If you think of them like that it will help. You see, when they were alerted to the presence of life in our dimension, they simply presumed that it was *life like theirs*! Which was natural, of course. Their particular brand of intelligence was all they knew existed, so how could they have anticipated anything else? They were expecting to encounter another Multitude, or an analogue of the same. Another mind the size of creation. Imagine their surprise… Though, at first, they didn't realise the difference at all.

"That was what those first incursions were all about, the autopsied Canadians, the stripped-down cars, the killings at Village Zero. They weren't hostile. They didn't intend to invade — as the Inner Council mistakenly believed — it was just that they didn't see their victims as individuals, and so were unable to appreciate the crimes they'd committed. They just thought of their activities as inquisitive communication on their part. The natural response of a hive mind encountering the unknown. They just bit off small chunks to see what the whole might taste like. For them there was no difference between one chunk, and the whole. One person and a universe. They believed our universe was another Multitude—"

Fade paused and rested his cheek against the tea chest. Jacob wondered if he was trying to get the story straight in his head? His skin was mottled by subtle tongues of green light, as were the walls and ceiling, results of the Weapon's alien lambency. The air rustled lightly with its presence, as if the very molecules were squabbling. Fade cleared his throat to continue.

"Eventually they became aware that they were dealing with an entirely *other* form of life. Their previous methods of investigation — which we mistook for expansionist aggression — proved inadequate. They couldn't learn what they wanted to know that way. They needed to devise a more direct form of observation. So they attempted to *create* an individual— Lila. The Nexus."

The walls of the boxroom grumbled menacingly, the tortured bricks grinding together like teeth. Tiny squirts of mortar foamed out from between the cracks as the Multitude tightened its lasso. Fade licked his lips with a delicate tongue-tip, flakes of rusty colour falling from his face as Icarus's Wing sponged up the last flecks of his life-force.

"What is more, they literally invested the nucleus of their power in her creation. In that much the Order was quite correct. Such huge exertion was necessary for such an ambitious project to succeed. You see, it was a vast undertaking for them. An unknown leap across fundamental barriers of comprehension, daunting even for a force as mighty as they."

Curious bands of living shadow strobed along the ceiling, dashed over smutty flooring tiles while the creaking from the brickwork ramped up to an ear-shredding crescendo.

"Afterwards, they leaked knowledge of her existence to the Order, and allowed your team access to their domain so that you could 'capture' her. They hoped that she might learn what it is to be truly individual by living amongst us. It was a dreadfully high-risk strategy. Without that bulk of their power, they *were* vulnerable. But they were fascinated by us. By singularity—"

"Is that why I'm here? Why all this is happening to me? Because I was the one to kidnap the Nexus?"

"You mean, you don't understand yet?" Fade asked wearily.

Jacob shook his head slowly, fearing the worst. Fade eventually smiled back at him, but he didn't look especially happy. The walls of the boxroom crumpled and the Multitude roared in to claim them.

Again…

## 28. Everything Is One.

"Fade," said a voice from the darkness. "It's started."

Jacob found himself at the top of a grassy slope overlooking the perimeter of the forest, a new elevation on that now-familiar clearing. He was back in the moment before the kidnappers embarked on their suicide mission.

Church Zero hulked behind him, a 2-D shadow, stark against the demented sky. A gale was tugging insistently at his shoulders, as if trying to rouse his attention. Other than the adepts inside their protective aura, and himself, the church grounds were deserted. Neither bird nor beast nor man risked exposure to the Multitude's storm. Within the spiral he could hear Fade laying down his final pep talk for the troops. He thought they looked a little more scared this time.

Jacob bit his lip. He'd already managed a dialogue with Fade once, he remembered that much. This must mean something. It implied that there *was* still some kind of hope left, still time. If Jacob could manage to break the frame and talk with Fade, he might be able to persuade him to abort the mission — stop the "kidnapping" — and then the whole experiment with Lila would never begin. Would never *have* begun. And all the disastrous events that spun out from that single instant would not occur.

Ignited by fresh hope, he dashed down the incline towards the adepts. The wind shoved at him but he refused to be diverted. Garish highlights from Vanguard's counterattack streamed over his shoulder, burning his cheeks with panels of soft cerise. He screamed as he barrelled onwards. Branches scrabbled through his hair, drew blood. His scalp felt wet. He was sprinting at full tilt by the time he cannoned into the protective dome.

It was like running into a steel wall. Blood exploded everywhere as his nose broke across his face, sparks scattered through his vision. He rebounded, and almost fell. Righted himself, then came at the barrier again. Rebounded… again.

Time after time he slammed his shoulder up against that hazy boundary, but to no avail. There was no way in. No breach to be made.

"FADE!" he shrieked at the top of his voice. "LISTEN TO ME! DON'T DO IT! DON'T GO THROUGH WITH THE MISSION!"

But no one noticed. Not one flicker of attention darted his way. He was a mime you couldn't see, playing Walk into the Wind, and Help, I'm Trapped in an Invisible Box. Only there really was a box for him, an iron cell that imprisoned his volition. He'd been locked outside of this timeline. He couldn't effect it one iota. He beat his fists against the dome, for all the good it did him.

Finally, bloody and battered and despairing, he fell away. Making small noises he crawled a short way off and collapsed onto a neatly clipped verge. He lay on his back and wheezed.

"They just want to understand," said Maria, dropping down

lightly onto the grass beside him, "what it's like to live alone, as singletons."

"What's happening?" whimpered Jacob. "I don't understand."

Maria watched the action unfolding inside the circle with interest. They were lighting up their braziers now. Fade looked stern. Battalion was nervous.

"Experiments," she replied.

"What?"

"Tests. Reruns. Different versions, different finales. Different ways to try to know humanity…" She looked up at the impenetrable canopy of the trees, and sighed very softly, a lingering breath of relaxation. Darkness crowded round them, gradually eclipsing the garden — the church, the world — leaving them stranded within a single shivering spotlight of reality.

"You see, they're interested in everything alive. They're curious, ravenous for information. But they had no way of interpreting humans — individual minds — because we are so alien to them…" She looked a little sad. "Mutual incomprehension, Jake... Imagine something so different that you could never understand it, something so radically removed from every reference point you've ever had. How would you try to understand that thing? How could you even begin to communicate with it?"

"Like trying to attack jealousy with an axe," whispered Jacob. Maria nodded enthusiastically.

"Exactly. That's the Multitude's dilemma. They're still trying to solve it. But what's really ironic is that they *envy* us. This characteristic of ours. This thing that they can't understand. They think it would improve them." She giggled, as if this were a terribly funny observation, fair wriggled with the silly pleasure of it.

"I don't get it," Jacob raged. "What kind of experiments are these? The story doesn't happen this way round. If Fade's in there — in the casting spiral — then where am I?"

"I think we're going to swap your roles this time," she observed. "Wipe his personality instead. See what that throws up, what insights emerge. Turn, turn."

The activity in the spiral was getting more desperate now. Adepts hunkered down to trace out the sigils and runes, little realising how truly futile those defences would be. Fade barked out his orders, keeping time with a stopwatch.

"But where are we right now?" Jacob demanded, glancing wildly around. "Where is here? Everything was destroyed. We lost. You— *they* invaded. What happened to the Earth?"

"Your place was... *consumed.*"

"So where are we?"

"Here."

"Where?"

"Where we are."

"I don't understand. We're inside the Multitude? A part of it?"

Maria frowned as if she couldn't articulate this profound difference.

"Everything is one," she finally intoned.

"Tell me the rest of the story… please?"

"Silly, but you know it already."

"*Please*?"

Maria's expression turned strangely tender, as if she'd suddenly taken pity on him. He felt like a chick with a broken wing.

"Lila lived with you for years, observing you, watching you play with your dogs. Watching you love, and hate, and scheme. In that time she became very good at mimicry, but copying a thing doesn't *make* you that thing. Despite all her years of observation — the lab rat analysing the scientists — she never truly understood.

"Frustrated, the Multitude decided to invade instead, to subsume our world and its individuals. It was hoped that, when humanity was a part of the collective consciousness, maybe they would finally understand the concept of independence. Only in order to mount such an invasion, they needed back that mass of their power which had been ceded to the girl. That was where you came in. You managed to return the Nexus to the primary incursion point, and she was assimilated back into the hive. Then they were free to return and claim their prize.

"Yet even after consuming the human race, *still* they did not understand. So they play games. They conduct experiments, running events time and again, tweaking episodes, making tiny changes to see if it brings them any closer to enlightenment. To revelation.

"But none of this is malevolent, J. Don't ever think that. They are simply so alien that they *had* to do this. It was the only way for them."

"When? When did all this happen?" he shouted.

Maria looked blank.

"How long ago?" Jacob pressed. "How long has all… *this*… been going on?"

She seemed about to answer, then frowned. Couldn't summon the words. Tried again. Then, finally:

"Time is meaningless. It isn't real any more. You can't put before before after or the middle in between. Everything is one."

"*Try*. Pretend that you're human again. How long?"

There was a long wait before Maria hesitantly replied:

"Two thousand years?"

His strength deserted Jacob in a rush. He almost passed out.

"No," he croaked. "*No*."

Maria shrugged helplessly, and smiled at him. She seemed so… *normal*. Was she real? Was she a mirage? Was she one of them, or was there even a difference any more? If he strangled her, would she die?

His eyes darted away to Battalion's face inside the spiral. He could see her trembling, sweating, wan and skinny. Behind her eyes, he saw her thoughts. He saw her willing herself not to be afraid, to be brave and not to let everyone down, not to run away.

An awful suspicion began to grow in Jacob's mind. A fear that, maybe, he hadn't even been in that circle during the original version, the first time this scene was ever played out? That he wasn't even the protagonist here.

"But what about the Weapon?" he stammered. "It was meant to rip up time by the roots. Roll everything back and start again. A second chance, Fade said."

"Ah," Maria's lips pursed into a delicate oval. "Hmmm, well, we devoured that, too. We contain first chances, second chances, absolution *and* paradise already." The wind ruffled Jacob's hair affectionately. "You mustn't worry," she urged sweetly. "I've told you, there's no malice to them. They love us. They want us. They only came here to understand us better. That's why they did all of this—" she gestured around herself simply.

"Then what you're really saying is that we've been destroyed by *curiosity*?" Jacob was incredulous. It was difficult to keep the soul-drowning panic in check.

"Nothing is *destroyed*. Everything is saved. Everything is precious. Everything is one," she chanted. "Everything is useful, everything is used. You are part of us, and we are part of you. Closer than lovers. Closer than parent and child, mother and foetus. Everything. Is. One."

"No," Jacob sobbed in terror and despair. "No, no. It can't just end like *this*."

"But it does end like this. It *will* end like this. It has *always* ended like this." She frowned deeply. "You still do not understand— and we still do not understand you. So we must try again, play it all over. From the beginning… or the middle… or the end. Turn, turn. Events are altered, the timeline rejigged. It makes no matter. It makes no sense. All over, again and again, until maybe, finally, we might truly know each other and be free. To be one... or many... or neither. With time."

"I thought you said time didn't exist, that it was meaningless," he gasped.

"Time is everything. Everything is one."

Jacob buried his face in his hands and began to weep. Something was coming through the trees, he could hear it. Battalion screamed again, and stepped back over the perimeter of the spiral…

Jacob feels a soft touch on his shoulder and opens his eyes.

The girl — Lila, the monster, the Multitude — is standing over him, peering down. She appears very young, so human, but he cannot tell whether her expression is sad, or indifferent, or affectionate. The darkness seems to swell around his shoulders, broadening out into ravines of singing night.

So many voices.

"*Hush*," she says in a thousand tongues. "*Don't be afraid. We are here for you.*"

Her eyes are black: infinite, eternal, and his sight is drawn down into them, along the longest darkest tunnel in the whole of the universe.

"Lila," he says in a tiny voice.

"*Hush*," she says.

They all do.

**

Jacob awoke to disorientation. The bedroom was dusky, the curtains closed still, which lent the gloom a strangely granular quality. Early morning, he concluded.

Startled, he realised that Maria was standing, motionless, at the foot of the bed. The light was so poor that he couldn't make out her face properly.

Still, he thought that she was probably smiling.

**The End.**

Also available from RazorBlade Press:

**razorblades**
*edited by Darren Floyd*
*ISBN: 0-9531468-0-4 £3.99 144pgs*

**Faith in the Flesh**
*by Tim Lebbon*
*ISBN: 0-9531468-4-7 £4.99/$9.00 144pgs*

**The Dreaming Pool**
*by Gary Greenwood*
*ISBN: 0-9531468-7-1 £4.99/$9.00 136pgs*

**Lonesome Roads**
*by Peter Crowther*
*ISBN: 0-9531468-1-2 £5.99/$13.99 154pgs*

**Hideous Progeny**
*edited by Brian Willis*
*ISBN 0-9531468 4 1 £6.99/$11.00 310pgs*

**The Ragchild**
*by Steve Lockley and Paul Lewis*
*ISBN 09531468 2-0 £4.99/$9.00 182 pgs*

**coming soon:**
The King Never Dies
*Gary Greenwood*
*ISBN: 0-9531468-9-8 £8.99/$13.00*

For more information about RazorBlade Press visit our website at:

www.razorbladepress.com